Belle

EDEN FRANCIS COMPTON

WITH J.G. DUBY

Published by:
Level 4 Press, Inc.
14702 Haven Way
Jamul, CA 91935
www.level4press.com

Library of Congress Control Number: 2019944201

ISBN: 9781646300747

Printed in the United States of America

Other books by
EDEN FRANCIS COMPTON

Emily
Death Valley
Catch and Kill

For Tom

—J.G.D.

Prologue

A gibbous moon throws milky light over the gables of a Victorian mansion, stealing the color from its red brick and cream-colored trim. An apparition moves in the shadows, passing the hog pen outside the kitchen. Three sows lazily lift their heads from the muck to watch the figure cross the yard to the barn and re-emerge with a can of gasoline.

The form returns to the mansion and mounts the grand staircase. The night is silent save for a soft creak of the stairs.

And then, a muffled whimpering leaks from behind a door. The door swings open, revealing a woman tied to a carved wooden column. Her eyes are wide above the gag over her mouth.

The figure lets out an irritated "tsk." "You should have drunk more of the tea."

The woman screams through the gag.

"Would you shush? It's your own fault you're not sleeping through this."

The figure traverses the room, spilling gasoline across the polished hardwood floor, over the furniture, splashing the bedclothes and mattress, and finally soaking the trailing end of the rope binding the woman's wrists. The noxious liquid pools at the captive's feet, soaking the hem of her fashionable but ill-fitting gown. Her nostrils flare as she catches the thick odor. She shakes her head and screams again.

Head aslant, the malefactor considers the tableau and, with a nod of satisfaction, removes a box of matches from a pocket. A strike, another strike, and the flame catches. A toss of the match, and it carves a dazzling flare as it soars and lands in a puddle.

A poof, and then flames dance across the floor.

A scream erupts, growing in pitch and volume. It frantically searches the night, soaring as if to chase an opera diva's high C, until it is lost in the roar of the inferno.

Part I

Seed Money

1

*L*ong and high, punctuated by gasps, a shrill cry erupted from a building behind Belle Sorenson, pulling her to the windows to peer inside. A lobby, a ticket kiosk with an attendant, and as Belle watched, a finely dressed couple dashing in from the street.

Belle's eyes greedily followed the tardy couple. The lady's toilette was impeccable. A velvet gown, deep ruby red, hugged her bodice and draped full length to the floor. The square-cut neckline was trimmed in taffeta of old rose, and a wide pearl choker accentuated her slim neck. A showy dyed-to-match aigrette crowned the soft pile of her brown hair. So grand. Her gentleman, equally resplendent in his black tailcoat and snow-white shirt with stand-up collar and white bow tie, passed their tickets to the clerk before extending a hand to her elbow and escorting her toward a grand doorway.

The singing crescendoed as he opened the door, and a glance through the widening gap explained all to Belle: a stage, lit for performance. On it were a man in chicken feathers and a woman similarly costumed. "Pa. Pa pa. Pa," sang the boy chicken. "Pa. Pa pa. Pa," sang the girl chicken.

Belle peered down at her own shirtwaist and skirt, so plain and a little tattered at the hems. Despite marrying a business owner, she hadn't yet managed a life much grander than what she'd left behind in her village in Norway. How she wished she could see the show, bedecked in a stunning gown and fine jewelry. A night out on the town, wouldn't that be something? Someday, when Mads delivered on his promise that she would be his queen . . .

She curled her fingers one by one into her palm, clenching her fist until it ached. Then she released it and calmly stepped back and scanned the crowded Indianapolis sidewalks for her husband. She spotted him right away. He was hard to miss.

At six foot four, Mads was broad as an ox and half as smart, and that was giving him some credit because oxen are not dumb. Towering over the sea of people flooding the sidewalks, Mads slouched against a lamppost, draining the last drops from his whiskey flask. His dark brows crowded low over his eyes, a scowl of impatience stamped on his face. Passersby gave him a wide berth, like low clouds swirling past a forbidding mountaintop. He wiped his mouth with the back of a meaty hand, and as he restowed the flask in its accustomed spot in his inner coat pocket, Belle saw his eyes finally find her. He straightened, a telltale sign that he was ready to light into her for being late.

Belle smiled.

She wasn't a classic beauty, she knew, her blue eyes set perhaps a tad too wide and her cheeks a shade too ruddy, but her smile—over the years she had learned it set her apart. Her smile was capable of making promises that resided in the eye of the beholder. Whatever desires its recipient harbored, Belle's smile said, "Yes, you shall have it." Her smile was her passport, a tool or a weapon to wield as necessary, depending on her situation. Right now, she needed it to calm a beast.

Mads's coal-black eyebrows, barometer of his moods, relaxed a fraction.

"You're late," he greeted her gruffly. "Wasting time with some scoundrel, no doubt. Who were you with?"

"Don't be silly." Reaching his side, Belle stood on tiptoes to kiss his cheek. "Who could ever compete with my Mads?" She gazed up at him with the adoration he needed. "I just heard the most remarkable thing. A man in a chicken suit, and a lady with him, singing on a stage at the opera house."

"You were at the opera?" he demanded.

"Of course not, Mads. I was looking in the windows. Come, look here."

Belle pulled Mads over to the front of the English Opera House. A large poster decorated with colorful drawings announced the current show. "*The Magic Flute*. By Wolfgang Amadeus Mozart," Belle read off the bill.

"I've got a magic flute for you," Mads's voice rumbled in her ear. His bulk crowded against her, his breath hot and reeking of whiskey.

Fantasies of velvet gowns and nights at the opera evaporated. Stifling annoyance, she turned to Mads, devoted smile in place. To it she added a promise of heat and said, "Shall we go home, husband?"

As Belle and Mads left Governor's Circle behind and progressed down the wide boulevard of Meridian Street, the city around them slowly declined. Fancy shops like the milliner's that sold only imported fashions, its proprietress a perfect advertisement for Parisian sophistication as she departed, were reduced to neat but simple storefronts, a tired-looking hotel, and a bank where a stern-looking banker locked the front door and drew a long shade over the window. A tall facade in the next block proclaimed "cheapest and best funerals," and outside a dilapidated rooming house, four men leaned along the porch railing, smoking.

As the neighborhoods deteriorated, so did Belle's mood. At an intersection with a beer garden on one corner and a saloon opposite, men spilled outside, tankards in hand, their drunken arguments sputtering into the night. So foul. Carriages and streetcars flowed past as Belle and Mads waited with the crowd for an opportunity to cross. On the other side, they made a left and entered their own neighborhood, where the buildings were even more squalid, the inhabitants more downtrodden. Belle sighed. Someday, they would move to finer lodgings.

In front of J.M. Wilde's Grocery, shop boys dragged barrels of apples and potatoes back inside to close up for the day. One little boy pitched rotten squashes and lettuces into the gutter, nearly splashing Belle's skirt. Mads grabbed a fistful of the boy's shirt. "Watch yourself, you little fool!"

"Sorry, mister," the boy squeaked. "I didn't see you there, honest!"

Mads let the boy fall to the ground. "Be more careful with your duties, or I'll pound you good," he growled.

"Here now!" The squat shopkeeper, wider than she was tall, came stomping outside. "Keep your mitts to yourself, Mads Sorenson, and let me boy do his work! I'll thank you to keep walking before I call me man out here."

"Go back inside and tend to your squashes, Mary Wilde, you fat cow." Mads sneered. "And tell your man I'm sorry for his troubles, married to the likes of you."

Belle stifled a giggle and busied herself examining her skirt for stains. Mary *did* resemble a cow, and she had the personality of a shrew. Belle wouldn't want to be married to her any more than Mads did. But still, Wilde's Grocery was their neighborhood shop, where Belle got all their fresh food and dry goods. It wouldn't do to make an enemy of them.

"Why, you!" Mrs. Wilde shook her fist at Mads, who waved her away as he continued down the street. It was far from the first time Belle had to sweeten a situation Mads had soured with his domineering ways.

"Up you get, Sammy," Belle said to the little boy. "No harm done, you see?" She spread out her skirt to show the unmarred fabric, then turned a sweet expression on his mother. "Mrs. Wilde, I see you are closing up, but perhaps you have a pint of milk I could buy?"

Seeing Belle's consideration of her littlest boy, Mrs. Wilde softened. "Since it's you asking." She nodded at Belle, then waddled inside and returned with a pint of milk in a mason jar.

As Belle handed coins to Mrs. Wilde, she asked, "And how is Mr. Wilde? Is his cough any better?"

"You're good to ask, Belle Sorenson. God's truth, the cough keeps him up all night and stops him in his tracks during the day. Can't hardly cross the store without stopping to catch his breath."

"I keep him in my prayers, Mrs. Wilde, as I keep you all." Belle did no such thing, as she was not a woman of faith, but Mrs. Wilde was.

"God bless you, Belle Sorenson. God bless you and keep you."

Belle hurried to catch up to Mads, who had nearly reached their own storefront halfway down the block. This far from the city center, no streetlamps kept the dark at bay. She was grateful that she couldn't see the dinginess of the white letters spelling out MADS'S CANDY SHOP. The hanging bell jangled when Mads threw the lock and opened the door for Belle to pass.

She made her way through the darkened store, past the long counter behind which rows of shelves held jars filled with brightly colored candies—drops of lemon and horehound and cinnamon, twisted peppermint sticks in green and white. In the morning, she would fill the counter's glass cases with fresh-baked cakes and delicacies. Skirting the stacks of magazines and newspapers that would need to be straightened before the store opened, Belle made for the rear door. She mentally inventoried the packets of cigarettes and pouches of smoking tobacco displayed on racks at the back.

Belle knew the shop was a little shabby. But Mads assured her they were on their way up in the world. "Mark my words, Belle," he'd say. "Someday, I'll be the candy king of Indianapolis. And you will be my queen."

The rear door squeaked as it opened onto the alley that ran behind the shops. Narrow, smelly, and dark, the cobbled lane was a shortcut that saved them going all the way around the block to reach the ramshackle house that passed for their home.

Belle led the way up the back staircase to their small apartment, Mads clomping up behind her. Unsteady from drink, he yawed from wall to wall, his shoulders knocking the sides of the cramped stairwell and bringing a squalling to life behind the thin walls; the youngest child of their first-floor neighbors had woken. Belle knew she'd be speaking to the child's weary mama tomorrow, to apologize and cajole once again.

Mads was a very easy husband to manage. His wants and needs were quite simple: Food. And sex. In the five years they'd been married, sex had never failed to calm him. And when Mads was calm, life went along much more smoothly.

She threw a look over her shoulder, and Mads came to a lust-stunned halt. She let out a giggle and hastened her steps, trotting lightly ahead of him. Mads lunged after her and stumbled on the stair tread. "Oof," he grunted as he crashed down like a felled oak, goggling up at her.

Belle posed at the top of the stairs with her fingers on the top button of her blouse. She slowly loosed it, drawing the fabric open just so.

Mads pushed himself to his feet and lumbered up the remaining stairs, chasing Belle into the kitchen, where kettles for boiling sugar, hand-cranked candy-rolling machines, leather gloves, oversize shears, and steel stirring paddles were piled haphazardly on a shelf under a large worktable.

Before Belle could lead him through to the bedroom, he crammed her against the table, fumbling at her clothing, doing more to slow her disrobing than speed it up. Why did he always have to be so forceful? "Mads, if you just—" But his mouth crushed her words, and as he kissed her lustily, he pinned her hands behind her back. His day-old whiskers roughed her skin, and the edge of the table pinched her hip. She had to get this situation under control.

She took his lip between her teeth and nipped hard.

"Ow! Dammit, woman." He recoiled, and Belle sprung free from his tight grip. She wiggled her hips, both to relieve the pain and to distract him from his anger.

"Did that hurt you, you big lug?" Belle untucked her shirtwaist and reached behind her to undo the buttons of her skirt, letting it fall to the floor. Shirtwaist, chemise, and knickers followed.

It was too easy. His eyes raked over her, lingering on her plump hips and following the curve of her waist to her breasts. Amused, she watched his gaze skitter away from the reddish-brown splotch over her left breast. Unable to hide his disappointment the first time he saw the thumbnail-sized birthmark, he'd said, "I thought you were perfect." As if he were one to talk.

Picturing the somewhat softer surface of their mattress, Belle tried again to lead Mads to the bedroom, but he grabbed her by the waist and plopped her atop the worktable. Son of a Benjamin! "Don't you want to take me to the bed?" she encouraged.

"No time," he grunted, climbing up and mounting her like a rutting boar. The candy-making gear beneath them rattled, every thrust sending kettles and spoons and rollers clattering to the floor. Belle knew it wouldn't be Mads putting it all away after. Speaking of responsibilities that would fall to her, Belle recalled that the fifty-pound sack of sugar was close to three-quarters gone, so she'd better have a new one delivered before the end of the week.

"Oooh," she squealed, although his thrusting made her feel anything but excited. The more noise she made, though, the quicker he came. She resumed mentally reviewing their inventory, visualizing the jars of candy in the shop. Lemon acid drops always did well, so they'd need a new batch soon. "Yes!" Maybe some more root beer barrels, also? "Oh, Mads, you're a beast!"

Mads roared and thrust and collapsed on her. "Uggh," he finished. One last bowl clanged onto the floor, and then all was silent, save Mads's hot breath puffing in her ear. His weight sagged, crushing the wind out of her, as a snore erupted from his mouth.

"Mads?" Belle jostled his shoulder. No response. "Mads, you have to get up." He was a deadweight.

Belle had forgotten the golden rule of sex with Mads when he was drunk: always finish on top.

2

Mads handed a paper sack of lemon acid drops across the counter to Mrs. Sanderson and gritted a smile. Belle watched the exchange from the back doorway, a cup of coffee and slab of bread in hand. A slight shudder rolled Mads's shoulders, and Belle could just about hear his thoughts: *This old bat's just a dried-up prune that no man's ever taken for a ride. Who'd want to?*

Poor Mrs. Sanderson had dithered over how to spend her five cents on candy but finally requested the sweet and tart lemon drops, just like every week. She took the bag with a satisfied nod, then asked, "Have you heard about the new candy shop going in down the block?"

"Yes, I've heard." Mads's smile hardened. "I wish them the best, of course, although I think the owner may find there is more to the candy business than he is prepared for."

"Oh?" The old lady leaned in, eager as ever to hear any stray tidbit of neighborhood gossip.

"Of course, he may well know a thing or two," Mads said. "But you know he's from back East. Do you know what he worked at before his current venture?"

Mrs. Sanderson practically quivered to hear more.

"I've heard it said, and this didn't come from me"—he paused—"but my understanding is he was an investor with Rough on Rats."

"Do tell!" Mrs. Sanderson's eyebrows climbed to meet her bonnet. "The rat poison people?"

Mads leaned back and made as if turning a lock on his words. "I'm sure he knows what he's doing, and there will be no interaction between the two companies that would result in an unfortunate, perhaps fatal, mistake."

The bell on the door jangled as Mrs. Sanderson scurried away, certain to broadcast Mads's seeds of innuendo among the wider neighborhood. There were two things Mrs. Sanderson could always be counted on for—her love of lemon drops and her desire for scandalous gossip. The more improbable, the better.

"Mads, have you been fibbing?" Belle teased as she finally approached the counter.

"Serves the bastard right," he said, taking his morning snack with greedy hands. "Putting that jumped-up devil's den on my doorstep. Have you seen what he has done? There is more brass going in there than the governor's mansion."

"Yes, it's—"

"And how did he get through the permitting process so quickly? Greased a few palms, no doubt."

"Perhaps there was—"

"No, don't make excuses for him. He's crooked as a corkscrew, no question about it."

"I'm not making—"

"Hush, woman, and let me think." Mads tapped his finger against the chipped coffee cup. Belle folded her arms across her chest. Mads never listened to a word she said. Why did she bother trying?

Mads launched himself away from the counter. "I'm going to go down there and have it out with him. Man to man."

That didn't sound good. "I'll come with you," Belle said. "I'll just get my hat."

"Be quick about it, and get my hat and coat too."

Belle returned moments later, her simple poke bonnet tied snugly and her arms laden with Mads's coat and bowler. He scowled by the door and snatched his things as soon as she came close, before barreling out the door.

The new candy shop was a short walk down the block, and Belle had to almost trot to keep up with Mads's pique-driven pace. As she hurried along, she tried to caution him against his usual bullheaded approach. "Remember, Mads. You will catch more flies with honey than vinegar. He may be a blowhard with more money than sense, but it won't do to antagonize him. We should lull him into false security with friendly words. And then when he least expects it—"

"Enough, woman. I don't need business advice from you."

Belle snapped her lips closed on the retort that came to mind. *Stubborn ox!* True, Mads had more experience in business than Belle, but surely her ideas had some merit?

Their competition was new from the foundation up, a square building fronted with large plate glass windows. Gold lettering on the glass proclaimed NORTHERN INDIANA CANDY EMPORIUM. Workmen bustled out carrying tools, ladders, and barrels of construction debris. On the sidewalk, gold pocket watch in hand, a portly man in pinstripes and spats monitored their exodus.

"Put a hustle on, boys!" He spoke around a large lollipop wedged in his cheek. "I'm only paying you for five more minutes, so you better grease your boots."

Mads pasted on a friendly grin and extended his hand. "Welcome to the neighborhood, sir."

"Not now, man," the businessman replied, his eyes glued to his watch. "Can't leave these bums unattended, or they'll rob me blind."

Mads's hand hung in midair a moment before he shoved it into his pocket. The candy shop owner bellowed directions at the departing work staff. When they had finally all gone, he turned to Mads and Belle. "Now. Who are you?"

"I'm your competition," Mads said.

The shop owner furrowed his brow. "I didn't know I had any."

"Why, you son of—"

Belle cut in, "We are Mr. and Mrs. Mads Sorenson, proprietors of Mads's Candy Shop." She pointed. "Just down that way."

The businessman took in Belle for the first time. "Why, madam, what a pleasure to make your acquaintance." He pressed his fat lips to her knuckles. "I am Cornelius J. Lickinpoofer. My friends call me Corny."

I bet they do, she answered silently. If eyes are windows to the soul, then mouths must be the gates of hell. That's how it seemed to Belle, confronted with the churning, chocolate-besmudged maw of the candy man. Cavernous and liver-colored, it gaped as he talked, the blood-red sucker bobbing around his tongue like an impetuous imp beckoning them in.

"Mr. Sorenson, I kid." He reached to pump Mads's hand. "Of course I know your shop. It's a quaint little place. Come, let me show you inside."

The interior of Lickinpoofer's store gleamed. The soda fountain behind the marble counter, the floor-to-ceiling wooden shelves lined with rows of empty glass candy jars—everything sparkling and new. The flooring was recently laid black-and-white checkerboard tile, and the ceiling was lined with ornately designed tin. Belle reminded herself the store hadn't yet seen any actual customers to reduce its shine.

At the back of the room, behind a door, a factory of industrial-sized candy-making equipment sat quiet. Lickinpoofer led them among the steam-powered machines, proudly describing each one. Vats for boiling sugar, great big taffy pullers—"Does the work of two men," he boasted. "Now, over here is the real moneymaker." He showed them a machine able to eject individually wrapped candies "at one hundred and fifty pieces per minute. Put that in your pipe and smoke it! Ah-hahaha!"

"A hundred fifty? Not possible," Mads muttered.

Lickinpoofer popped the sucker from his mouth, pointed it at Mads. "More than possible, man—a fact. And at forty pieces per one-pound box, that adds up to more than three boxes of candy every minute. It's practically a license to print money!"

Belle saw the expression on Mads's face and knew he recognized the threat Lickinpoofer's business posed. They would never be able to compete.

Lickinpoofer led them farther into the maze of machinery, gesturing as he went. Belle trailed after, observing from a distance. The man was fat. There was no other way to put it. His trousers strained against ham hock thighs; his waistcoat threatened to throw off its brass buttons like the rivets off a blown steamer. Concentric folds of fat draped from his jaw; his dark eyes compressed to coal shards.

"Always had a sweet tooth, me," he was saying. "Even as a schoolboy. The help couldn't keep me out of it. And when I retired from the oil business—a very rich man, I don't mind telling you—I said to myself, Cornelius, you can have anything you want. En-ee-thing. What do you *really* want?" He paused, looking from Mads to Belle and back. Mads leaned in as if it were a mystery.

Candy. Good Lord, Mads, wasn't it obvious?

"Candy, of course! Ah-hahaha!" More sucker-bobbing laughter. "And then I was struck by genius. Why not open a candy store? Surround yourself with it, Cornelius, I told myself. I'm never without a bar of chocolate and a pocketful of suckers. I'd *bathe* in it if I could! Bah-hahaha."

Bathe in it, indeed. The taffy puller behind Cornelius was plenty big enough to accommodate the entirety of him, tip to toe. Just a step or two back and in he'd go, a great jollocks of jowly, bobbing blubber. Pulled and stretched by gnashing levers, the candy man's pin-striped pants straining thinner and thinner, his flashy brass buttons pinging off like popcorn. Fat Corny Lickinpoofer stretched to nothing, his laugh swelling and fading with every heave of the machine.

***

The walk back was subdued. Mads went straight through the shop and across the alley to their apartment. Belle followed quietly. It seemed the shop would remain closed for the afternoon.

Once upstairs, Mads collapsed into a chair. "Bring me a bottle," he said.

Belle poured him a glass of whiskey and went to put the bottle back on the shelf, but he held out his hand. Reluctantly she set the bottle on the table. She wanted to share what she thought were sensible ideas for fighting to hold their head above water as the battleship that was Northern Indiana Candy Emporium threatened to swamp them in its wake. She couldn't do that once Mads was insensible with drink.

"What if we advertise?" she suggested. "We could emphasize that our candies are handmade, from your grandmother's recipes." Mads had no hope of competing with Cornelius Lickinpoofer and his modern efficiency. Instead, Mads should promote his candies as carefully handcrafted, based on old-world family recipes and long tradition. People were hungry for connections to golden days gone by.

"Bah," he grunted.

In the morning, she tried again, offering bits of advice as she made his breakfast. He gave no reply and grimly tucked in to the bowl of porridge when she set it before him.

"Mads, dearest," she finally said, "there is no harm in trying a different approach when what worked in the past works no longer."

Mads shook his head derisively. "When I decide to take business advice from a woman, I will be sure to seek you out," he said, scraping his chair back from the table. He donned his coat and trudged downstairs to open the shop for the day.

Belle fumed as she tidied the kitchen. Surely her ideas had worth, even if she was a woman? Filling the basin with water from the kettle keeping hot on the stove, Belle plunged the plates in and scrubbed, thoughts swirling in her head.

Yes, Mads had been at the candy business since before they married. And yes, she was just a girl who grew up on a small farm in Norway.

Yet Belle felt sure there was more they could do. After all, for all his years of experience, Mads had never managed to build enough capital to expand beyond the one shabby shop.

She dried the dishes and stacked them in the sideboard, emptied the stove's ash box, and fed the fire, tamping it down carefully. She then took the water pails down the back stairs to the alley. They were lucky to live not far from a pump, and Belle always felt a moment of gratitude for the clean water just outside the door, rather than a half mile away like the river in her hometown.

Still . . . grand houses had plumbing inside, sinks that ran water—even heated water!—and toilets that carried away waste in a clean and odorless network of pipes. Imagine that! So unlike the outhouse she and Mads shared with the family downstairs and three other households on their street.

The pails were heavy and awkward to carry up the narrow stairs, the wire handles cutting into her palms. Out of breath by the time she reached her kitchen, Belle set the pails down next to the stove and shook out her hands. What would it be like to live in a grand house? Like the one in the painting she liked to walk past on her errands in the city center. One time, risking Mads's impatience, she had stopped in at the gallery to inquire about it.

The gallery owner had told her all about the mansion and its mistress, the celebrated wife of a judge, who always dressed impeccably and was beloved by the community.

Belle had gone into a reverie; she saw herself gowned in lush purple velvet, presiding over a stately house, heads turning with admiring smiles whenever she promenaded through town.

"Indeed, much respected," the gallery owner had continued. He guided her closer to the painting. "Notice the fine brushwork. As if the paint were laid down by the wings of angels, don't you think?"

"I suppose," Belle said. The artistic qualities of the picture were beside the point. What she wanted was what it depicted. "I'm surprised the painting doesn't hang in their home still."

"Ah, well." The gallery owner smoothed a finger along his mustache. "You see, I acquired the painting in an estate auction."

"Oh?"

"Yes, yes, um." He brushed invisible lint from his sleeve. "You see, it was, um. Quite tragic, as I understand it. The owner, Judge Quilleran, died quite suddenly, and with no will."

"What about his wife?"

"Well, this was, um, not long after his beautiful lady succumbed to, um . . . yellow fever."

"Yellow fever," Belle repeated. How exotic.

"The painting is very affordable, as you can see." He gestured to a small card pinned to the wall. "And we offer very reasonable lay-away plans."

"Tell me, what happened to the home?"

The gallery owner furrowed his brows at her, but she didn't care. She understood full well that he wanted her to buy the painting, but what Belle wanted was the house.

"I'm not a real estate agent," he quipped. "My understanding is that it stands empty even now."

Stands empty even now. The man's words rang in her head, sending her thoughts spinning. "Really?" she breathed, alive with hope. "And where is this incredible home? Is it very far away?"

"If you must know, it's in a town called La Porte." He had given up all pretense of politeness.

Belle forged on. "Where is that?"

"A few hours north of here, I think. Look, are you going to buy it?" He closed his eyes and, with a deep breath, visibly calmed himself. "That is to say, would madam care to make a purchase? Bring this beautiful painting home with her?"

Belle ignored the gallery owner's last words. She fixed "La Porte" and "a few hours north" in her mind and drifted out the door, lost in a dream of reigning over the Quilleran mansion.

Now, Belle retrieved the broom from the corner and slowly whisked it over the floor, stirring up puffs of ash. In her mind's eye she visualized the painting. Such a beautiful brick home, elegant in its narrow windows and pointed arches, with the gable trimmed in lacy wooden filigree. The turned wood columns that supported the porch were painted a creamy white, and a square turret rose above it all like a crown. It was fit for a queen, and Belle pictured herself as the celebrated lady of the manor.

Mads had promised her when they wed that one day he would lavish her with riches. He'd *promised* her.

Someday that beautiful brick home would be hers.

3

Belle sawed thick slices off the loaf of bread she'd made the day before and slathered them with butter. She carved several pieces of chicken and layered them on top. Arranging a napkin over it all, she paused at the door to take a breath, reminding herself of her own advice: honey is what catches flies, not vinegar.

In the shop, she found Mads still in a foul mood. Judging by the emptiness of the shop and the sullen scowl on his face, he'd made no sales yet. She set his mid-day meal at his elbow and steeled herself to begin her crusade, but he began talking before she could.

"Look at this." He spread his arms wide, taking in the whole store. "What do you see?" Belle surveyed the uninspired decor, the second-hand counter with its nicks and gouges from long use, the walls needing a fresh coat of paint, not to mention Mads's unwelcoming expression. "It's candy perfection," he continued, not waiting for her answer. "If I didn't know better, I'd think someone was out to get me. Where is everybody? This place should be jammed with people. Because I ask you, Belle, who makes the best candies in town?"

Me, she thought, because truth be told, it was Belle who did the lion's share of the work.

"I do," he said, jabbing at his chest with his thumb. "I do. And mark my words, Belle. One day soon, everyone will know it. I will be known as the king of candies. And you will be my queen."

Now we're getting somewhere. "Yes, and I will be queen." Belle visualized herself standing regally on the porch of the vacant Victorian. "And we shall live in the Quilleran mansion."

Mads drew the plate she'd brought closer and flicked the napkin off. "The what?" he asked with a disapproving frown toward his lunch.

"The Quilleran place," Belle said. "Remember, I told you about it? The painting? It's still available."

"Oh, that," Mads said, waving her off. "What did you bring me? Chicken on bread again?" He pushed the plate away. "I'll have lunch at the tavern. Watch the shop."

That's all? *Watch the shop?* Living in the Quilleran mansion would mean success, the success Mads claimed to want, and he simply waved it away like a fly off his soup. Waved *her* away. And sailed off to lunch at the tavern, which would spill over into the rest of the day. Lunch at the tavern meant many hours, many pints, and many coins. It meant Mads spending money they did not have and coming home drunk and demanding. And for Belle, it meant another evening catering to those demands, no closer to her own dreams.

It was a quiet afternoon with few customers, due in part to a dreary rain that leaked out of a leaden sky. The only significant purchases were made by a young servant girl, sent to buy a selection of sweets for a dinner party being hosted by her employers.

"And how did you hear of us?" Belle asked as she rang up the girl's purchase.

"I pass by on me way to visit me mam, on me day off," she said. "Cook burnt one of the cakes this morning. She always burns the bread pudding. I told her I could get some sweets quick and cheap. So she sent me."

The door swung shut behind the girl, leaving Belle alone again.

She used the quiet to take stock of the business. It did not surprise her in the least to discover that the candies they made right upstairs and packaged by hand did better than the prepackaged factory-made treats they ordered from a wholesale supplier. And yet they sold them for the same price. Mads argued they needed to keep the cost down to stay competitive with the inexpensive candies, even though it meant their handmade goods sold at a loss. Belle had to wonder if the opposite might work better. Raise the price—only a little—and promote them as specialty items.

And the fact that better-class families were willing to send their servants into this neighborhood to shop meant there was an opportunity to exploit. Why did they never advertise?

She spent a few minutes straightening the stacks on the floor in front of the counter. Magazines and newspapers, feed and seed catalogs, these were important moneymakers for the shop. The *Indiana State Sentinel* and *Chicago Tribune* were always in demand, along with *Peterson's*, *Harper's*, and *Ladies Home Journal*. The pile of June 10, 1890, *Indianapolis Journal* had fallen over, spreading papers across the floor. Belle scanned a copy as she gathered and re-stacked them. "SILVER DEBATES IN CONGRESS, Consideration of the New House Bill Begun Amid Howls from Opposition," proclaimed the headline. There was a long article about the Sherman Anti-Trust Act that would soon go before the House. Belle skipped those and continued scanning. "DEVIOUS DEEDS IN DAYTON, Fraudster steals, kills 4" told about a man who swindled the life savings out of several old women before killing them with arsenic. "COWS DESERVE BETTER, ingenious device humane way to slaughter" explained that a German scientist, Dr. Hugo Heiss, had invented a special pistol that would kill livestock quickly and painlessly.

"Who would have thought such a thing was necessary," Belle muttered. Didn't a poleax do the job well enough? How hard could it be to slaughter a cow with an axe?

The door jangled, and a dandy gentleman waltzed in, doffing his bowler and greeting her with a wide grin. "Good day, madam. What beastly weather," he said, slapping his dripping hat against his thigh.

"Come in, come in," she said. "What better place to hide from that horrible drizzle than inside with the sweets?"

Henry Simpson was only too glad to get out of the rain. He'd been slogging up and down the streets of this miserable neighborhood for hours, cursing his boss whose bright idea it was to canvas the businesses in this part of town. He hadn't gotten a single bite and doubted he ever would. The shops didn't seem to have a pot to piss in.

"Sweet indeed," he said to the woman behind the counter, answering her remarkable smile with one of his own. "Mr. Henry Simpson, at your service."

"Mrs. Belle Sorenson, proprietress." With a pretty little laugh, she sketched a curtsy.

Despite her wide-set blue eyes and dainty lips, Mrs. Sorenson wasn't exactly a beauty. But her smile took his breath away. The whole soggy morning suddenly seemed worthwhile. Too bad she was a "Mrs."

"Pleased to make your acquaintance, Mrs. Sorenson, proprietress. Do you run this charming shop all on your lonesome? Or is there a Mr. Sorenson about?"

"My husband, Mr. Sorenson, just stepped out. I expect him to return momentarily."

"I see. Well, what do you recommend, Mrs. Sorenson? Some peppermints? Or the chewing gum?"

"Those are popular choices. But if you want something a little more"—she met his eyes boldly—"indulgent, I have something I can show you."

"You have my undivided attention," he said. He couldn't take his eyes off her rosebud lips.

"I made these myself this morning." She indicated a tray of flat cakes in a glass display case. She paused, cocking her head, a delicate finger tapping her chin. She seemed to come to a decision and leaned in to say conspiratorially, "I can't reveal too much as it is a secret recipe passed down in my husband's family. But it gives nothing away to say that you will notice a subtle cinnamon flavor. Of course, we use only the freshest ingredients."

"And worth every penny, I have no doubt." She was a vision. He'd be happy to spend eternity gazing at her enticing curves as she moved among her wares behind the counter. "Do you make all of your confections?"

"Many of them, yes," she said. "Mr. Sorenson and I work side by side, just across the alley in our apartment upstairs, so you know everything is fresh, unlike some shops whose goods may be stale—or worse."

That brought him out of his fantasies. They lived close by? He seized the opening. "Right across the alley, you say? Have you considered what calamity might befall you if, God forbid, there were to be a fire? Or an accident resulting in catastrophic injury? Some unforeseen eventuality that not only robbed you of your business and livelihood but tossed you out of your home?"

"I pray such a thing never happens!"

"Of course, of course," he hastened to assure her. "And an upright, God-fearing woman such as yourself no doubt has little to fear. Still, accidents do happen, even to the most righteous among us. Every day in my work, I see accidents that wreak havoc, and it is my responsibility and great pleasure to protect people such as yourself from the harm these accidents cause."

"Are you a fireman?"

"No, ma'am, not at all." He laughed. "I am an agent with Indianapolis Life and Casualty, and I protect the innocent and unwitting through insurance. Your purchase of a simple policy through Indianapolis Life and Casualty can mean the difference between the security of knowing you are protected and the life-altering eventuality of being out of house and home, not to mention your livelihood, due to fire."

"Oh." Mrs. Sorenson seemed to deflate before him, taking his hopes of a sale down with her. "I'm afraid you've wasted your time. We don't have the funds to purchase insurance right now."

"I see," he said. "And are you the controlling owner of the business?"

"Well . . ." She paused. "Not exactly. Mr. Sorenson is the owner, but I assure you he would tell you the same thing."

"Of course," Simpson said. It never paid to talk to the wives. However comely, however enticing, the fairer sex simply had no head for figures. "I understand completely. May I leave you with my card?"

"Thank you. I'll be sure to tell Mr. Sorenson you came by. Please, take some of our homemade candies with you for your trouble." She scooped horehound sweets into a paper sack and handed it to him with a twinkling eye. "I'm sorry I can't be more helpful."

"Not at all," he said. "It's been a pleasure to while away a few moments with you. Good day."

Belle tore up the card and thought nothing more of Mr. Simpson of Indianapolis Life and Casualty until a few days later. It was a fine afternoon, but despite a bright sun and mild temperatures, Belle trudged home from errands in a low mood. Would a queen be consigned to this miserable neighborhood, with its grime and poverty? Would Mads ever be able to move them away from here? He still was refusing to listen to any of her ideas.

Ahead of her, a group of people blocked the way. As she got closer, she saw Mrs. Wilde gesturing wildly as a policeman took down her words on a little notepad. Around them, nosy onlookers craned their necks to get a better view.

"We're ruined," she heard Mrs. Wilde wail as she neared the knot of people. "Knocked me man down and made off with the cash box. In broad daylight! What are we coming to?"

What, indeed? Belle agreed silently as she edged around the rubberneckers.

Belle's mood brightened a shade when she arrived at the candy shop and found Mads deep in conversation with a well-dressed man. Thinking perhaps he was placing a large order, she called out, "Good morning, gentlemen."

"Ah, here's my wife," said Mads. "I've got good news, dearest. Come see."

Good news? They could certainly use some. Perhaps this would be a recurring order from a household with the means to pay them regularly and well.

When the man turned, Belle's fantasies of a reliable income evaporated.

"This is Mr. Henry Simpson," said Mads. "Of Indianapolis Life and Casualty. He says he came by the other day when I was out."

What a lowdown, conniving snake of a man! But she couldn't let him see how she really felt. "Why, hello," she said, pasting on a delighted smile.

"It's a treat to see you again, Mrs. Sorenson," said Mr. Simpson. "I think you'll be pleased to hear your husband has just made the wise decision to invest in the protection of your greatest asset."

On the counter between the two men lay a sheaf of papers. Belle could see Mads's scrawl of a signature at the bottom.

"Now the store is protected in case of fire, theft, or flood," Mads said proudly.

"Wonderful," Belle lied. "Mr. Simpson, would you give us just a moment?"

"Of course. I'll just take my copy of the policy." He quickly gathered some of the papers and picked up his case before moving away and making busy packing up the documents.

"Mads," Belle said, drawing him aside. "I thought we were saving up so we could move to a larger place? That home we talked about, don't you remember? Won't this be a delay?"

"It's all part of the plan, my dear, don't you worry," he whispered back. "I've got it all figured out. Soon I'll be in a position to give you everything you've ever dreamed of."

Belle felt a spasm of doubt. How would spending money help them save money?

"Thank you for coming in, Mr. Simpson," said Mads, rounding the counter and extending his hand.

Mr. Simpson approached, and the two men shook. "Before I go," said Mr. Simpson, "I'd like to offer you another opportunity to invest in the protection of that which you hold most dear. Your business—your livelihood—is protected, but what about your home? The one place you should be safe from harm. You mentioned that you live just across the way. With these buildings so close together, if one were to catch fire, they'd all go up like a box of tinder. I'd like to tell you about our home insurance."

"Mads, I'm not sure that's a good idea," Belle whispered in Mads's ear. "We can't waste our nest egg."

Mads waved her to silence. "The man is talking, Belle. Let him finish."

Mr. Simpson set his case down and affected a soulful pose. "Is there anything more precious than life itself? Imagine yourself in the future. Your business a success, surrounded by the pitter-patter of little feet"—he beamed at Belle in what he probably thought was a winning way, but his words failed to entice her—"your wife the envy of everyone she meets."

That's more like it . . .

"And then, bam!" Mr. Simpson slammed his hand on the counter, and Belle jumped, as did Mads beside her. "The worst happens. A late-night fire, and all is lost. Who can predict the exigencies of fate?"

Belle cast a glance at Mads. He was rapt, absolutely drawn in by Mr. Simpson's spiel. "Mads, let's stop this," she whispered. "His silver-tongued drivel is meaningless. He's attempting to fleece us out of our savings. We can't afford this. Think of the Northern Indiana Candy Emporium."

"Woman, that's exactly what I'm thinking of. Now be still."

Be still? She wasn't the one behaving like a child. She kept her placid smile in place, yet inside her mind she saw Mads in a dunce chair, wearing the short pants of a schoolboy. His bulk overwhelmed the little three-legged stool, his knees crowding his body. *Smaller.* As he swiftly shrank before her eyes, his knees dropped away from his chin, then his feet swung above the floor, then he was no bigger than a mouse cowering on the seat of the stool. She plucked him up with two fingers and dropped him in her pocket.

"This is why women have no head for business." Mr. Simpson chuckled. "They just don't have the drive to be competitive. Now you, Mr. Sorenson, I can tell you are a man of exceptional drive. A man who recognizes opportunity knocking at the door and opens it wide to welcome it in. I'll tell you what. You're a customer in good standing now that you have the business policy. Take advantage of the protection of the home policy—right here, right now—and I'll throw in a life insurance policy as well."

The day the Northern Indiana Candy Emporium opened, a line formed down the street of patrons eager to discover this new source of delectables. "Fools! Sheep!" Mads raged from their shop, which remained empty all day.

As customers continued to choose new over long-standing, Belle was forced to scale back her production of goods. She alternately commiserated with Mads and tried to convince him to take action against the success of their competition. But, as always, he would hear none of it. If things continued like this, their business was doomed. Belle's mind boiled over with ideas to try to save the shop, each one throttled by Mads's defeatism. At night she would collapse into bed, exhausted with worry, and every morning she would rise again, determined to find a solution to their problem.

One night she awoke to thick smoke choking her lungs, the room lit with a red glow.

"Up, Belle, up!" Mads was shouting. He pulled her from the bed, and she stumbled after him, coughing and blinking away tears from the acrid smoke that filled the air.

In the main room of their apartment, flames crawled the wall behind the stove. Belle cowered at the bedroom door. They'd never make it out!

Mads shook her. "We've got to go!"

"No, no, no!" she screamed.

The floorboards were hot against her bare feet as he dragged her after him, and they reached the door just as flames began racing across the ceiling. She scrambled after him down the back stairs and out into the alley, which was filling with families pouring out of the buildings, mothers carrying babies, fathers shouldering small children, their fearful cries echoing off the walls as they pushed away from the inferno.

Belle clutched at Mads's arm as they were carried along with the throng. It swept them out of the alley and down the lane, spilling them onto the main street. The sickly sweet smell of wood smoke and burning sugar clotted the air. Screaming and crying punctuated the deafening roar of the fire that consumed Mads's Candy Shop from within. Shattered windows breathed yellow and orange tongues of fire like some terrible god of the underworld, and thick smoke disappeared into the dark sky. The searing heat pulsed away from the building, pushing at Belle like a malevolent force. Frozen in horror, she stared wide-eyed as everything she had worked for was destroyed. All their candy-making tools, their inventory and ingredients—everything.

Neighbors had gathered at a nearby pump, passing buckets along one to another and splashing water ineffectually onto the conflagration.

"Good God, woman," Mads exclaimed. He swatted at her head and legs, and she realized flames were licking at her nightdress. Mads swirled his coat off and used it to smother the last of the tendrils along her hem.

A shout went up from the crowd, "Here comes the steamer! Make way, make way!"

Powerful black horses galloped down the street, pulling the Indianapolis steam-powered fire engine. Its boiler puffed steam into the night, and its gears churned madly, throwing off glints of red in the firelight. But Belle knew the fire brigade was too late to save their home and livelihood.

Numb and bewildered, Belle stood barefoot in the street while Mads draped his coat over her charred nightdress. Her throat burned; tears streamed from her eyes. They had nothing left, not even a bed to sleep in.

"Look at your hair," moaned Mads. He slid her braid over her shoulder so she could see. It was several inches shorter and smoking at the end. It smelled horrible.

She burst into sobs.

"There, there." He produced a handkerchief.

"Thank you." She sniffled into the snowy linen. Then something occurred to her. Mads was barefoot but somehow had had time to put on pants and a shirt. She tugged his coat closer around her, thinking about the implications.

"Mads," she said. "You're fully dressed."

He wrapped her in a close embrace and whispered in her ear. "Ssh. Remember I told you I had a plan?" She stiffened. "I hired a man to do me a favor."

Belle struggled in his arms, trying to pull away. "You son of a skunk! You madman! We could have died! Look at my hair!"

Mads hugged her tighter, pressing her head into his chest. "Hush, now, you're overwrought," he said loudly. Into her ear, he whispered, "Keep your voice down. We're rich, Belle. The insurance covers us in case of fire."

Belle stilled. Rich? "Truly?" she mumbled into his chest. He nodded.

Laughter bubbled up inside her. She pressed her mouth against his shirt, trying to stifle her glee. Her shoulders shook with the effort.

It was finally time for the reign of Queen Belle.

4

Belle reclined naked on the bed. Atop her, with whipped cream in his ear and honey smeared in his mustache, Mads nuzzled between her breasts, sucking and biting while she giggled and squealed. "Num, num, num," he said, his whiskers scratching her skin. "Two perfect cream puffs."

"Mads, you sticky, sticky boy!"

"That's right, sweetest. I'll make you sticky everywhere." He plucked the jar of honey from a table next to the bed and tipped it over, globbing the amber goo over her breasts and down her stomach, where it pooled in her belly button. When he lapped it up, it tickled, and Belle squealed some more. He drizzled even more honey, letting it pour lower and lower until it mingled in the soft patch of hair between her thighs.

"Something's missing," he said, dragging a bowl of whipped cream closer. He scooped his paw in and plopped a dollop on top of the honey. He tipped a ladleful of melted chocolate all over her sticky torso, smearing it from her groin, up her belly, and across her breasts. "There. That's covered that birthmark."

"Oooh, it's so warm!" Belle said. It was just how she imagined it. It all was. She'd spent the entire afternoon setting up this whole scene. She'd visited several groceries to buy just the right ingredients, while

Mads and some men from the neighborhood moved hastily bought furniture into their new—temporary—apartment. Just until the money came in and they could move, Mads had promised her. And so this was his reward. Why not indulge his mad fantasy of dressing her in everything sweet and sticky and letting him lick it all off? His gamble with the fire had made them rich—finally.

"And with a cherry on top." He dropped a maraschino on the goopy mound, then paused to admire his handiwork.

"Look what you did to me," Belle cooed. "Such a sloppy, sloppy mess."

"Yumm." Mads leered as he dipped a maraschino in honey. "One for you," he said, sticking it to one of her nipples. He dipped another. "And one for you." He stuck it on the other and grinned. "I don't want anyone to feel left out."

He made a show of sucking off one cherry and then the other, while Belle gifted him with squeals and giggles of delight. And when he lowered himself to her, smearing the gooey mixture between them, she moaned and cried louder and louder, just how he liked it, until he roared his explosion.

The next day, with chocolate still in her hair, Belle was up to her elbows in sticky laundry when Mads came home raging after a visit to Mr. Simpson of Indianapolis Life and Casualty. The company wanted to investigate the fire. It seemed the timing, falling so closely on the heels of purchasing their policy, had aroused suspicions.

So Mr. Simpson was a snake and also a weasel. This would not do. She calmly finished pinning the last sheet on the clothesline and closed the window. "Tamp down the stove, Mads. I'm getting dressed. And then you're going to take me to Indianapolis Life and Casualty." She would talk to Mr. Henry Simpson herself.

And talk she did. She spun a dramatic tale of their midnight brush with death, playing up Mads's turn as the hero rescuing his damsel from certain death in a hellish inferno. Tears were shed. Sobs were stifled. "Where will we go, Mr. Simpson? What will we do?" she cried, beseeching him with liquid eyes.

As they walked back to their temporary apartment, their payout check tucked safely in Mads's inside pocket, Belle wondered if she could have made a career on the stage. *Sarah Bernhardt has nothing on me.*

Belle awoke with butterflies of excitement tumbling in her stomach.

In a few short hours, Mads would bring her to their new home. He'd been silent on the details, wanting to surprise her. No matter how she tried to wheedle the location or size or anything else about it, Mads stayed mum. Her mentions of the painting had always seemed to fall on deaf ears, but she'd brought it up so often, surely he'd heard her. Might it actually be the Quilleran mansion in La Porte?

Belle's excitement only increased as they left their grimy old neighborhood near the busy wholesale district on a streetcar. But it dimmed a tad when, instead of disembarking at the train station, they continued on and entered Fletcher Place. Maybe he had an equally beautiful home in one of the finer neighborhoods of Indianapolis ready for her?

They passed neat single-family homes with small but tidy yards. Well-dressed folk strolled on the sidewalks. As they approached each stop, Belle looked to Mads to see if this was where they would get off. But they passed them all by.

As the quality of the houses began to ebb, so did Belle's enthusiasm. She tried to remain optimistic, telling herself they were just traveling through this neighborhood to get to another, finer one. But no. Ten minutes farther on, Mads finally escorted her off the streetcar, Belle's hopes utterly dashed. The neighborhood was . . . well, it wasn't *quite* as grimy as the one they'd left behind. The single-family homes were respectable, if somewhat run-down. But they were a far cry from her mansion in the painting.

Mads unlocked the front door of a small mint-green house with black shutters, and Belle braced herself against sure disappointment.

The house was plain and square with a simple layout: a living room in the front right corner, an office in the front left corner, a dining room in the back left, and a cramped kitchen and tiny water closet in the back right. A narrow hallway divided the house down the middle, with a set of stairs leading up to two bedrooms. The taps all had running water, which she couldn't deny was an improvement, and a patch of grass fronted the house.

"Well?" In the kitchen, Mads spread his arms wide with a proud grin on his face. "What do you think?"

Belle surveyed the room, observing the peeling wallpaper and dingy linoleum floors. "It's . . . bigger," she said, casting about for something positive to say.

"Are you upset?" Mads asked. "Listen, this place was a bargain. And with what I have left over, I can invest in a candy store on Meridian Street. Pickwick's Picks, it's called. The foot traffic there is ceaseless. We'll make our money back in no time. And then, in a few more years, I'll have the money to buy you anything you want."

Belle stared at Mads. A few more years? Was he insane? She'd been waiting all five years of their marriage, his promises for their future among the reasons she'd said yes in the first place, that and his status as a business owner. The insurance money should have finally been their big chance. How could he have wasted it on this shabby embarrassment?

"Don't be upset, Belle, please," Mads said. "Investing in this candy shop is a once-in-a-lifetime opportunity. I learned of it not long after we came into the money. Just wait and see. We'll be in the clover before long."

Just wait and see. A few more years. Before long.

Phrases that broke her heart.

But he was her husband, and he made the decisions, for better or—usually—worse. What could she do?

* * *

Belle tucked away her disappointment and set to work turning their new house into a home. Over the next days, she scrubbed the previous occupants' dirt from the linoleum. She washed the kitchen cupboards and polished them with beeswax. She wiped the windows until they gleamed and sewed new curtains, choosing bright, joyful prints. She didn't stop until the house was a place of comfort and welcome, despite her own misery.

Mads, by contrast, couldn't have been happier. He gave every appearance of a man without a care in the world. With the infusion of cash from the insurance payout, it seemed the pressure to succeed was off his shoulders. It had bought him a share of a flourishing business, and, as baffling as it was to Belle, that was the beginning and end of his ambition. He left the house each day with a spring in his step to spend his hours at the various barrooms, poker tables, and horse races in and around their new neighborhood.

The dividends from their investment in Pickwick's Picks were not the windfall Mads claimed, and within weeks Belle discovered they barely covered household costs. But that didn't stop Mads from making rash purchases. He sent away to Minneapolis for a decadently large bed of carved mahogany and an oak rolltop desk. The thing had rows of cubbies hidden behind a locking roll front, but Mads never bothered to close it, much less lock it. Just another example of extravagance he was happy to lavish on himself.

Her queries about Mads's timeline for when they would be "in clover" were brushed aside with "You wouldn't understand" or "Why don't you trust me?" or, most often, "Bring me the whiskey."

It was a blessedly cool day. The recent heat had abated somewhat, and the sunshine streaming in the windows buoyed Belle's attempts to stay positive. Mads had left for the day, and Belle set to her chores with vigor, cleaning up the morning's meal preparations before moving on to Mads's office.

Mads was not a tidy man. The surface of his desk was strewn with papers, bits of tobacco and ash from his cigars, a bottle of whiskey and a dirty glass, a discarded neck collar, and a single rather smelly sock.

She collected the laundry and dishes and brought them to the kitchen, setting them in the sink to wash later, and then resumed her excavation of Mads's desk. Gathering the papers together, Belle tapped them into a neat pile. As she did so, her eyes took in the words on the top page. "This opportunity of a lifetime won't come again, Mr. Sorenson," she read. "We're happy to welcome you aboard this exciting venture, and with an investment of only five hundred dollars, you can be part of the Pickwick's Picks team." She shook her head at the letter, resigned to where this supposed "great" opportunity had landed them.

Until her eye fell on the date. Six months prior.

Mads had been negotiating to invest in the new store *six months ago*? He told her the offer came *after* the fire. Not several months before.

Belle dropped into Mads's leather desk chair. Disbelief fell over her like a suffocating blanket.

Mads had *lied* to her.

Hadn't she been his devoted helpmeet, right from the beginning? Cooking for him, making the candies, washing his drawers, sewing and mending their clothes, so they didn't have to buy new—all to save money for the future? *Their* future? Hadn't she been faithful to him, only him, spurning advances of the young dandies and old lechers who bought their tobacco and newspapers at their shop?

Hadn't she only weeks ago allowed him to make sport of her body in an orgy of dessert toppings?

Mads had promised her everything she wanted. *Promised* her. Time and again, he'd told her he idolized her, worshipped her, wanted to give her everything she desired. "You're my queen, and you deserve a castle to rule over." The only true thing he'd ever said.

And this was her reward. Not the elegant home of her dreams, but this pathetic house in a jumped-up neighborhood with delusions of grandeur.

She would not be treated like a passenger in her own life, a dumb ornament, incapable of thought or speech.

No more, Bell promised herself.

"Ow!" she exclaimed. She had crushed the papers in her fist, slicing her finger on an edge. Blood welled up, and she raised her finger to her mouth, sucking the red away. She needed a cup of tea.

In the kitchen, she put the kettle on and scooped India tea into the pot. A shaft of sunlight streamed in through the window, casting a glow off the cupboards she had brought to life with beeswax and her own hard work.

Another surge of anger flooded her. All the time she was making this shambles of a house livable, they could have been living in that mansion in La Porte. Mads could have bought it for her, and he didn't. He simply didn't want to.

Suddenly a thought struck her.

If Mads lied to her about this, what else was he hiding?

She took her tea into Mads's office and sat at the great rolltop desk. She spent the afternoon poring over page after page of letters back and forth, proposals and counter-proposals, contracts and binding agreements. Most of it was very dull, but two documents caught her attention. She read them twice through and then a third time to make sure she understood correctly.

Belle let the papers fall. What she had just read was a truly remarkable stroke of luck. And it changed everything.

The piecrust was out of the oven and well-cooled, filled with a sweet and creamy chocolate pudding and topped with frothy peaks of whipped cream. The house was tidy, and the table set. The box of Rough on Rats was safely re-stowed in its cupboard in the kitchen.

Mads came home smelling faintly of beer, grinning with good spirits. "Belle! Wife! I'm home," he bellowed as he burst through the door, sending it crashing into the wall.

She greeted him sweetly, gently closing the door behind him. She hung up his hat and coat and helped him to his seat at the table. "I've got something special for you tonight," she said, placing the pie in front of him. "Mads, have I told you how happy I am?"

"What's this?" he asked. "Where's my dinner?"

"No dinner tonight. I'm putting you to bed with just dessert."

His brows furrowed. "What kind of homecoming is this? I work hard all day, I deserve—"

Belle put a finger to his lips. Not only did she not want to hear it, she didn't want his rant to derail her plans. Her carefully orchestrated, date-specific plans.

"Ssh," she said, stroking her other hand up her body. His pique dissolved into a look of wonder and greedy lust as she began to slowly unbutton her shirtwaist. "Mads," she purred, "I want you to know how utterly"—she unbuttoned a button—"completely"—another button came undone—"*delighted*"—another button popped open—"I am with our life in this new house." All the buttons were freed now. She spread the fabric wide, revealing her naked breasts. "You deserve a great reward for how you've treated me."

Mads stared, eyes agog, mouth agape, practically drooling. He reached for her.

"No no, not yet," she said, shaking her finger at him. She tapped him playfully on the nose. "You have to eat what I made you first. Be a good boy and do as you're told, and then we can play."

He grabbed a spoon and dug in. "I want to feed you," he said, bringing a scoop of chocolate to her face.

She jerked back, reflexively batting away his hand. The poisoned pie fell to the table with a plop. "Naughty boy!" she recovered. "That's my job." She grabbed a serving spoon and dug out a large helping. She raised it toward her own lips but tipped the spoon, spilling it down her front and giggling coyly. "Oops." The chocolate felt cold and sticky on her chest.

Wait. Did rat poison work through the skin? Surely not.

She scooped another huge serving and brought it to his mouth. "Take what you deserve," she said, and he gulped it down.

Belle watched to see what would happen. She hadn't been sure how much poison to use. The directions on the tin didn't specify the quantity that would take down a full-grown man—why would they?—and she didn't want to put in so much that it was noticeable. Mads was smacking his lips. Evidently, she'd gotten that last part right, at least; the poison hadn't affected the flavor. It also didn't seem to be affecting Mads.

"Mmm, more," he said, pointing at his open mouth like a baby.

She pushed another spoonful at him, and he lapped it up. Still no reaction. How long was this going to take? She scooped out more pie, spooning mouthful after mouthful at him, making a sloppy mess. Chocolate pudding and whipped cream spattered on the table and over Mads's shirt. He opened his mouth wide and gobbled each bite, laughing as it went all over his face. If the poison didn't kick in soon, she was going to be out of pie, and Mads was going to want to take this circus to bed. She certainly was not going to let him kiss her and get any rat poison in her mouth.

She scraped another scoop of pie out of the dish. "Open wide, big boy." She made a game of it, waving the spoon toward him and then away as he lunged after it with gaping lips.

"Gimme, gimme," he said, nipping toward the spoon, but his eyes stalled on her cream-covered breasts. As she shoved the spoonful into his mouth, he grabbed her wrist and started pulling her toward him. "Now for the real fun."

Saints above, was the poison ever going to kick in? She should have bought ox poison. She should have dumped the whole box in. She had to stall him.

"Oh, is this what you want?" She leaned forward, offering her chocolate-covered breasts. He laved his tongue over her skin, slurping the creamy pudding off her body.

He was laughing, but his face darkened and his breathing stuttered. Suddenly, he froze. "I— Ah—" he choked out. His back arched, and a terrible grin stretched his chocolate-smeared mouth before he pitched face-first into the messy remains of the pie.

Finally! She plucked a napkin from the table and scrubbed the chocolate and cream off her chest, then rebuttoned her blouse and stared at her deathly still husband. She threaded her fingers into his thick, dark hair and raised his head. Underneath the cream and chocolate, his satisfied grin of delight was fixed in place. His glazed eyes saw nothing.

Belle changed her clothes and wrestled Mads into a clean shirt, no easy feat with his body limp and uncooperative. She wiped pudding and cream off the table and floor, flushed the remains of the pie down the sink, and double-checked that the rat poison was secure in its usual place. Then she ran out into the night.

"Help! Help!" she screamed, bringing tears of hysteria to her eyes. She raced to the house across the street and pounded on the door. "Help me! Please, someone, help me. Call the doctor! My husband is sick."

Dressed in widow's black, Belle gathered her holdall and briskly mounted the waiting carriage. Her trunk, packed with her clothing and personal belongings, was already strapped to the back. The carriage lurched forward, and Belle sat straight-backed, not sparing a backward glance at the home she'd briefly shared with Mads.

On the way out of town, she directed her driver to the art gallery and made a purchase.

"Enjoy," the gallery owner said as he handed over a painting wrapped in brown paper.

"Thank you," Belle said. "I will be hanging it in the very home it depicts. I intend to resume where poor Mrs. Quilleran left off."

The gallery owner froze, brows knit together in puzzlement. "I beg your pardon?"

"Yes, you told me all about Judge Quilleran and his beautiful wife. And then poor Mrs. Quilleran died of yellow fever, and grief took Judge Quilleran not long after."

"Did I now?" A smile broke out on his face, and he stroked his palm over his mustache, after which his expression was sober once more. "And so you went to La Porte and bought the place?"

"I haven't been to La Porte even once. I completed the transaction by mail and telegram."

His eyebrows rose a fraction, a hint of surprise that Belle caught before it was swiftly exchanged for one of admiration.

"I see, I see," he said. "Very bold of you. Not one to hesitate, I see. Fortune favors the brave, as they say. Well, best of luck to you."

"Thank you," Belle said, basking in the man's appreciation.

At the curb, she let the driver load her painting into the carriage. "Take me to the train station."

Once on the train, Belle watched Indianapolis pass slowly into the background. She was leaving all this behind, the grime and poverty, Mads's lies and selfishness. The holdall at her feet contained some very important papers.

The first was the $3,000 life insurance policy Mads had purchased from Mr. Henry Simpson of Indianapolis Life and Casualty. The policy went into effect on July 30, 1890, the very day of Mads's death. The second was an older document, a life insurance policy from the Home Life Insurance Company. Belle hadn't known this second policy existed until her hunt in Mads's desk. It was a three-year policy that covered Mads for $2,000 in case of untimely death. The last day of its term was July 30, 1890.

At the bottom of her holdall, carefully stashed beneath thread and needles, a pen and bottle of ink, some changes of underclothes, and seven linen handkerchiefs, was the remainder of the $5,000 insurance payout. After selling the house in Indianapolis and purchasing the Quilleran home and arranging her travel, she still had over four thousand dollars. More than enough to start a new life.

Hereafter, July 30 would be like a birthday to her. More than that, it would be her Independence Day.

Part II

First Quarter

5

Belle rode the train to La Porte insensible to the discomforts of a one-hundred-fifty-mile ride that required several train changes, buoyed by hopeful anticipation of her new life. The beautiful home in her mind's eye awaited, patient and idyllic, the repository for her dreams of the life she deserved. No more would she be beholden to a husband who lied to her and used her. Belle would be the master of her own destiny.

The painting, carefully wrapped in layers of brown paper, leaned against her knees. A porter in Indianapolis had offered to stow it, but she insisted on keeping it with her.

The jam-packed train leaked passengers, a few at every stop, as it traversed the northern quarter of the state. As they neared Belle's destination, there remained only a handful of other passengers sharing her car. Two proper gentlemen in suits faced resolutely forward in the front of the car, their derby hats perched dead level on their heads, so unlike Mads. No rakish, devil-may-care angles for these fellows. On the other side of the aisle from Belle, a matron sat crowded between two school-age children, their heads sleepily resting on her shoulders, making Belle thankful to be traveling alone. One row in front of her, so close Belle could smell her lovely honeysuckle perfume, a woman sat in the window seat, watching the plains and farms and little villages roll by. Her dark brown hair was swept up under a brimless hat decorated with jet beads and two erect bird wings arranged in a V, iridescent purple and green feathers catching the light. Very chic. Belle might just have to get a hat like that herself.

Directly across from Belle, a washed-out miss dressed in plain gray serge read a small black book. Belle took it for a Bible until the girl closed it, marking her page with one finger, revealing the title: *The Strange Case of Dr. Jekyll and Mr. Hyde.*

Catching Belle's curious glance, the young woman said, "I suppose you think me addle-headed, reading fiction? Mama says only the Bible is fit reading for a young woman."

"Not at all," Belle replied. She had grown up reading the Bible, although she hadn't laid eyes on one since marrying Mads. Belle loved to browse through the fashion plates in *La Mode Illustrée*, but she had never had the chance to read fiction. Maybe she would take it up in her new life. "What is the story about?"

"It is the story of two men, one good and one evil, a murderer of the innocent."

"That sounds Biblical after all," said Belle, but the young lady seemed not to hear and carried on.

"And this evil man has some kind of hold on the good man—as if he were blackmailing him. But do you know what I think?"

"Indeed, I do not," said Belle, wondering if the girl always spoke so frankly with strangers. Her eye wandered to the woman in the fashionable hat. With her face turned to the passing scenery, only the curve of her jaw was visible.

The young woman leaned forward conspiratorially. "I think they are the same man."

Two men, very different from one another—opposites, even—and they are the same man? "How could that be?"

"The good man pretends to be the evil man, or maybe the evil man is his true self and he pretends to be good. Or tries to be good. I'm not sure yet."

"You have your work cut out for you," Belle said.

"Thank you." The girl nodded gravely. "My name is Miss Alice Longacre. Are you a resident of La Porte?"

"No," Belle said. "Well, yes. I am Mrs. Belle Sorenson. I am moving to La Porte."

"Why, then, we are both newcomers to the town! It is so good to make your acquaintance. Is Mr. Sorenson not traveling with you?"

"Mr. Sorenson has passed. Just recently."

"Oh! How tragic. I am sorry. Was it the grippe?"

"His heart gave out."

The train whistle screamed, and Belle chose not to view it as comment on her elision of facts.

They'd been rolling through empty prairie for much of the last hour, dotted with the occasional farm, but now buildings cropped up on either side of the train. A gasworks came into view, its stacks churning smoke into the sky. Then came a tall brick woolen mill with rows and rows of glass windows, followed by a large wooden building proclaiming itself a feed mill and cider press. A foundry, a furniture factory, a wheel works, on and on it went, building after building, markers of industry, commerce, and prosperity.

Miss Longacre peered out the window and Belle followed her gaze to the upcoming station, a two-story brick building with a single-story wing on the nearest side. A long portico shaded the platform. As the train pulled abreast of the station, Belle could read a sign above the portico that said, simply, LA PORTE.

A handful of travelers and their luggage clustered near the station entrance, while one man stood apart from the crowd, waiting with his hands behind his back, gazing up at the sky. His black suit was rumpled, and the collar at his neck signified his role in the church. He started as if struck by something and hastily took out a stack of papers and a pencil from his coat pocket and began scribbling something down, the papers braced against one knee, which he held up like a stork.

"That must be my patron, Pastor Bauer," Miss Longacre said. "I will live with his family in their home and teach at the local schoolhouse. He looks kind, do you not think?" She looked to Belle for reassurance.

Belle took in the man's ridiculous posture and mad scribbling and thought that kindness was the last feature he called to mind. Absentminded and quite possibly mad, more like. "Kind to his core, no doubt," she offered. The train lurched to a stop. "Best of luck with your charges."

"Thank you ever so much. I expect I will be very busy. I hope the children are not too unruly." Miss Longacre kept up a stream of chatter as they disembarked the train. They exited from the rear door while the businessmen and the matron and her children and the mysterious woman in the feathered hat left by the forward door.

On the platform, the pastor approached to collect his protégée. "Miss Longacre?" he inquired. "I am Pastor Bauer. You are to come with me."

"Yes, sir," she replied. "Pleased to meet you. May I present Mrs. Belle Sorenson? Mrs. Sorenson, this is Pastor Bauer."

Behind him, the woman with the bird hat made stately progress across the platform toward the station. Her gown was magnificent. Fashioned of iridescent purple silk almost identical to the wings on her hat, it fit the woman perfectly, as if made for her form alone. She looked neither left nor right as she moved toward the station entrance with an assured stride. Her face was composed and serene.

"I met Mrs. Sorenson on the train," Miss Longacre said, drawing Belle's attention back to Pastor Bauer. "She is new to town as well."

"Ah yes, I see. Welcome to La Porte, Mrs. Sorenson. Will I see you in church this week?"

Undoubtedly not. "Perhaps."

The pastor and Miss Longacre departed, and Belle enlisted a porter to find her a carriage and load her steamer trunk. The boy was young, with ears that stuck out from his head like wings, and he gawked at her with big calf eyes. She treated him to a smile, and he fell over himself, scrambling to show her the way to the street.

"Right this way, ma'am," he panted. He hefted her trunk, with the painting perched on top, in scrawny arms.

When he offered to balance the holdall atop the painting, Belle declined. "I'll carry it," she said.

The station lobby bubbled with activity. Arriving and departing passengers hurriedly bypassed each other as they navigated around rows of chairs populated by wilted travelers. The porter led Belle past an overstuffed baggage room, a ticket office, and a telegraph office. On the right was a concierge desk with a sign that read LA PORTE HOTEL AND RESTAURANT. Behind the concierge, a sign pointed up a flight of stairs: ROOMS. Through a door next to the stairs, the smell of roasted meat and baked bread wafted under Belle's nose, reminding her it had been some time since she had eaten.

"Hold a moment, young man," she told the porter, retrieving the painting and instructing him to safeguard her trunk in the baggage room.

The dining room held more than a dozen square tables surrounded by ladder-back chairs and dressed in white linen tablecloths. Belle approached the host's desk and asked the man there for a table.

"Right this way, madam," he said. "Can I stow your belongings behind the host's desk?"

Belle was not going to be parted from her painting or her holdall for even a second. "No, thank you. I'll keep them with me."

The host led her through the grid of foursquare tables, each topped with neatly aligned place settings. Sunlight streamed through tall windows that ran along the front and rear walls. The dining room was partially full, with diners at various stages of a midday meal, and waitresses in starched white uniforms circulated the room. The food aromas were even more pronounced, and Belle felt her stomach grumble. The host showed her to an empty table in the center of the room, and as she took her place, she realized that seated at a neighboring table was the woman in iridescent silk from the train.

The woman studied Belle with an appraising gaze, and Belle couldn't help feeling thoroughly examined and judged. She straightened her shoulders. Someday, she would have gowns even more beautiful than this lady's.

"You are new to town, yes?" the woman said. Her voice was low and throaty, with a hint of a French accent. "I saw you on the train."

"Yes," answered Belle. "I've just moved to La Porte."

"Ah. Come, sit with me." She gestured to the empty chair opposite her with a gloved hand. "It is odious to dine alone, yes?"

The woman waited with cool reserve while Belle rose and stowed her holdall underneath the new chair and leaned the painting against it as she sat down.

"I am Della Rose Thornton, dressmaker." She made it sound like a pronouncement, eyeing Belle while she loosened her gloves finger by finger, sliding them off to reveal delicate white hands. Smoothing the fine kid gloves, she seemed to come to a decision. "You may call me Della Rose. Thornton was my husband's name, and if I could shed it, I would. You must come visit me. You are too attractive to dress like this." She gestured with her gloves at Belle's out-of-fashion poke bonnet, her plain traveling dress, her dusty black boots.

"I've just got off the train," Belle said.

"As have I," Della Rose said pointedly as she arched a brow at Belle. The waiter approached, and she told him, "We will have the veal cutlets with braised celery and lima beans." Everything about her suggested a woman who did as she pleased without concerning herself with convention. And she was a businesswoman no less. Belle was impressed.

They made polite observances on the weather and the train ride until the waiter brought their food.

"Now, tell me your name and what you are doing here in little La Porte," Della Rose commanded as they settled into their meals.

"I am Mrs. Belle Sorenson. I have bought the Quilleran mansion and have come to take possession of it and move in." She sat tall in her seat, pride at her accomplishment straightening her shoulders.

Della Rose laid down her fork and knife and eyed Belle with an assessing look. "Have you? And did you visit the Quilleran home before signing your papers?"

What a silly question. How could she have? "No, it was all done by mail."

"So. You have a surprise awaiting you, then."

Was that all the woman had to say? Did she even know the house? "Yes, I can't wait."

Della Rose tipped her head with a slight nod of acknowledgement. "Will Mr. Sorenson be joining you?"

"No, I am a widow. Mr. Sorenson passed away a few weeks ago."

"Ah. I detect from your tone that perhaps you are not the grieving widow. Perhaps, like me, you feel you are better off without a husband."

Della Rose's forthright manner gave Belle pause. Perhaps this woman was a kindred spirit. "I wouldn't say I have not grieved my husband," she replied cautiously.

"Of course, of course," Della Rose assured her. "But you will soon see that life as a widow is far superior to that as a wife."

When the check came, Della Rose insisted on paying for both meals. "It is my welcome gift to you as a newcomer to La Porte. And," she added with a sudden twinkle, "I admit I hope it will encourage you to come see me in my shop. I would love to dress you in something that enhances your appearance rather than hides it. You may not be the great beauty, but I know just what would suit you."

A new wardrobe to go with her beautiful new house sounded ideal to Belle. "Yes, I would love to come see you. Thank you very much."

6

The baggage room was staffed by Belle's big-eared shepherd from earlier, who jumped up eagerly and ran outside when Belle asked him to find a carriage to take her to her new home. He reappeared in minutes, breathless but grinning. "This way, ma'am," and he beckoned her to follow as he turned back around and led her through the station to the street.

Outside, the midday sun was blistering. Belle shaded her eyes against the glare. Carriages and wagons rolled along a busy industrial street. Belle noted a sleigh manufacturer, a plow works, and a machine shop, with more businesses farther down the street in both directions. It somewhat reminded Belle of the industrial sections of Indianapolis, but on a smaller scale.

Her escort took her to the corner, where an open farm wagon waited. The wagon bed was loaded with sacks of feed and farm implements, and a grizzled farmer sat on the driver's bench. His lower lip bulged with a plug of tobacco.

"Just over here, ma'am. Here you go," her porter said with pride.

"What is this?" Belle stopped short.

"A buckboard, ma'am?" The porter sounded puzzled.

"Is there no carriage? A closed carriage?"

"Um. No, ma'am. This is all I could find. But Mr. Nilson is happy to take you where you need to go."

Mr. Nilson grunted.

It was not how Belle had pictured arriving at her dream home, but never mind. What did it matter how she got there? Once she was at the Quilleran place—her place—all would be well.

Belle supervised the loading of her trunk onto the wagon, which required some shifting of seed bags, and then let the porter hand her up to the bench seat next to the driver, followed by her painting and holdall, which she awkwardly stowed at her feet. When the porter kept his hand out for a tip, she leaned down and patted his cheek. "How can I ever thank you?" She beamed. "You are my hero."

He blushed to his ears and stammered something that might have been "thank you" but sounded like "I love you."

"Take me to the Quilleran place," she told Mr. Nilson, enthusiasm overtaking the sting of being stuck on a buckboard.

"The what?" He shot a stream of tobacco juice into the street.

"I said"—Belle shifted away slightly—"the Quilleran place."

"Heard you," he said. "You don't want to go there."

"I beg your pardon? I will decide where I go, not you."

"Hmmph." The farmer's wagon remained stubbornly still.

Was she in some kind of farce? Was this monosyllabic farmer making fun of her? Did he not know of Judge Quilleran's stunning Victorian home? "Sir, if you are from out of town, perhaps there's someone else who can assist me."

"Lived on the prairie hereabouts my whole life." The farmer fell silent. Apparently, that was all he was going to say.

"Here, boy," Belle called to the porter, who was loitering nearby. When he heard her, his face lit up and he ran over.

"Please give this man directions to the Quilleran place," she said sweetly.

The boy tipped his hat back and scratched his head. "Well, now, you take Michigan Street here to, um . . ." He paused. "The what now, ma'am?"

Where had she landed? Was this town populated entirely by fools? Belle took hold of her patience and said, "Is there someone who would know all the properties in town? Someone who could give us directions?"

"Um." The boy did some more head-scratching. "Sheriff would know, I should think."

"Thank you. Your help has been invaluable."

Mistaking her tone, the boy blushed again and backed away, ducking his head in bashful adoration.

"Kindly take me to the sheriff," she directed the farmer.

"Git up now." The farmer rattled his reins, and the buckboard lurched forward, hauled at a plod by a squat brown horse. Mr. Nilson maneuvered the wagon into the flow of traffic, made a right at the next street and proceeded along the block past a cigar factory, a boarding house, and some modest dwellings. This is where Mads would have had them live, were he still alive and in charge. *But he is not. I am*, Belle thought with determined pride.

At the intersection they waited for a chance to cross. There was so much to look at that Belle wished she had eyes on all sides of her head. Directly across the street stood an imposing red stone building with arched windows and peaked gables. Shops sat cheek by jowl all up and down the street, advertising marble, harness repair, saddlery, groceries, tobacco, and more. Belle realized this street's offerings were more mercantile, and everywhere the businesses were busy and thriving. It set up an eager thrum in her heart. La Porte was a place where an industrious woman could find success.

They finally crossed, and immediately on the other side, Mr. Nilson called "Whoa," bringing them to a stop.

Now what? "Is there a problem?" Had he decided he wanted to be paid?

He nodded his head at something over her shoulder. She turned to look, finding them parked in front of a red stone building next to a hotel. "Sheriff," he said.

"Oh." Belle realized the imposing red stone building she'd seen a moment ago was big brother to this smaller one and was now just visible behind this little building. "What is that larger building there?"

"La Porte County Courthouse."

"Ah." She shifted her holdall and painting to free her feet. "Perhaps you'd be so kind as to help me down?"

He grunted and released the reins, clambering to the ground with a great deal of grumbling and muttering before offering her a gnarled and dirty hand. Belle didn't waste one of her smiles on him.

"Wait here," she commanded, hefting her holdall and the painting out of the wagon seat.

Inside the sheriff's office, the air was stifling, but at least she was out of the brutal sun. A man sat behind a desk, eyes on the papers before him. Soft white hair fell in a wave from his forehead over the back of his neck. A sheriff's star was pinned on the black vest he wore over a white shirt. Belle approached and said, "Good afternoon, sir." The sheriff gave no response. He was either a very intense concentrator or a very rude man. "Excuse me," she said a little louder.

Still nothing.

Just then, the door behind the sheriff's desk opened, and a younger man came through, his sandy blond hair brushing the lintel. He greeted her with a sunny grin as open and guileless as the prairie. "Good day, ma'am. How can the sheriff's department help you?"

"I was trying to speak to . . ." Belle gestured questioningly at the man at the desk who still maintained his intense concentration on his papers.

"That's Sheriff Johnson. Finest lawman the county's ever seen. He comes over tired nowadays, though." He leaned down to the old man's ear and shouted, "SHERIFF? SHERIFF JOHNSON? A LADY'S COME TO SEE YOU."

The sheriff snorted and picked up his head. A string of drool dripped onto his desk. "What's that?" The deputy took a handkerchief from the sheriff's pocket and wiped his face. The sheriff batted it away. "Off of me, boy. What you doin', Little Jimmy?"

"A lady has come to see you," Little Jimmy said loudly.

"What now? Who's this?" He peered up at Belle with watery blue eyes. "Hello there, pretty lady."

"Hello to you too," she said. "My name is Mrs. Belle Sorenson, and I am in need of assistance."

"Heh? What's she say?" the sheriff asked. "Little Jimmy, tell her to speak up."

"Yes, sir," Little Jimmy said. "Sheriff asks you to speak up, ma'am."

"I heard." Belle raised her voice. "Sheriff, I need your assistance."

"Heh?"

"I NEED DIRECTIONS TO THE QUILLERAN PLACE," Belle shouted. "I BOUGHT IT."

The old man stared at her so long she thought he'd had a seizure. Then he let out a long and wheezy burst of laughter, his face reddening to the color of a toadstool. His eyes screwed up into wrinkled wedges. He coughed and cackled, slapping his hand on his desk. Little Jimmy watched the display with a frown of confusion.

Belle was starting to think this whole town was in on some kind of joke. She appealed to the deputy. "Little Jimmy, is it? Perhaps you could help me?" She gave him her smile, sweetened with vulnerability and helplessness, certain he would be driven to rescue her.

She was pleased to see his neck flush. "It's, um, Deputy Hofstetter," he corrected her. He spread his hands and shrugged. "I don't know the place, ma'am, I'm sorry to say."

The sheriff held up a finger, gasping for breath. He fumbled in his pocket for a handkerchief and wiped his eyes. "It's out the McClung Road," he wheezed.

Belle looked to Little Jimmy to explain, but he seemed just as puzzled as she was.

"Past Clear Lake," the sheriff added.

"But that place is—" Little Jimmy stopped. He rubbed the back of his neck and inspected his shoes.

"Is what?" Belle demanded.

"Well, now, ma'am. It's not my place to say. It's yours now and, well. That's all there is to it."

He refused to tell Belle anything more as he escorted her outside.

"Of all the!" Belle exclaimed. The farmer had unloaded her trunk and left it on the sidewalk. He and his buckboard were nowhere to be seen.

Belle was not a complainer, but it had been a long and tiring day. She was bone-weary, and being abandoned by the farmer and his wagon swept the last lick of strength out of her. She sank down onto her trunk and let the painting fall against her knees.

Deputy Jimmy Hofstetter's heart broke to see his charming visitor so distraught. She drooped like a wilted cornstalk after the harvest. "Don't take on now, ma'am. What's happened?"

"Mr. Nilson was to drive me to my new house. But he's gone and left me."

"Old Farmer Nilson? I can't say that's a surprise. He's a solitary one, used to marching to his own drummer. But you don't need to fret. I can drive you out there. You rest awhile inside while I hitch up the wagon."

Deputy Hofstetter settled Mrs. Sorenson inside and went to ready the patrol wagon. When he returned, she had her head nestled lightly in one hand. She was a picture of all that was sweet and good. How Nilson could have up and left her, Deputy Hofstetter couldn't say.

He leaned down and whispered, "Mrs. Sorenson?" Her lids fluttered open, and for a moment, Deputy Hofstetter was inches away from the widest, bluest eyes he'd ever seen. He felt a blush creep over his face. He hated the way he reddened whenever he tried to talk to a lady, which only made him blush more.

"Oh, Little Jimmy! You surprised me. Do you have a carriage ready?"

Gosh, how he hated that nickname. People had called him Little Jimmy since he was still in short pants, and when he grew and started to take on the height he was now known for, they just kept calling him that. Because it was funny now, wasn't it? Calling a tall man "Little"? Well, it wasn't funny to Jimmy, and he wished he could convince Sheriff Johnson to call him Deputy Hofstetter. If the sheriff would show him that respect, then surely other folks would follow suit. But the truth was that Sheriff Johnson was pretty well into his dotage and not likely to change.

Deputy Hofstetter wanted to explain all of this to the pretty lady, but his tongue was so tied up in knots, all he could do was gesture for her to follow him. He was such a fool. What could a fine lady like Mrs. Sorenson ever see in him, anyway? Besides, she was married.

She let him take her elbow and guide her to the wagon outside. When she caught sight of it, she stopped short.

"First a farm wagon, now a patrol wagon," she said.

"Sorry, ma'am, it's all I have. Is it all right?"

"It's fine, it's fine. Better than a ragpicker's cart, I suppose." She held out her hand to him. "Here, help me up."

The drive out to the Quilleran place was not far, only a couple miles. Deputy Hofstetter tried to think of something to say, but the more he tried to force thoughts into words, the dumber he became. When the wagon bumped into the weed-choked driveway, Deputy Hofstetter noticed Mrs. Sorenson tighten up beside him, and when he pulled the horses to a stop in front of the house, he felt more than heard her intake of breath.

This can't be right, Belle thought. The place was a ramshackle mess. Weeds and brush clogged the driveway and yard, and the house was a symphony of neglect: broken windows, the front door hanging off its hinges, the covered porch listing badly on collapsing posts.

"Is it not what you expected, ma'am?"

She glared at the deputy with disbelief and lifted the wrapped painting to her lap. "See this?" She tore at the brown paper, peeling it back. "*This* is what I expected." His eyes widened. "Well? Don't you have anything to say?" The big oaf stared at her, his face reddening. "How long has it been this way?"

"Ma'am, it hasn't looked like that since I was a boy." He seemed embarrassed to be the one to tell her.

Energized by her own indignation, she climbed down from the wagon, kicking her skirts out of the way. She started trying to get down her heavy trunk but could only tug at it ineffectually.

"What are you doing, ma'am?"

"What does it look like? I may have bought a cat in a bag, but it's my cat. *Mine.* I'm unloading my belongings. They're not going to trot inside on their own, are they? And you're too busy catching flies to help me."

That got him unstuck. He reached over her head and plucked the trunk and then the holdall down with ease.

"Come on," she said, and headed toward the front door.

"But ma'am, you can't stay here," he blurted out.

"Oh, I'm staying here," she called back. "I bought this place, it's mine, and I'm not leaving."

Little Jimmy rushed ahead, mounting the stairs two at a time and reaching the door first. The door had, in all likelihood, been magnificent once upon a time. Wide, sturdy, and imposing, with elegant scrolling enhancing its four panels, it would have announced to all who entered the Quilleran home that here lived an upright man of rectitude and judgment, a man uniquely qualified to dispense justice, and a wife of great taste who merited respect all her own. Now it sagged off its hinges and hung slightly ajar, faded flakes of once-black paint littering the floorboards.

"Allow me," Little Jimmy said and pushed the door inward. An ominous groan scraped the air as it swung wide, and Belle found herself staring into the dimness of the front hall. Behind her, the buzz of grass-hoppers filled the heat of the day. Before her, the house was silent.

Then with a crack of splintering wood, the door sagged away from the jamb, and, without bothering to announce its retirement, fell to the floor like a diva denied her last demand. The crash was deafening, the result final. Dust and rotted wood filled the air in a choking, blinding cloud. Belle refused to see it as a metaphor for her situation.

"Well, that's a fine mess," Little Jimmy commented.

Belle cast a withering glance at him, then took hold of herself and bustled inside.

Little Jimmy followed. "Are you sure about this, ma'am? This house has been neglected a long time."

Belle wasn't sure at all, but she had finally arrived at her dream home, and she wasn't about to give up on it now.

To the right, a staircase rose to the second floor, its balusters broken and missing. To the left, an arched doorway led to a parlor or sitting room. Glass and rocks littered the floor, remnants of mischievous boys breaking windows, no doubt. The remaining panes were coated with grime, blocking out light. Piles of mouse droppings were mounded in corners, and cobwebs were strung like bunting.

Belle drifted, stunned, through the rest of the downstairs. The library contained empty, dust-covered bookshelves and shredded leaves and fibers, the vestiges of some animal's nest. The water closet was a nightmare. Water damage marred the wood flooring. The exterior of the porcelain commode was stained and dingy, and the wooden seat and lid had been torn away. Belle dared not step beyond the doorway. She leaned forward from her toes to see inside the bowl. Something dark and nasty filled the toilet. The stench was overpowering. "Is that what I think it is?"

"Well, ma'am." Little Jimmy blushed bright red to the roots of his hair. "I'm afraid, um, it may be." He drew her back and let the door close. "Maybe the kitchen is in better condition."

The kitchen was the last room on the ground floor. She took a breath and pushed open the door. It could have been a snug room and probably was once a perfectly functional kitchen. But now trash and debris were strewn across a grimy floor and heaped into corners. An old iron cookstove brooded against one wall, its formerly fine filigree accents rusted solid. Cupboards stood agape, their shelves empty except for more mouse droppings and nest remnants. A back door leading to the yard hung open.

And in the corner, a dark, shaggy beast hulked like an escapee from the gates of hell. It grunted and snorted, rooting in the debris, then jerked up its head and directed a malevolent glare at Belle.

Belle froze. Fear squeezed her throat, and her heart pounded in her ears. The beast grunted a threat.

Suddenly she was jerked backward by Little Jimmy, who pushed ahead of her, smoothly drawing his revolver. He blasted off a shot, and the beast scuttled across the floor and out the back door. He followed it to the threshold, craning his neck.

"He's gone, ma'am. Best see if we can get this door to stay closed." He put the door to, but the latch wouldn't catch.

"Wha— wha— what. What was that?"

"Wild boar, ma'am. Quilleran kept hogs. When he died and no one claimed the place, the herd reverted to wild over the years. They're mean as the dickens. Best to steer clear of 'em if you can." He went back to fussing with the door, pushing at it with his shoulder, forcing it to latch.

Belle felt the last ounce of will leach out of her. It was as if the strings holding her up had been severed. She slumped against the wall as tears began to well up. She hated the loss of control and scrubbed at her eyes, pressing back the emotion.

"Oh, hey now." Little Jimmy approached her. "It's all over now. No need to fret. He's just a little old boar. They're mighty fierce—"

Belle let her tears escalate to a wail of distress. Little Jimmy wanted to be the hero, console the little lady? Belle could easily play that role.

"—but he's gone now," Little Jimmy blurted. "He's gone now, and it's all fine. There, there. There now." He patted her shoulder awkwardly.

Belle turned and pressed her face into his chest and clutched at his shirt. She sobbed and hiccupped. The deputy stood stiffly as she huddled into him. With shy hesitation, he put an arm around her shoulders. Her sobs slowed, and she melted her body into his. Belle felt the deputy sink into the embrace before catching himself and stiffening again.

"There now, ma'am," he repeated as he eased back, putting space between them.

"Thank you, Little Jimmy." Belle tilted her face up to him with wide eyes. "I don't know what I would have done without you."

"It's no trouble at all." His neck and cheeks were blotched bright red. "Um. Do you want to see the rest of the house?"

Playing the reassured heroine to his strong hero, Belle gave him a smile that was warm but with a touch of shyness. "Yes, I think I'm ready now." She straightened her back and led the way to the foyer with its grand staircase.

When she went to mount the stairs, he barred her way with his arm and said, "Careful now, ma'am. You'd better let me go first." He tested each tread before putting his full weight on, and their ascent was slow but uneventful.

The upstairs rooms were in somewhat better shape, as no rocks had sailed this high and most of the windows were intact. There were four bedrooms and a water closet, and Belle chose the largest bedroom for herself. It might be a wreck right now, but she would transform it into a room befitting a queen.

A narrow door toward the front of the house opened to a claustrophobic, winding staircase that led up to the square turret. A sharp odor of ammonia assaulted Belle as she leaned in to peer up the dark stairway. "Oh!" she gasped, covering her mouth and nose.

"Probably bats up there, ma'am."

Belle closed the door firmly. A problem for another day.

"Well, ma'am," said Little Jimmy. "I've been gone from the sheriff's office for a spell, and it's time I get back. If there's nothing more I can do for you."

"Just one thing, if you wouldn't mind," answered Belle.

"Of course, ma'am."

"I'm going to need to hire men to fix up this place," she said. "Perhaps you know someone?"

"Well, now." The deputy laughed sheepishly. "It'll take an army of workers to make this place livable."

Belle scowled at him.

"But it happens I might know one or two men who can help. I'll see what I can do."

She rewarded him with an approving smile. "Thank you, Little Jimmy.

7

I'm in hell. I'm in hell, and I put myself here.

Belle spread out a pile of clothes as a bed of sorts and lay down to sleep. It wasn't comfortable but would have to do until her furniture arrived from Indianapolis. She couldn't see a thing once she blew out her candle, and there was not a sound of human habitation, not a whisper of traffic or neighbors or industry. It was dead silent. And Belle was completely alone.

Sometime in the night, coyotes set up a yipping howl, singing a devilish call and response that chilled her heart. It seemed to go on for hours, and Belle only realized she'd slipped into sleep when a cock crowed at the first glimmer of daylight.

With the morning sun shining in, she assessed her bedroom. She'd chosen it because it was the biggest, and in the early light, she saw it was also beautiful. Spacious, with large windows, the room had an alcove perfectly sized for a master bed, framed by support columns that were gracefully turned. True, the columns and the matching paneling on the walls needed refinishing, but that would be easily solved.

She went to the second-floor water closet. It was grimy but nothing like the one downstairs, which seemed to have been used by every passing hobo in the county. Belle opened the tap. The long-disused pipes protested with a groan, and Belle stared at the reluctant taps, willing them to give her water. She heard a grumble, and then a gush of brownish, fetid liquid splashed violently into the sink, rebounding against the porcelain and spraying directly into her face.

Son of Benjamin! Foul water dripped from Belle's brow onto her chin as she stood frozen in disbelief. Repulsed, she hastily stripped off her soiled nightdress and found a patch of unsoaked fabric to scrub away the filth from her face and arms. She put on yesterday's clothes—no point dressing in a fresh outfit—and went downstairs, leaving her sodden, smelly nightdress on the floor of her room. With the plan of taking stock of what tools and provisions she would need, she headed for the kitchen. Swinging open the door, she was confronted with the reappearance of the feral hog. It trained its beady eyes on her and snorted. Then it charged.

With two clenched fistfuls of skirts, Belle tore back down the hallway and leaped up the stairs, chased by a terrible shriek. When she reached the top of the stairs and stopped to catch her breath, the shrieking ceased, and she realized it had been her.

The swine trotted out the front door. Belle could have sworn the fiend was smiling.

I'm in hell, she thought again. She sank down onto the top step of the staircase. What had she gotten herself into? The house was nothing like what she had pictured, what she had been promised. She wanted independence and the castle she deserved. Instead, she was in a dilapidated, run-down dump. She couldn't face the fears lurking in the depths of her mind: Was this all a mistake? Should she never have bought the house?

Her reverie was broken by a knock at the door—or rather, where the door had been before it fell off its hinges.

"Hello?" The man standing in the doorway was gray. Everything about him was drab—clothes, complexion, spirit, and manner. He slouched with apologetic shoulders, as if asking for the right to exist. He peered in. "'S there a Miz Sorenson here?"

"Yes, I'm Mrs. Sorenson," Belle called down. "Who's there?" She rose and descended the stairs.

The man swiped a beaten and dusty gray cap from his head and crossed the threshold. "Name's Ray Lamphere, ma'am. I heard you was looking to hire a handyman?"

Belle approached the man slowly, taking him in. He was so skinny he must be malnourished, every bit of him washed out and colorless. He blended into the space around him, as if the color been drained out of him by a life of drudgery and neglect. What could he possibly have to offer? There was only one way to find out.

She smiled.

For Ray, setting eyes on Belle Sorenson was like the clouds parting, a shaft of light beaming down, and an angel descending. Her hair was dusky brown, her skin translucent, her posture regal. It was as if he were seeing in color for the first time. She floated down the stairs, and it was all Ray could do to remain upright on his feet.

"I'm so sorry. I think there's been some sort of mistake," Mrs. Sorenson said, her smile sweet as blooming milkweed. "Little Jimmy must have misspoken. I'm afraid I can't afford to hire anyone. But thank you so much for coming by. I'm sorry you've wasted your time."

She couldn't have crushed him any harder than if she'd taken a sledgehammer to his skull. "Aw, shittagoddam," he muttered under his breath. The thought of walking away and never seeing this angel again sucked the color out of his world once more.

But it figured. Nothing good ever happened to him.

Belle watched the handyman slump into himself and turn to go. The man seemed to have no fight. Had no one ever believed in him or given him a purpose beyond merely breathing? This was going to be far too easy. "Perhaps there's one small thing you can do for me, before you go?" she gently requested. "If it's no trouble to ask?"

He spun back around with hope brimming in his eyes. "No trouble at all, ma'am. What can I do for you?"

He looked like a hungry puppy. And there was nothing more loyal than a rescued dog.

"I have a painting I want hung. I know, don't gawp at me like that. The house is a wreck and needs a great deal more than decorating. But when you see the painting, you will understand. Here, look." Belle went to where the partially unwrapped painting leaned against the wall next to the stairs. She tore the rest of the brown paper away and turned it toward Mr. Lamphere.

He came closer. "Well, shittagoddam— Uh, sorry, ma'am. Just airin' my lungs. What I mean to say is, ain't that this place? Ain't ever seen it looking like that, though."

"Exactly right, Mr. Lamphere. This is what I thought I was buying. And somehow, by hook or by crook, I want to return it to its glory. I don't know how I'll do it or how long it will take. But I want this painting to be where I can see it every day, where it will remind me of what could be and inspire me. Does that make any sense?"

"Yes, ma'am, it surely does."

"And I want it to hang right here." Belle indicated the large wall on the left of the hallway, which separated it from the parlor. "Can you do that for me?"

"No trouble at all, ma'am."

And Ray Lamphere was as good as his word. He went to his wagon and fetched a hammer and nail and had the painting up on the wall in minutes.

Belle stood back to take it in. If she focused only on the painting, ignoring the clutter and debris and broken glass that surrounded her, she could envision what the mansion should be. *Would* be. "Thank you, Mr. Lamphere. I'm very grateful."

"Like I said, no trouble at all." He paused at the empty doorway. "You ain't got no door, ma'am."

"Yes, I know. It fell right off its hinges when we opened it yesterday. I suppose I'll try to board it up today."

Mr. Lamphere inspected the damage. He moved his hands over the door jamb, picking at the rotten timber. He fingered the rusted hinges. Finally, he knocked on the door itself. "Be a shame to throw away a perfectly good door," he said.

"It may well be, but I can't spend another night here with the house open to the all outdoors. The feral hogs keep wandering in and out. And I simply can't afford a new door."

Mr. Lamphere's eyebrows popped up at that. "No, ma'am, that won't do. Leave it to me." He nodded his commitment to the job.

"Mr. Lamphere, I couldn't impose on you. As I said, I can't pay you."

"Won't be no trouble," he said.

"Well, then. Thank you so very, very much. I just don't know what I would do without you . . . Ray." She gave his name a shy spin, as if asking permission to be familiar with him.

He didn't object, as she knew he wouldn't. A loyal puppy likes to hear its name.

While Ray worked on her door, Belle returned to her bedroom and approached her holdall, stashed in the corner and closed tight. The metal clasp was held fast with a lock, its key hanging from a chain beneath her shirtwaist, nestled against her heart.

An unfamiliar despair had begun to creep up on Belle. Doubt plagued her—doubt about her choices, doubt about her plan, doubt about how she had ended up in this wreck of a house in a tiny town in the middle of the northern Indiana prairie. It wasn't at all what she had envisioned.

Belle resolved to stow away those doubts. She had allies. Little Jimmy had been so eager and protective, saving her from the hog and making sure she would be safe for the night. And now there was Ray. Capable, sweet, desperate Ray, working steadfastly to repair her door. Plus there was the one thing she could always count on, no matter what. Something that would never desert her or let her down.

Belle took the key out from under her clothing, slipped the chain over her head, and inserted the key in the lock of the holdall. It snicked softly, the sound of secrets. Spreading the sides of the holdall wide, Belle inspected the contents. Nearly four thousand dollars. It was a beautiful sight, the tidy bundles of twenties and the handbag containing loose notes and coins. How lovely it had felt at the Indianapolis train station to withdraw a bill from her purse to pay her fare, to have money on the train to enjoy a cup of tea in the dining car.

But after all her yearning, her dream house had turned out to be a cat in a bag. A cat with ragged fur, notched ears, and snaggle teeth.

She should have suspected it when the asking price was so close to the selling price of the house in Indianapolis. It was almost a one-for-one exchange. She was so eager to acquire this house that she didn't stop to think. A foolish mistake, and one she would take care not to repeat.

But she had the cure to turn this raggedy alley cat into a lioness.

Belle took her handbag out of the holdall. The handbag itself was new, one of her first purchases after coming into her money. It was wine-colored satin, decorated with green velvet cutouts and stitched with moss-green floss and thread-of-gold. Tassels of green and gold silk cord dangled from its bottom. It was the loveliest item Belle had ever owned. She fortified it with a fresh ten-dollar note and looped the gold and black silk drawstring cord over her wrist. Relocking her holdall and restowing the key under her shirtwaist, she rose from the floor, dusted her skirts off, and went downstairs.

Ray lurked awkwardly at the foot of the stairs, twisting his cap in nervous hands.

"Ray! What a sight for sore eyes. It feels like an age since I saw you," Belle sang out brightly as she descended.

Ray perked up at the greeting. His shoulders straightened and relaxed, and his arms fell to his sides. "Miz Sorenson, I wanted to tell you. I need to go into town for supplies to fix your door."

"Perfect! I shall accompany you. There are things I need in town. You can regale me with the story of your life on the way."

"Oh, Miz Sorenson, that's a story no one wants to hear." Ray ducked his head, shying his eyes away from her.

"I'll be the judge of that," she said. "Now hurry, go get your wagon ready."

The day was fine, the sky a cornflower blue Belle had never seen before. The sky in Indianapolis always seemed begrimed with coal smoke and industrial exhaust. Here, it stretched away to the horizon, infinitely open and beautiful. Ray drove the wagon slowly along the lane. Leafy trees lined the way, and through them, Belle spotted water. Two little lakes, throwing off sparkles of sunlight just as bright as her mood.

Ray sat stiffly on the bench, struggling to think of how to make conversation. Mrs. Sorenson was so pretty next to him, driving all thought from his brain. What could he possibly say that she would be interested in? Not a thing. So he drove the horse in tortured silence.

Until Mrs. Sorenson broke it. "Ray, you have to help me."

Ray started, then darted a look to her. *Anything*, he thought. *I'll do anything to help you*. But the words stuck in his throat.

"You've lived here your whole life, have you not?"

Ray nodded mutely.

"Ray, I have a problem, and I think you can help me. Maybe you're the only one who can. You see, I've just moved here, and I know nothing about La Porte. But you, you are an expert. Ray, I need you to tell me about La Porte."

La Porte was the only place Ray had ever lived. How could he explain what it was when he knew nothing else? He didn't know where to begin. Thoughts stalled in his brain and words clotted his throat.

"Um. I. Gosh, Miz Sorenson. I don't . . ."

"I understand completely," she said, patting his arm and leaving her hand there. His skin tingled with electricity from her touch. The power of it made him want to both run and pull her to him. Instead, he held himself very still. "You love it so much you don't know where to begin. Let's do this: I'll ask you a question, and you give me an answer. All right?"

Ray nodded, grateful for her consideration.

"Let me see." She tapped a finger on her lips. "I know. Tell me about where we are. What are these two pretty lakes I see through the trees?"

"Oh, that's easy." Ray pointed to his left. "This one is Lower Lake. And"—he leaned forward and gestured beyond her to their right—"that one is Clear Lake. Cleanest water in the county," he finished proudly.

"I see. And what about my neighbors? What can you tell me about them?"

"Back that way"—Ray gestured behind him, toward a neat white farmhouse protected by a screen of trees—"that's Hank Philips. He owns almost seventy acres, including that pasture across from your place. He's a good man. You need anything, you can ask him. Now up ahead here, on the left, this cabin, see?"

The Dirt Troll's little cabin was coming into view. Its eaves hung low over a single story of unpainted clapboards, presenting a cramped, forbidding appearance. Unkempt grass and weeds grew wild in the front yard, and brambles lined the road. On one end of the building, a stone chimney looked like it had been thrown together rather than thoughtfully constructed.

"Yes, I see it."

Ray spat in the dirt, thinking of the last time he'd seen the Dirt Troll. Ray was walking back to town from an odd job when a group of boys descended on the place, hooting and hollering for Dirt Troll to show his face. When he appeared from nowhere and plucked one child off the ground, holding him aloft as if to throw him, the other boys screamed in terror and ran off. Dirt Troll carried the unlucky boy to the road and set him down ever so gently, giving him a tender pat on the head. The boy stared at him in wonder, no doubt surprised to find himself still alive. Until the Dirt Troll closed the space between them, put his face a hair's breadth from the boy's, and screeched, "And don't come back!" The boy fell on his backside, scrambled to his feet, and took off. He never once looked back, so he never saw the Dirt Troll chuckle gleefully at his retreat.

"That's the Dirt Troll. You don't wanna talk to him. He's loony."

Mrs. Sorenson craned her neck to get a look at the place as they passed by, but Ray didn't see any sign of life. The Dirt Troll was usually in his fields working, or he was off somewhere unknown. Probably trucking with the devil.

As they neared town and more houses appeared, tidy homes with smaller lots only big enough for a kitchen garden and some chickens, she asked, "How many people live in this good town?"

Ray took one hand off the reins and rubbed the back of his neck, thinking hard. "Not sure exactly. Maybe eight or nine thousand?"

"That's quite a bit smaller than I'm used to. You may know I came from the big city, Indianapolis. So many people, so much bustle. It's not peaceful like it is here. You are a lucky man, Ray Lamphere, to call La Porte your home. Tell me, is there a Mrs. Lamphere? Do you have a passel of little Lampheres?"

Ray's cheeks burned. "No, ma'am," he choked out. "No Mrs. Lamphere except my mother, and no little Lampheres."

"Never fear, Ray. You're a young man yet. I'm sure there's a pretty little miss out there for you, just waiting on her knight in shining armor to appear. Because that's what you are, aren't you? You're my knight in shining armor. I don't know what I'd do without you to help me with my door problem. I'd be sleeping with the feral hogs if it weren't for you!"

Her laugh tinkled merrily in his ear, and Ray thought he could die a happy man right then and there. No woman had ever paid attention to him, given him compliments like this. He drove the rest of the way into town listening to Mrs. Sorenson's friendly chatter. When they crossed the railroad tracks and came into the heart of La Porte, she instructed him to take her to the "shopping district." He wasn't sure what a shopping district was, but Knowlt Fisher's mercantile was a good place to start.

"I need to buy provisions, Ray. I'm going to make you a proper supper after you finish boarding up my door. It's the least I can do to thank you. No, I won't hear it. No buts. Not a word of it. You wouldn't hurt my feelings by saying no to my hospitality, would you?"

"Oh, no, ma'am. I would never hurt you. That's a promise."

She beamed at him and patted his arm. "Go on now, get your supplies. Start an account for me at the lumberyard and charge it to that. Pick me up here in, say, an hour?"

"Yes, ma'am."

Mrs. Sorenson climbed down from the wagon, and it wasn't until shouts of impatience roused him that Ray realized he had stopped traffic to stare after her.

Knowlt Fischer was not a bad man. At least, he didn't think of himself as one. He ran Fischer Mercantile as a straight shooter, honest and trustworthy. He was a friend to man and a good provider. He never beat his wife.

The bell over the door chimed as Mrs. Bauer, the pastor's wife, left with her weekly shopping and a new customer entered. Knowlt observed the lady swaying gently as she walked, her gaze direct and sure, unlike the mousy looks Mabel gave him still, even after all these years. What would it be like to be married to a woman who could hold her own? Knowlt would likely never find out.

Whose fault was it that Mabel was as suited to him as a fish is to the prairie? He had courted her in the traditional way: gone walking after church, danced at the church suppers, even visited her family at home. He'd taken her, properly chaperoned, for afternoon drives in his one-horse carriage. And then they'd married. How could he have known how different it would be after their nuptials? Does a rat get inside the trap and think, I didn't know I don't like bland, insipid cheese?

And if no one knew the truth, the misery that lay locked inside his heart, then he counted himself a successful man.

"Good morning, ma'am," he said as the woman approached. "It's a fine day today, isn't it?"

"Hello," she said, adding a wide smile to her greeting. "Very fine, indeed. I need to open an account. Can you help me?"

"If I can't, nobody can," he said with a wink. "What with me being the owner, don't you know." He produced a ledger from under the counter. This woman was as different from Mabel as could be. Thick, dark hair, where Mabel's was colorless and fine; strong and tall compared to Mabel's wispy frame. And that smile—it was so sweet, it slipped inside his soul and took up residence. If Mabel had ever smiled at him like that, well. Wouldn't that be something?

"Mr. Fischer, is it?"

"Knowlt Fischer, at your service." He gave a short bow.

"How do you do. I am new in town. My name is Mrs. Belle Sorenson."

"Pleased to meet you, Mrs. Sorenson. Welcome to La Porte. You've come to the right place to supply a new household. Who's your mister?"

"There is no mister."

He tapped his pen on the ledger and eyed her. "I need your husband's name to open an account."

"His name won't do you any good from the great beyond."

A widow? Well, now. Knowlt's interest was piqued. Not that he would be unfaithful or put Mabel out. But a man could dream. "You're a widow? Why didn't you say so? No need to make things difficult." He wrote her name on a new page in the ledger. "Place of residence?"

"I just moved to town. I own the Quilleran mansion."

"Do you, now? What'd you do to earn that punishment? Heh." She didn't laugh back, but her smile held its place, letting him know she didn't think him too much the fool. "What can I get you?"

Mrs. Sorenson placed a suitably large order, everything from wheat flour, sugar, and coffee to canned peas and tomatoes, a new oil lamp, kerosene, a broom and dustpan, laundry soap, and a washtub. Given what he knew of the old Quilleran place, she'd need a lot more than a few cleaning supplies.

"Drive your wagon around to the back of the store on Jefferson

Avenue," he said, "and my boys will load it up. Unless you need it delivered?"

"I have a wagon," Mrs. Sorenson said. "My hired man will drive us around before we leave town."

"Very good. Best of luck to you," he said as she departed. *You're going to need it*, he didn't say out loud.

Belle spent the remainder of the day in the kitchen, clearing out the accumulated trash and debris, and scrubbing the floor and surfaces. After getting the crotchety old stove to light and then struggling for hours to create a meal on it, she found Ray packing up. "Ray! That door is still wide open to the all outdoors! I thought you said you could board it up for me?" What had the man been doing all afternoon?

He said nothing but reached for the door handle and swung it shut. It closed with a solid thunk.

Belle clapped with delighted surprise. "Why, Ray! This is more than I could have dreamed. You fixed it!"

"It's nothing, Miz Sorenson. Just a few hours work." Ray shuffled his feet awkwardly and looked everywhere but at her.

"Nothing? Nothing, you say? I say, 'hah' to that! I could just kiss you." Belle closed the space between them, crowding Ray against the newly functional door.

"Oh, um, gosh, I . . ."

"Oh, don't worry, Ray." She laughed, patting his shoulder and dancing away. "That wouldn't be appropriate, now would it?" Poor Ray didn't reply, and Belle could practically see him falling in love with her. "Ray, I have a surprise for you. I promised you supper. Come to the kitchen."

Belle had roasted a chicken she'd purchased from the butcher in town and was serving it with potatoes and turnips mashed with cream, canned tomatoes warmed on the stove, and a slightly burnt apple pie.

The stove was old and drafty and impossible to keep at an even temperature, but she had done her level best.

They took their plates outside to sit on the porch steps. The sun was sliding down to the horizon, and the day was beginning to cool. As they ate, Belle alternately thanked and praised and then teased Ray, keeping him on uncertain footing. He plowed through the meal like a starving man and, if he noticed the pie's burnt crust, said nothing about it.

"Thank you, Miz Sorenson. I don't get a feast like this all too often, I can tell you that. My mama is . . . Well . . . She don't cook like you, is all."

"It is I who should thank you, Ray," Belle said. "Those hogs would be here stealing my supper and trying to get into my bed if it weren't for you. Now I can shut the door and know I'm safe. All thanks to you."

Ray stood up. "I should get on home now. My mama will be wondering where I am."

"How lucky you are to have a mother who worries about her boy like that," Belle said, putting a touch of wistfulness to her tone. Her own mother brought no such feelings of loyalty or fondness. The woman had been far too busy taking care of Belle's demanding father, too worn out from years of farming and raising children, to give Belle more than cursory attention. Belle had practically raised herself.

"I don't know about that," Ray muttered.

His hesitation was plain as day to Belle's eye. "Would you care to visit me again tomorrow?" she offered.

Ray stopped his awkward shuffling and looked up earnestly. "I believe I can do that, ma'am."

"How wonderful." She blessed him with an approving look. "You are my only friend in this town, Ray. I'll see you tomorrow."

Ray nodded, unable to hide his shy pleasure, and took his leave. Belle watched his wagon rumble down the weedy driveway. Ray Lamphere was a treasure she hadn't expected to find. Such a sad, needful man.

Things were looking up.

***

The following morning when Ray arrived, Belle greeted him with biscuits hot from the oven, almost not burnt. Replacing the old stove was high on her growing list of improvements. But drizzled with honey, the biscuits became perfectly edible, and Ray's gratitude was plain. He devoured three before setting to work on her rear door.

With Ray well-fed, she directed her attention to the rest of the downstairs. A thorough cleaning of every nook and cranny needed to be done, so all would be ready when her furniture arrived. As she swept up glass in the library, she mulled over the problem of all the broken windows. Was that something Ray could fix? After dumping her full dustpan into the kitchen trash bin, Belle took a break to visit Ray. She loaded a few more biscuits onto a plate and poured honey over them. "Hello?" she called out the back door. "Are you hungry?"

The August air was steamy hot. Ray had his sleeves rolled up, and sweat stained his shirt. He was a lanky man, not well-formed, with narrow shoulders and long limbs. Beads of sweat glistened on his sinewy forearms. As she got closer, she could see scars under the sweat, crisscrossing the skin of his arms, all the way up to where they disappeared under his shirtsleeves.

"Always hungry for your cooking, Miz Sorenson." He helped himself to the biscuits.

"You sure know how to flatter a girl, Ray." If Ray thought her singed biscuits and burnt pie were something special, she couldn't imagine what passed for a meal at his home.

"Good news, Miz Sorenson," Ray said. "Your rear door is fixed." He demonstrated by pushing it shut. It latched easily.

"My, that was fast," Belle said. "Let's sit awhile."

Ray tried to focus on what Mrs. Sorenson was saying as they sat side by side on the back stoop. She had patted the boards next to her and insisted he rest for a spell, but his mind kept drifting to what she'd said the day before. She hadn't meant anything by her comment about his mother, he knew. Most people had fond feelings for their mothers. But to call him lucky to have a worrying mother, well, Ray wasn't too sure about that. There was a lot about his mother that most people would find unlucky at best, maybe even downright cruel. But he wasn't about to tell Mrs. Sorenson about that. Beautiful, kind, thoughtful Mrs. Sorenson. Belle, though he couldn't possibly call her by her given name. He hated to leave her and go home to his mother, who would be waiting for him with nothing but criticism.

"What about you, Ray?" she asked.

"Me?"

"Yes, you, you silly goose," she said. "I've told you all about me. Now it's your turn. That's how a conversation goes. Tell me something about you."

"Nothing to tell, Miz Sorenson. There's nothing interesting about me."

"Ray, don't talk about yourself like that. There's something interesting about everyone. Let's see. Where were you born?"

"Here."

"And do you have family? Brothers and sisters?"

"Just my mother. No brothers or sisters."

"What about your father? Did he pass away?"

"Couldn't answer that, Miz Sorenson. He left my mother and me when I was just a tyke."

"I'm sorry, Ray. That must have been difficult."

Ray shrugged. He didn't remember anything about his father, but his mother had told him plenty, and none of it was good. "We're better off without him." That's what his mother always said. Although Ray wasn't sure how much worse things could have been.

"Is that how you got these?" Her voice was gentle, and she delicately touched his arm where his scars were, igniting an electric thrill that traveled straight into his brain. As with the last time she touched him, Ray forced himself to hold very still. Just talk normal, he coached himself.

"No, Mama did that." As soon as he said it, he was full of regret. Stupid, stupid, stupid. He could hardly think straight with her fingers tracing those damn scars. Mrs. Sorenson wouldn't want to hear about how his mother beat him. He should have made up a story. A brave story about bronco riding or fighting Indians or tackling a wild boar.

"Oh, Ray. You poor thing." He glanced up and saw real sympathy in her eyes.

"Aw, it's nothing. I probably deserved it."

"They're so faint it must have been a long time ago."

"Maybe a few years now," he said. "I walked a girl home from church one Sunday. Mama didn't like it. She said only a harlot would want to marry me. And I would go to hell if I married her. I'm ashamed to say it, Miz Sorenson, but I got mad, and I told her to shut up."

"What a horrible thing to say to you. Of course, you stood up for yourself."

"M—maybe." Ray stumbled over his words in confusion. He'd never had anyone take his side. "But she went and cut a willow switch and came at me. I put my arms up and got all cut up."

"Takes strength to carry on, if you ask me," Mrs. Sorenson said quietly. "You're very brave."

Ray shrugged. He never thought of himself as brave. More like the opposite. He'd never fought in a war or gone adventuring out West. He'd lived his whole life in his mother's house in a tiny little town in northern Indiana. What was brave about that?

Belle let her compliment sit with Ray as she stared out over the long grass of the pasture. In the middle of the field, at the top of a slight rise, grew a solitary cherry tree. She stood and stretched and gazed up at the house she'd taken on. Time to sink her hook even deeper. "Just look at

this place, Ray. It needs so much work. And then there's the barn and
caretaker's cottage on top of it. What am I going to do?"

"Ma'am?"

"I need your advice. Tell me what you think about my house.
Come." She tugged him by the arm to the front of the house. The
cream-painted trim was peeling badly. Flakes littered the ground and
the overgrown shrubs like snow. "I'm going to need to paint all this
wood. The trim, the shutters. And these bushes! I should tear them out.
What do you think?"

"Nah, they just need a good trim, and they'll bloom again. These
here are lilacs. You prune 'em, and they'll be full of flowers next spring.
And a painter can scrape and paint this trim for you."

Hmm. Pruning she could handle. Or get Ray to handle. But painting was another story.

Ray fingered a brick, and bits crumbled away. "Humph. That's bad."

"What? What's bad?"

"See here." He pointed at the white stripes between the bricks.
"The mortar's failing. You need a bricklayer to come and repoint all
these bricks."

"Oh no." Belle had visions of dollar bills flying out of her holdall
and sailing away on the winds. "What if I don't repair the bricks?"

Ray scratched the back of his neck. "Well . . . I'm not a bricklayer,
but if you don't take care of it, it will only get worse. Bricks may start
to fall out."

"Ray! That's awful. Can you fix it?"

"No, ma'am, I never learned bricklaying."

"This is terrible." She cast her eyes over the house again, this time
landing on the broken glass. "What about the windows? I need those
fixed before the cold weather comes."

"That's a fact, Miz Sorenson. But I'm not a glazier either," Ray said.
"I may know some fellas can help you."

"Do you really?" More dollar bills scattered to the wind. "Please, tell
them to come by."

"The thing is, Miz Sorenson, I don't think they'll work for free."

"Oh, Ray, don't you worry. You just tell them to come by."

"Um, Miz Sorenson, I think we ought to discuss—"

Belle leaned forward and planted a light kiss on his mouth. Then she gasped and drew back. She let a little surprised laugh escape her lips. "Oh, gosh, Ray, I'm sorry. I've been wanting to do that since I first saw you."

"Um . . ." Ray was beet red.

"I've embarrassed you. I'm so sorry. Let's pretend it never happened. I promise never to mention it. Now, what did you want to ask me?"

"Never mind." He jammed his hands in his pockets and stiff-walked to the porch, where he picked up his toolbox, toted it to his wagon, and heaved it inside. He swung up onto the buckboard and jangled the reins, prompting his horse into a startled trot.

Belle watched the dust swirl in the air as the wagon rolled away. Poor Ray. He never knew what hit him.

9

The mansion on McClung Road was bustling, and Belle felt alive and in her element. Ray had enlisted a crew of men who had jumped into her projects with enthusiasm. A glazier circumnavigated the house, dictating measurements to his boy. Two bricklayers swore at each other as they dug out crumbling mortar and troweled in fresh. A team of housepainters arrived in a flashy wagon loaded with ladders and tarps and brushes and cans of paint. A plumber swore at the clogged pipes and made them run again. Belle couldn't have been more delighted.

And Ray, who she'd appointed foreman of the whole operation, strutted from one team to another, chivying the slow and praising the swift. When he wasn't supervising the workers, he answered her every beck and call.

"Ray, the floorboards in the parlor are loose. Fix them, won't you?" she'd say. Or, "Find some boys from town to clean out the caretaker's cottage and barn, Ray." One morning she decided to keep hogs, saying, "I need you to fix the hog pen, Ray."

Most of the time, Belle swept from room to room, observing the workers as they slowly transformed the house, restoring some of its old glory. The men responded readily to her high-spirited friendliness. She took the time to learn their names and the names of their wives and sweethearts and children. She was following her own advice about honey catching flies, even though she knew these men wouldn't accept kindness instead of wages. Still, it couldn't hurt.

"Your boy is the spit and image of you, Mr. Herman," she said to the glazier as he arrived with his thirteen-year-old son, Walter. She stood in the entrance hallway, platter of fresh-baked biscuits in hand. "And a hard worker. Biscuit?" Mr. Herman declined, but Walter hungrily snatched two. "And how is Mrs. Herman? Bearing up all right?" Belle had previously learned that Constance Herman had given birth to their fourth child recently and was recovering slowly. "I'm making a chicken stew today. You'll take some home with you at the end of the day."

"I don't like to impose, Mrs. Sorenson," replied Mr. Herman. He seemed taciturn on the surface, with his severe black mustache and stern eyes, but Belle saw the devoted way his son followed him around and realized he must treat his family well. He was the kind of man whose family was everything to him.

"I won't hear of you refusing me, Mr. Herman. A healthy stew will do your wife good, and she can't be up and about cooking for the rest of you. So you'll take the stew, do you hear? Now, don't say no and break my heart!" Belle finished with a laugh.

Mr. Herman gave her a short, stiff bow and thanked her. "Come, Walter, we start in the library today."

As the boy passed her, Belle whispered, "Psst, Walter. Here." She slipped a folded napkin from the pocket in her dress. "I also made oatmeal cookies this morning. There's more on the table in the kitchen. Help yourself to as many as you need."

Walter took the package with a grin. "Thank you, ma'am!" He inhaled two of the three cookies before he got to the library door. It seemed he'd put on another inch or two of height in the three days he'd been working for her. The route to any man's heart went through his stomach, and that was no less true of a growing boy.

Of all the men on her team of laborers, Belle's favorites were the bricklayers. They were twins, although they looked nothing alike. One was tall and lean, a Jack Sprat with a trowel and a hod, and the other was as round as he was tall. Ed and Fred Roman bickered every minute of every day and couldn't get through a sentence without a swear or two. They were unabashed unless Belle surprised them, in which case they blushed like little girls.

Belle loaded a plate with biscuits and sidled around the corner of the house to where the brothers were setting up. Fred spilled lime and sand from sacks into a two-wheeled barrow, seeming to measure by eye and experience.

"Ed, you get them sons a bitches on the fuckin' second floor. I got these down here," said Fred. Fat and florid and not shy about his place in the world, Fred always took the lead.

"Fuck if I will, Fred. I was up the ladder yesterday." Ed was smaller and though he seemed to have no less of a sense of his own importance, he was the follower. But only after putting up a fight. He dragged the ladder off the back of the wagon.

"Who's the fuckin' king today? You too good to get up a goddamn ladder?" Fred poured in water and stirred the mixture with a long paddle, gently at first and then with great swooping turns as the ingredients became one thick mass.

"Not so good I can't spend a day on the ground," Ed said. "I was up the ladder yesterday, and the day before. And the day before that. I'm always up the fuckin' ladder. It's your damn turn. You climb the fuckin' ladder." He leaned the ladder against the wall and retrieved some tools—which Belle learned from the brothers yesterday were called trowels and hawks—from the wagon.

"With my knees? Look at me. Do I look like I'm meant to climb a fuckin' ladder?" Fred spread his hands wide, encompassing his tremendous girth. He grabbed a trowel and a hawk from Ed and said, "Quit yer bellyachin' and get yer sorry ass up that fuckin' ladder before I stomp you—Oh, pardon me, ma'am, good morning to you," Fred greeted Belle when he finally noticed her.

"Good morning, Fred. Good morning, Ed." Belle took in their discomfiture with silent glee. "How are you fellows today?"

"Fit as a fuckin'— I mean fit as a fiddle, Mrs. Sorenson," said Ed as he scooped a load of mortar onto a hawk and mounted the ladder.

"He's a scoundrel with the mouth of a sailor, Mrs. Sorenson. He don't mean no offense," added Fred.

"Fuck you, Fred."

"You make my point for me, little brother."

"Now, boys," interrupted Belle. "Behave yourselves. I made biscuits. Are you hungry?" She held out the platter to the two men.

Ed came scuttling down the ladder at the word "biscuits."

"None for me, thank you," said Fred.

"These biscuits are awful good," said Ed around a mouthful.

"Help yourself to as many as you'd like," Belle said, and Ed snatched three more for good measure. "How much longer do you think the job will take, boys?" Every night, she retrieved her ledger and carefully recorded each worker's hours and the supplies purchased by Ray or herself, fretting over the numbers.

"Takes what it takes," said Ed. Crumbs tumbled down his front as he talked.

"I can see that," Belle agreed. "But I wonder if you can estimate a time for me?"

"It's work that can't be rushed, ma'am. Scraping out the old mortar, mixing the batches, filling the lines. Then there's the drying time. If the air is holding water like it likes to do this time of year, could be another week, or it could be longer."

A prickling of worry tickled the back of Belle's neck. What if she ran out of money before the men finished? *No.* She would see this house restored. No matter what. "Well, I can't have these bricks falling down around me. So get the fucking job done."

Fred and Ed froze and stared at Belle with goggling eyes. Ed's jaw dropped, and a big chunk of biscuit fell to the ground. Belle winked. As she sauntered away, she heard them break into guffaws.

"Brother, did you hear what she said?" came Fred's voice. "Get the fucking job done! Ha ha ha! Fucking hell, she's a bold one! Ha ha ha!"

Belle rounded the corner to the back of the house, where Ray was working on the enclosure for the swine. "Hello, Ray. Are you hungry? I made more biscuits."

"Thank you, Miz Sorenson. Don't mind if I do."

"Now, Ray. When are you going to quit being so stuffy, calling me 'Miz Sorenson'? Aren't we a team now?"

"Well . . . I . . . gosh, Miz Sorenson, I—" He stopped short at her raised eyebrow. "I mean, Miz Belle."

"That's better. Here, take a biscuit."

Ray dropped his hammer in the grass and swiped his forearm across his brow. He took a biscuit and bit into it. "Should have this finished in a day or two. A lot of the timbers are still in good shape. I just needed to replace some of them and shore it up."

"Well done, Ray." Belle beamed at him. "Before long, we'll be dining on pork loin."

"And curing bacon," Ray chimed in.

"All thanks to your hard work and dedication. You're a godsend, Ray."

Belle left him to his work and returned to the kitchen, where she set a kettle on her poor excuse for a stove to make a pot of tea. A sense of well-being settled over her. Yes, everything was going along just perfectly.

Belle would bind these men to her, every one of them, through their love of food or devotion to family or sense of humor or whatever little show of kindness unlocked their hearts. She would bind these men to her, and they would love her and do as she asked, and one day she would be queen of not only this house but all who came here.

In the afternoon, a delivery wagon arrived from the train station with Belle's furniture.

"Ray, have the delivery men store everything in the barn," she instructed. "Except I need my bed. Have them bring that upstairs."

They'd arrived as a prairie rainstorm swept in, soaking the crew of four while they unloaded each burlap-wrapped piece. The men grunted and sweated the enormous bed up the stairs in parts, enlightening Belle about a number of inventive oaths.

Ray fussed through the whole thing. "Miz Sorenson, that is, er, Miz Belle, you might want to consider—"

"Easy now!" Belle cautioned the men. "That bed came all the way from Minneapolis. It's mahogany! Don't damage the finish!" It was bad enough they were tracking mud and water inside; they'd also gotten stuck halfway. The stairs made a tight turn at the landing, and the men on either end of the heavy, carved pieces were wedged against the walls.

"Lift, you limp prairie hog fuckers!" the foreman said. The men strained under the load, sweat beading on bulging arms, trying to hoist the piece high enough to get around the corner without jamming against the walls and the railing.

"Lift it higher," Belle called. "You have to go above the balustrade."

The men stopped. Heads swiveled to her.

"Miz Belle," said Ray, taking her gently by the arm and coaxing her into the parlor. "Please, ma'am. I'm not sure it's a good idea to put that bed up there yet."

"Oh, don't be silly, Ray." She smiled at him and patted his cheek. He was such a worrier.

He blushed but persisted. "Ma'am, remember I told you that roof needs fixin'? It would be a shame if a bed fine as this one—

"Now, Ray, stop your worrying. This house has stood here for thirty years and was built solid."

"But for twenty of 'em, the house was open to the all outdoors," Ray pointed out.

Belle pushed past him to march up the stairs after the movers. She wasn't going to waste time listening to Ray's old-womanish frets. She was the master of this home and nothing would stand in her way.

10

Sun streamed through the windows, rousing Belle from a lovely, dreamless sleep. She stretched and snuggled down in the covers. "I may never leave this bed," she said to the empty room.

But there was so much still to do. She needed to see about getting some hogs. And chickens, too, so she could have eggs. If only she knew how to wield a mortar trowel or glazing knife. The more work she did herself, the less she had to pay someone else. But she could sweep and clean and scrub, and it was time to tackle the bat-infested turret. She threw back her covers and dressed.

Belle was finishing her breakfast of tinned plums and tea when she heard the work crews arrive. Wagon wheels and men's voices rumbled into the yard, and there was a knock at the front door. She swung it open to find Ray, good old Ray, with his cap twisting in his hands. In the yard, men were getting down from their wagons, ready to set to work.

"Good morning, Miz Sorenson, that is, Miz Belle." Ray still had that shy, hangdog look about him, but being the boss of her workers had put a little starch in his spine and some color in his cheeks.

"Good morning, Ray."

"The fellas are getting to work. And I'm fixing to finish that hog pen today."

"Very good, Ray. Thank you." She started to push the door to, but Ray raised his eyebrows and interjected, "Um . . ."

"Yes, Ray?"

"Mr. Paris, at the sawmill? He has a message for you?" Ray's tone was full of apology.

"Yes, what is it?"

"It's, um, the matter of the bill? Um. Your bill?"

"Oh, that. Not to worry, I'll take care of it."

"Yes, ma'am, of course. It's just that I won't be able to get any more lumber until it's, um. Until it's paid."

"Oh." Belle thought a moment. "How much more lumber do you need to finish the pen?"

"Well, none," Ray said. "I got everything I need this morning, but—"

"That's fine, then." The bill could wait until the next time she needed lumber. "I'll visit Mr. Paris at some point and take care of it."

"I don't know . . ." Ray's brow furrowed.

"Stop your fretting, Ray!" Belle's laugh tinkled brightly. "I don't see what the problem is. I swear, you are like an old woman with your frets and worries!" She began closing the door again, when inspiration struck. "Oh, Ray? One more thing."

"Yes?"

"At the end of the day, please see me. I've got something for you."

"Yes, ma'am," Ray said. He blushed and nodded before trotting down the porch stairs.

Ray unloaded the latest supply of lumber, thinking about Mr. Paris's words. He'd been very clear with Ray about the bill and almost hadn't let him take the load away. But Ray had explained—again—about Mrs. Sorenson's situation as a widow of limited means. She was only trying to get her homestead set up to support herself. She'd surely pay her bill as soon as she had a moment to bring the money by.

Mr. Paris wasn't completely reassured. "I'm trusting *you*, Ray Lamphere," he'd said. "Not some widow from out of town."

Ray believed in his soul that Belle was a woman of her word. But he hoped she'd stop by the sawmill soon.

The hog pen was in good shape. Ray had gotten a strong start the day before on the final wall, and today he would add on the gate.

As he set to work, he felt a rare sense of pride. The hog pen had been in a sorry state a few days ago but now look at it. Fit for kings, it would be. It was a pen Belle—he was still soaring on the fact she wanted him to call her Belle—could be proud of. Proud of his work. That had a mighty good ring to it. Was it wrong of him to want to take care of her, make her proud of him?

She said she had something for him, and Ray figured that meant she was about to pay him. Not that he couldn't use the money, but part of him didn't want to take it. It seemed as if this place, Belle's home, was where he was meant to be.

There was a thought that kept creeping into his mind in quiet moments and the dark of night. What really felt right, and good, and true, was the idea that he was meant to be with Belle. As her man. Her husband.

As soon as the idea erupted in his thoughts, he quashed it. That was just crazy. Mrs. Sorenson—no, Belle. She had *asked* him to call her that—she was a fine lady, and he was only a hired hand.

But. Maybe someday?

Ray pounded the last nail home. The gate was hung and the latch installed. He nudged it closed and the latch caught. The pen was complete.

Ray stowed his hammer and tools in his toolbox, surprised to find that the sun was close to setting. The gate had been fiddlier than he'd expected, but he'd finished the work, just like he'd promised Belle. As he came around the front of the house, he realized all the other workers had gone. He put his toolbox in his wagon and did a circuit of the house to inspect the work.

Fred and Ed were a vaudeville act, but they knew what they were doing. The mortar drying between the bricks looked tight and smooth. As far as Ray could see, the glazier had only a couple more windows to do. And the house painters had finished the trim and the last of the shutters and rehung them. The fresh coat of creamy white paint did wonders for the appearance of the house. Belle would surely be pleased.

Ray knocked on her front door and swiped his cap off his head. When the door swung inward, he about lost his breath. She had taken down her hair. It fell past her shoulders in brown waves. Was it as soft as it looked? Ray clenched his hat in his fists to keep from reaching out to touch it. "Evening, Miz Belle," he said.

"Ray, you gave me a turn! I thought everyone had gone. You caught me at my toilet."

She spoke sharply, and Ray felt shame bloom on his cheeks. "I'm awful sorry, ma'am. You asked me to see you at the end of the day."

"I did? I don't remember that."

Ray didn't know what to say. Had he misunderstood her? "I'm sorry," he said again. He waited, unsure what to do. "I inspected the fellas' work."

"I expect so," she said. "Surely this can wait until morning."

"Oh. Yes, ma'am. If you say so. Yes, ma'am." He finished to the closing door, feeling desperately crushed.

Suddenly the door yanked back open. "Actually, Ray, I do have something for you." Belle's voice flowed over him like honey, sweet and soft.

"Yes, ma'am," he said, hope reigniting.

"It's this way," she said, leading him up the staircase.

The treads creaked under Ray's feet. Why did he have to be so loud? He placed his foot carefully on the next step and eased his weight onto it. There. That was better. A little quieter. He lifted his back foot gently off the lower tread, winced when it creaked, and put it gently on the next one up. Eased his weight on. Nice and quiet.

"What on earth are you doing?" Belle was looking at him from the hall above.

Ray froze. "Uh."

"Never mind," she said and disappeared into her bedroom.

She wanted him to follow her into the bedroom. Strange feelings warred with each other in his gut as he finished climbing the stairs. He'd never set foot in a lady's bedroom.

He stood rooted by the door, his eyes roving around the room. Clothing spilled out of a large trunk in a corner, and a small table supported an oil lamp. His eyes landed on the great four-poster bed, which was now dressed in richly colored covers. Images of Belle in the bed invaded his mind. He saw her dressed in a white cotton shift, her hair down, an angel. His angel. Her wide blue eyes gazing up at him with innocent passion. She would say to him, "Ray, I need you—"

". . . to move this bed."

What did she say?

"Ray, did you hear me? I said I need you to move this bed." She stood there, hands on hips, elbows out like angel's wings, waiting.

"Ma'am?"

"Am I not speaking plainly?" She laughed. "I think you've been working too hard, Ray. This bed needs to be moved."

"But . . . why?"

"Ray, did you drop a hammer on your head today? I already explained all this. You haven't been listening to me."

"Sorry, Miz Belle. I guess I'm running out of steam. I've been working more than twelve hours."

"I know, and I don't know what I'd do without you." Her smile took the sting out of her earlier impatience. "You are a knight in shining armor. Sir Ray, I need the bed centered between the columns. The movers must be blind. Look how off-center it is."

"Well, all right, Miz Belle. I'll get one of the fellas to help me move it tomorrow."

"Ray, I want it moved tonight."

"It's a mighty heavy bed, Miz Belle." Ray scratched the back of his neck. He was plenty weary from the day's work. He was ready to hit the hay himself.

"Oh, but Ray. I've seen you working," she said softly, her eyes pleading. "I know how truly strong you are."

Her compliment sent his heart soaring. That's how he knew she was an angel: she always knew how to lift him up. She saw his strength, appreciated it, like nobody else had ever done.

"Well," he said. "I'll try." He reached under the footboard with a sturdy grip. Her belief in him filled him up, bringing him the power he needed, like the strength of many men. He heaved on the bed, gritting his teeth and putting his legs and back into it. The bellow of a beast emerged from deep inside him.

The bed remained firmly affixed to the floorboards.

Ray was trying, Belle had to give him that. And she was appreciative that he'd remembered to come see her at the day's end, when she herself had plumb forgotten she'd invited him. Cleaning the turret had proved to be so foul, so disgusting, so exhausting, that she'd sunk immediately into a hot bath, trying to eradicate the day from memory entirely. Her plan for Ray had washed away along with the grime.

He stood up, winded, and rubbed his hands together. Grinned at her. "Not to worry. I'll get 'er this time."

He bent down again. But instead of trying to lift it, he jerked his weight sideways, attempting to drag it across the floor in short tugs. A horrendous screech accompanied every millimeter of progress. Most likely accompanied by deep scratches in the wood floor, but Belle put that out of her mind. He was doing exactly as she asked, and that was the point.

After several shrieks of protest from the bed, Ray stopped to check his progress.

"Must be almost there," he said, standing up to catch his breath. The bed was a scant inch from where it had begun. "Oh. Not quite there yet, I guess."

Belle smiled sweetly. "I know you can do it, Ray."

He moved to the head of the bed and repeated his efforts. By incremental tugs and shoves, Ray managed to haul the bed the few inches necessary to center it between the columns. He arched his back, stretching his overused muscles, gasping like a landed fish.

Belle clasped her hands together with glee. "You did it, Ray! I knew you could." She actually hadn't known, but his success filled her with a sense of her own power. She wanted Ray to move the bed, and he did.

Her whole time with Mads had been an exercise in bottling up her power, ignoring her desires, and managing Mads by trying to direct his. It had reminded her of trundling a hoop as a child, guiding the ring of wicker along with well-timed and gentle nudges—only Mads and his passions had been the hoop, barreling ahead heedless, and she'd spent years trying to keep him rolling in a direction that would benefit her, or at least not send them into catastrophe. She'd been a fool to marry Mads, she knew now. But she'd solved that problem, hadn't she? And just like freeing herself from Mads, she was beginning to suspect she could master any problem.

With Ray, she had the sense she could direct men to do her bidding, like pawns on a chessboard, and not just guide and hope as she had done with Mads. Her heart swelled with the feeling that her true path lay ahead of her. It was intoxicating. "Ray," she whispered. "Come here."

He crossed the room but stopped with several feet still between them. "Closer."

He took a single, timid step nearer. She could easily close the gap, but that would not do. He would do as she told him.

"Closer still," she commanded. He inched forward as she crooked her finger, beckoning, requiring he obey her words, until he was close enough she could hear his heart, still beating hard from the exertion. She wanted to hear it instead racing with desire for her. "Tell me you want me," she whispered.

"I— Uh—" A red flush crept up his neck.

"I know you want me, Ray. Don't deny it. You wouldn't lie to me, would you? Tell me you want me."

"No, ma'am. I mean. Yes, ma'am."

His eyes bounced from her eyes to her lips, down to her breasts, and then back to her lips. He was desperate to kiss her. She could see it plain on his face.

"Admit it," she whispered. "Say the words. You want me."

"I want you." The words emerged from deep in his throat, choking out as though against his will.

"Kiss me, Ray," she told him.

He leaned down, and his lips brushed hers. She teased her tongue against his lips and exulted at his groan of desire. Then she pulled back. "Ray, I want you to do exactly what I tell you."

"Yes. Yes, I will."

"Light the lamp. There are safety matches in the drawer."

Ray did as he was told. The lamp cast a glow into the darkening room.

"Take the cover off my bed."

He dragged off the spread, dumping it on the floor.

She pouted. "I didn't say to put it on the floor. Don't make me cross, Ray. Fold it across the foot."

He scrabbled it up, struggling to fold the bulky material, and spread it across the foot of the bed.

"Good. Now take the blanket."

He bundled the old wool blanket, brought from Indianapolis and destined to be replaced as soon as possible, into his arms.

"Good boy." She smiled. "Follow me. Don't forget the lamp."

11

Belle brought Ray out to the one-room caretaker's cottage and bid him spread the blanket on the floor.

"Kiss me," she told him. He moved his lips softly over hers, gently coaxing open her mouth and teasing her with his tongue. He drew her closer with a hand at the small of her back. His other hand cupped the back of her head, tilting her mouth so he could explore. He tipped her head back, exposing her neck, and slid the tip of his tongue along her jaw, down to her collarbone. He grazed her skin with his teeth, and a growl rumbled in his throat.

She pushed him back, shocked by the heat in her cheeks. Parts of her body she'd never been aware of were responding in surprising ways. She didn't know nipples could want so badly to be touched.

"I'm sorry," he said. "Was that too much? I won't hurt you, I promise."

"No, it was—" Belle paused. She had to regain control. "It was very good. Take off your shirt."

Ray fumbled at his buttons and drew the shirt over his head. His bare chest was narrow, his pale skin rising and falling with his uneven breaths. He waited for another command.

"Now your pants."

He attacked the buttons and dropped the trousers and then drawers to the ground.

Ray's penis was quite different from Mads's. Longer, maybe? But narrower? And it seemed to have a bend at the end, a crook. Did that hurt him? Would it hurt her?

Ray slowly lowered his hands to cover himself.

Belle pulled the chain with its key over her head and let it drop, then began unbuttoning her blouse. Ray closed the space between them and gently removed her hand. "May I do that?"

His eyes were wide in the lamplight. She'd never noticed before, but they were a chocolatey brown, a deeper, warmer color than she had ever credited. There was safety there, and comfort. It wouldn't be so bad, would it, to rest in that oasis for a time?

His hands at her buttons were gentle, delicate even. He marked each undone button with a kiss, feathery soft. First on the plumpness of her cheek, next on her cheekbone, and one on the tip of her nose that made her laugh against her will. Then he dropped them lower, sliding a trail of tender kisses down her neck, a nibbling one on her collarbone. Did she have that many buttons? She had lost track.

Ray was pushing her blouse off her shoulders when he paused. "You have a birthmark." He was staring at the reddish-brown mark over her left breast, the odd, irregular splotch that Mads had always wanted her to keep covered. "It's shaped like the wings of an angel."

An angel? Was that how Ray saw her? "Mads, my late husband, didn't like it. He thought it made me 'imperfect.'"

"That just shows what he knows." Ray lowered his lips to the birthmark and gently kissed her there. He kissed the swell of her breast, and then he took his tongue to her nipple. The sensation ripped a gasp from her. It was delicate and fierce all at once, and she was held in place, all her focus on that one, lovely, melting location.

The control she so badly wanted evaporated. She was no more in control than a newborn kitten.

And Ray seemed equally powerless over the raw desire that sprang up between them. Belle assumed he came to the moment with the inexperience of an unwed, homely, shy man, but gone was his bashfulness and insecurity. His touch was full of confidence, and he made her body his to command. And, unlike with Mads, her body was all too ready to comply. They were hungry for each other, unable to get enough.

Belle banished all thoughts of Mads. What was happening between her and Ray was so different that comparison ceased to have meaning. It would be like trying to equate a trip to the shoemaker to luncheon with the queen of Siam.

They lay on the blanket, the hard floor beneath them unnoticed, skin upon skin, the two twined together. When Ray entered her, the thought blossomed in her mind that, no, his funny little crook didn't hurt. If anything, it introduced a novel sensation that only heightened the intensity. But as his rhythm increased, whatever conscious thought she'd been capable of faded away. Soon she was nothing more than an empty vessel, a space filling with pleasure, with sensation, with need that grew into something more. She needed. Desperately, achingly needed something. What was it? Where was it? How to get it?

She pulled at Ray, hauling him closer, deeper into her. Whatever it was she was looking for, she couldn't find it.

"Raaaaay," she wailed.

He stopped what he was doing. "Wha— what?" He was panting. "Am I hurting you?"

"Don't stop, don't stop. I don't know. Oh, help."

"Are you willing to try something?"

Try something? She couldn't think. There was only the unidentifiable, overwhelming need. "Yes?"

Ray held Belle tightly and rolled onto his back, bringing her with him so she was on top. He slid his hands down her back, over her hips, down to her legs.

"Now sit up," he said. "Like riding a horse."

She rocked up and as she did so, gasped, "Oh!"

It was not that she had never been on top before. Mads had placed her in numerous positions, like a doll in a tableau arranged for his pleasure. He sometimes situated her astride him and bade her bounce while he lounged with his hands behind his head and watched her breasts jounce up and down until he grunted and swore, and she knew she had done her duty.

This was not like that. As she rocked up, the pressure on her delicate folds was an awakening. She rocked forward. And back. Forward. Back. With each motion forward, Ray thrust himself into her.

As they found this new rhythm, the need inside of Belle grew again. She was the ocean, the swelling tide, a great power drawing ever fuller. A crashing explosion shook her. "Son of a Benjamin!" she yelled.

Ray's thrusts increased, his fingers pressing into the plump flesh of her hips. When his own explosion came, he marked it with a gritted "Yup."

As she returned to herself, Belle heard Ray muttering over and over to himself. "Thank you, thank you, thank you, thank you."

Belle opened her eyes and, looking down at the first man to bring her to satisfaction, discovered tears leaking down the sides of his face.

It was a beautiful sight.

The salty tracks on his cheeks marked him as hers, utterly and completely.

Belle's ear hurt and her hip did too. Her pillow and mattress seemed unaccountably hard. Her mind remained mired in sleep, which shrouded her thoughts as she gradually came to wakefulness. Sunlight pierced her eyelids, forcing her into full consciousness.

She heard snoring.

She peeled open her eyes and wished instantly to shut them against the sight of Ray Lamphere next to her. Her ear hurt because her pillow was his bony shoulder, and her hip hurt because she lay on the floor of the caretaker's cottage.

She had lain with her handyman.

She needed to get up to the house before the workers came. Traipsing across the lawn, half-dressed like a slattern, was not how she wanted to be seen. She only hoped it wasn't already too late. She eased away from Ray, and his snoring cut off. She froze. But he quickly resumed, and she was able to roll away and rise. With her back to him, she dressed quietly and looped her key around her neck.

When she turned back, those warm brown eyes she'd taken so long to notice were on her.

"Good morning, beautiful," he said. He looked like he was in love with her, as if he had expectations she had to fill. That would not do. After all, he was her handyman. Best to nip that right in the bud.

"Ray, don't be a slugabed. There's work to do. Get yourself up." She tugged the blanket away from him and bundled it in her arms. "I'm going up to the house. I only hope I get up there before the workers arrive. I won't have any wagging tongues."

She marched to the door and wrenched it open. The rusty hinges squealed. Over her shoulder, she said, "Oh, and if you want, you can fix this cottage up and start sleeping here. I'm sure it's better than living with your shrew of a mother."

As she strode across the field, at first she was relieved to see no wagons hulking in her driveway, no workmen roaming about. Ray caught up with her, tucking his shirttails into his pants. But as they got closer to the house, Belle felt a thread of unease. Something was amiss. "Ray," she said. "Where is your crew?"

Then she spotted what was bothering her so much about her house. She picked up her skirts with one hand, the blanket wadded under the other, and tried to run. But the grass was long and tangled her feet. She crashed to the ground, and dew soaked her skirts. Her hands were smeared green. Ray helped her to her feet, and she pushed on, struggling with the trailing blanket and walking as fast as she could manage.

All the while, she kept her eyes on the house, straining to make sense of what she was seeing. Her rear door was missing, as were a number of windows, sashes and all. "Ray!" she shrieked. "What happened?!"

A furious horror lanced into her. Who could have done such a thing? After all her efforts to make repairs to her house, someone had come along and vandalized it. Terrified of what she might find inside, she ran the rest of the way. At the threshold of the kitchen, Ray pushed in front of her. "Best let me go in first, Miz Belle."

He entered the kitchen, disappearing into the hallway beyond. Belle waited anxiously on the steps. In a few moments, Ray returned, saying, "Everything's clear. No one's here."

"Look what they've done!" Belle wailed. "Someone has come and stolen my brand-new doors and windows! What lowdown, sneaky thieves. Who would do such a thing?"

Ray rubbed a hand down his face.

"And where are my workers?" Belle demanded. "They should be here by now."

"I don't rightly know, Miz Belle," Ray said. On the table rested a piece of paper folded in quarters. Ray picked it up and unfolded it. "Look here, ma'am. There's a note."

"What? Hand it here." She crowded his shoulder and took the letter. "'Dear Mrs. Sorenson,'" she began reading. She skimmed it, reading aloud bits for Ray's benefit. ". . . 'behind in payments' . . . 'new construction job in town' . . . Well, of all the— Those sneaky rats took my doors hostage and left me high and dry for some other job in town. What job could possibly lure them away from me?"

"That's probably the Charles Gunness job."

"And who is this Charles Gunness?"

"Bigwig in town," Ray explained. "His company makes musical instruments. He's building a big ol' concert hall in honor of his late wife. He's hiring workers left, right, and center to get it done. I hear he's a real son of a bitch too. If you'll pardon my language."

"How did you hear of this, Ray?"

"Well, I live in town, and you hear things is all."

"What did I ever do to deserve to be treated so cruelly? What could make them abandon me like this?"

Ray scratched the back of his neck. "Well," he began with hesitation, "it's like this. This Gunness, he pays real well. And he guarantees wages. And, well, Miz Belle, like it says in the note, you're a little behind in payments. Men've got families to feed. Maybe you could . . . pay them?"

Belle planted a fist on her hip. "Are you giving me financial advice now, Mr. Handyman?" Even as her harsh words spilled out, she knew Ray was right. It was just good business sense: you had to pay employees in a timely fashion. The problem was, unlike a successful business, she didn't have an active source of income. And she'd been kind and thoughtful to her workers, where many employers were downright cruel. Was falling behind in payments justification for abandoning her? For stealing pieces of her house? No, it most certainly was not.

Ray put his hands up in a pacifying gesture. "Listen, Miz Belle. I know these fellas. They would gladly come back and work for you if you pay them. That Gunness, they hate 'im. And they adore you. But the fact is, money talks."

Belle crumpled the note in her fist. "So they want to be paid, do they? Fine."

She stalked upstairs to her room and lifted her holdall onto the bed. She unlocked it and snapped open the catch, spreading the sides wide apart. She stifled a desperate sob. The stacks of money had dwindled to almost nothing. She only hoped there would be enough to get her workers back. She folded some bills and tucked them in her handbag, then returned to the kitchen.

"Let's go, Ray."

12

There was something different about La Porte today. As Ray's buckboard brought them toward the town center, strangers on the street were meeting Belle's eye and nodding. A man in a smart brown bowler grabbed its brim and gave a solid tip of his hat as she passed. A pair of women going about their shopping smiled and nodded.

A great balloon of emotion swelled in Belle's breast. When they'd left the house, she'd felt angry as a fiddle, as they said in Norway when she was a girl. But now, her fiddle played a happy tune, and she waved to townsfolk as they passed. She'd never been noticed and appreciated like this in Indianapolis. It was about time.

"You seem in fine spirits this morning, Miz Belle," Ray observed.

"Little La Porte is starting to grow on me, Ray," she said. "Good morning to you!" she called to a matron and her daughter approaching the mercantile, empty baskets swinging from their hands in rhythm with their steps.

They waved and smiled back. The young lady even dipped a curtsy. "Mornin', Mrs. Sorenson."

They knew her name! As they should, what with all the jobs she'd created with her renovation efforts. Her reputation clearly preceded her. How delightful! Yes, La Porte was quickly growing in Belle's affections.

Ray drove the wagon to a large building at the end of Michigan Street with GABRIEL'S LIVERY painted on the side. "Don't be taken in by his looks, Miz Belle. He's got the face of an angel, but he'd steal the pennies off a dead man's eyes."

A man approached from the dark interior of the livery barn. His denim coveralls and brown work shirt were well worn but clean, and he had the big blue eyes and golden hair of an angel, just as Ray had said. The arrangement of his features conveyed sweet innocence. "Good morning," he called. "Who you got with you, Ray Lamphere? I think my eyes have died and gone to heaven. Ma'am, you put the sun to shame."

"You're laying it on a might thick, Gabriel," said Ray. "This is Miz Belle Sorenson. She's new to town."

"Ah, the magnificent and mysterious Mrs. Sorenson, who bought that wreck out the McClung Road. I'm pleased to make your acquaintance."

She graced him with one of her most glowing smiles. "Pleased to meet you, Mr. Gabriel."

"Just Gabriel will do." He swept an exaggerated bow.

"Thank you, Gabriel. How courteous you are."

"Ma'am, it is my considered opinion that good manners are the grease that smooths the waters among folk," Gabriel said. "Welcome to La Porte. I hope I can be of service to you somehow."

"You can be of service by taking my horse and wagon," Ray said. "And don't think I don't know exactly the state of my tack. I don't expect to see it any different when I come back."

"I'm cut to the quick, Ray Lamphere," Gabriel said with exaggerated woundedness.

Ray guided Belle by the elbow off the wagon. "Right this way."

Town was bustling, with carriages and buckboards and one-pony traps clogging the streets and citizens navigating the sidewalks. Belle felt almost like royalty as she waited at the corner while Ray waved traffic to a stop, narrowly missing getting run down. Once drivers realized who he was escorting, they pulled up, tipped hats, smiled, and waved. Belle processed across the little street like Queen Victoria herself on her way to inspect the guards.

But when Belle and Ray arrived at the Gunness construction site, she was a little put out to find that work did not come to a halt like traffic had. A huge crew, including numerous familiar faces, were deeply engaged in their various trades. There were Fred and Ed, laying down brick after brick, sweat dampening their shirts. Her house painters were doing duty as carpenters, banging boards together with heavy swings of their hammers. A few men glanced her way, and when Ed saw her his expression perked right up, as though anticipating the usual tray of biscuits.

A grizzly foreman noticed and shouted, "Whatcha sons a bitches lookin' at? Never seen a lady before? Nah, come to think of it, you probably ain't. But today ain't that day. Keep your lousy eyes on your work. I'm talking to you, Ed Roman. She ain't for the likes of you, and if you'd rather go gallivantin' with a lady, then lay down your goddamn trowel and get the hell out of here."

Poor Ed tucked his head down and increased his speed, slathering mortar and snugging bricks on at a rate that would have that wall built by midday.

The foreman kept up a stream of abuse, chivying the men to go faster and finding fault with the quality of their work. He ranged back and forth on the site, inspecting the bricklayers here, the carpenters there, always moving, always criticizing, always bellowing in a bear-like growl.

Belle could see her workers glancing sheepishly at her and quickly away so she couldn't catch anyone's eye.

"This won't do," she finally said. "Come on, Ray." And she traipsed across the dusty site, weaving around work wagons and piles of lumber and bricks and buckets of nails. She marched up to Fred and Ed, who devoted their attention to their bricks and trowels, the sky, the ground—anything but her approach. "Hello, Fred. Hello, Ed."

"Er, hello there, Mrs. Sorenson." Fred looked around warily. "Didn't see you there. What a surprise to see you."

"A pleasant one, I hope," she said with a conciliatory smile. "Imagine how sad I was this morning to find everyone gone. I've grown accustomed to the bustle of having you men about. It was so quiet I could hardly hear myself think. I was completely abandoned." She laughed, as though it was all a silly joke rather than a betrayal.

Ed was busy inspecting his feet, hunched in on himself with one arm across his chest, supporting the other elbow. At Belle's gay laugh, his eyes rose to meet hers. She beamed at him, coaxing him back into her graces.

Fred was struck dumb, seemingly unsure how to respond.

"Well," she teased, "what do you have to say for yourselves? Don't tell me you don't miss me too."

Fred gaped, a fat fish out of water, gasping for air.

Ed blurted out, "Fritz Herman took 'em down."

"Took what?" Belle feigned indifference.

Fred apparently found his voice and took over for Ed. "The doors and windows, Mrs. Sorenson."

Behind her, a voice said, "I took 'em as what you might call ransom, Mrs. Sorenson." The glazier approached, trailed by his son Walter, both of them bearing down on their former employer with determined ire. "I do a job, I expect to get paid. Got a family to feed. Two more young 'uns at home besides this one." He jerked a thumb at Walter. "Not to mention the babe and my wife who's still recovering."

His voice was hard. The glazier and his boy stood poised for battle. With the same clothes and identical pose, Walter was a copy of his father in miniature.

"Oh, that." She dismissed it—the missing doors, the lack of payment—with a negligent wave. "Just a misunderstanding among friends. Of course, you must provide for your family. Mr. Herman, I must tell you, in all honesty, I believe you are the most noble of men. I admire you. No, I really do. You are a hard worker, devoted to your family to

the point you take this humiliating job working for a terrible man like
this Gunness I've heard about, who hires brutes like that foreman over
there. All of you"—she gestured to the men gathering around her—"I
respect your integrity and devotion. I respect men of character like you,
even when they make poor choices."

Belle drew some bills from her handbag, counted and folded them
in half, and handed them to Mr. Herman. "Here you are." Fred and Ed
perked up, and she produced another fold of bills. Like chum in the
water, the money drew her other workers, and she handed out bills to
each of them.

"Hold up now, ma'am," said the glazier. "This ain't all of it."

"Now, Mr. Herman, you have to leave me with something to live
on," she said sweetly. "You'll have the rest of your money in due time.
Consider this earnest money. As far as I'm concerned, this little misunderstanding is behind us, and you are all welcome to come back to
work for me any time. Ray, of course, may have a problem with it. You
put him in a terrible spot, having to carry on the work all on his own,
but that's in the past. Good day, men. I trust I will find my doors returned before tomorrow. It's been a delight seeing you again."

She swept away, head high. Behind her, Ray stammered out, "I'm
not— It isn't me—" She could almost hear the blood rushing to his
face. Then he said, "Like she said, come back any time," and his hurried footsteps followed her.

Belle was striding confidently down the street, headed away from where
the wagon was parked, by the time Ray caught up with her. "Where
you goin', Miz Belle?"

"Go make yourself busy, Ray. I am going to visit the dressmaker." A
woman of means and reputation needed to dress the part. "Bring the
wagon to pick me up in an hour."

"Yes, ma'am. Er. What should I do while I wait?"

"Honestly, Ray. I don't know. Surely you have someone you could visit. Your mother?" She knew that was a little vicious, but she was in such high spirits she couldn't help herself.

Ray shrugged uncomfortably.

Okay, maybe that was a step too far. "Or an errand to do? Do we need supplies? Lumber? Nails? I'm sure you'll think of something." She smiled and turned on her heel.

The directions Della Rose had provided were straightforward. Her shop was on the corner of Jefferson and Michigan streets, next to a confectioner's with a Chinese laundry just around the way. "Very convenient, darling," she'd told Belle when she'd described the area. "They do the best work. I send all my clothes there."

From the construction site on Main Street, it was a short walk. Pastries and breads beckoned through a glass front on the confectioner's, but Belle was more taken in by the discreetness of the dressmaker's place, which announced itself simply by DELLA ROSE in gold letters on the wooden door.

The shop was decorated in sophisticated, muted tones, chosen, Belle presumed, so they wouldn't compete with whatever dress a lady might try on in front of the full-length mirror. Bolts of cloth filled shelves on one wall, and two comfortable chairs were provided for shoppers.

"Finally! You have come to see me." Della Rose appeared from a door leading into a back room. "I thought perhaps you had forgotten your promise."

"No, of course not. I have been delayed by unforeseen circumstances. You would not believe—" Belle was suddenly overcome by the drama of the past hours, the past month, and couldn't finish.

"I see." Della Rose crossed to the front door, locking it. "Come. Into the back. We shall have tea."

Belle followed Della Rose into a busy sewing room. A plaid fabric of gray and maroon wool draped in a pile around a sewing machine, waiting for the dressmaker to resume her work transforming it into a

garment. Another sewing machine was being piloted by a young woman, making what looked like a chemise. Her foot pushed the treadle at
a steady pace.

"Carrie, you may take a break. Go have a pastry next door."

Carrie brought the flashing needle to an abrupt stop and left the
chemise where it was. She jumped up from her seat and then stopped
short at the sight of the visitor. "Who's this?" she asked. "You're not
replacing me with—"

"Don't be ridiculous, Carrie. Your imagination is getting the better of you. I've given you the afternoon. Say thank you and be off
with you."

Carrie shrugged, and said, "Thank you, Della Rose," before escaping to the street.

Della Rose turned her back on the departing girl and ushered Belle
in. "My assistant. She likes to imagine drama where there is none. The
man who operates the laundry around the corner is a runaway prince
of China; her landlady is in league with rebel terrorists. You see how
it goes?" She ushered Belle to a small table snugged against the wall,
covered in a fine damask tablecloth and embraced by two chairs. "Sit,"
she told her, as she stoked up a small stove and set a kettle on it. "Tell
me everything."

And so Belle did. Or, at least, almost everything. She started at her
life with Mads, the candy shop and the labor that went into trying to
make it successful. Della Rose was suitably impressed with her business
ideas and appropriately dismayed at Mads's resistance to them. She
told Della Rose of Mads's promises of wealth and his callous treatment
of her. She finished with his death, carefully skirting mention of exactly
how he met his end. She mentioned the gallery owner's story of the
Quilleran mansion and her dreams for it, and of arriving to find it a
derelict mess.

"One moment," Della Rose interrupted. "What is this tale the owner of the art gallery spun for you?"

"I was admiring a painting of the mansion. He told me it had been owned by Judge Quilleran, whose wife was beloved and esteemed by everyone in town. Until she died of yellow fever. Tragically, grief took Judge Quilleran not long after.

Della Rose stared. Then she tipped her head back and began to laugh. The unabashed outburst went on for a time, punctuated by Della Rose clapping her hands together in delight. Belle couldn't imagine how death had inspired such mirth.

"He has told you such a fairy tale," Della Rose finally said, wiping her eyes. "I can tell you, that story is a lot of nonsense. Judge Quilleran was a cruel, closefisted miser. There was never a Mrs. Quilleran—my dear, you can't even get yellow fever here. Quilleran hired workers to perform repairs and never paid them, claiming they hadn't done the job right. Eventually, no one would work for him anymore." At this, Belle shifted her weight uneasily and reached for her teacup. The nerve of not paying them at all! What a dreadful man. "When he died, the place had fallen into such disrepair no one would buy it. This was many, many years ago, of course."

Belle pictured the slight rise in the gallery owner's eyebrows when she'd told him about buying the house without visiting first. Perhaps what she'd construed as admiration for her boldness was actually admiration for his own guile.

"Della Rose, I believe I have been swindled."

"I am afraid so, Belle. Men cannot be trusted. This is not news. It is not news to me, nor is it to you, I think."

Belle nodded thoughtfully.

"Men will always let you down. What can we do?" Della Rose said with a philosophical shrug. "So. You must find it within *yourself* to become a success. Decide what you want. Then go after it."

Belle had never heard a woman speak like this. She appraised the dressmaker with new admiration. It seemed she had found a kindred spirit. Della Rose, with her magnificent attire and fashionable Gibson girl hair. Her feminine beauty hid a spine of steel.

13

When Ray arrived to pick her up, Belle mounted the buck-board with determination. She needed to solve her financial problem. That four thousand dollars hadn't gone as far as she had hoped, taken up by unexpected repairs and wages. But first things first, she needed to see about the concert hall owner, usurper of all her construction workers. "Ray, where does Mr. Charles Gunness live?"

"Maybe an hour outside town, on the way to Elkhart."

"Take me there."

A bolus of envy lodged in Belle's gut when they arrived in front of the Gunness home. It was a true mansion, built in the Queen Anne style and painted in fashionable, bold colors. Coral for the main siding, dark green for the trim, with taupe and sand accents, the house occupied the crest of a slight hill, presiding over a view that spread for miles. So this was how the rich of La Porte lived. Belle's own Victorian might not be so large, but soon it would be as grand. Assuming she could get her workers back.

When Belle knocked on the door, a maid answered. A maid. This Charles Gunness had house staff, like some kind of lord of the manor. The maid brought her into the front parlor while Ray waited in the hallway. "Mr. Gunness will be with you shortly, ma'am."

Belle sat on the sofa, smoothing her fingers over the horsehair-stuffed cushions in teal blue silk. The sofa Belle had shipped from the house in Indianapolis was covered in affordable taffeta.

The parlor was magnificent. Every bit of it was the height of fashion, from the patterned wallpaper to the oriental carpet and the dark mahogany furniture. Astonishingly, the house had been electrified. Electric wall sconces would illuminate the room after dark, and not a single oil lamp could be seen.

Even more astonishing were the figures. Paintings on the walls showed Greek gods and nymphs, all nude, and sculptures of naked men and women graced every surface. A low table in the center of the room held a colorful bowl decorated with more figures. Leaning in closer, Belle realized they, too, were nude. There was even a life-size statue of a creature with the head and torso of a man and the legs of a goat, playing a flute. Looking around, Belle realized every single painting or sculpture featured a musical instrument.

Indeed, distracted by all the nudity, Belle hadn't realized at first that the entire room was full of musical instruments. Two corners were taken up by very tall stringed instruments, and a trumpet rested on its bell on a side table, surrounded by another smaller trumpet, a triangle, a tambourine, and a pair of wooden clappers held together with colorful string, sized to fit in one's palm. There were other objects that Belle couldn't identify, perhaps instruments from foreign lands: a long tube riddled with holes, strangely shaped drums, and a long horn that curved at the end like a giant's candy cane.

A gramophone took pride of place on a small table next to a wing-back chair by the fireplace.

The door burst open, and a short, rumpled man cloaked in impatience stalked in. His waistcoat was misbuttoned, and his coat hung askew on his shoulders. He was completely bald, but what he lacked on top was more than made up for by a single eyebrow of mixed black and white hairs that colonized the space above his eyes like a large and spiky caterpillar. Long, wiry hairs spiraled from it haphazardly. And he had a mustache to match.

Belle felt her own eyebrows rising in wonder, but she yanked away from the wild display and focused on his eyes, which were a nondescript and safe brown.

"What's this about, then?" he demanded. As he spoke, the untamed hairs of his mustache fluttered.

"Hello." Belle smiled warmly. She was determined to win this man over. "I'm so pleased to meet you. My name is Mrs. Belle Sorenson."

"Yes, yes," he said. "Pleased to meet you and all that."

So impatient. Well, even if he had no time for conversational pleasantries, she would find a way past his gruff exterior. However busy and important he was, he was still a man, and there was a key to every man's heart. She had only to find it. "And you are Mr. Charles Gunness?"

"Naturally."

"I've just come from your concert hall construction site. What a magnificent project." Belle injected her words with admiration, trying to get the frumpish old man to unbend a bit.

"Magnificent, yes," he agreed. "And monumental. I'm afraid I don't have time for social visits. Good day." He turned to go.

Belle thought quickly. "How long do you expect the project to take?" she asked. "I'm from Indianapolis, and though I do love my new home, I find myself missing the cultural opportunities of a large city."

He paused, and she knew she'd found her mark. Always make it about him. That was a maxim Belle knew by heart. Every man—and woman, really—was motivated by self-interest. To find the key that unlocked this man's heart, she had to find what moved him. His grand vanity project seemed the place to start.

"Are you," he asked, "a devotee of the musical arts?"

"Who can fail to love music?"

"Many, it seems," he said. "Judging by the resistance I've had to my project. Which will only improve La Porte and bring enlightenment and joy to this Midwestern outpost." He checked his pocket watch.

"Speaking of which, I'm pressed for time. Thank you, good day." He nodded with a slight bow and turned the doorknob.

She couldn't let him leave. She cast about for something to keep him engaged, and her eyes landed on the gramophone. Perfect. Belle gave a gasp. "Is that . . . ? Could it be?" She moved across the room to the table. "Is this a gramophone?" She reached toward it.

"Don't touch it!"

She jerked her hand back and gave him a wounded pout. "I'm terribly sorry. I've always wanted to hear one. This is the first one I've ever seen. It must be lovely to have music any time the desire strikes." She closed her eyes and swayed as if to a tune in her head. "I can just picture you here, in your chair, warm by the fire on a chilly autumn night, with beautiful sounds right by your ear."

"You sound like my late wife," he said. "It was her idea. To put the gramophone next to my chair."

"A brilliant lady, evidently. You must miss her." Belle filled her voice with sympathy.

Bringing Mr. Gunness's wife to mind seemed to have sent him on a reverie. Belle watched his face as it softened ever so slightly. He must have been wholly devoted to her. His business duties momentarily forgotten, he quietly said, "Her name was Calliope. Like the Greek muse."

"You're building the concert hall in her memory, aren't you," she said softly, putting some of Ray's information to use. "She loved music and you love her, and giving the public a chance to experience concerts will keep part of her alive."

Coming back to himself, he fixed her with an unblinking gaze, and Belle feared she had put a foot wrong. But then he broke out of it and marched across the room toward her. "Yes, that's right." He wasn't much taller than Belle, but he loomed over her, his eyes intent on hers. Belle held her ground. The eyebrow and matching mustache vibrated as if transmitting his intensity, and she caught the glimmer of a tear in his eye. She relaxed. He was moved. "You understand. No one has made that connection before."

Belle's eyes fell on the record on the gramophone, reading its label. She let them widen. "Is that Brahms? The Clarinet Quintet? It's one of my favorites." Belle had never heard of it before in her life.

Mr. Gunness's eyes moistened. "That piece of music was Calliope's favorite. Would you care to hear it?"

"It's my dearest wish to hear that music and see how a gramophone works, but—" She hesitated. "I don't want to impose on you. I know how busy you are. I've already taken up so much of your time." She cast her gaze wistfully on the music player, as if she were a little girl longing for a new doll.

"If we don't take time for music, what meaning in life is there at all?" He blurted the words out on puffs of air that disturbed his mustache. With soft, pudgy hands, he cranked the gramophone to get the disc spinning and gently set the needle arm on the track.

There came a few beats of scratchy noise, and Belle had a moment of panic. Was she going to have to pretend to like scratchy nothingness? But then, no.

First strings, starting high and descending, then a clarinet swooping in. Belle really was transported. The sounds coming from the gramophone were beautiful, swelling majestically to fill the small room, creating feelings in Belle of tenderness and yearning. She didn't even have to pretend in order to bring a few tears to her eyes.

Ray, hands folded behind his back and eyes cast at the ceiling as he waited in the hallway, was perplexed to hear soft music emanating from the parlor. Hadn't he heard, just moments before, the jiggle of the doorknob? Hadn't he seen the knob turn with his own eyes?

When Mr. Gunness had emerged from a room toward the back of the house and marched down the hallway to the parlor where Belle was waiting, he seemed a man with little time and less patience. He checked his pocket watch and re-stowed it with a shake of his head. His every move spoke of a man who had no desire to visit with curious widows.

The pretty music floated out to Ray. Soon it came to an end, and a new tune started. He resigned himself to wait. Time went on, with no way for Ray to know how long, except for the rumble in his belly and the slow slide of a patch of sunlight across the floorboards.

It came to him that he really didn't know the purpose of this visit. Belle's goal in setting out this morning, gathered from her muttered comments, was to get the fellows to return to her house to continue the work. And when she had left the dress shop, she had said, "Let's go see this Mr. Charles Gunness. Who does he think he is, taking up all the workmen in the county." But was music a usual part of a business visit? That didn't seem fitting.

The music changed again, to a popular tune Ray recognized. A bellowing erupted from the room. Was that singing? What on earth was going on in there?

A reawakening was happening inside of Charles Gunness. His face ached, and it dawned on him he hadn't smiled like this in years. He felt light, buoyant, a brigantine set loose from her anchor and free to sail the open seas. He'd been toiling for decades—forty-seven years, to be exact—creating and building his musical instrument manufacturing business, providing for Calliope and their children, without a break or pause. Storm clouds, low, heavy, and dark, had obscured his horizon, so all he saw was the work in front of him, the next deal, the next conquest. Those clouds had closed in suffocatingly when Calliope passed.

But a break had unexpectedly appeared, letting in the warm glow of the sun. This woman, this Mrs. Belle Sorenson, had pushed aside the shroud of dedication, duty—and, yes, grief from Calliope's passing. Mrs. Sorenson—would she let him call her Belle?—was sunlight in a dark land.

She was clearly moved by the music. Just as he was, and just as Calliope always had been. He was not one to indulge in flights of fancy or believe in that spirit nonsense. Dead was dead, and there was no bringing his beloved Calliope back, but there was a tiny corner of his heart that held onto the notion that perhaps, just perhaps, his late wife had guided Mrs. Sorenson's footsteps somehow. That Calliope brought her here, to this house and this room and into his life.

When the final notes of the quintet died away, and the needle scritched to the center of the turntable, Charles lifted the needle off. A moment of reverence hung in the air. Were those tears in Mrs. Sorenson's eyes? Truly, she was a rare one. Just as his Calliope had been.

"I've never heard anything like that in my life," she whispered. "It was beautiful. I didn't just hear it with my ears. It was as if I heard it with my heart, my very soul."

"It hits me like that too," Charles said. "Would you like to hear another?"

"Yes, please," Belle said. "Perhaps something more lighthearted?"

Calliope had abhorred popular music. She called it facile, but Charles enjoyed the popular songs just as much as he loved Brahms and Beethoven and Mozart. Was there any chance Mrs. Sorenson would enjoy a popular tune? Or would she be offended? Fortune favors the brave, his father had always told him. It was a motto that had served him well in his business dealings. He only hoped it wouldn't fail him now.

He replaced the Brahms with a record of baritone Steve Porter singing "Sweet Rosie O'Grady," cranked up the turntable, and set the needle on the track.

While Belle had been prepared to feign a love for Brahms, almost from the first notes she had been transported. The music reached inside her and created a longing, not painful but sweet, for something she couldn't quite pinpoint.

But this next tune was completely different. A man's voice sang out words she'd heard many a time, raucously spilling out of taverns as she passed by, sung by crowds of drunken men. Mads, too, had sung it more than once, usually after coming home from one of those very taverns. Unlike Mr. Gunness, Belle had no desire to honor the memory of her dead spouse. She pushed that unwelcome remembrance aside and focused on the upbeat, swinging notes and the story about the "cutest little girl," Sweet Rosie O'Grady.

Belle clapped when it came to an end. "What fun!" she exclaimed. "Play another!"

So Mr. Gunness did. He put on record after record, choosing all the most popular tunes—"Turkey in the Straw," "Ta Ra Ra Boom De Ay," and more. When he put on "Daddy Wouldn't Buy Me a Bow Wow," he taught Belle the words, and they sang along, "Daddy wouldn't buy me a bow wow, bow wow!"

"Again, again," cried Belle. She was having fun, and winning over her mark.

"Let's try it with accompaniment!" Mr. Gunness's color was high, and beads of sweat gathered at his temple. His fussy, militant composure had dropped away. He grabbed the smaller trumpet—a cornet, he'd informed Belle earlier—and handed Belle the triangle. He tootled along with the music—evidently, his enthusiasm outran his talent. But Belle played along with him, enthusiastically whacking the triangle on every "bow wow."

"Now costumes!" Mr. Gunness shouted. He plunked the bowl decorated with naked people on his head, and his wayward eyebrow crept out from under the rim as it sloshed around his temples. He offered the lace table runner that had been under it to Belle, saying, "Your royal cloak, your majesty!" and swirled it around her shoulders. He took her by the hands and pulled her with him to dance around the room. It was all so silly and fun, and Belle couldn't help but laugh along.

Ray had been waiting for what had to be hours. It seemed Belle had completely forgotten him. His feet grew tired from standing in place, so he took to pacing the hallway. The pair in the parlor played song after song, growing louder as the afternoon wore on. When he started to hear the awful toots and blats of a horn and then tuneless singing, he found his way to the kitchen. The cook was hard at work preparing for the evening meal. The maid who had let them in was at the worktable, cutting up a pile of onions.

"Stay by the door, you," the cook told him. She was a plump, rosy-cheeked woman but eyed him like a shrew. "This isn't a public house."

"Yes, ma'am. I wonder if I could trouble you for a glass of water."

"Do I look like I have time to wait on you hand and foot?" she said crossly.

The maid rolled her eyes and set down her knife. "I'll get it," she said.

"Hmph," said the cook.

When Ray got back to his post by the parlor door, it was strangely quiet. Maybe they were finally done. About time. He had better things to do than wear out the floorboards in a rich man's house.

Several moments passed, and it was still quiet. Ray listened at the door, expecting to hear the murmurings of a polite goodbye, but there was nothing. Should he knock? He raised his fist. Hesitated. He had no business questioning the likes of Belle and especially not Mr. Gunness. It would be the height of impertinence for a lowly handyman to intrude.

Had Belle forgotten he was waiting for her? Maybe he should just take the wagon and go home. But where was home? Belle had invited him to live in the caretaker's cottage on her property. If he abandoned her, she'd fire him before he even had a chance to move in. That he could not bear.

So he waited.

But as the silence stretched on, Ray grew more impatient. A tiny worm of resentment niggled its way into his brain. She was always like this. Selfish. She bossed him like she was a queen and he was a peasant. *Do this, Ray. Do that, Ray. Ray, fix my hog fence. Ray, fix my door.* And did she pay him? Not one red cent. She didn't even pay the other workers all of what she owed. It was probably true what he'd heard Mr. Cox tell

Mrs. Snyder outside Knowlt's place, that she was as rich as Rockefeller. The only reason she didn't pay was because she was stingy, just like all rich people. She only cared about herself. Here he was, working like a dog for her day after day, fixing this and building that. Driving her wherever she wanted to go. And for what? So he could stand in a god-damn hallway all day long while she listened to "Ta Ra Ra Boom De Ay" a thousand times in a row with a man old enough to be her father?

Ray had boiled up a good head of steam. He stalked the length of the hallway, back and forth, up and back, pounding his fist into his palm to the beat of his angry, wounded thoughts.

Then the music started up again. Ray raced to the parlor door and leaned an ear to it. "Papa, papa, treetop tall, Hear your lovin' mama call," he heard a man singing along with a banjo. It was a song any-body with ears would recognize: "Hot Time in the Old Town Tonight." Belle's laughter and Gunness's awful singing accompanied the music.

This was the limit. Ray's head of steam drove him to action. He wrenched the door open and burst into the parlor.

And there they were. Belle on the sofa, her blouse open. Gunness kneeling on the floor before her, shirtless. His head buried against her chest, his hands squeezing her lovely breasts like playthings. His lips on that tender skin, buzzing raspberries and bouncing one breast and then the other to the beat of the music. He had a bowl on his head.

And Belle, what did she do? Laughed. She laughed with delight, like this was the most fun she'd ever had. "That's right, you naughty bugle boy! Play that tune!" She took the bowl from his head and put it on her own.

The music blared from the horn of the gramophone, and Gunness squeezed a breast so her nipple jutted out, then wrapped his mouth around it and blew a fat raspberry. Belle laughed uproariously. "Play them! Play them like trumpets!"

The song came to its end, and then there was silence, just the scratch of the gramophone needle.

Belle finally noticed Ray. "Oh!" She jumped up and turned away from the open door. Gunness, on his knees with his back to Ray, said, "What, my darling? What's wrong?"

Belle hastily buttoned her blouse. "Close the door, Ray Lamphere," she shouted over her shoulder. "Right now!"

Gunness turned. His mouth dropped open.

Ray backed out of the room like an overmatched terrier out of a rat's nest. He blasted out of the house and ran to his wagon. Jumping up on the buckboard, he grabbed the reins and lashed them at his horse. "Git up, now! Git up!"

What the hell had he just seen?

14

The cut glass bottle was the prettiest little thing Belle had ever owned. She withdrew the dropper and touched a dab of scent below each ear and one on each wrist. The smell of roses surrounded her.

Charles Gunness loved roses. The perfume was a gift, one of several he had given her in their few weeks together. An ivory bracelet carved with roses had been the first, and then a box of chocolates that she had passed along to Ray. How could Charles know of her distaste for candy? From there, his gifts grew more and more extravagant, including a light gig and a sweet and docile white mare named Gwen to pull it. No more relying on Ray and his dingy buckboard for trips into town.

Belle sat at her vanity and smoothed a stray hair into place. Charles would be arriving in his carriage within the hour. They were spending part of almost every day together, Charles taking time out of his busy work schedule in order to be with her. They would listen to music on his gramophone or take drives along the pretty country roads near his home. Today they would have a picnic, serenaded by the gramophone while they lunched in the grass.

And, if Belle wasn't mistaken, today's gift would be small, but precious. Just the right size to slip on her finger.

Everything was going to plan. It was a new plan, admittedly. The morning Belle had gone to meet Charles, her only aim had been to reclaim her crew of workers. But thanks to his amorous response, she found herself with an irresistible opportunity.

A clattering downstairs told her Ray had brought the day's workers into the house. Charles had been easily convinced to siphon some of the laborers off his project to return to their work for Belle. He had even paid their wages and her bills in town. The exterior jobs were finished, and the focus had moved to the interior, with workers stripping and refinishing floors, and removing faded wallpaper and replacing it with fashionable paper carefully selected by Belle.

In the evenings, once all the men had left for the day, Belle would roam through the rooms and out into the yard, admiring the transformation she had wrought. From a decrepit, abandoned disaster, the Quilleran mansion was slowly but surely being returned to its proper glory. No, not the Quilleran mansion. *Her* mansion.

One last appraisal in the mirror told her all was in place. Satisfied, she gathered her shawl and went downstairs, where she found Ray working in the pantry, a small windowless room off the kitchen. It had been empty save for an old hutch containing a few broken dishes and crockery. Ray was supposed to be installing a new cupboard, but it was taking an awfully long time.

Ever since that day he had barged into the parlor at Charles's house, he'd been in a sulk. It had taken constant praise and coy, lovesick glances to get him to move into the caretaker's cottage, but now despite his proximity he would arrive at the main house late in the morning instead of at the crack of dawn. He performed his work at a desultory pace, ghosting about like he was dead already. He clearly hadn't gotten over his hurt feelings. Poor Ray. It was a delicate balancing act, coaxing him out of his moods with kind words and good cooking without leading him to think he could replace Charles.

Belle paused at the doorway, unnoticed, and watched Ray work for a moment. He may be an odd, awkward, heartbroken man, but his carpentry was first-rate. "Well done, Ray!" she exclaimed. "This is wonderful!"

When Ray turned, his hangdog look set her teeth on edge. But where would she get another handyman who would be so devoted to her and work for free?

"Ray, don't look that way." Belle tried to tease him out of his mood. "Didn't your mother ever tell you your face would freeze like that?"

He gave a half-hearted laugh and set his hammer down. "I suppose you're off to see Mr. Gunness."

"Yes, I am. His cook has made us a luncheon, and we're going to have a picnic. I'll try to bring you back a little dessert." Food was always a good way to brighten a man's mood.

"Thank you, ma'am," he mumbled, but he kept his eyes lowered, as if he couldn't bear to look at her.

That wouldn't do. "Oh, Ray." Belle stepped forward and placed her hand on his arm, leaving it there as she felt his resistance begin to soften. She cocked her head, giving him a small, sweet smile. "Don't be like that. I can't stand to see you so sad. Whatever happens between Mr. Gunness and me, you still have a special place in my heart. My feelings for you haven't changed."

Ray raised hope-filled eyes to her, and she rewarded him with a kiss on the cheek.

"That's better," she said, then, twirling her skirt, "Well, what do you think. Do I look all right?"

"You're awful pretty today, Miz Belle. Just like always." But then his brow furrowed. "You're injured."

Oh, bother. Why had she worn a dress with three-quarter-length sleeves? "It's nothing." Belle jerked the sleeves down and swirled her shawl around her shoulders, completely covering her arms. "Charles likes to roughhouse a bit, but it's all in fun. No harm done."

"Miz Belle—"

A knock at the door announced Charles's arrival.

"Must go," Belle sang. "Carry on, Ray. The work looks very fine. Well done." She dashed to meet Charles at the door.

"Good morning, my lovely." Charles took Belle's hands and kissed them tenderly.

"Good morning, Charles dear." She glanced over his shoulder at the coachman standing at attention by the barouche, the front seat of which was piled with boxes and blankets for their picnic. "Three of us for luncheon?"

Charles tipped his head back and roared with laughter. He tucked her hand in his arm and escorted her to the carriage. "You are a delight," he said as he handed her into the back. "Since the day is so fine, I had Dominick put the top down. But if you prefer, I can have him put it back up."

"No, this is perfect," Belle said. "We can see the whole sky above us. It's so clear and blue. The sky in Indianapolis was never like this. I can't get enough of it. Where are we to have our picnic?"

"There is a spot near Fishtrap Lake I want to show you. It's very romantic."

The barouche exited right out of Belle's driveway, catching her by surprise. "Charles, does your coachman know the way to Fishtrap Lake? I thought it was to the left."

Charles laughed and patted her knee. "Yes, my lovely, it is to the left, but we are making a stop in town first. I wanted it to be a surprise, but I might as well tell you know. I'm taking you dress shopping. You are so beautiful, I hate to see you dressed so plainly. There is an excellent dressmaker in town. I had her make some dresses."

Belle kept quiet about her friendship with Della Rose and when they arrived at the dressmaker's shop pretended to meet her for the first time.

Della Rose, quick to catch on, played along. "Mr. Gunness, you spoke the truth. The lady is indeed lovely. I believe the dresses will suit her perfectly."

Della Rose had four dresses for Belle to try on and present to

Charles: two morning dresses with tulip bell skirts, high necks, and long sleeves; a pale rose tea gown with a lace bolero; and most magnificent of all, a white silk ball gown decorated with black silk rosettes.

The ball gown took Belle's breath away as she stared at herself in the wall mirror of the little back room. "Della Rose," Belle gasped. "This is the most beautiful dress I have ever seen."

"Yes, I knew this one would please. It will make a man fall in love with you." She fussed with the skirt, spreading it around Belle's feet. She straightened and met Belle's eyes in the mirror. "If that is what you want."

"I believe I have already achieved that," Belle replied.

"Remarkable that you have fallen in love again so soon after losing your last husband."

Belle made no reply. She kept her eyes on her figure in the mirror, turning to look over her shoulder at the back.

"You are playing a dangerous game, Belle. Do you really want to trade your freedom for money?"

Belle spun away from the mirror and fixed the dressmaker in her sights. "There is no freedom without money, Della Rose."

Charles sighed with contentment. Both his belly and his heart were full.

His cook had packed them a feast—cold chicken and potatoes dressed in oil, slices of beef and ham, fresh bread and a small tureen of butter, a mélange of vegetables seasoned with fresh herbs, sliced apples tossed with cinnamon and sugar, clusters of imported grapes, and bottles of white wine. And, of course, a small box of salt. No matter how the cook prepared the food, he always added salt. Belle had joked that he should have been a fish, he liked his food so salty.

The blue water of Fishtrap Lake threw off sparkles of sunlight as he and Belle lounged on the blankets and cushions Dominick had left for them before taking the barouche out of sight. Birdsong hung in the air. The heat of high summer had abated, leaving the days golden and warm. It was a perfect late September afternoon.

And Belle sure was a picture. Skirts spread around her, hair piled softly atop her head, the field and forest in the distance, and in the foreground: her, focused solely on him. He hadn't ever felt at the center of anyone's world, even with Calliope. Especially once the children came.

Charles had brought Belle out to this lovely spot as part of a plan—he was a man of action, after all—and this moment and how he felt in it confirmed his decision was the right one.

The gramophone he'd brought along played the Brahms quintet that Belle had exclaimed over their first day together. Charles, reclining on a pillow, balanced his wine on his breastbone and, eyes closed, drew musical figures in the air with his finger. He'd told Belle that if he could have been anything other than a businessman, he would have been a world-famous conductor. Or a virtuoso violinist. Or a renowned tenor on the stage.

"You look like a pasha of the east," Belle teased him. "Propped up on your pillows, supping on wine and grapes."

He peeled one eye open. "Then you must be my harem girl." Belle giggled. "Girl, I have wine but no grapes. Prepare me a grape."

Belle found a small knife in the picnic basket and pared the skin off a grape. "Your grape, master."

He leaned back, and she popped it into his waiting mouth, squealing when he nipped her finger. How he longed to take this game further! Once they were married, they would don costumes and act out the pasha and his harem girl. He'd play a tune on his horn and watch as Belle danced for him.

"Close your eyes, Belle," he told her.

Immediately, she did, laying the knife down first and folding her hands in her lap.

The ring was specially made, a gold band set with a cabochon ruby. He chose a ruby because red captured her spirit in a way that sapphires and emeralds and even diamonds never could. He held it out for her and said, "Open your eyes." When her lids fluttered open, he said, "Be my wife, Belle Sorenson."

Her eyes widened and she threw herself into his arms. "Of course, I'll marry you, you old stinker!" Charles slid the ring onto her finger, and the red stone glowed in the sunlight. "You've made me the happiest woman in La Porte."

"And you've made me the happiest man on the planet," he answered. "We'll be married at my home on Saturday. I don't see any reason to wait. Your house should sell very quickly after the work you've put into it. And tonight my children are coming to dinner. You'll join us. It's high time they got to know you."

A slight squint creased her features—she was probably nervous about dinner—and then she smiled and murmured, "I'd be delighted."

Charles eyed the sun sinking lower in the sky and sighed. "The day is getting on."

Belle took his hand in hers. "All good things must end," she said gently. "But that doesn't mean they won't come again. Now we are promised to one another, it is only a matter of days before we will be together always."

Belle's thoughts churned as she greeted Charles's family. It was just like a man to make assumptions about how things would go in a marriage. He'd stated how it would be, not bothering to ask her opinion or even permission. Sell her home, would they? There was only one possible outcome now.

She flashed a warm smile as introductions were made. Henry, the oldest, was a captain of industry, a busy man who Charles said took after him and was his lieutenant in the Gunness empire. Henry's wife, Elizabeth, was pretty enough, but distractedly fussing over their three teenage boys.

Henry's sister, Sarah, seemed to have married the nearest replacement for her father that she could find. William was a rumpled, soft-looking fellow who must offer more to his wife than appearance, though he was only a junior man at the Gunness company. They had no children, and given their age, Belle could only assume they never would.

Belle knew she was a good thirty years Charles's junior, so she wasn't entirely surprised his children's reception of their soon-to-be stepmother wasn't all smiles and well wishes. She was, after all, even younger than they were.

All nine of them sat around Charles's dinner table in polite awkwardness. From the foot of the table, Belle could feel an icy wall of tension separating her from Charles at the opposite end. His staff served them duck a l'orange, a dish Belle had never eaten before, and the table was even more laden with food than their picnic had been earlier in the day. Sarah, a slight woman with dark hair that made her fair complexion seem ghostly, picked at her plate, seeming to eat almost nothing. Her husband indulged eagerly next to her. Conversation was stilted, with long pauses filled by only the sound of silverware clinking against china.

Even Charles was quiet, focusing on his meal and contributing little to breaking the uncomfortable mood. Belle wondered if he even noticed it. Perhaps this was how dinners in the Gunness household always were. Quiet, reserved, and stuffy.

No wonder he was so desperate to play.

Belle was never so glad when the evening came to an end. As the family members filed out of the dining room, Henry caught Belle's attention.

"A moment please, Mrs. Sorenson." He let everyone leave and when they were alone, he fixed fierce eyes on her. "You need to know that it won't work."

"What?" His comment caught her by surprise. "What won't work?"

"It's an old ploy, madam, and one I've prepared for. All of the Gunness holdings are in my children's names. When my father dies, there will be no windfall inheritance for you. You should get out now while you can."

Ah, so that's what was at the root of her icy reception. She'd thought it was simple resentment of her as a usurper of their mother's place, but now she saw there was a sense of entitlement to their father's fortune as well. She should have expected it.

"I see you cannot imagine someone loving your father for who he is, not for his money," Belle said. "I won't try to move you from your cynical position. But I will tell you this. May God above forbid, should the day come that Charles passes, I would not dream of fighting your children for their rightful inheritance. Your father worked hard for his money. You and your children are his family and heirs and deserve the money he worked so hard for all his life."

She turned on her heel and stalked out. That ought to convince him.

15

After the vows were said and toasts drunk, and the guests had shared their well wishes, sincere or otherwise, and gone home, Belle was alone with Charles. In the presence of others, Charles Gunness was acutely polite to the point of being stiff. He never said a wrong word and laughed little. But with Belle, he loosened up and became the child she knew he'd never had the chance to be.

He took several days off from work—Belle was sure he hadn't done such a thing in years, if not decades—and the two of them slept in and ate breakfast in bed, strolled his gardens, and talked of everything and nothing. Through it all was the music. Nearly every room in the house had its own gramophone and music played constantly, whether they ate at the dining room table or talked in the parlor or made love in the bedroom. In the evenings, Charles brought a gramophone outside so they could listen to music as the sun went down.

Charles was a vigorous lover, eager to explore this new life of games and play. Like a little boy, he'd say, "Let's pretend!" And so they would—pretend they were the pasha and his harem girl, pretend they were doctor and patient, pretend he was lord of the manor and she but a meek serving girl. He always chose the roles, and he always put himself in power over her. He was an important man in the business world and had a deep need to stay in that role in the bedroom as well.

For Belle, the role-playing and silliness were a gift she was happy to give to her new husband. She saw that he had lived many long years in a dry spell of duty and work, and he deserved to finally have a chance to revel in gaiety. He may not be the most appealing or attractive man, with his unkempt facial hair and the flaccid skin and plump form of a man who had spent his life sitting in an office chair. And so what if he sometimes got carried away in his power plays? He was clearly devoted to her and meant her no harm. A few bruises were nothing compared to what she had gained in marrying him.

Belle wasn't blind to how worn out Charles would get by the end of each night, lying next to her, sweaty and catching his breath. But a good night's sleep and he was a new man in the morning, waking refreshed and refueled by passion.

On the third night, however, when Charles said, "Let's play," Belle had to take a pause. She examined him closely. Did he seem a little pale? Worn? Dark smudges had appeared under his eyes. Their robust lovemaking was catching up with him, and he looked every bit of his sixty-seven years.

"Are you all right?" she asked. "Maybe we should have a more restful night tonight. We have many years together, Charles. You've worked so hard in your life, I'd like to see you have some rest."

"Nonsense," he said. "I'm fit as a fiddle. And I want to play!" He positioned a record on the gramophone and turned the crank to set it spinning. When he rested the needle on the record, harmonies from light strings and woodwinds twined together. "Stand there," he told her, pointing to the center of the bedroom.

She took her place as directed, arranging the skirts of her gown, then looked at Charles expectantly.

"Don't look at *me*," he said. "You're a maiden in the middle of a forest glen. Your attention is far away, and you take no notice of what's happening right at your feet."

Belle let her vision soften and pictured a forest around her. Out of the corner of her eye, she saw Charles remove his jacket and tie, his collar and cuff links. Off went his shirt and trousers and every stitch of clothing until he was completely naked. He dropped to his hands and knees and crawled across the floor to the hem of her skirt.

"The maiden is innocent and has no idea what's about to happen to her," he said. "She's gazing off into the forest. She sees a stag, a majestic stag with an impressive rack. She can't take her eyes off him. She's drawn to his masculine power, his virility, even though she doesn't know why." As he spoke, Charles lifted her skirt and crawled under the wide bell of it. "The maiden doesn't notice the forest elf right at her feet." His voice was muffled by layers of skirts and petticoats and knickers.

Charles's hands slid up her legs and fumbled at the ribbons tying her stockings on. The delicate silk slipped down, and his whiskers brushed against her thigh. It tickled, like a cluster of spiders had climbed inside her drawers. "Oh my," Belle giggled. "What is that strange sensation?"

"Just the wind, my dear," Charles said.

"The wind is very strange in this forest." He kneaded his fingers into the flesh of her thighs. "It feels . . . strong."

"Strong enough to carry you away, little maiden."

"Carry me away? Oh, no," Belle said in mock horror. "But I'm just an innocent maiden, and I must get home. I must get away." She began to take a small step.

Teeth nipped at her thigh and held on, while Charles growled and shook her flesh with a muffled, "Be still!"

"Ow!" Belle froze in pain, but he released her skin, kissing and stroking away the sting.

"You'll stay here with me, maiden," Charles said as he emerged from her skirts, "if I have to tie you to a tree." He drew her toward the bed. His bathrobe lay at the foot, and he stripped it of its sash.

Belle was all for fun and games, but if her new husband was going to bite her and tie her up, she needed to take things in hand.

The gramophone had long since stopped spinning. The silence gave her an idea.

"Oh," she gasped suddenly. He dropped her hand. "Charles, what happened to the music?"

She sashayed slowly toward the gramophone, unbuttoning her blouse and skirt along the way. As they came undone, she dropped them to the floor. She cranked up the gramophone again, replacing the record with a popular tune called "The Laughing Song." As the first lively piano notes sprang into the room, Belle stripped the rest of her clothes. Fully naked, she swung her hips in rhythm with the music. She wriggled and swayed as Charles watched in mesmerized glee, his cock now standing out straight as a flagpole.

When the chorus came, Belle joined in with the singer's laughter. She gave great, exaggerated laughs from her belly, rocking back with her mouth wide open.

Charles jumped up on the bed, bouncing with the beat. He grabbed the bedpost and thrust his groin at it in a wild rhythm. "I'm a wild man of Borneo!" he said and swung around the pole. He bent over and stuck his ass out toward Belle, then thrust his hips again at the bedpost, grinding in time with the music. "It's a hot time tonight in the jungle!" He hopped from the bed and danced toward her, his whiskers shaking exuberantly.

He looked absurd. Belle burst out laughing, quickly covering it by turning the laugh into part of the song.

Charles closed the gap between them, taking her hands and spinning with her around the room. He drew her close, squeezing her in his arms and kissing her neck and shoulders, burying his face in the softness of her flesh. He licked her birthmark and murmured, "pretty little spot," while kneading his fingers into her plump breasts. Then he slapped her fanny.

On the last chorus, Belle and Charles laughed along breathlessly, swinging closer and closer to the bed. When the song ended, they flopped down on it, side by side, chests heaving. Belle listened to her husband's ragged breaths. She rolled up on her elbow. His face was flushed, and beads of sweat gleamed on his shiny dome head. "Charles? Are you all right?"

"Never better, pumpkin. Come here, and I'll show you." He laughed.

His skin was pasty, and he was still gasping for air, but his cock-stand hadn't flagged. He rolled her onto her stomach and hauled her hips up so she was on her knees, facing away from him.

"Let's revisit this spot." He slammed his hand down on her bottom. "See how it quivers!" he shouted and smacked her bottom again.

A little roughhousing was one thing, but it was time to bring this game to an end. Belle glanced back and, with a coy wink, waggled her hips. "What are you waiting for?" she teased. "Or are you too tired?"

He took the bait. "Tired? Too tired?" he roared. "I'll show you, little maiden. You'll be the one who's worn out when I'm done with you."

He drove himself into her, and the thrust rocked Belle forward on her palms. He reared back and slammed into her again, his hands gripping her hips greedily.

"Come on, now!" Belle urged him. Had he ever been given this much license to indulge in his own pleasures? She doubted it. Only she was able to give him what he craved, what he deserved. "Yes, darling! Yes! Your little maiden can hardly take any more! Please, have mercy!"

Charles found a rhythm, driving into her again and again, pitching Belle forward with every thrust. Their skin slapped together, growing sticky and wet, squelchy sounds filling the room.

It was taking longer than usual for Charles to reach his release. He thrust and thrust and thrust, but no relief came. She looked back at him. His face was red and contorted in intense exertion, almost like he was in pain, his mouth turned down and his chin dimpled with tension.

"Uh, uh, uh," he grunted as he continuing banging away. "Goddamn. Goddamn!" Sweat dripped off his fierce eyebrow and down his nose, falling onto his mustache.

He needed more encouragement. "Come on, big boy! Do it!" she squealed. "You're so big. So powerful. Now! Now! I can hardly take it you're so big!"

More grunts and swearing from Charles, and then with one last big thrust and "Uuuhh!" he finished. He collapsed on her back and rolled off to the side, panting, the flush fading fast from his skin. "Uunh," he groaned, and then coughed. His face was now pasty white. He curled up on his side, clutching his hands to his heart as wheezing coughs racked him. Then he was still.

Belle stared. Was he—? She reached out and touched his shoulder, and he flopped onto his back, eyes staring blankly at the ceiling. "Charles?" she whispered. "Charles? Dear?"

All at once, he dragged in a long, gasping breath.

"Heh heh heh," he chuckled. "That was a big one, old girl. Haven't had a blowout like that since my salad days. Heh."

Belle stared at her husband who was, incredibly, still among the living.

"Good night, dear," he said, patting her rump. He rolled over and slid under the covers. In moments, his breathing became snores.

Belle lay awake for a while. That was too close of a call. If she was going to come out ahead, she needed to take action. Quickly.

16

At breakfast the next morning, Belle set her plan in motion. Carefully. "Darling," she began as they ate poached eggs with a rich, creamy sauce, a cello concerto accompanying their meal from the gramophone, "I forgot to tell you yesterday, I have a buyer for my house."

Charles looked decidedly peaked, his skin pale and shadows darkening his eyes. The creases by his mouth had deepened, as if in just three days he had aged ten years. But despite this physical change, he was as lighthearted as he'd been since Belle met him.

"Wonderful news, my dear." He beamed at her. "Just wonderful. What shall we do today? How about a little dip? I know it's September, but the days are still warm. I know a quiet little water hole where we can shuck our clothes and swim as God made us. Like Adam and Eve." He waggled his giant eyebrow at her.

"Charles"—Belle knew she needed to proceed with tact—"I need you to understand what a big step it is for me to sell my home. And now that I'm going to make a break from my life as an independent woman, I have to admit I'm a little worried about giving everything up for you when you're so clearly . . . slowing down in advancing years. You know how devoted I am to you. How much I adore you. But . . ." She showed him pleading eyes. "Last night gave me a terrible scare. It would tear me to pieces to lose you. And if, on top of that, I lost my home and everything I need to keep me, what would become of me?"

Charles was busy shadow-conducting with one finger the low, deep tones of the concerto. The only sign that he was paying attention was the frown that pinched his mouth after she said "slowing down."

"Nonsense, Belle," he replied. "Nonsense. I've got decades left in me. You've got nothing to worry about." He brightened, then rose from his seat and tossed his napkin on his plate. "Now, how about that swim?"

How dare he swat away her request like an annoying fly, and then expect her to succumb to his every whim. He was no better than Mads. But it wouldn't do to tip her hand just yet. "Perhaps this afternoon would be best," she said, concocting a fond smile. "This morning, I have to go to my home to get things in order for the buyer."

"It's a date, then," he said, leaning down and planting a furry kiss on her mouth.

Belle returned home in the warmest part of the afternoon, quite ready for a cooling swim, even though she still felt a bit cross with Charles. He wasn't in the parlor, though, and she couldn't find him in the bedroom either. Back downstairs, she heard voices in his office, so she knocked and poked her head in, then immediately pulled it back out. Charles was in the middle of a meeting with an insurance agent—the very same man who'd sold Mads his policies: Mr. Henry Simpson.

Well now, wasn't that interesting? Charles *had* heard her fears at breakfast. But how would she explain to Mr. Simpson that she was now married to *another* man about to sign a life insurance policy? No matter, she'd think of something.

She sailed into the room with a bright "Hello!"

The two men rose, and Charles beamed, delighted to introduce her. "This is the light of my life, my darling wife, Mrs. Belle Gunness. We've been married only three days. Darling, this is Mr. Henry Simpson of Indianapolis Life and Casualty. Mr. Simpson, my wife is the reason I called you in. I want her to have the security of knowing she will be taken care of."

Belle came to Charles's side and clasped his hand to her chest. "Thank you, Charles," she whispered to him. "You have no idea how much this means to me." He cupped her chin fondly and stroked her cheek. Belle put all her focus on Charles but kept Mr. Simpson in her peripheral vision, alert for a spark of recognition to cross the man's face.

"I couldn't bear to think of you left with nothing," Charles told her. "This policy will take care of you, and I've seen to it that you will have my house as well. You will want for nothing, my darling."

"You have nothing to fear now that this policy is in place, Mrs. Gunness," Mr. Simpson put in, grinning enthusiastically. "You are well set up for a perfectly comfortable existence should the unspeakable happen."

To Belle's relief, Simpson showed no sign of recognizing her. Which was a miracle, given he'd paid out not one but three policies to her just a few months back. It just proved what Belle already knew: when she turned on her charm, as she'd mistakenly done when she first met him in La Porte, she was irresistible. But if she dawdled by a man's side, playing the subservient wife and drawing no undue attention to herself, a fool like Simpson barely even took note of her. There was no reason for Belle to enlighten him.

"Pleased to meet you, Mr. Simpson. Do carry on. I will leave you two to your business. Charles, I will be upstairs waiting." At the door, she gave her husband a sly wink before leaving the room. He would know to conclude his meeting swiftly. He had a reward awaiting him.

Belle greeted Charles from their bed, toying with a lock of her hair. "What shall we play today?"

He donned lederhosen and a Tyrolean hat and put Strauss on the gramophone, posing heroically for her. She laughed and clapped. "Now take it all off."

By the end of the afternoon, going for a swim was long forgotten. Belle was worn out, and Charles even more so; he lay beside her, panting and pale, and his racking cough had returned. Belle watched him struggle through it, wondering if his moment had finally come. That insurance policy had been issued just in the nick of time. But the coughing eventually subsided, and he insisted he was "fine, never better, fit as a fiddle."

"I never doubted it, my darling," Belle told him, acknowledging to herself that she was going to have to take matters into her own hands. "I have an idea. Let's bring a picnic supper to my house and eat there. You have never really seen my home, and soon it will be too late. I want to share it with you before it's gone."

So out they went in a carriage packed with a feast of Charles's favorite foods.

"By the bells of St. Cecilia," Charles breathed as they entered the house on McClung Road.

Yes, Belle thought. This was the reaction she wanted from people when they arrived at her masterpiece.

She showed Charles around, eager to point out all she had accomplished so far. In the hallway, she stopped at the painting of the house in its glory. "This is what I expected when I bought this house. Imagine my dismay at finding it such a wreck. But I knew I could restore it. And with your help, I have." She smiled up at her husband sweetly, feeding his ego. Not that it really mattered. He'd sealed his fate the moment he decreed she'd sell her home.

"Hah! It only shows what a fool I am for you, throwing good money after bad. You'll be well shut of the place when it's sold, and you can recoup at least some of what you lost. Silly girl." He bussed her cheek fondly. "It's not your fault. Women have no head for business. You see a thing and take a fancy to it and buy it with no thought for the hard practicalities."

"Yes, dear." There was no need to argue. Charles's opinion was no longer of any import.

"Now, where's that dinner I was promised. I'm famished. And I know what I want for dessert," he said with a wink.

Belle laid plates on her dining room table. In the kitchen, she unpacked what Charles's cook had prepared: raw oysters and deviled eggs, lamb chops, green beans, and whipped, creamed potatoes, and a banana mousse.

Belle had readied a special salt cellar just for Charles, and she set it right next to his plate as she served. He began ladling the white crystals liberally on his food, as he always did. The addition of arsenic, taken from the very same box of Rough on Rats she had used in Indianapolis, meant the salt had less of an effect than Charles wanted, and over the course of his meal he kept sprinkling more and more.

When Belle returned from the kitchen with the banana mousse, she found Charles curved over his plate, arms clutched across his midsection, moaning. She rushed to his side. "My darling, what's wrong?" she cried.

"*Hrrrk.*"

"What's that? I can't understand you."

"I—*hrrrk*," he repeated and then hunched over again and spilled the contents of his stomach back onto the plate it came from.

The smell was extravagant. Belle reeled back. Steeling herself, she returned to Charles's side. "Charles, how can I help? Perhaps some bicarbonate of soda?"

A fresh wave gushed out of Charles, joining its predecessor on his plate and spilling onto the table, his lap, and the floor. "Please . . . help me," panted Charles. Sweat beaded on his pale forehead and his breath came in pained gasps.

"Yes, Charles. I am helping you," Belle murmured, stroking his back. "It will be over soon."

Charles may have been none the wiser, but their contract was almost fulfilled. She'd given him the one thing all his riches never could: the gift of play, freedom to let loose and experience simple fun and pure joy, both in the bedroom and out of it. She knew as clearly as she knew her own name that his days with her were his happiest and most fulfilling. And her final gift to him, the perfect resolution to his life—reunion with his lost Calliope—was imminent. Indeed, a last gasp marked his end, and he slumped back in his chair before tumbling to the floor.

In return, in a matter of days, her holdall would again be filled to the brim and ready to keep funding the restoration of her dream home. And to think he'd said women have no head for business.

She ran to the caretaker's cottage. Pounding on the door, she cried, "Raaay! I need you!"

Ray flung open the door on the second knock and stared in wonder. Belle had never come to his cottage before. Her face was wrenched as if in agony, and tears threatened to spill down her cheeks.

"Come in, come in," he said. "What's happened? Did he do something? Leave you?" That would be like a gift from heaven. Charles out of the picture, with Ray ready to take over and console Belle. From there it was a short hop to love and togetherness.

"He's dead," Belle said. "He died, Ray. What am I going to do? I need help."

"There now. It'll be all right." Ray patted her back while she sniffled into his shoulder. The old bastard was dead? Ray wasn't sorry, not one bit. No, he was glad Gunness was gone, him with his cruel fists and more money than he knew what to do with. Now maybe things between Ray and Belle could go back to the way they were. He would treat her better than Gunness ever had. He rocked her and murmured into her hair, "I'm sorry for your loss, Miz Belle. But he was an old-timer and when your time comes, that's it. Let's go on up to the house, and I'll help you lay him out."

But when they got there, Ray saw the situation was a horse of a different color. He and Belle fetched up on the threshold of the dining room.

"Shittagod*dam*." Poisonous odors assaulted Ray. The stench crawled inside his mouth and nose, blocking out any breathable air. He jerked the collar of his shirt up over his nose. "What the hell happened? I ain't never seen anything like this in my life." He inched closer, gruesome curiosity luring him forward. Gunness lay curled on the floor, surrounded by a mess of puke. "Boy, he sure did shoot the cat."

"What?" Belle asked from the doorway.

"You know, puked. Spewed his guts." The stench wasn't so bad now. He could handle it. Not like some people.

Ray took in the table set for two and the remains of the meal. "I always did like your cooking. Not sure what his problem is."

"It wasn't my cooking, Ray."

"All right, all right. No need to snipe at me."

Ray leaned down and peered into the old man's lifeless eyes. "What a way to go," he mused. "Poor old bastard."

It was clear that whatever had happened had affected only Charles. It didn't take much of a leap to figure out that something wasn't quite right.

Belle hovered in the doorway. "He's better off now," she said quietly. "He deserved a happy ending to his life, and now he can be happy forever with his first wife."

Ray thought that was a mighty strange way to look at things, but when Belle began to softly weep, he went to her and held her and stroked her hair.

"If it hadn't been for you, Ray, I wouldn't have done it. I told you things were still the same between us. But you didn't believe me. You should have believed me. I need you, Ray. I need you now more than ever. You have to help me clean up this mess."

He hesitated barely a moment. He would do anything to have her back.

Ray carried Gunness's body upstairs but paused on the landing. He couldn't lay the messy body on the bed, as you would with a normal death. Coming to a decision, he put the body in the bathtub. They'd have to wash the mess down the drain.

Leaving Belle to tend to her dead husband, Ray returned downstairs. As he rolled up the soiled carpet and mopped up the slop in the dining room, he pushed away thoughts of what the hell he had gotten himself into and instead put his mind on getting the job done.

In the earliest hours of the morning, before the first cock crow, Ray returned to the caretaker's cottage and cleaned himself up. Belle joined him there with a tender passion. She was a wonder, his intoxicating flower. Ray had Belle back, and he could breathe again.

The sun sent its first tendrils of light over the horizon, and Belle nestled in the crook of Ray's arm, lazily stroking circles on his chest. "You know, Ray," she whispered, "Charles lived his life as a mean, miserable man. He died a happy one. I made that possible for him. I gave him the gift of joy."

As she spoke the words, Belle realized Charles had given her a gift as well. He had exposed her to a world of music she had never before had the chance to appreciate.

Soon she would see the reward for all her efforts—once Charles's insurance policy paid out and the proceeds from selling his house came through. Then the security of financial independence would be hers. The very thought brought a monumental relief. Her limbs felt heavy, and her mind floated into visions of luxury and comfort, of eating off expensive china and wearing soft silks, surrounded by the fine furnishings of an exquisitely renovated home.

17

In celebration of her recent business deal, Belle had bought three almost-grown hogs and a flock of six chickens from a foreclosed farm in the next county. They arrived on a wagon late one Tuesday afternoon, and the driver unloaded the animals with little fanfare while Belle and Ray supervised.

It had been a taxing time, notifying Charles's children of his death and arranging his funeral. "So unexpected," she had told them. "Right in the middle of—well. I'm sure you understand." There had been some tense moments when they realized their childhood home would go to her, but no one could argue that Charles didn't have the right to do that. And he hadn't altered any of his financial or business holdings, just as Henry had predicted, so in the end, everyone was satisfied.

The relief of returning to her home had been sweet. In her absence, Ray had accomplished a fair bit of work. In addition to finishing the swine enclosure and her pantry cupboard, he had toiled outside, clearing brush, fertilizing and clipping the grass, and pruning the shrubs around her house. Still, there was much to be done. The proceeds from Charles's insurance policy and the sale of his home, totaling almost $10,000, revitalized the restoration project—and her spirits.

She embarked on a mission to decorate her home in the style it deserved, with furniture, drapes, lamps, throw pillows, carpeting, and more bought in a studious bout of catalog shopping. A new stove, an icebox, and a complete set of pots and pans made the kitchen more functional, and a beautiful new buffet and hutch of polished maple transformed its appearance.

Top of her list, though, was to change Ray's lingering sulk. Despite her return to his bed after Charles's passing, Ray moped from task to task, always completing his work but forever with the gloom of a condemned man. Belle knew what he wanted. But what did he expect? That she was going to move him into the house with her? That she would *marry* him? It was actually quite endearing.

Ray had come to the harsh realization that living at the house, even at the remove of the caretaker's cottage, was simply too painful. After that wonderful night together after Gunness's death, Belle had made it clear she had no intention of making their relationship more formal or permanent. She came to him in the cottage several times a week, and she was generous with her compliments to his work, but anything beyond that was a fantasy.

Even more than that, he couldn't shake the images of what he'd seen the night Gunness died, or the dread of knowing Belle was responsible. She'd *killed* a man. Still, the idea of leaving her stabbed him with guilt. How would she manage without him?

He couldn't worry about that. He'd done enough to get her on her feet. The house was in decent shape, and the land was coming along. The hogs had an enclosure to keep them safe from predators and a three-sided shelter to provide shade or warmth. She'd just have to manage on her own.

So once he'd settled the new hogs with feed and water, Ray retreated to the cottage to pack. It didn't take long. A couple pairs of pants and some work shirts, a bowl, a spoon, a pan, and his coffeepot. It all fit into a single canvas bag.

Ray closed the door firmly behind him and slung his bag over his shoulder. He wouldn't look back up at the house. Couldn't. He knew Belle was still admiring her new drove of pigs, and he just couldn't bear to see her. He set off for town.

"Raaay!" Her cry stopped him in his tracks before he reached the end of the driveway. He should keep on going, he knew he should. But the sound of her voice cut right through him and welded his feet in place. He fixed his eyes on the woods across the way. Their leaves had turned golden. It wouldn't be long now before they dropped to the ground. Summer had gone. He heard her footsteps running up to him and braced himself.

She arrived breathless at his side and grabbed his arm. "Ray! Where are you going?" Her cheeks were pink, and the breeze swept a tendril of hair across her face. She impatiently brushed it away.

"It's time for me to move on, Miz Belle," Ray said, trying to keep his voice neutral. "The hogs have a home, and they've been fed. The pantry's finished. The fence line up to the brook is secure. You can hire someone to fix the rest. Don't forget to feed and water those hogs every day. They'll eat a lot." Ray gave her a tight nod.

"Ray, please," Belle said. "You can't leave me. I need you. What will I do without you?"

Ray's feet were still cemented to the earth.

"Please, Ray," Belle said again, softly. "I killed a man for you. For us." Ray winced. "Ray, you know it's true. You know my true feelings. It was just too painful to see all of your hard work abandoned, just because I'm a poor widow with no one to care for me. I couldn't let that happen. Don't you see? Ray, you need to know that I was going to begin paying you. Now that I have money, I can afford it. But I understand it may be too late. For us." Belle paused, struggling to remove something from her pocket. "Please take this, as a parting gift. I know it's not much, but—" She sniffled. "I'm sorry. Goodbye." She ran back up to the house.

Into his hand she'd thrust several bills. It wasn't close to covering all his labor, but it was still more money than he'd had at one time in his whole life.

Ray woke up in his old bed in the house where he grew up. He could hear noises in the kitchen, vexed grumbling and the banging of a fire being lit in the old stove. He threw off his covers and stood, drew his pants on, and tucked in his shirt. And then he went to face the bitter old woman who was his mother.

"Well, look who's decided to get out of bed," she sneered as he entered the kitchen. "I guess you're used to lying abed all the day long up at that scarlet woman's house."

"No, Ma," he answered her. "And she's not a scarlet woman. Belle Gunness is a fine and kind woman."

"Pah!" She plunked the coffee pot on the stove to boil.

It was pointless to argue with her. She never had a good word to stay about any living thing. She spread bile wherever she went, even in town, where even though she was behind in almost every bill she owed, few merchants would confront her on it. It was worth more to their own equilibrium and self-preservation to let this particular sleeping dog lie.

"Well, what are you waiting for? Ain't you going to get in some wood? How can I keep this fire going with no wood? Can't you do anything right?"

"Yes, Ma," Ray said automatically and went out to the shed. It was a rickety lean-to structure, giving shelter to stacks of logs and a few tools. With axe in hand, Ray reduced a log to sticks of kindling in a blaze of fury. He grabbed another log and slapped it on the splitting stump.

The last thing Ray wanted was to be back with his mother again. As lovelorn as he'd been in the caretaker's cottage at Belle's, it was a happy dream compared to the misery of life in the mean, two-room house with his callous mother. But he was tormented by his part in the death of Charles Gunness. The scene had been messy and gruesome.

The grimace frozen on Gunness's face had been one of total agony. Ray didn't believe she meant what she said, about doing it for him. No, sir. That was absurd. She must have done it for her own selfish reasons, without a single thought for his feelings.

Ray was working up a fine state of outrage along with the sweat as he swung the axe down again and again.

What had she seen in Gunness in the first place? All she'd needed was to get some of the workers back. But no. She had to go and marry the old bastard. Ray's axe flew, and the pile of kindling became ever larger. What had her life been like with Gunness? Did Ray even want to think about that? Not really, but he couldn't stop his mind wandering into imaginary scenes of the two of them together, her young and beautiful, and him old and wrinkly. Belle insisted she was happy with him, but happy women don't murder their husbands. And there were those bruises.

Ray's axe hung in the air. He lowered it slowly.

Clearly, Gunness was hurting her. What kind of man puts a hand to his wife like that? Especially a woman so rare and fine as Belle? Ray knew all too well what it was like to live with someone whose first and last resort was violence. A cuff to the head, a pinch of skin squeezed between cruel fingers. The paddle, the willow switch. Anything handy, really.

The truth was, you reap what you sow. Gunness's own brutality caused his death. The Belle Ray knew wouldn't hurt a fly. She could never have done this if she hadn't been pushed to the brink.

Belle was a lonely widow in a state of extreme financial need, and Gunness took advantage of her. Seduced her, brought her into his home. And then beat her.

Poor Belle, keeping up appearances the whole time, insisting that everything was fine when it obviously was not. She must have longed for the sweet way Ray treated her. It must have seemed like a poor bargain, to marry a violent man when a kind and gentle one had been right under her nose.

It was suddenly so clear: Belle had done what she had to. And she had done it for him.

No one ever in his life, not one single person, had ever done anything for him. Let alone something this monumental. A strange feeling of dark exhilaration overcame him.

The bucket of slops was heavy and awkward. Belle lugged it with two hands, the bucket braced against her hip and the handle biting into her palms. The contents sloshed as she trudged, with bits of garbage slopping onto her skirt. Good thing she had put away her fine clothes for the day.

At the pen, she set the bucket down and undid the gate. Hefted the bucket again, shuffled inside, and dragged the gate closed behind her. There, managed that without letting a single pig out. She heaped the slops into the trough and smiled triumphantly. Farm life wasn't so hard. Maybe she *could* do it on her own.

Suddenly, the pigs raced over, dumping Belle on her behind. She was jostled from all sides as trotters pressed her fingers into the ground and hairy hog bodies battered her head and torso. Terrified she was about to be trampled to death, she pushed and rolled away from the trough. She scrambled to her feet and ran to the gate, unlatching it and escaping the pen as fast as she could. Breathless, bruised, and filthy, she bent at the waist to recover.

She stumbled back to the kitchen and collapsed into a chair. Who was she fooling? She couldn't do this on her own.

On the table was a stack of money. Sounds of banging echoed down from the second floor. Could it be?

At the kitchen sink, Belle took a moment to clean up. She swiped bits of garbage from her skirt, then washed mud off her hands and face and smoothed her hair into place. She took the stairs swiftly, wings of hope lightening her steps. Upstairs, she found Ray on his knees, prying the scuffed and worn baseboard away from the wall in one of the bedrooms.

"Ray?"

"Mornin', Miz Belle. I'll have this baseboard off of here and cleaned up real nice. Make a world of difference to this room."

"You came back," she gasped.

"Well," Ray said, getting up off his knees. "It's like this. I figure you couldn't hurt a fly. Unless that fly was really a hornet fixin' to get you good. Anybody would swat a hornet like that. And you only did what you had to do. And the thing is, I'd rather be here with you than anywhere else in the world."

It was a long speech for Ray, and Belle was impressed. He deserved a reward. She flung herself across the room and into his arms, covering his face and neck with kisses. "You came back to me."

Belle grabbed at Ray's shirt, ripping the ends out of his trousers and sliding her hands up his torso. For a lean man, he was very muscular, and she reveled in the feel of his strength. A frenzy of fingers sent their clothes to the floor, and they collapsed there, too eager for each other to seek out Belle's comfortable bed. The bare floor was good enough.

September turned the corner into October, bringing the first hints of fall. Ray felt a level of happiness he'd never known before. Not only was Belle coming to his bed several nights a week, but she was paying him a small weekly wage for all his work on the farm. Truth be told, he would do the work for free, had done it for free for months, but the fact that Belle was paying showed how valuable he was to her.

He began his days early, feeding Belle's hogs and chickens along with the sweet mare, Gwen, that Gunness had given her with the little gig. Then he turned his attention to the unending list of jobs to do on Belle's home. He'd finished improvements to the baseboards in two bedrooms before deciding to tackle the sagging front porch before the winter snows arrived.

He was just stopping for a drink of water when Belle returned from town with the gig.

"Hellooo!" she sang out as she reined Gwen to a stop in front of the door. "Come help me unload, Ray."

The back of the carriage was packed with boxes and parcels. Belle was full of high spirits as they ferried the packages into the house, telling him news from town. "Ray, you won't believe what they're saying about me in town. Knowlt Fischer, you know, proprietor at Fischer Mercantile, told me I'm very much admired. Those are his words, not mine. 'Very much admired,' he told me. The ladies of town have taken to looking to me for style guidance. And everyone was so kind, offering their condolences on Charles's passing."

Ray helped Belle bring the packages to the dining room, where they piled them on the table. "I only bought the necessities," Belle explained. "I needed needles and thread, and writing paper and envelopes. And I got some books for the library—those empty shelves look ridiculous. And a standing mirror for my bedroom. Of course I ordered some new dresses from Della Rose; after what Knowlt Fischer said, how could I not? I have to keep up my appearance. Perhaps I should buy a piano? It would look perfect in the parlor. Oh! I almost forgot—" Belle selected a parcel from the pile, wrapped in brown paper and tied with string. "Here, Ray, do you have your pocketknife? Cut this string. This one is for you." She clasped her hands together and bounced a little on her toes.

A package for Ray? He couldn't recall receiving a present in a very, very long time. The string came away easily, and he unfolded the paper to reveal a set of clothes. A work shirt and pants, the fabric stiff and new. The shirt was blue and the pants brown, a departure from the worn-out, graying clothes he always wore.

"Well," Belle asked, "do you like it?"

"Yes, ma'am," Ray said. "Very much. You're a kind woman, Miz Belle."

"Oh, good, I'm so pleased. Now look at this!" She tore into a different package and revealed a large hoop decorated with long ribbons and two pairs of sticks. "Have you ever played the game of graces?"

No, but he'd seen schoolgirls playing it before. It was like catch, without a ball. Ray frowned, fingering the colorful ribbons trailing from the hoop and realizing he'd never seen any boys play it. "That's a girl's game."

"Oh, don't be silly," Belle said. "Only if two girls are playing. If it's you and I, then it's a people's game. Don't you think? Come, let's play."

"Play? Me?" Much like receiving a present, he couldn't remember the last time he'd played a game.

"Yes, you, silly Ray." Belle laughed. "It will be fun."

"But I have work to do," Ray protested. "I'm working on the porch."

Belle got cross. "What do I look like to you?" she said. "Do I look like that awful foreman at the Gunness Music Hall construction site? A great ogre of a man who will howl at you and dock your pay for taking a break?" She put on a scowl and hunched her shoulders and stomped around the room. "Work harder! Work harder, Ray, you sonuvabitch! Grr!" she growled at him in mock aggression. Then she dropped her shoulders and let out a peal of laughter, which he couldn't help but echo. "Ray, the sun is shining, and it will be winter soon and too cold to be outside. Life is short. Let's play."

How could he say no to that?

The game was harder than it looked. He crossed his sticks in an X and looped the hoop over them, then drew the sticks apart so the hoop flew into the air. Getting it to go straight was easier said than done. A little stronger effort from the right or left side sent the hoop off course. And when Belle returned the hoop, aiming his sticks so they'd catch the hoop was no easy feat either. But after a few tosses, Ray started to get the hang of it.

"I don't believe you, Ray," Belle teased as she struggled to fling the hoop to him. "I think you *have* played the game of graces before. You're too good at it! You must have played it in the schoolyard with all the other children!" He sent the hoop into the air with a snap of the sticks and watched as it sailed across the yard to Belle. Who missed it, again. But she laughed and stooped to reclaim the hoop. "What are you looking at, Ray?" she called. "Wait, there's something funny on your face." She started walking toward him.

"What, me?" He knew he screwed up his face when he was concentrating, plenty of people had made fun of him for it—was he doing that now? He hadn't thought so. He was having a good time, playing this little kid's game.

She was right in front of him now, peering up into his face. He could feel the heat coming off her from running around. Her cheeks were rosy, and her hair was threatening to come down from its pile on her head. He wanted to sink his fingers into its glossy softness and release it from its pins. Her lips seemed so close and inviting. He wanted to kiss her.

"Is that—I think it is. Why, Ray, I think you're smiling." She reached up and traced the curve of his lips.

That was too much. He scooped her close and lowered his mouth to hers. He kissed her slow and sweet, until she murmured, "Take me to your cottage, Ray."

18

elle snuggled down in her covers, enjoying the languorous contentment that saturated her body after sex with Ray. It was still as much a means to an end as sex had been with Mads and Charles. Her compliments alone wouldn't keep Ray happy, she knew that. He was such a needful man, so starved of human touch, human kindness, and it gratified her to provide that for him while it bound him to her incontrovertibly. But with Ray, unlike with the others, Belle *received* something in return: he touched her with her pleasure in mind, not just his, and the experience of being loved physically gave her a feeling she couldn't quite name, a sense of being truly seen, of *wholeness.*

A thunderous rainstorm had swept through at some point during their lovemaking, and it kept up all evening, the rain slackening just long enough for Belle to race back to the house. As she settled into her own bed, the storm picked up again, sheets of water pouring from the sky and roaring down her gutters. The sound highlighted how warm and snug she was.

Belle yawned. She had to give it to Mads, he'd chosen a spectacular bed. Its mahogany frame gleamed darkly in the soft light of her bedside lamp, with the queenly headboard rising behind her and the footboard a distant six feet away. The plush mattress supported on modern steel coils felt like sleeping on clouds. The bed linens were the finest available, bought with money she earned from Charles—and worth every penny, she thought as she drifted into sleep.

With a sudden howl, the storm renewed its assault, jolting Belle awake. Rain washed down in torrents, and a restless wind hammered at the roof.

Plop.

A drip spattered her nose.

Plop.

Belle squinted up at the ceiling, dismayed to see a stain of wetness seeping across the plaster.

Plop.

"Ray!" Belle wailed.

Plop. Plop.

The drops were getting bigger, splashing on her forehead and nose. She sat up and cupped her hands to catch the drips. She needed a bucket, fast, before her new linens were spoiled.

"Stop! Stop dripping, dammit!" she cried. But the rain didn't listen, instead leaking through her fingers, dampening her precious sheets.

"Ray!" This time she hollered, scrambling out of bed. She ran downstairs to get a bucket from the kitchen. In the hallway, she yanked her front door open and screamed into the dark morning, "Ray! Come quick! I need you!" She remounted the stairs at a gallop and leapt onto the bed to center the bucket under the leak.

The caretaker's cottage wasn't that far away. Why didn't he come? "Ray! Get up here!" she screamed again.

A creaking moan split the night, stopping Belle's heart. Was the ceiling sagging?

Plop, *plop*, *plop*, the drips rang hollowly in the tin bucket.

Another long, ominous creak, and suddenly a gush of water poured down on her along with an explosion of plaster and rotted timbers. "Noo-oo!"

* * *

Ray woke with a start. He'd crashed into a deep sleep the moment his head hit the pillow, and now he awoke from a dream where Belle had been standing before him, dressed in a gauzy robe that veiled her body. The folds of fabric swayed in a gentle wind, revealing her nakedness underneath. "Ray," she beckoned him, her voice soft. He grasped at the dream as it slipped away.

He heard his name again, this time a sharp cry: "Ray!" It floated across the yard, from the direction of the big house. As another wail sounded faintly through the tempest outside—"Raaay!"—he realized these calls were real.

Belle needed him!

He leapt out of bed and scrabbled for his boots. He hopped one-footed to the door as he struggled to tug the boots on. He dashed across the yard, pelted by the rain and pushing through wet grass. The front door hung open, and Ray barreled through it, then up the stairs. His heart hammered in his throat. He should have thought to bring a weapon. What if she was being attacked? He burst into her bedroom and stopped short. A ghost was standing beside her bed.

No, that was Belle. Covered in white plaster dust, surrounded by roof debris, rain pouring down through a gaping hole in the roof.

"Ray," she wailed and burst into tears. "Look at my beautiful bed!"

"That can't possibly be right," Belle stated, working hard to keep the anxiety she was feeling out of her voice.

The man waited, impassive in the face of her incredulity. He was tall and bearlike, with a sandy-red beard and redder hair.

"He's one of the best in the county," Ray had told her that morning after the roof collapsed. They'd hovered in the doorway of the bedroom, gaping at the sodden debris decorating her bed and the floor all around it. Sunlight streaming through the gap in the roof raised steam from the wet sheets and timbers. "You need a real good fellow for this job. It's much too much for me. I can help him, but you need an expert. Hugh Anderson is your man."

Now Anderson said without heat, "I'm afraid so, ma'am. Two thousand dollars, thereabouts, for supplies and labor." He navigated the debris-strewn floor to the calamity in the ceiling and looked up through the hole. "You've got not only the damage to this ceiling and the attic floor above it, plus you've got the roof itself. You'll need to replace joists, subfloor, rafters, roof sheathing, roofing tiles. And that's just what I can see from here. No guarantees I won't find more damage as I go along."

A fury crackled along Belle's skin, listening to this so-called expert standing there calmly while shattering her world. It was more than the broken timbers and drenched interior, more than brick and wood and plaster. This house was the first space she'd ever created for herself, and the assault to it cut into her very soul. She didn't just need to fix a hole in her roof to keep out the elements, she needed to restore wholeness to her sanctuary.

In her mind's eye, a hammer swung at Hugh Anderson, tap-tap-tapping to nail his lips together. Instead of cruel words, his mouth could produce only muffled grunts. His eyes widened, and his hands scrabbled at the nails but they melted into his skin, sealing off any hope of talking ever again.

There, that was better. Belle turned away from the roofer and his devastating diagnosis. She leaned a hand against the hallway wall. This was not part of the plan. She was so close! So close to bringing her house and her life to the state of perfection it—no, *she*—deserved. Why did this have to happen now?

Two thousand dollars was an astronomical sum. The payout from Charles's insurance and the sale of his home had been generous, but that money was spoken for. Well, it was spent, as a matter of fact. She had calculated that the remainder would be enough to live on. But now this.

She could pay Hugh Anderson, or she could continue to eat. She couldn't do both.

But she would starve before she would abandon her sanctuary.

"Will you accept payment in installments?" Belle asked. "I don't have a lot of savings. Everything is in this house."

"I'll need half down to get started," Anderson said. "I'll bill you for supplies as I go along. Too many disreputable folks back out on paying their bills, and I don't have time to chase 'em down."

"But surely you don't think *I* look disreputable." Belle bestowed one of her most winsome expressions on the man, widening her eyes and parting her lips slightly, like a lost waif in need of protection. "Just this once, can't you make an exception?"

"No, ma'am. I can't."

He was implacable as stone, this man. And heartless. He'd probably let an urchin freeze in the snow.

"I'm sure you're an honorable woman. But I have one policy for everyone. Saves me a lot of headaches."

"I see," Belle said. "I need to think about it. Thank you for coming by."

Anderson nodded and took his leave. Belle closed the door after him and sank against it, leaning her forehead against the cool wood.

"That's a lot of money, Miz Belle," Ray said.

Belle straightened up, stiffening her backbone in both a real sense and a figurative one. "That is *all* my money, Ray. Or close enough. Come, we have work to do."

She marched upstairs toward the mess in her bedroom. The first task in this project had to be clearing away the debris, and she might not be trained as a roofing carpenter, but she could surely tote and carry.

"What are you gonna do about the roof?" Ray asked from behind her on the stairs. "How will you pay for it?"

Belle halted in place two steps above him and swiveled on her toe.

"Hear me, Ray." She towered over him and pitched her voice low and fierce. "I will not let all of my hard work be wasted. I have put too much of myself into this house to just walk away." She paused, and softened slightly. "I mean we, Ray, of course. We have put so much into this house. You see that, don't you? Tell me you're with me, Ray, because I need you."

"You oughta know by now, Miz Belle, I'll never desert you. If you're stayin', I'm stayin'. I'm with you. I just don't know how you're gonna pay for it, is all."

Belle bent down and swiftly kissed his cheek. "You let me worry about that."

Truth was, she didn't know how she was going to pay for it. But work seemed to be a good lubricant for thinking, and she let her mind ruminate on the problem as she and Ray dug into the mess. They carried armload after armload of timbers downstairs and outside. Ray brought up a barrel from the barn, and they filled it with small pieces of wood and plaster, and then Ray used ropes to lower it down to the first floor.

Belle built a fire in the yard and set the huge laundry kettle to boil, then gathered her bedding, muddy with plaster dust, and dunked it into the kettle. When each piece was clean and rinsed, she hung it on the line to dry. It was a blustery fall day, the night's storm swept away, and the wind would do the job quickly. As she worked, she pondered her situation. She had a head for business, she had no doubt, despite all the men in her life who'd told her otherwise. But there was no way she was making candy again, and what other skills did she have? The only way she'd ever succeeded in earning real money was by marrying it. But how could she turn marriage into a business? Where was she going to find a wealthy man eager to jump into matrimony? It was too bad she couldn't write away to Sears and Roebuck for a husband as if he were a bicycle.

Of course! An idea struck Belle. It was brilliant. *She* was brilliant. She rushed inside, passing Ray on the porch as he brought another load outside. "I've got it, Ray! I've got it!"

She sat down at the desk in the library, the big fancy thing with its cubbies and locking roll top that Mads had insisted on buying with part of their fire insurance money. She scrounged in the drawers for a sheet of letter paper and a fountain pen. "Dear Sir," she began.

Ray peered over her shoulder. "Miz Belle, what are you up to?"

"Ssh, now, Ray. Let me write." His breath tickled her ear as she formed the words on the page.

"Are you sure that's a good idea?" he asked. "No telling where it might lead, who might show up here."

Belle froze her pen and pinned Ray with a stern look. "Stop your whining, Ray. That roof needs repairs and to do them I need money. Do you know how to fix a gaping hole in the roof? No? Do you have piles of money lying around that I don't know about? No? I thought not. Remember, everything I do, I do for us. Now, are you with me, or are you against me?"

"I'm with you, Miz Belle. I'm always with you."

"Good. Now you go back to work and let me do this."

"Yes, ma'am," Ray said and shuffled off.

Belle returned to her task, her pen nib scratching softly as she crafted a letter that would set in motion a plan to solve all her problems. "WANTED: A good and reliable man to become a partner in a profitable farm. Matrimony in mind."

Part III

Scaling Up

19

The crossroads, when he came to it, was impossible for Andrew Helgelien to ignore. Not because of its scenic beauty or bustling commerce. No, it was just the intersection of two dusty roads in a featureless stretch of plains, with one small building to mark that any civilization at all was nearby.

But it mirrored precisely the state of Andrew's life: a crossroads.

He was outside his territory as a traveling salesman, and it wasn't by chance. His usual route took him from his brother's small apartment above his saloon in the heart of a Norwegian neighborhood of Chicago, along the bend of Lake Michigan as far as Michigan City and branching out away from the coast as his mood struck him. On this trip, though, when he'd reached Portage, he'd taken the east road instead of arcing north. He'd told himself this was simply the direction his whim was taking him that particular day.

As he reined his wagon to a stop in front of the little building, he still carried the melancholy he'd picked up on his last farm visit. It was a two-room house on a few acres three miles before this crossroads, home to an old man and his missus. Their children had all grown and gone, and now it was just the two of them. They listened patiently while Andrew showed them his wares, but Andrew didn't think he'd make a sale. It was as if they had invited him in to be polite and to have something new to talk about at breakfast the next day.

But Andrew pressed on, showing them his tinctures and tools. Things changed when he brought out Rawleigh's Mineral Liniment. Made by Irma Rawleigh, an old herb healer from his neighborhood in Chicago, it was one of his top sellers. "It'll do wonders for any aches and pains you might have," he told the couple.

The old fellow perked up. "Mother," he said. "Do you think?"

"Could be, could be," she answered. "Might I try a bit?"

She poured a few drops on her hands and rubbed the liniment all around. "Oh, my. Isn't that nice. Don't get old, young fella. Arthritis pain lives in every joint all day long. But this takes the pain right away!"

She lowered herself to the floor and tugged her old man's boots and socks off. She poured a few more drops of Rawleigh's in her palms and tenderly smoothed it over his feet. Up and down the soles, between the toes, the works. The mister closed his eyes in relief as the liniment began to soothe.

The silent exchange the two mates shared then was something Andrew knew he would remember for the rest of his life. Their eyes met, and they were the only two in the room. All the years, all the memories, all the love and hardship, flowed back and forth between them, with not a word spoken.

That was the moment Andrew decided. His correspondence with a widow in La Porte had been going on for weeks, with her encouraging him to come meet her. She'd even given him her address, describing exactly how to find her house.

But Andrew had thought it was too much to hope for that a match from a lonely hearts advertisement could work out. He was closing in on forty years old, a confirmed bachelor with no prospects to change that status. How could he, traveling from town to town most weeks of the year? For many years, he'd thrived on the adventure of it, the novelty of new faces, new places. But the last year or so, that novelty had become more tiresome than adventurous.

When he first saw the ad, a little flicker of something had sparked in him. *I'll just answer out of curiosity*, he'd told himself. What were the chances an ad in the paper could lead to love? But then she had written back with questions about his life on the road, and they had taken to writing frequently. He eagerly anticipated her letters and wrote her long ones in reply. In the light of day, he still thought a true love match would be too much to hope for. But in the darkest part of the night, sleeping in a field or a barn with only Odysseus for company, he could admit that he hoped for a happy ending.

Watching the two old lovers communicate so much without a word, he realized he wanted that kind of intimacy for himself. And so, here he was at this lonely crossroads, faced with a choice: turn north and return to his regular territory, or continue east, to the unknown?

Andrew got down from his wagon and tied up his horse. "That's the boy, Odysseus. I'll be only a moment, and then we'll be on our way. I've made my decision." Who was he kidding? His decision had been made back in Portage.

The unimpressive building was a box built out of rough, unpainted boards. Above the doorway, letters in black paint proclaimed its purpose: POST OFFICE, FARBUT I.N. Inside, a counter lined the back of the square room, with shelves and cubby holes on the wall behind.

"Afternoon, sir," the postmaster greeted him. His colorless hair and pale eyes gave him a ghostly appearance. "What's news?"

"Good afternoon, Postmaster," Andrew replied. Like most who lived in a rural area, the postmaster appeared ready to indulge in a little chin wag with anyone who came through. Andrew always made sure to have a story or two at the ready. Today, though, he couldn't hold back his real news.

"I'll tell you what's new, my good friend." He withdrew a letter from his breast pocket and waved it in the air. "I'm heading off to meet my fate. I'm meeting a woman. I don't like to count my chickens before they're hatched, but I'm a hopeful man. Could be she'll turn out to be the love of my life."

"You don't say?" The postmaster took the letter and inspected the address. "La Porte, Indiana. Well, now. That deserves a toast." He disappeared behind the counter, then reappeared with a jar in his hand. A pale yellow liquid sloshed inside. He unscrewed the lid and offered it to Andrew. "Aquavit, my own make, from a still I built myself. I admit it doesn't hold a candle to the stuff from the old country, but it gets the job done."

"Aquavit! Well met, fellow Norwegian. I haven't had a taste of aquavit in too long. *Skål*." Andrew took the jar and downed a sip. The harsh liquor burned his throat. "Whoo! That puts hair on your chest!"

He passed the jar back to the postman, who nodded, then winced on a swallow of his own. "Tell me about your lady love, then."

"She's a widow, sitting on forty-two acres of good farmland. Claims to be good-looking, but time will tell on that score. I'll make my way there, stop in at the homesteads on the way. I expect it'll take me a week or thereabouts to get there."

"You gonna settle down, then? I see you've got a traveling wagon out there." The spirits sloshed in the jar as he gestured out the window.

Andrew chuckled. "For the right woman, I'd retire old Odysseus there, sell my wagon. Put down roots." He sighed. "I've been on the road for many years now, my friend. The romance of the open road has worn a little thin. It might be time for a change."

The postman raised the jar to Andrew. "*Skål til lykke.*"

"*Skål!*" They passed the jar back and forth, Andrew no longer noticing the liquor's bite, with its numbing effect well in place. "I should be getting along. Oh! Before I forget. I must write my brother." He patted his pockets. "You have paper and a pen?"

The postmaster produced the necessary materials, and Andrew bent over the counter to scrawl a few words to Asle back in Chicago.

"Brother," he wrote, "I've met someone. Don't want to jinx it. Fingers crossed that she's all she claims to be." Andrew paused to think. The words he'd written swam lazily in his aquavit-hazed vision. As circumspect as he'd been to the stranger at the crossroads post office,

Andrew was in fact full of hope for his future. A giddy, golden feeling swelled inside him. He set pen to paper again. "I'm heading to her tonight, the sun at my back and hope in my heart. I'll write to you in a week to tell you all about it." He sealed the note in an envelope and addressed it.

"Thank you, good sir. In a month's time, I may be a married man. Wish me luck!"

"Good luck to you, sir."

Andrew returned to Odysseus. "Let's go, old fellow. We've got a lady to meet." He regarded the dusty road he'd be traveling. Ahead, on the horizon, heavy black clouds filled the eastern sky, promising storms. "Better get on and find a place to shelter before we're soaked to the skin, Odysseus. I know how you hate the rain." Andrew woozily clambered up on the driver's bench and clicked to his only companion. The lowering sun behind him lit up the road ahead, a golden spotlight illuminating his destiny.

Wind gusted down the chimney, making the fire in the kitchen stove roar. Belle put a kettle on for her first cup of tea of the day and wondered what time Andrew Helgelien would arrive. His last letter had been short and sweet, telling her to look for him today.

Her tea ready, she brought it to the library to begin her correspondence for the day. To ward off the chill, she started a fire in the grate. Settling down with pen and paper, she paused to think of just the right turn of phrase that would encourage her suitor to divulge his net worth. The ideas came, and she wrote steadily for several minutes until she heard the clip-clop and rattle of an approaching wagon. Instead of trundling on by, it sounded like it turned in. She went to the window, and there, plodding up the driveway, was a horse and peddler's wagon. As it drew nearer, Belle could make out the words painted in gold lettering on the tall side of the black wagon: W.T. RAWLEIGH COMPANY. It was early, but Belle didn't mind. A thrill of anticipation

inflamed her. She was about to meet the first man to answer her lonely hearts ad.

The driver drew his horse to a stop with a gentle "Whoa there, Odysseus" and stepped down from the wagon. Belle was pleased to find his build tall and lean and his face appealing, with a strong jawline that bloomed into a huge grin as he approached her door. She wouldn't have to feign attraction like she had with Charles.

He knocked, and when she opened the door, she was greeted with a hearty, "Halloo there, madam!" The man doffed his derby to reveal a thick head of dark hair, and placed it over his heart, making a little bow. "Could I trouble you to find the lady of the house, Mrs. Belle Gunness?"

"I am Mrs. Gunness," Belle answered, already evaluating his words, his demeanor, trying to figure out what made this man tick and how she could best meet his needs.

He gaped extravagantly. "Impossible! The lady I seek is a widow, not a fair young beauty such as yourself." He took her hand in his and bowed low over it, placing a respectful kiss on her knuckles. Straightening but not loosing her hand, he said, "My name is Mr. Andrew Helgelien. Could you possibly be the lady herself?"

No need to overdo it, Mr. Helgelien. The man was certainly suited to his profession, both in temperament and image. His smile was broad and toothy, the perfect picture of a friendly traveling salesman who has "just the thing you need, madam," and he was dressed the part, with his derby and black suit, his brocade vest with its watch chain looping across. But a closer examination revealed frayed cuffs at his wrists, a button missing from his vest, pants that bagged at the knee, and the watch chain only tarnished gilt. Perhaps this was a clue to his deepest needs? She knew from their correspondence that he had some means—or she wouldn't have invited him to come to her. Why dress so shabbily? Was he in need of someone to care for him, truly and deeply?

Belle met his gaze directly, conveying warmth and comfort. "You are too kind, Mr. Helgelien. Yes, I am Mrs. Gunness. Drive your wagon up to the barn, and be welcome to my home."

* * *

"Charming and a good cook too," Andrew said, tucking into the dinner his hostess had made. Mrs. Gunness had put on a real spread, pork loin with creamed potatoes and boiled greens. From the hint of cinnamon in the air, there was a pie cooling somewhere for dessert. He sat at her elbow at a fine table laid for two, the mid-day light streaming in from the window. "I must have landed in heaven."

So eager to meet his lonely-hearts correspondent, Andrew had pushed himself and Odysseus long past sundown to arrive in La Porte last night, bedding down in a nearby barn. He'd tried not to arrive too early at her house; nevertheless, the sun was still low when he'd pulled into her driveway. But Mrs. Gunness was the picture of gracious hospitality and didn't bat an eye at his questionable manners. Once he had found a place for Odysseus in the barn and rewarded him with a bucket of oats and fresh water, Mrs. Gunness gave him coffee and breakfast. Then she'd told him to make himself comfortable in her home, as she had some correspondence and cooking to attend to.

Unused to leisure time, he'd returned to the barn to tidy up his wagon and review inventory. Now he was dining with his correspondent, who'd turned out to be as wonderful as her letters had promised. A sense of comfort and peace wrapped around Andrew, and he felt cautiously optimistic that his leap of faith would be rewarded.

"You may revise that judgment when the workers arrive tomorrow morning and commence banging," Mrs. Gunness commented drily, although a twinkle of merriment shone out from her blue eyes. She was not a beauty in any classical sense, and at first glance, he had even found her rather plain. It was only when he saw her smile transform her face and curiosity brighten her eyes that he realized how lovely she truly was.

"Oh, that won't bother me. In all honesty, I am very impressed with the work you're doing here. It must have been quite a project to restore the house to this point, given what you said about the state you found it in. From the outside, it's just about like the painting you showed me. But it will be quite a showplace when you're done."

"I like a man who's ready with a compliment. Too many men are quick with a harsh word when things are not to their liking and forget to share a kind word when they are happy."

"Well, ma'am, on the road, I've discovered a kind word goes a long way toward making a sale. You know what they say—you catch more flies with honey than vinegar."

"That you do," Mrs. Gunness concurred with a smile, then gestured questioningly at the pork loin with the server and heaped his plate with seconds in response to his nod.

"Now, that's not to say I'm trying to make a sale here." He laughed around a mouthful of food. "I guess I've just gotten in the habit of always having a nice word for folks, always looking on the bright side. When I come upon a farm, knock on the door, the first thing I do is tell a joke. Get them laughing. A happy farmer's wife is more likely to open her purse than a sour one."

"Oh!" She clapped her hands. "Tell me one of your jokes! I love a good joke."

Andrew jumped at any opportunity to put on a show. As he stood up from the table, he felt a change come on subtly, an alteration in his being as if he were shifting from human to something more. His spine straightened, his chest broadened, the set of his face became open, encouraging his audience to pay attention. He doffed an imaginary cap and bowed at Mrs. Gunness. "Good day, madam. Lovely to see such a friendly face in the middle of this otherwise dull day." He enlisted the special tone he took on sales calls, making his voice more resonant.

Mrs. Gunness jumped up and began to play along. "Good day to you, sir. Is this your wagon of goods?" She gestured at the table.

"Indeed, madam. Full of every conceivable tool, and some that defy common understanding, and drawn by this remarkable horse." Andrew patted an imaginary steed next to him. "Aren't you, boy? What's that?" Andrew leaned closer to the invisible beast. "Yes, yes, I'll tell her."

Addressing his hostess, he said, "Yes, quite an amazing horse. When I first set eyes on him—it was at a county fair in Ohio—he claimed he was born in the far Andes, mountains down in South America, don't you know. Seeking opportunity, he immigrated to New York City and joined the mounted police force. Captured many a fiendish criminal. After a decorated career, he retired to spend his days at that fair, giving rides to the kiddies. And then his ungrateful owner put him up for sale, saying he'd better fetch a good price or it was off to the glue factory.

"Astonished, I was!" Andrew went on. "I asked the owner, 'How could you sell this amazing horse?'" He paused for effect. "Do you know what he said?"

"Tell me!"

"Now, this fellow was a crusty old farmer in Ohio." He leaned toward Mrs. Gunness and said conspiratorially, "You know how they are. Anyway, this old fellow spat in the dirt and said to me"—here, Andrew put on a country twang—"'He's a big fat liar. He never did any of those things.'"

The good lady burst out laughing. Her eyes crinkled up, and she bent over, her laughter like a bell pealing. Andrew was utterly charmed. When her laugh died away, it left her breathless and flushed. She lowered herself to her seat, and Andrew took his. "Now, if there are kids around, they're sure to ask me one question. Can you guess what it is?"

Mrs. Gunness shook her head, still catching her breath.

"Picture a little fellow of seven or eight. He'll look up at me, all suspicious. 'Mister,' he'll say. 'If your horse can talk, how come he don't talk right now?'" Andrew winked at Mrs. Gunness. "'Well, young man,' I'll say, 'He'd talk your ear off except for one thing. He's a little hoarse today.'"

She set off laughing again, leaning back in her chair with her hands on her belly.

"That little pun usually gets the young 'uns on my side. That and my pocketful of penny candy." He winked again and withdrew a wax-wrapped disc from his coat pocket. Stamped on the pale-brown wrapper were the letters I.R.

"Sweet," Mrs. Gunness commented. "But your teeth must suffer for it. Having a pocket full of candies is hard for most to resist."

"Oh, no, not me," Andrew protested, slipping the candy back into his pocket. "Do you know, I have them with me always but I've never so much as tasted one."

"I admire a man with such strength of will," she said. "You must have an encyclopedia of stories in your head."

"I know quite a few, that's a fact. But that one is my old reliable. I might change the story up depending on my audience. Now, if I'm in Illinois, I'll say the horse's owner is from Indiana. Or instead of the New York City Police, I might say my horse worked for the Royal Canadian Mounted Police. Little changes like that, just to make it more interesting for me and more effective on my audience. But I use that story at just about every farm I go to. Works a charm."

"My word. You are quite an entertainer, Mr. Helgelien. You must make a sale at every stop."

"I'll allow that I make a fair living at my trade." Andrew felt no need to brag about the tidy sum in his bank back in Chicago.

"How interesting." Mrs. Gunness rested her elbow on the table and her cheek on her fist, gazing up at Andrew, who flushed with delight. "You must have met so many people in your line of work."

"More than I can count, Mrs. Gunness. More than I can count."

"Many encounters, but few that last, I'll wager," she observed. "It sounds quite lonely."

She had no idea how right she was, and the observation left him feeling exposed. "Beautiful, a good cook, *and* observant. Your list of accomplishments grows with every minute." That was another thing he'd learned on the road: plentiful compliments were like a protective cloak that kept others at a distance, kept him safe.

"Tell me about your family," she said. "You said in your letters you've never married and that you live with your brother between travels. He has a family, your brother?"

Relieved at the change of topic, Andrew answered, "Yes, my brother, Asle, in Chicago, married a lovely girl name of Matilda, and they quickly produced a perfect family of two boys and a little girl. Harry, Gordon, and Christina. Everybody dotes on Christina. She is her mother's daughter and the light of her father's eye, and she has two capable protectors in her older brothers. She need fear no man with those two at her side."

Mrs. Gunness laughed. "She sounds like a bit of a handful, really."

Andrew shook his finger at her. "There's that observant wit again. You've hit it on the head. She's a redhead through and through. What she has a mind to do, she does." He laughed fondly.

"And your brother? He's a saloonkeeper?"

"Indeed. Keeps him busy morning, noon, and night. There's nothing like a saloon to teach you about humanity." Andrew paused, casting his mind back. "Not that he needed lessons. He was always very clever. Knew me better than I knew myself, it seemed."

"He sounds like a good brother."

"Oh, he is. Do you know, he rescued me from a fire when we were boys? It was right before we were to leave for America. It had been a hot, dry summer, and a wildfire started in a field. It was a very close thing. There was smoke everywhere, and it was hard to breathe. If Asle hadn't dragged me away, I might well have died that day."

"My goodness! He must be quite a man now, to have been so brave as just a youth. You sound very proud of him. But for him to do what he did, he must love you very much, Andrew. May I call you Andrew?" She leaned ever so slightly closer.

Andrew was charmed through and through. "I'd be honored. On the condition you allow me to use your Christian name."

"Of course, Andrew. Call me Belle."

20

Belle settled Andrew in a guest room on the second floor, the first room on the left, just across from her own, unusable, room. She had moved her things to another guest room down the hall until the roof was fixed.

"It's not much, I know," Belle said. She and Ray had worked hard to make the room habitable in time for Andrew's arrival. Ray scrubbed the floors and cleaned out the fireplace while she shined the windows. The scent of fresh paint still hung in the air. Belle had a new bed delivered from town and bought linens to put on it.

"It's like a palace compared to where I usually bed down, in some farmer's back field or hay loft. What a remarkable quilt. Did you make it?"

Belle had sewed the last stitch on the white quilt with its black eight-pointed star in the center late last night. "I did, yes. This is the selburose, a pattern famous from my hometown of Selbu."

"Ah! Yes, of course. I know the selburose. This is beautiful work."

They said good night in the hallway, and Belle retreated into her room and waited through the noises of Andrew's nighttime preparations, the doors opening and closing, the rush of water in the sink, and the flush of the commode. She sank onto her bed with a sigh of contentment. Things were going so well. Better than she could have hoped for, really. Andrew was an entertaining companion and fun to be with. But she could tell that behind the jokes and tales of the road, underneath his performer's bravado, his heart beat a lonely tattoo. The wistfulness in his voice when he talked of his brother's family spoke volumes. She could picture him doting on his niece and nephews, pining after the wife he thought he would never have. His charisma and performances were a protective wall he hid behind.

She was determined to breech those defenses and give him the intimacy he both craved and feared.

Andrew woke to the soft glow of morning sun creeping into his room, and he lay snug underneath the hand-sewn quilt for several moments, letting his body slowly come to life after such a sound night of sleep. "Better than a night under the stars, however bright they are," he muttered to himself as he rose and dressed.

After breakfast, Belle invited Andrew to walk the fence line with her. "My handyman tells me the fence is secure up to the brook, but I want to check the rest." The sun was still low and the air outside had a bite to it, signaling winter was on its way. On the porch, Belle slipped her hand into the crook of Andrew's elbow and pressed close, saying, "I hope you don't mind. The chill eats into me, and you are so warm."

Andrew didn't mind, not one bit. The feel of her softness pressing against his arm and her small hand tucked under it presented him with a new experience. He could envision taking care of this beautiful, kind woman, beyond keeping her warm during their perambulations. He had never been anyone's protector.

He chanced a look down at the marvel by his side. Her hair, its color the light brown of a robin's wing, was piled softly at the back of her head. The faint wind played with a stray tendril just the way he would like to. Her dainty shell of an ear was blushing in the chill, and he longed to draw her closer and kiss the tender skin there. How she would be shocked to know his thoughts.

As they descended the porch steps, a lanky man emerged from a smaller cottage a short distance from the main house. Belle waved and called out, "Good morning, Ray! Come meet Mr. Helgelien."

The man paused a moment, uncertainty clear in his stance.

"Come," Belle said to Andrew. "He's a shy man but good at his job." She led Andrew toward the man, who reluctantly turned their way. "There now," Belle said brightly. "Andrew Helgelien, this is my handyman, Ray Lamphere."

"Hello, Mr. Lamphere," Andrew said, extending his hand. "Pleased to make your acquaintance. Mrs. Gunness has been showing me some of the improvements you've made to the house. You do fine work."

Lamphere nodded slightly with a frown. His manner was cool, almost unfriendly. Ignoring Andrew's offered hand, he said to Belle, "Thought I'd paint the porch today. Don't want to leave it bare over the winter. I'll need to go into town for paint."

"Good idea, Ray. I know I can always count on you. Thank you."

"Yes, ma'am." Lamphere stalked off.

Andrew watched him go, bemused. "Did I do something to offend the man? He seems to have taken an instant dislike to me."

"Oh, don't be silly, Andrew. Ray is a good man, but he has his quirks. He's shy and awkward and sometimes doesn't know how to act with people. Don't take it personally. He'll warm to you in time. Please try to be patient with him."

Andrew was used to having to win people over. Eventually, he would break through with Lamphere, he was sure of it.

As he went to the barn to hitch up his wagon, Ray nursed hurt feelings. He didn't like the look of Andrew Helgelien, with his slicked-back hair and fancy duds. Snake oil salesman. But along with his jealousy, Ray feared for the man. Did Belle have plans for him—deadly plans? Ray hated the idea that Belle might marry this man and live with him forever after, removing any possibility of being with Ray, but he also hated to think that she would marry Helgelien and then do to him what she did to Gunness.

He wasn't sure which was worse.

"What are your intentions for this farm, Belle? I believe you mentioned something about cattle in your letters?"

Belle was winded from their walk up the slight hill that led to the dry streambed at the corner of her property, and she paused to catch her breath while she answered. "Yes, dairy cows. I want to make a business of selling milk and butter and cheese." She had no such intentions, having chosen another line of business, but it made for a good story. "I need to make some improvements to the property, like putting in a real fence." She pointed to the rotted timbers they'd been following, the remnants of what had once been a split rail fence. "This whole fence will have to be replaced."

"Yes, indeed," Andrew replied. "If I may suggest . . . ?"

"Go on," Belle said, pleasantly surprised that he asked before assuming she wanted his opinion.

"You might find barbed wire a faster and more economical way of fencing for cows. Barbed wire is quite affordable now."

All the better if he could save her money while also making her money. "Thank you, Andrew. That sounds like good advice." She would make a point of comparing the price of lumber against that of barbed wire.

Andrew grinned and tipped his hat with a flourish. What a show-man. When he held out his hand to help Belle over the brook, she took it with a grateful nod, even though she had crossed it on her own many times, including when the streambed was full. He wanted to be a gentleman, and she would let him. On the other side, he tucked her hand in his elbow as she led them onward through the long grass. She decided to turn the conversation back on him.

"Andrew, you must have seen some very interesting things, bedding down in people's fields and barns, as you mentioned last night."

A grin spread his lips wide. "Oh, yes. I have indeed. You'd be surprised what goes on when people think no one is looking. I've seen some knockdown donnybrooks in my time on the road. One time, it started while I was still in the house. This home was occupied by the mister and missus and their five children, plus an old grandpappy. He sat there quiet in the corner the whole time I was there selling the missus some new shears and a tonic for the mister's digestion and a syrup for the littlest one's cough. And I'd showed the middle girl a storybook, told her she could read it while I was there, and if her parents agreed, they could buy it. Well, you should have seen her eyes light up at that. She took that book like it was made of butterfly wings and opened it up right there and started reading. Attention glued to the page, she started to walk over to the window, I guess to see the words better.

"Now, that old codger just sat there the whole time, quiet as a church mouse, corn cob pipe in his teeth leaking smoke like a banked fire. And just like a banked fire that suddenly bursts aflame, out of nowhere, this old fellow up and snatched her as she passed by and gave her a good wallop. Started hollering, 'Who do you think you are, Miss High-and-Mighty, reading a book? I guess you think you're too good for the likes of us? Nose in a book all the time like some kinda know-it-all.' Poor little thing was cowering away from him, afraid to talk back or run away.

"Well. The girl's daddy didn't take too kindly to that. He reared up like a bear with his fur on fire and pushed himself between his father and his daughter. 'Nobody hits my little girl but me!' he hollered and started pummeling his father. That old codger looked like skin and bones, like he would just blow away in a strong breeze. But you know what they say—looks can be deceiving. He was strong. And *fast*. And he came after his son, who had to be twice the size of him, like a whirlwind. Punches windmilling through the air. The two of them fought like cats in a sack. Knocking over crockery and scattering the family.

It couldn't have been the first time because as soon as it started, that mama scooped up all her chicks and herded them into the back bedroom. Over the ruckus, I could hear the sound of a large bureau or the like scraping across the floor to bar the door."

"My word, Andrew! What did you do?" Belle suspected at least some of this story was fabricated, or at least exaggerated. But his manner in telling it was so engaging, she didn't mind. In fact, his creativity and theatricality only added to it, and she admired him for it.

"I was as quick as the missus to protect my chickens. That is to say, my wares. As soon as that grandpappy started the ruckus, I got to packing up all my things. I was crawling on the floor under the table, gathering items that had gotten knocked over, like some kind of mole in his tunnel. And then I crawled right out the door."

Belle laughed at the absurd picture he painted. "What a shame you didn't make your sale, though."

"Oh no, I made my sale."

"But, how?"

"What I did, you see, was I went around the back of the house and found the window of the bedroom where the missus and her brood had barricaded themselves in. Tapped on the glass, and she came and slid it open. I gave her the tonics and the shears, and she paid me. And all the while, we could hear the shouting and crashing and banging coming from the other room.

"Before I left, I called that little girl over and gave her the book. The missus protested, saying they couldn't afford it. I said, 'No charge, ma'am. Hide it if you have to, but that girl deserves a book.' Well, the tears of gratitude and joy that brought were better than any payment."

"Oh, Andrew!" Belle exclaimed. "How kind of you."

They walked quietly for a time. Belle was struck by Andrew's story. He told it the way he'd told his stories the night before, as an entertainment, full of exaggerations, she was sure, all toward making the story humorous and diverting. But there was a deeper truth in there. Andrew was a kind man. Someone who would put himself out for another.

Such a man deserved happiness of his own, deserved a family and intimacy. He deserved someone who understood that he was more than an entertainer, more than a purveyor of trinkets and tinctures. He deserved someone who loved him.

Belle would see to it he got what he deserved.

After another satisfying meal, Andrew followed Belle to her library, which was snug, with two leather wingback chairs grouped in front of a fireplace. There was a chill in the air, and Belle moved to build a fire.

"Here, let me," Andrew said, taking the matches and poker from her. "I love to get a fire going."

Belle went to fetch a tea tray, and Andrew quickly stacked logs and kindling together and set a match to it. As it took, he wandered the room. The library was sparsely stocked; of the pair of floor-to-ceiling bookcases, only two shelves were full. Andrew ran his finger along the rows, perusing the titles: *Great Expectations, Moby-Dick; or, the Whale, The Portrait of a Lady, Pride and Prejudice, Strange Case of Dr. Jekyll and Mr. Hyde, Vanity Fair, The Count of Monte Cristo* . . . his lady was quite well-read. Andrew was acquainted with some of these books, but not many. He would have to remedy that if he was to keep up with her in conversation.

With the fire roaring, he drew the chairs close together before the warm light and settled into a wingback. How cozy. Perhaps one day soon, he could buy Belle some more books for her shelves. They could sit companionably by this fire, reading and conversing. He would help Belle turn this property into a profitable ranch, put Odysseus out to pasture and his wagon in the barn.

Belle brought in a tea tray, and Andrew spooned sugar into his mug, stirring thoughtfully, lost in his musings of the future. He tapped drops of tea off his spoon and set it on the table.

"Tap, tap, tap." Belle laughed.

"What's that?"

"Three taps," she said. "Always three taps. You tap your spoon three times after stirring in your sugar. Never two, never four. Always three." Fondness glowed in her eyes as the firelight cast a warm blush upon her.

Great God, she was beautiful.

"A penny for your thoughts, Andrew," Belle said.

"I'm thinking about the moment I decided to come to La Porte to meet the lady in the letters."

"Oh? You must tell me." She pivoted in her chair to face him directly and folded her hands in her lap. All her attention was focused on him. Her bright eyes were lit with curiosity, and she leaned slightly forward as if to catch his meaning as soon as possible. Andrew had never met such a good listener.

"Well, I was at a home in a little town way out on the prairie. To call it a town is generous. It's little more than a crossroads." Andrew told Belle about the old couple, the way they listened patiently to his spiel, and the loving way the wife tended to her husband's feet. He described the way they finished one another's sentences and communicated with no more than a gesture. "The thing that stands out most in my mind is the way they looked at each other. So much was said, but not a word spoken.

"There I stood, Belle, watching this in silence. I felt something drip on my hands, and I realized I was crying. I'd received quite a few letters from you by then, sometimes two a day. I had doubts. Could it possibly work? To marry a woman you've met through the mail?

"But that day I saw the love between those two old folks, and I said to myself, 'Andrew, even if her lovely name should prove ill-suited to her, even if she has the face of an ogre, if Belle should be lovely in nature, then that will be enough for me.' That very day I wrote you to say I was coming."

Belle listened with her whole being to Andrew's long tale. She was mystified by the couple's lasting devotion to one another and fascinated by the impact their connection had on him. But the fact that he shared their story was telling, and it inspired Belle.

Without saying a word, she moved from her chair to the floor and began unlacing Andrew's boots. She held his gaze as she pulled off one boot and then the other, ignoring his protests.

"What are you doing? I didn't mean— No, my feet are horrible, you can't—"

"Ssh," she said. "I can. I will."

She pulled off his socks and had to stifle a gasp at the grotesque sight that was revealed. His feet were huge, deformed with bunions and hammer toes, and his toenails were thick as planks. But she was sure this was the quickest way to his heart. Belle began slowly caressing his soles, then gently and firmly rubbed his feet all over, ignoring their monstrous ugliness and focusing on working away the soreness. She kept her eyes locked on his, where she would find what she was looking for. Before long, she was rewarded: an expression of incredulous gratitude suffused his features.

"Oh, my God," he murmured. "Heaven. This is heaven." He slid from the chair and kneeled on the floor with Belle, taking her hands in his. "Marry me, Belle. Please. I want to be your husband and take care of you for the rest of our days together."

Belle leaned forward and dropped a delicate kiss on his lips. "Yes, Andrew. I'll marry you."

21

The ceremony the next day was simple, just how Belle wanted it. When Andrew told her of a small chapel north of La Porte that he knew of from his travels, she agreed it was the perfect location.

Once the vows were spoken and congratulations bestowed, Belle let Andrew lead her to her gig—no reason to parade his peddler's wagon about—and help her onto the bench. As he drove, she snuggled next to him underneath a blanket, wondering what her wifely duties might entail with this new man. He was kind and gentle, unlike her previous husbands, but she had yet to share his bed and you just never knew. The disappearing sun set the horizon on fire, and the water of Clear Lake was ablaze with reflected color. She took the display as a sign of celebration that her business plan was proceeding so beautifully.

"See here, Belle. A wedding present." Andrew pointed to the fiery display. "Isn't it beautiful? I'll tell you, my dear. Sleeping under the stars and waking to a beautiful sunrise is a gift. Some fine night next summer, when the warm weather is with us again, I'll take you out into our fields, and we'll sleep under the stars. I want to share that with you."

Sex under the stars—that would be new. "That sounds lovely." Belle squeezed Andrew's arm fondly. "But why put our joys off to tomorrow? We must have enough blankets to spend a night out tonight.

It's not too terribly cold. We could celebrate our wedding night under the stars. Wouldn't you like that?" Belle needed Andrew to have his every wish met.

They enjoyed a light supper and then gathered up all the blankets in the house, carrying them out past the barn and into the pasture. Belle led him toward the cherry tree and they found a spot to spread the blankets on the dewy grass. Twilight had engulfed the sky, stealing away the last of the sunlight. They lay on their backs under the covers, her head resting on his arm, as the stars made their debut, one by one. She had concluded Andrew would want to take the lead, so she waited patiently for his advance.

"Belle?" His voice was low and quiet, making a ceremony of the moment. "May I kiss you?"

"Yes," she answered simply.

Andrew rolled over and framed her face with his arms, then lowered his lips to hers. His mouth was warm and soft, and Belle raised her hand to stroke his cheek.

Andrew rose up on his knees and pulled Belle to sitting. "I want to see you. May I?" Belle nodded, letting him push her suit jacket off her shoulders and offering her arms so he could tug the sleeves free. He unfastened the long row of buttons down her blouse, pausing to kiss her lips. He worked slowly, carefully, treating her body with reverence. She might actually enjoy this.

Once her blouse was undone and lying discarded next to them, her corset and chemise, her knickers and skirt followed quickly. Kneeling naked before Andrew, skin pebbling from the cold, Belle reached up and plucked out the pins holding up her hair, letting it fall in soft waves.

Andrew caressed her tresses, sliding the strands through his fingers. "So soft," he said and moved his hands to her shoulders. A shiver— excitement? The chilly air?—twisted her spine. "You're so cold!" He snugged the blankets around her. "Are you sure about this? Maybe we should go inside."

He really was a gentleman, but she needed to do this for him. She shook her head. "No, let's stay. Here, let me." With the blankets as a cloak, she helped Andrew out of his clothing. His jacket went first, and as Belle removed it, she noticed something in his pockets.

"What's this?" She extracted a handful of candies. "You really do carry them everywhere. Are they good?"

"I don't rightly know," Andrew said. "Remember, I've never had one myself."

"What does 'I.R.' mean?" Belle asked, noting the letters stamped on the wax paper wrapping.

"That's for Irma Rawleigh, who makes them. Irma and her husband, Winston, ran the W.T. Rawleigh Company for many a year. Winston traveled the route, and Irma made most of the tinctures and balms he sold. When he passed on, Irma sold the business to me. Her wares are so good, and in such demand on my route, that I'll continue to sell her products as long as she's able to make them. Everyone in Chicago knows that I.R. stamp. Although, I doubt anyone in these parts has heard of her."

What a clever idea. She should have made Mads do something like that. As if she could have made Mads do anything.

Inside the wax wrapper was a brown disc. Would it be sarsaparilla? Horehound? She popped it in her mouth and let the sweetness begin to dissolve. "Oh! It's molasses. How unexpected! And you've never even tried one? How can this be? They're very good. Here." She unwrapped a candy and slid it past his lips. He nibbled her finger, holding it in his mouth and swirling his tongue around it and the candy.

"Delicious," he said, stripping off his shirt and pants.

When they were both naked, he kissed her again and made to ease her down on her back, but she resisted. It was time for her to take charge. "Lie back," she told him.

"What—?"

Belle burrowed under the blankets and began to massage and stroke the length of his body. She started with his big, ugly feet, kneading and pressing away the aches. Thankful for the dark that obscured the callouses and yellow toenails, Belle pulled on his toes and kissed them one by one. Andrew sighed, a gusty release of tension and worry. She felt his whole body relax. Perfect.

Belle moved up his calves, marking her way with kisses. She found that he was ticklish behind the knees, so she paused there and teased the tender skin with her tongue and lips. She worked her way higher and found his hard cock.

"Belle, I— Ohhh, God. Please, Belle." He groaned when she took him in her mouth. She stroked and licked while he moaned, begging her to wait, please wait, no, never stop.

When she judged he couldn't handle any more, she moved to his torso, trailing kisses along his stomach. She nipped gently at his skin and licked away the sting, and when she reached his neck, she buried her face in the hollow, nuzzling and kissing. Her body rested along the length of his, skin to skin, as his hands traced lacy designs on her back.

"Good Lord, wife," he said with awe.

"Did that feel good?"

For an answer, he rolled her to her back. Using his knees, he pushed her legs apart and pressed his cock against her folds.

"Oh!" she gasped. She rotated her hips up and gripped his buttocks with a desperate greed. They moved together slowly, finding a rhythm that was their own. When Andrew reached his climax, Belle cried out with him, their voices mingling and echoing across the night, witnessed only by an audience of stars.

Belle awoke, shivering and damp. A thin crescent moon hung overhead, and the night was still. Damp had soaked into the blankets above and beneath her, stealing away the warmth she and Andrew had made together. And what warmth it had been. She hadn't expected her marital bed to be so satisfying.

Her shivering woke Andrew, who pulled her close. "We should

go inside. It's not going to get any warmer. Trust me, I know from experience."

So they gathered up their love nest and, not bothering to don their damp clothes, picked their way naked through the dewy grass, across the pasture, past the barn and the snoring hogs in their pen, and into the house through the kitchen door. It was quite liberating, traipsing through the night in her birthday suit. They dressed in dry night clothes and she snuggled into the curve of Andrew's body under the selburose quilt in his room.

In the morning, over a breakfast of sliced apples and fresh bread, Andrew announced he had an idea.

"Do you? What is it?" Belle passed him the sugar bowl and watched with amusement as he stirred sugar into his tea and tapped his spoon three times.

"Let's build you a fence. We'll send Lamphere to town for supplies, and then I'll help him put in the posts and string the barbed wire. Then you'll be well-fixed to bring in that dairy herd you want. Plus, it will give me a chance to get to know Lamphere a little better. See if I can get him to warm up to me."

Belle hesitated, putting just the right amount of shame in her tone when she answered. "Andrew, that is a wonderful idea. And don't think I'm not grateful for the help. But the truth is, I don't have the money for fencing right now."

"Oh, don't worry about that. I thought it would go without saying. I'll pay for it."

Worked like a charm.

Ray returned from town with a wagonload of barbed wire and lumber, grumbling to himself about this sudden plan to build a fence. He hadn't even finished painting the porch, like he'd told Belle needed to be done before winter. And now they were starting a whole new project? For nonexistent dairy cows? Was this how things would be from now on? This Helgelien fellow coming up with harebrained ideas, and Ray having to follow his orders?

Stringing barbed wire was a brutal job with a tendency to beat up a man's hands. Ray had heard Andrew try to convince Belle it was man's work, but she would hear none of it. She donned a shorter-length work skirt and a man's shirt with long, loose sleeves and heavy work gloves, saying, "I've poured hours of my own blood and sweat into this property, and I won't stop now. I may not have your strength or the skill of a trained man like Ray, but I can help."

Ray worked alongside them with sullen reserve. He disliked Andrew Helgelien on principle, as the intruder who'd taken away his beloved Belle. Ray was cut out and cast aside, and not just cast out of her bed, but seemingly out of her world. Whereas before, they laughed and joked all day together while they worked on the house, now she lavished her humor, kindness, and attention on Helgelien.

On top of all that, Ray disliked Helgelien in his person. He resented the man's easy charm and open friendliness.

At the end of the day, the trio were exhausted, dirty, and sporting numerous punctures and scrapes from the wire. Even Ray, with his toughened workman's hands, found it impossible to avoid getting hung up on the sharp barbs.

Helgelien insisted on treating not only his own wounds and Belle's but Ray's as well with one of his patented liniments, refusing to accept Ray's protestations. "Come now, let me see," Helgelien said, taking hold of Ray's wrist and examining the scrapes up and down his forearm. He held out his own arm to show nearly identical wounds. "Like we've been in a fight with a cat. I have just the thing for it."

Ray followed Andrew and Belle to the barn, where Andrew's traveling wagon was parked beside Belle's gig. Andrew opened up one of the side cabinets and rummaged among the boxes, bottles, and tins.

"Ah! Here it is. Morehouse Wound Liniment. 'Cures all manner of scrapes and cuts. Strong enough for a man's cuts but gentle on baby's scraped knees,'" he read off the label. "I've sold many a bottle of this and used it myself. Here." With a clean cloth from his stores, he gently daubed the liniment on Belle's cuts first, then treated himself the same.

Ray was reluctant, but Andrew's good humor was an unstoppable force. Ray let Andrew apply the medicine, and though he didn't like to admit it, the liniment did soothe the sting. He bit out a begrudging "thanks" and retreated to the caretaker's cottage to stew about what would be going on in the house that night.

He tortured himself with images of Belle as he had known her in their intimate moments, with himself replaced by Helgelien. He barely slept.

In all his life, Andrew never expected to attain the kind of happiness he had found with Belle. She was everything he could ever have hoped for, the very woman he longed for all those lonely nights on the road, catching glimpses of other families' happy lives as he moved from town to farm to outpost and back again.

Belle took pains to take care of him and to care for him, going out of her way to do little things like helping him into his clothes in the morning, trimming his hair with her sewing scissors, and learning his favorite foods.

It came home to him again just how much she must love him when she produced from her pocket a bottle of Rawleigh's Mineral Liniment that night in his bedroom. "Where did you get that?" he asked.

"I saw it in your wagon today. You didn't notice when I took it." She looked proud and impish both, pleased to have surprised him, and it charmed him anew. "I recognized it from the story you told me our first night. The old woman who massaged her husband's feet?"

"I recall," he said. She was a wonder, his wife.

"Sit," she said, pointing to a rocking chair in the corner. She left the room and, after several minutes, reappeared with a basin of steaming water and a pile of towels. She knelt in front of him and peeled his socks off. They were green wool and showed signs of wear. His gnarled big toe poked through a hole. "I see I shall have to knit you some new socks."

She rolled up the cuffs of his pants and lifted his feet into the steaming water. Blissful relaxation flowed from his soles up into his whole body.

"Tonight, I'm going to tell you a story," Belle said.

"Ah!" Andrew's eyes brightened. "I don't often get to be on the other side of a story. This will be a delight!"

She was sure it would be, for him though not her, but not in the way he was expecting. Belle unscrewed the cap of the liniment bottle and let a few drops fall in the water. She swirled it in and then slid her fingers under Andrew's feet, cupping his heels and stroking up the lengths of his arches. Her tale was far uglier than his feet, a remembrance she never indulged. But allowing him a true piece of herself was the only way to give him the intimacy he longed for. She would do this for him and then return the experience to the recesses of her memory.

She spread a towel across her lap and pulled Andrew's left foot to her, patting it dry. With a couple more drops of liniment, she set to work, smoothing the lotion into his skin with slow and gentle motions.

"As you know, I grew up in Norway. I came to America when I was twenty-two and married my first husband almost right away. We never had children, and doctors told me I never would be able to. All this you know, because I told you in my letters. But I never told you about my girlhood in Norway, or why I will never bear children."

As she spoke, Belle caressed Andrew's feet, giving him the comfort that meant so much to him. Andrew stayed quiet, letting her tell her story in her own time.

"The place I grew up is very beautiful. Selbu lies in the floodplain of the Nea River, and everywhere are green fields and pastures, with the river twisting its way through them to the Selbusjo lake. We are famous for our knitting, especially the selburose pattern. You know, the black star on the quilt."

Andrew nodded. "It sounds beautiful. I grew up outside of Bergen, and I never made it farther than the next town until I left Norway for America. I would like to go back some day and see Selbu. You make it sound magical."

"When I was just a girl there, I was very foolish. I was the youngest of eight, and we were very poor. My father was a stonemason, and my mother knitted goods for sale. But there were many of us, and never enough to go around. Never enough food, and never enough attention. I was left very much to myself. My older siblings went to work and moved off as soon as they were able. By the time I was a teen, I was alone and very lonesome.

"Until one day, I met a boy and fell in love. He was from a good family and made many promises to me. Soon enough, I realized he had made them for one reason only, which was to have his way with me. I thought we were in love. But I was nothing to him.

"I know this because when I fell pregnant, he refused to see me. There was to be a dance, and I knew he would be there, so I went. But he was cruel to me, ignoring me and dancing with all the other girls and laughing at me behind his hand.

"When I came close and tried to talk to him, he kicked me away like you would kick a dog. I fell, and then he kicked me again, hard, in the stomach. Later that night, I started to bleed. And I lost the baby."

A cramp squeezed her insides, and Belle gasped in pain and shock. She hadn't expected letting these memories resurface would bring back the physical pain as well. But it only strengthened the gift she was giving Andrew. She met his eyes and finished with the words she knew would bring him eternal satisfaction. "I have never shared this story with anyone. Not my first husband or my second."

Andrew's eyes shone. "Oh, my darling." He pulled her into his lap and caressed her face, brushing her temple with tender kisses.

"I was afraid to tell them," she said. "But I felt that, with you, finally I had found someone I could share my true self with."

"I'm honored. Thank you. We are two lost souls who have finally found one another," he whispered against her lips.

And with that, Belle knew that her husband understood the magnitude of what she had just given him.

22

*I*t was late the next morning when Belle was awoken by bars of sunlight from the window. She and Andrew had made love late into the night, falling asleep cozily entwined under the selburose quilt. They lay with legs still linked, face-to-face, and as Belle's eyes fluttered open, she was met with Andrew's sleepy-eyed gaze.

"Good morning, wife," he said.

"Good morning, husband," Belle replied. She stroked his face tenderly. "Are you happy?"

Andrew covered her hand with his and pressed kisses into her palm, eyes steady on hers. "I can say without reservation that I have never been happier. I feel . . . fulfilled. Does that make sense? It's more than a feeling of happiness, Belle. I feel a sense of rightness, that I am in the right place with the right woman, and my destiny is to be here."

Belle was warmed by Andrew's admission. It was exactly what she hoped for, what she was trying to give him. To bring a man as lonely and on the outside of life as Andrew into the circle of human connection felt like a higher calling, and she glowed inside to know that she had succeeded.

"That is just how I feel," Belle said. "That you were meant to come to me."

Belle fixed a breakfast of fried bread and soft-boiled eggs, with canned pears and hot coffee. "Today, I want you to work with Ray alone," she told Andrew. "I think it would be good for you two to try to get along without me."

"You think he has some kind of attachment to you?" Concern furrowed Andrew's brow.

"Nothing like that. But I think he is a little protective and wants to be reassured that you deserve me." She laughed. "Now go," she added and pushed him out the door.

Once he had gone, Belle hooked a gathering basket over her elbow and strolled out on her property away from where the men were working. She had noticed a number of interesting plants on her walk with Andrew the other day. Blackberry bushes were plentiful along the tree line that bounded her property, where they thrived in the dappled light. Mint grew near the brook in the woods beyond the boundary line. And jimsonweed, with its spiny seed pods beginning to open, was just about everywhere. After her experience watching Charles's suffering, Belle was determined to find a better way.

Andrew slipped off his soiled boots as he entered the kitchen, which was warm and toasty and smelled of fresh herbs. He greeted Belle with a kiss on the cheek. "Well, I'm not sure your plan to have me and Ray work together made a difference. That man may never warm up to me. But he's a good worker, and his job is secure as far as I'm concerned. Good God, but it's cold out." He rubbed his hands together and held them out to the stove.

"You brought a wave of cold air in with you and your nose is red," Belle admonished kindly. "Here, leave your boots by the door and take this and go sit in the library while I finish supper. I made a fire in there, so it should be cozy by now."

Andrew took his tea and sank into one of the wingbacks before the fire. He stretched out his legs, letting the heat soak through his woolen socks to bring life back to his numb toes. He blew steam from his mug and took a sip. Delicious. Strong mint, sweetened just right, with a hint of something extra he couldn't identify. The hot liquid slid down inside him, warming him from the inside. "Aaah," he said.

He was bone-tired from a long day of hard work. Lassitude washed over him as he sipped at the sweet tea and let the fire soothe his aching body. How satisfying physical labor was. So different from traveling and meeting people.

His slipped into a half-waking reverie in which he regaled Lamphere with the story about his talking horse, and Lamphere laughed so hard he expanded into a balloon. As Lamphere floated away, Andrew felt a tickling at his feet, only to discover a cat licking his toes.

He woke groggily to find Belle removing his socks. "You'll set your feet on fire," she scolded him, brushing cinders off a sock.

"I was dreaming."

"You're a tired boy, aren't you? All that hard labor. Here, I brought you fresh tea." She handed him a full mug.

He sipped at the delicious sweet mint tea. As it went down, his stomach answered with a growl. He was ravenous.

Belle laughed. "Yes, supper is ready, so don't fret. No, don't get up. I'll bring a tray."

How could Andrew have gotten so lucky? He needed to write to Asle and share his good fortune and apologize for marrying without telling him first.

"Andrew," Belle called, and he rose to meet her at the door. He realized she held no tray of food, and more than that, she was naked. He was puzzled, and so tired. But there she stood, an invitation and promise. He crossed the room to take her in his arms but grasped only air. Confused, he spun around, searching. He must be overly exhausted to be imagining things. As he returned to the fire, a wave of dizziness stole strength from his knees, and he collapsed clumsily into the chair. He'd feel better after he ate, surely.

He slipped into sleep again, this time dreamless, and woke when Belle shook his shoulder.

"Eat, darling. And then I'll help you to bed." She held a steaming tray, and the savory smell of roasted meat and vegetables swirled toward him. His stomach growled again.

He reached out hesitantly for the tray, fearful it might be another vision. But no, it was solid and real. With the tray situated on his lap, he took Belle's hand and kissed it. "Thank you," he mumbled. He shoveled his meal in, eager to satisfy his gnawing hunger. He alternated bites of food with sips of tea. Belle massaged his feet while he ate. Heaven.

Except for the dizziness. He put down his fork, as Belle's form swung in front of him, doubling and swaying. He shook his head. "I wonder if I'm coming down with something," he said. Or thought he said. Belle's mouth moved, but Andrew heard no sound. Instead, a roaring filled his ears. He closed his eyes.

When he opened them, the tray was gone and the fire had burned low. Its light cast a dim glow into the darkened room. A figure wavered before him in robes of white, her hair cascading over her shoulders. Everything was confusion in his mind. Where was he? Was this Asle's home? Where were the children? Had he fallen ill at a house on his route, and this figure was a farm wife tending him?

The figure shimmered before him, wavering like a candle flame in a draft. Her form was insubstantial, otherworldly, but he felt a powerful sense of calm radiating from her. It penetrated his senses, bringing him a feeling of profound well-being. He knew to his marrow that despite his momentary pain, all would be well. She was an angel.

"You are loved, Andrew." Her words echoed inside his head as if she spoke not with a voice but conveyed her thought directly to his mind. A pain he had always lived with, as present as the hair on his head, subsided and was replaced with relief. Tears flooded his eyes. He felt newborn. He was loved. Deeply and completely, for who he was, to his very core.

On the heels of that revelation, a wave of pain racked him. His muscles locked, and he shook like a rag doll. The roaring in his ears became overwhelming, and the pain grew stronger, then stronger still. He would have cried out, but even his breath and voice were frozen. The anguish and shuddering crested, then subsided, only to be followed by another wave, stronger than the first, leaving him panting and weak. His mouth tried to form words. "Help me," he wanted to say, but more waves of pain convulsed him.

As his angel watched, her face resolved into the image of his wife. It was Belle. Belle was his angel. Just as he had always known. An angel had come into his life to save him. She had given him his every wish, and filled his life and heart with a purpose it had lacked before.

He wanted to tell her thank you, wanted her to know he understood her and was grateful. Before he could make his tongue and lips form the words, more convulsions shattered him. The pain was great.

23

All in all, Belle was quite pleased with Andrew's death. She had chosen mint tea laced with ground-up jimsonweed seeds to give him a more peaceful ending than had befallen Charles. The gratitude in his eyes at the end told her she had succeeded.

The violent convulsions notwithstanding.

After covering his body with a blanket, she had rewarded herself with her own cup of mint tea—freshly brewed, after a careful cleaning of the teapot. She'd curled up in the wingback beside Andrew's to reflect on the success of her first client. But she must have fallen asleep because now the fire was out, and faint gray light filled the window.

Belle rose and stretched, then slipped on her boots. Frost crunched under her feet as she crossed the yard to the caretaker's cottage. Her breath steamed in the chilly air. A long silence answered her knock, and she pounded twice more before she heard sounds of Ray rising.

The door opened.

"I need help."

* * *

"What is it?" Ray blinked into the near-darkness of early dawn. What was Belle doing on his doorstep in the middle of the night? The roof couldn't have collapsed a second time.

"Andrew has died," she said quietly. "I need help with the body."

Ray's shock was quickly followed by a sense of inevitability. A part of him knew from the moment he saw the man what Helgelien's fate would be. "I'll get my shovel."

Belle led him to the library, where a blanket shrouded a tall body seated in one of Belle's new wingback chairs. He considered asking Belle what happened, but thought better of it.

As though she'd anticipated Ray's question, Belle said, "He was sleeping in the chair by the fire. He died in his sleep."

Ray didn't comment on the believability of that statement. He stooped and shoved his arms under Helgelien's knees and shoulders, and was surprised to find that the body retained its seated shape after he lifted it. How long had Helgelein been sitting here? What had Belle been doing all that time?

Helgelien was a tall man and the weight of his dead body bore down on Ray as he carried it out of the library and down the hall. Every step toward the kitchen was a gritted effort.

The blanket fell away from Helgelien's face, and his blank eyes stared up at Ray. Ray tried to quicken his pace. *It wasn't me. I didn't do it.*

Belle held the kitchen door for Ray, and he clomped down the steps, his breath heaving. The farm cart he'd positioned by the back door waited to receive its load. Ray had to wedge Helgelien's head in the corner, and the dead man's massive feet protruded from the end. "Where to?"

"The hog pen," Belle answered.

She carried a bucket of slops to divert the hogs and held the gate open for Ray as he brought the cart through, closing it behind him. She poured the slops into the trough, and the three hogs trotted over and rooted gleefully in the mess.

Ray began digging in a corner, breaking through a thin crust of frozen mud to get started. He worked methodically, enlarging the width of the hole and then deepening it. After devouring their meal, the hogs came over to inspect his work. They bullied their weight past Ray and rooted their snouts in the unearthed soil. Goddam swine!

Ray gave up and threw the shovel down. "Let's get 'im in there. These hogs are the devil to work around."

He lifted the cart handles up, levering the body toward the hole. It toppled in headfirst, ass and feet to the sky.

It barely fit. Ray tossed shovelfuls of dirt on top, slowly erasing the head and torso, the hips, the legs. But when he got to the end, one foot remained stubbornly visible. A purple heel and gnarled toes stuck out of the ground, mocking Ray's efforts.

Belle kneed the hogs away, and Ray tried to shovel more dirt on, mounding it over the exposed foot. But the hogs swarmed back in and quickly found Andrew's toes. One took a bite.

"Ray!" Belle cried, giving the nearest swine a kick. Meanwhile another darted in behind her. "The damn hole's too small. It needs to be deeper! Don't you know how to dig a grave?"

Ray pinned Belle with a pointed stare. "Never had a call to do it so much before, Mrs. Helgelien."

Belle narrowed her eyes at him. "Well, get him out of that hole and dig it deeper before these hogs take another bite." She shoved another hog away.

"You want me to dig him up again?" Ridiculous.

"It's either you dig him up and do it right, or these hogs will do it for you."

"Shittagod*dam*," Ray muttered and took up his shovel, eyeing the hogs with loathing.

Belle went back to the kitchen and returned with a basket of apples and a loaf of bread. "This won't last long, so go fast," she said. She tossed an apple across the pen, and the hogs chased after it. The quickest sow got the fruit, and Belle tossed out more, one at a time, trying to keep the beasts busy while Ray dug. "Faster, Ray!"

Instead of removing Helgelien and digging the hole deeper, Ray realized it would be easier to dig a new hole next to the first and then roll the man in. He doubled down, his shovel digging and pitching at a rapid clip. Sweat rolled off him despite the morning chill. When he had finally dug deep enough, Ray took hold of the protruding foot and used it to lever the body out of the softly packed earth, which gave way easily, and into the new grave.

"Hurry, Ray, I'm running out of bread!" Belle had disbursed all the apples and was breaking hunks off the loaf and tossing them to the hogs.

Ray shoveled and scraped dirt over Helgelien's body as fast as he could. When the hole was finally covered and Helgelien safely interred, Ray tamped down the gravesite with his feet, and Belle joined him.

The hogs, still curious, still hungry, milled around, hunting for treasures.

Ray set the shovel in the farm cart and wheeled it out of the pen while Belle closed the gate behind them.

"Ray, I want you to get rid of his wagon and horse. Drive it off into the woods and hide it. If anyone ever asks, Andrew drove off to be a salesman again."

Ray harnessed up Helgelien's horse and climbed into the driver's seat of the wagon. As the sun climbed above the horizon, he grabbed the reins. The wagon creaked and rattled as they set off, and an uncomfortable feeling crept up on Ray. He was sitting in Helgelien's seat, driving his horse. A vision of the man's blank eyes flashed into Ray's mind, but he shook it away.

What was one less snake oil salesman? Was it really that much of a loss?

His conscience whispered an answer: *That wound liniment worked wonders on your barbed wire cuts. That's not snake oil.*

Maybe so, maybe so. But what about the rest of it? Helgelien with his big laugh and slick words, making up stories. Lies is what they were. Wasn't lying a sin? It was in the commandments, just like murder. "Thou shalt not bear false witness."

And besides, Ray committed no murder. All he did was bury a body. And it was illegal to *not* bury a body properly, so really, he was just following the law.

What did he care about Andrew Helgelien? He probably had it coming. And who knows, maybe he really had died of natural causes.

The question was, what choice did Ray have? Would he leave Belle? March his way into the sheriff's office and make a clean breast of it, see Belle arrested for murder? Just the thought of it froze the breath in his lungs, making him dizzy enough to stop and drop his hands to his knees and blurred his vision. He shut his eyes, letting the horse find his own way for a minute.

No. He could never do that.

He would never, *never*, leave Belle.

Asle Helgelien held a stack of mail in one hand and a cup of tea in the other. At his feet, Christina peered up at him, her red hair having escaped the braids Matilda had put in that morning, giving her the wild look of a street urchin. She was small, always had been. Born too early, she almost didn't survive her first week. But she had made up for it in the years since. The girl had more life in her than most adults.

"I don't want to," she said. Her chin jutted out, and her fists were planted on her skinny hips. "I want another one of Uncle Andrew's sweets."

When his brother was away, Asle kept a stash of molasses candies in his pocket to remember him by. The children were allowed one after supper, and the boys were still sucking on theirs, making the treat last as long as possible. Christina had crunched hers up immediately.

He exchanged a look with Matilda, washing dishes at the kitchen sink. They both knew a storm was coming. But the Bible said "Spare the rod, and spoil the child," and Asle firmly believed that no good would come from letting this little tornado of whims and emotions have her way. "No sweets. You must go to bed, and you will," Asle told her firmly.

"They don't have to." Christina's arm shot out, one finger indicting her brothers, who sat at the table, heads bent over their schoolbooks.

"When you are big and going to school, you will be able to stay up too," Matilda said. "But you are four, and it is time for you to sleep."

"Now, do as you are told and listen to your mother." Asle put on his sternest look. "Or I will get the paddle."

Christina stomped her foot and glared at him. Then she stomped across the floor, fists still on her hips, her bare feet slapping against the linoleum. At the doorway, she pivoted and gave them all one final glare so they could feel the injustice of their treatment of her. They heard her stomp all the way upstairs and into her room.

"That child," Matilda said.

Asle sat across from the boys and began slitting open envelopes with a table knife. "She'll either rule the world one day or destroy it. Oh, here's a letter from my brother. Why—"

From her work at the sink, Matilda called, "Yes? He has some news?"

"'Brother, I've met someone,'" Asle read. "'Don't want to jinx it. Fingers crossed that she's all she claims to be. I'm heading to her tonight, sun at my back and hope in my heart. I'll write to you in a week to tell you all about it.' Oh, Andrew."

"But that's wonderful!" exclaimed Matilda. "Andrew happy and settled down, wouldn't that be lovely? Maybe a spring wedding? Do you think we could go? Of course, we don't know where he is. You must ask him when you write back so we can plan."

"Matilda," Asle cut in. "You are putting the cart before the horse. He has just met the woman. This is Andrew we're talking about. His next letter may tell a new story in a different town."

"Of course, you are right," Matilda agreed, fetching a towel to dry the supper dishes.

Asle folded the letter and slid it into its envelope. Would Andrew finally settle down and marry? Perhaps. On his last sojourn, he'd seemed almost melancholy, and reluctant to set out on the road, a place he'd always yearned for. If Asle's charismatic, impetuous, big-hearted brother was finally ready to put his wagon in the shed and tie the knot with a good woman, Asle would be only too glad to celebrate the union.

24

Belle no longer thought of the desk in the library as Mads's desk. It had sat empty after arriving from Indianapolis, but she claimed it as her own as she got her business under way and stocked it with writing paper and fountain pens that pleased her. There was a letter opener, mucilage, and postage stamps. A stack of newspapers from cities and towns throughout Indiana and the Upper Midwest. And on the corner of the desk, a vase of dried wildflowers, collected at the height of summer to bring a welcome bit of color to sustain her through the winter.

The desk had six columns of cubbyholes, and Belle had devised an organizational system to make her new process run smoothly. Letters filled the cubbies, ordered according to how far along in the process their correspondence was. The first row was for initial contact. The second row was for prospects who had responded favorably. If a correspondent failed to reply within two weeks or responded negatively, Belle began a new correspondence. (Old letters were filed in the lower drawers, alphabetically by last name.) The third row was for prospects who indicated they had means. The fourth row was reserved for suitors who were ready for the final push.

Belle was rather proud of her system, which showed far greater organization than anything Mads had ever done for the candy shop.

She retrieved the most recent letter, out of row four, column five, from Joseph Barber of South Bend. A Mexican War veteran and widower, he was a patriot, a farmer, and a very lonely old man since his wife died about a year ago. According to the letter, he would be arriving on the twelve o'clock train. His shaky handwriting led her to suspect he'd be frail, but she wasn't daunted. Her efforts with Andrew proved she had the skills to run a profitable business, and an elderly client's money was just as spendable as a younger man's.

In the hours before she had to leave to meet him, Belle wrote three more letters, continuing to sign them all Mrs. Belle Gunness, as she had when she began her advertising campaign. She replied to a professor of psychology from the University of Wisconsin in Madison who had asked about her dreams and to a zookeeper from Chicago who had regaled her with facts about sea lions. A butcher from Toledo was curious about her looks, wanting to know if she was "sturdy," so she wrote to him about fixing the barbed wire fence and caring for the hogs. But she also slipped in mentions of her soft brown hair and what a good seamstress she was, that she could never order pre-made clothes because they didn't fit her small waist and large bust.

She also penned a carefully worded query to the research librarians at the University of Chicago for information on poisons. She hoped to learn of one that was swift to kill but painless. She had tried to make death more comfortable for Andrew than it had been for Charles, but he'd still had to suffer through those convulsions.

A timid knock came at the door of the library. "Come in," she called.

Ray poked his head in, his cheeks ruddy from the raw cold of late November. With the weather turning toward winter, Belle had kept Ray busy indoors in the weeks since Andrew's passing. She had, of course, used Andrew's checkbook to write herself a check and deposit his funds into her account, and she had hired Hugh Anderson to fix her roof. He and his crew had worked swiftly to replace the timbers and shingles, making the roof good as new again. Meanwhile, Ray and a few of the house painters who'd tackled the exterior previously had repaired ruined woodwork and flooring in her bedroom, painted, and hung new wallpaper. Her room was even more beautiful now than it had been before the roof collapse.

"The carriage is ready, Miz Belle," Ray said from the doorway.

"Very good, Ray. Thank you." Belle signed her final letter and sealed it in an envelope. She cleared away her pens and paper, tidying her desk before she left for town. She drew the roll top down and locked it.

When Ray handed her up to the carriage, his hand lingered on her thigh. "Anything you need help with? You want I should come with you?" She was visiting his bed several times a week again, and he had left behind the moping he'd done during Andrew's time at the house. Belle much preferred this Ray, who spoke in full sentences and met her eye. It was unlikely to last, though, once she returned from her outing.

"Thank you, Ray, but no. I am going to meet a friend at the train station. He will stay with me for a few days."

Ray's expression darkened briefly before he retreated and waved her off. He would be upset, but he would be steadfast. Belle was sure of it. He was in too deep to abandon her now.

In town, Belle posted her letters and made her way to the train station. She arrived on the platform just as the locomotive rolled into place. Also waiting was Miss Alice Longacre, La Porte's young school-teacher. She had no luggage, but as was typical for the girl, she clutched a book in her hands.

"Miss Longacre, what a surprise to see you here," Belle greeted her.

"Why, Mrs. Gunness. Hello! Are you taking a trip?" Eagerness lit Miss Longacre's eyes.

The porters opened the doors, and passengers began to disembark.

"I'm expecting a visitor. And you?"

"Oh, not I," she said wistfully as travelers jostled by. "I like to see the trains come and go. I imagine it's me in the carriage, heading far away from here. Is Mr. Lamphere here with you? Driving your carriage, perhaps?"

"I'm afraid not."

"Oh, what a shame. Will you tell him I said hello?" The girl brightened at Belle's nod and dashed off through the swarm of travelers surging toward the station building.

Belle scanned the mass of people, but none of them could be Joseph Barber, and there was a long pause where no one else got off the train. Could he have missed it? Decided not to come? Belle would be vexed if her campaign to bring Mr. Barber had failed, considering he'd assured her his life's savings would accompany him.

But no, after a wait, one final passenger emerged from the middle car. He wore a black suit with a silk top hat that hadn't been fashionable since the middle of the century. He gingerly dropped one booted foot and then the other onto each step before descending to the next. His gnarled hands gripped tightly to the railing, and at the final step, his boot reached for the platform but was left hovering, tapping the air, unable to find purchase.

This had to be her man, but he looked as though he needed a nurse more than a wife. Oh, this one was going to be easy.

Nearby, two porters chatted, oblivious to the old man's struggle.

"Help him," Belle called out, pointing at the middle carriage. But before they could respond, the old man slipped. With one hand clenched on the railing, he swung out of the train, his top hat tumbling off his head, feet scrabbling for the ground. The porters ran to him and, hoisting the old man up on either side, gently righted him. The man tugged his suit jacket straight while one of the porters retrieved the top hat, dusted it off, and handed it to him. He jammed it on his head.

"Mr. Barber? Joseph?" Belle asked as she approached. "I'm Mrs. Belle Gunness. Welcome to La Porte."

"Thank you, er, thank you kindly, miss," he said, checking his pockets and glancing around confusedly. He was shorter than she expected, not even reaching her shoulder. Age pressed down on him, hunching his back and pushing his head well forward. Instead of a straight spine, his was a question mark. "My suitcases. I need my suitcases." He tottered in a circle, searching for his belongings.

"Fetch his cases, will you please," Belle directed the porters, who climbed into the car and returned, each hefting a large suitcase. "Carry them to my gig, please. On Michigan Street."

The two porters hurried off, the oversized cases easy work for young legs, and disappeared through the station doors.

"You got my letter, then," he said. "Never can tell with the mail. I thought I might get here and find no one to meet me. Half the letters I wrote to Fidelia during the war never got to her. Probably went to some other Fidelia in some other South Bend. Fidelia Barber of South Bend, Ontario, maybe."

"Is there a Fidelia Barber in South Bend, Ontario?" Belle asked, trying to follow his train of thought.

"Hell if I know," he answered. "Only one Fidelia, that I can tell you. Only one. Fidelia." He finished on a sigh.

This poor man missed his wife terribly, that much was clear. His suit hung on his stooped frame like scraps on a scarecrow, and his every labored step was accompanied by a small grunt of effort or perhaps pain. Belle slowed her pace to match his. "She must have been a very special woman."

"That's the plain truth, missy. Fidelia is—was the one and only. My Fidelia could sew a straight seam with stitches so fine they disappeared. She can bake any kind of pie you want and cook a feast to fill a man's belly. A good mother to the six children the Lord blessed us with. And she can shoot the toenails off a bear."

Belle noticed as Joseph slipped into the present tense. He missed her so much, it was as if she was still present in his life. Interesting.

"Maybe you're like some who are shocked a woman can shoot so well," he continued, "but she's a regular Annie Oakley. She gets a real pleasure out of hunting with me. And me, I'm a forward-thinking man. Always have been. Let the woman shoot, I say. If she can, she can. Wearing a skirt don't mean she can't sight a deer. What's a skirt got to do with it, I say."

"You were a good husband to her, I can tell," Belle said.

"Were?" he said sharply. Then softly to himself, "Yes, yes. Dear Fidelia. Gone too soon."

"How long has it been?" Belle asked gently.

Joseph sighed. "Last winter it was. Oh, it was bitter cold for months. We slept with every blanket and barely kept warm. Fidelia had a cough that just wouldn't quit. And then one morning, she woke up dead. I got out of bed, and there she was, standing next to the bed and in the bed at the same time. 'What are you doing, Fidelia?' I asked her. 'I've passed on, Joe,' she told me."

Was he suffering from dementia or just grief? Belle had to wonder if his mental state would make things easier or harder.

They arrived at her gig, where the two porters hovered, waiting for a tip. She drew them aside as Joseph eyed the high carriage step warily and quietly said to the boys, "Help Mr. Barber up, but treat him with great respect. He is a war veteran. Do not dishonor him by treating him like he is infirm."

The boys nodded and positioned themselves on either side of Joseph. One snapped a smart salute and said, "Good afternoon, sir. Permission to assist?"

Joseph straightened up slightly and saluted back. "Permission granted," he barked.

The porters clasped his arms and lifted him up to the carriage step, guarding his back as he navigated the lip of the carriage floor and settled himself into the seat. "Permission to depart?" they chorused.

"Good work, soldiers," Joseph said. "Dismissed."

The porters rushed back to Belle. She gave them each a coin and smiled warmly. "Good job, boys." They grinned and blushed and hurried back to the station.

Belle joined Joseph on the seat and settled a lap blanket over their knees. "The days are getting chilly," she said, guiding Gwen onto the roadway. "Before we know it, snow will be on the ground." She snapped the reins, getting the horse up to a trot. Next to her, Joseph quietly laughed to himself. "What is funny, Joseph?"

"Do you know where snowmen put their money?"

"What? Um, no. Where?"

"In the snowbank. Ha!" His shoulders jerked. "How do mountains stay warm?"

"How?"

"They put on their snowcaps. Ha!" More jerky laughter. "What's a snowman's favorite drink?"

"Tell me," Belle said, charmed by his childlike delight.

"Iced tea! Ha ha ha!"

"You are quite the jokester, Joseph." Belle hadn't expected such liveliness from the old fellow. "You didn't mention that in your letters."

"Not me, not me," he said, wiping tears from his eyes. He was somewhere between laughing and crying now. "My Fidelia. She had a joke for every season, every situation. Knew a million of 'em. She kept us laughing all the time."

"Tell me another," Belle encouraged.

Joseph obliged, keeping up a steady stream of jokes all the way out to Belle's house.

"Getting old isn't for the faint of heart," Joseph told the lady who had picked him up at the station. She had a terrific smile. What was her name, again? Billie? Ellen? He climbed down from the carriage with the help of a fellow who met them in front of the house. His hip had stiffened up after sitting so long on the train, and the ride to the house hadn't helped. And what a house it was. Twice as big, at least, as his house with Fidelia. Big, and fancy too. It had a turret.

"Mr. Joseph Barber, this is my handyman, Ray Lamphere. He is indispensable around here and will be happy to help you with anything you need. Isn't that right, Ray?"

"Yes, ma'am," the fellow said. Name of Ray, apparently. Hard to see how such a scrawny fellow could be indispensable. But then, Joseph had always been short and that didn't stand in his way.

"Ray, could you put the gig away and feed and water Gwen? And put a blanket on her. It's going to be cold tonight, I think."

"Right away, Miz Belle."

Belle! That was it. Pretty name for a pretty lady. But not as pretty as Fidelia.

"Come this way, Joseph. I'll show you your room," Belle said.

Joseph followed her onto the porch—he noticed there were no rocking chairs—and into a large entranceway with a staircase on the right. Joseph peered into rooms as he passed them but didn't see Fidelia anywhere. Would she be able to visit him here? Would he still be able to talk to her? He needed to know he'd made the right decision coming here. Fidelia had told him to, but did she still think so, now that he was here? How was he supposed to manage alone?

The staircase was long. He didn't mind it so much going up, but coming back down was going to be a trick, especially in the morning when his knees stiffened up and his hip was at its worst.

"Here is the water closet." Belle opened a door, showing him a room with a sink with running water and a toilet. Joseph and Fidelia had never seen the sense of spending money to bring that business inside.

Belle led him to a room with a bed big enough for two covered in a good homemade quilt, a fireplace already laid with wood, and a wash-stand with a basin and ewer. Joseph checked the ewer. Empty. Fidelia wouldn't think much of that hospitality.

"You won't need the ewer, Joseph," Belle said. "The water closet is just next door, remember?"

"Hmph."

"I'll leave you alone, Joseph. You probably want to rest after your journey. I'll come find you when supper is ready."

Joseph heard her but didn't reply. His attention was caught on the only other furniture in the room: a rocking chair.

* * *

Belle heard voices coming from Joseph's room and paused at his door to listen. She couldn't make out any words, just a low murmuring. Joseph talking to himself, or talking in his sleep, perhaps. She knocked and entered and found him sitting on the edge of the bed, still in his rumpled black suit, facing the rocking chair in the corner. A dress was draped there, as if it were sitting. Gray linen, with a high waistline, gathered neckline, and straight narrow skirt, the dress was decades out of fashion. It showed signs of wear, especially at the skirt hem, but was clean and obviously cared for. This dress was someone's best, and Belle guessed it was the dress Fidelia wore to be wed and for special occasions after that. Joseph had brought it all the way from his home, and it was the only thing he had unpacked.

Had he been talking to the dress?

"Joseph? Is everything all right? Are you rested? Supper is ready."

The lady made good grub. Not the lady; Belle. Her name kept slipping out of his mind. He almost called her Fidelia when she brought out the food. Seventy-five years of saying "Thank you, Fidelia" didn't disappear overnight.

"Chicken pot pie is one of my favorites. Fidelia used to make it."

"Is it now?" Belle said. "I hope mine lives up to hers."

Joseph didn't want to tell her that would be impossible.

"Tell me about your wife, Joseph," she asked. "Did she like to cook?"

"Jerusalem crickets, she's a fine cook. Chicken pot pie, anadama bread, good pot roast, biscuits and gravy, where the biscuits are so light and fluffy they could take you up to visit the angels. Pig's head cheese. Mm-mm. Yessiree, best cook in the county. Won the apple pie contest at the county fair seven years running. Only reason she didn't win the next year was on account of coming down with the shits on the day of. Pardon my French."

He glanced over at where Fidelia stood by the window. Joseph had been afraid she would only visit him in the rocking chair in his room, but she had followed him downstairs when Belle came to get him for supper. After his language, Fidelia was shaking her head at him. She had that look on her face like she wanted to be cross and scold him, but really she thought it was funny. He knew he better be more careful of his words. He didn't want this fancy lady kicking him out.

"Did Fidelia let you talk like that?" Belle asked.

"Ha! Fidelia was a frontierswoman. Wore breeches like a man when we went hunting and knew more salty words than a sailor, ha ha. She could swear a blue streak, but she had a tender heart. She wouldn't stand for no sass from our kids, but she cared for 'em and cried over 'em when they grew up and left."

"She sounds like a hell of a woman."

Joseph perked up at the swear word. Maybe this lady wasn't so fancy after all.

"That she was. Here, I have a photograph." He kept a leather billfold in his breast pocket and pulled out a small daguerreotype that showed Fidelia seated, wearing her wedding dress, and Joseph standing with his hand on her shoulder.

"How lovely," Belle said, drawing her chair close to his. He could feel her warmth right next to him. If he didn't look, it could be Fidelia sitting close by his side. "This is the dress you have laid out in your room, isn't it?"

"Yup, yup," Joseph said. "Oh, Fidelia. Pretty as a picture that day. I look at that dress, and that's what I see. My bride Fidelia. I took that picture with me when I went to war." He glanced up to share a fond look with Fidelia, but this wasn't his bride next to him. Where was Fidelia? Who was this woman?

For a moment, he endured a painful clarity: The silence and loneliness of the house with Fidelia gone. Cooking for himself in the kitchen that was so much Fidelia's he could hardly bear to stand in it. The lumpy bed they'd shared, the indentation where her body was meant to rest, empty.

He suddenly remembered the letters to and from this woman—what was her name again?—and Fidelia telling him to come.

"You were very lucky in your marriage, Joseph. You and Fidelia loved each other very much." The woman put her hand on Joseph's, the warmth of it good against his ever-cold old bones.

Fidelia was now standing behind her and had laid her hand over the woman's. Fidelia was giving him a stern look that he recognized. It meant, "Buck up, Joseph. Quit your squealing and get on with it." She was right, as always. He blinked away his tears and grasped their hands, giving a squeeze. "You're right, my dear."

The woman slid her chair over to her place, and they ate quietly for a spell. It was almost like the companionable silence of suppers with Fidelia after the children had grown and gone. Joseph was glad he had come.

When they finished, the woman began to clear their plates, Fidelia hovering close by as if to supervise. "That was a very fine meal, ma'am," Joseph thanked her.

"Now, Joseph, you promised to call me Belle."

Belle! That was it. "Thank you, Belle."

"You're welcome. I'll just clear these dishes and bring you some tea." Stacking Joseph's plate on hers, Belle said, "Joseph, can I ask you a question?"

"Sure you can," Joseph said.

"What did the elephant ask the naked man?"

Joseph looked from Belle to Fidelia, who gave him no help, and back. "I don't know, what?"

"How do you breathe out of that thing?"

It took Joseph a moment to realize he'd really heard what he thought. Then he burst out laughing.

"Ah, ha ha ha! How do you breathe out of that thing! Ha ha!" Tears squeezed out of his eyes. Fidelia bent over in silent guffaws, mirrored by Belle, both of them clutching their sides. The pair straightened, and Fidelia's form shimmered and expanded, growing in size to match Belle's height. Her image blurred and wavered like a candle flame, and when Belle gathered up the dishes and left the room, Fidelia was swept after her, imitating her movements, the two women moving like dancers in unison. When the other lady returned, bearing a laden tray, her hands were superimposed by Fidelia's hands as she set out the pot and mugs and began to pour tea.

It made Joseph dizzy to watch the two women blending together, then separating again, blending and separating, blending and separating.

Then Fidelia's figure snapped over the other woman's, merging with her completely.

Joseph was drawn from his chair, rising on shaky legs, desperate to get to his beloved. "Fidelia," he breathed. "You've come back to me." He threw his arms around her, and she was warm, so warm.

25

In the morning, Joseph followed his nose to the kitchen. The cookstove blazed with heat, and the sweet smell of baking cake perfumed the air, but the room was empty. Sacks of flour and sugar sat on the worktable, with a bowl of eggs and a crock of butter.

The back door burst open, and Fidelia came in, her nose red from the cold. She had on a heavy sweater and a pair of men's breeches. She strode with her familiar swagger and stood with a wide station.

"Good morning, sleepyhead." She tossed her sweater on a peg by the door and set right to work with the ingredients on the table. Her body shook with the rhythm of her spoon beating circles in the bowl. "High time you found your way out of the sheets. I thought I'd have to drag you down here by your ears."

"Good morning." Joseph stretched up to kiss Fidelia's smooth cheek. "Smells like you've got a cake in the oven."

The spoon stilled, and Fidelia said sternly, "Some of us have been up for hours. It's a pound cake. And now that you're up, I'll make you flapjacks."

Hot damn. He pulled up a chair to the worktable to watch his wife cook. His favorite cake was in the oven, and she was making his favorite breakfast. A long-absent contentment settled over him. Everything was gonna be hunky-dory.

***

Joseph Barber was much more confused in person than he'd been in his letters. Belle had expected an old, lonely man, and Joseph was that. But he was also a man so lost in his memories he seemed to forget where he was and who he was with. He thought she was Fidelia.

It was proving very easy to maintain that illusion. She'd slept beside him under the selburose quilt, not having to worry about catering to his sexual desires, since those had faded decades ago. When he'd stirred during the night, complaining of achy bones, she'd taken him downstairs for a cup of mint and chamomile tea. He was happy as long as he had his Fidelia by his side. So that's what she would give him: his final hours with his beloved.

She hummed "Arkansas Traveler," a favorite of Fidelia's she'd learned the day before, as she worked. The pan was plenty hot, and once her batter was mixed, she ladled it in, setting up a spattering sizzle. Over her shoulder, she called, "Old man, how many flapjacks are you fixin' to eat?"

"I'll take four, please," he answered, and joined her as she resumed humming. His creaky old baritone played a rough harmony to her soprano.

Belle set a plate in front of Joseph just as Ray knocked on the kitchen door and came in. "Mornin', Ray," she sang out. "Want some flapjacks?"

"Um, yes, please," Ray said, settling into a chair. Belle sure was acting funny this morning. She was talking different, walking different. And what was she wearing? She looked like she'd borrowed those clothes from the church box.

She plunked a plate in front of him and straddled a chair next to the old codger she'd brought home from the train station. Barber. The fellow seemed pleased as punch to be here. Enjoy it while it lasts, grampa.

The man was about as ancient as you could be and still be on this side of the grave. His eyes were cloudy with cataracts, and his gnarled hands looked like tubers. While Ray watched, Barber fisted food into his mouth, opening his maw wide to receive the shaking fork. He mashed the flapjack around with what few teeth he had left. Ray focused on his own plate. Was she going to marry this one? It was hard to credit.

Belle got up and stomped around the kitchen, humming an old tune while she stoked the fire and put water on to boil. She hefted the iron skillet from the stove and demanded, "You want more, old man?"

And when Joseph said, "No, thank you, Fidelia," Ray shot Belle a questioning look, but she avoided him, keeping her focus entirely on Barber.

"Get a move on, old man." Belle found she didn't mind bossing Joseph around like he said Fidelia used to. She could get used to bossing men around, truth be told. "I want to get to the bank when it opens, and then we can stop at the furniture store. I know you want rockers for the front porch."

"I'm movin'." Joseph handed his plate to Belle. "That's good eats, Fidelia."

"Look at you," Belle sighed. "You got syrup on your face. Here." She wet a cloth under the tap and dabbed at his chin. She was none too gentle, like a harried mother with her messy toddler. When she finished, he puckered up for a kiss. She laughed and planted her lips on his cheek, and he pulled her into his lap, surprisingly strong. Her good cooking and affection seemed to have given him new life. "All right now, that's enough," she said, pushing herself off and straightening her clothes. "We'll have time for that later."

"At my age, you can't count on later." He winked at her. "You got to take your pleasures now. You don't know—I could croak right there in the bank."

"Hush now, Joseph," she scolded him. "Don't talk like that. I hope you've got years left."

Belle slipped on her longest coat to cover the breeches—nobody in town needed to know she was mimicking a dead woman—and bustled them into her gig, which Ray had waiting out front, making sure Joseph was wrapped up well against the late autumn chill for the half-hour ride. Someday, Belle would have a motorcar. She would whiz into town, with a long white scarf blowing in the breeze made by her speed. It might still be chilly, but it would be fast.

When they arrived at the bank, Belle helped Joseph down. "Thank you, sweetheart," he said.

"You're welcome, sweetheart." She kissed him fondly on the cheek. "Now come along and don't dawdle."

The little bank building was a one-story square with a heavy door and no windows. There was one counter at the back, iron bars protecting the cashiers. "Good morning, Mr. Todd," Belle greeted the bank manager when he approached. With his round bald head and protruding eyes, she had to remind herself not to call him Mr. Toad, though she suspected she could have called him Mr. Turd and he wouldn't have minded. His overly enthusiastic greetings suggested he had a terrible crush on her.

"Why, if it isn't La Porte's most beautiful citizen, and aren't you looking lovely today," he fawned. "Good morning, Mrs. Gunness. What can I do for you?"

"Mrs. Gunness! What's this now?" Joseph exclaimed, straightening his age-hunched shoulders. "Who do you think you're talking to? This here's my wife, Mrs. Barber, and that's how you'll call her."

"It's all right, Joseph, I'm sure Mr. Todd just made a slip of the tongue. Why don't you sit here and be comfortable." Belle ushered Joseph to a carved mahogany chair in front of the banker's desk. Its leather seat squelched as Joseph settled into it. She squeezed his shoulder, then turned to Mr. Todd and said, "Perhaps I could speak to you a moment outside?"

Once outside the glass-windowed door, Belle leaned toward the banker and whispered, "I'm sorry about that. Please forgive his outburst. Mr. Barber is my great-uncle, and as you can see, he's a little confused. Such a dear old man. But he actually thinks I'm his dead wife, Fidelia."

"Oh, goodness, what a pickle." Mr. Todd chuckled.

"Yes, exactly. But you see, that's the reason we're here. Uncle Joseph is no longer able to care for himself since Aunt Fidelia passed on, and they never had any children. So I've taken him in." With a hand to her breast and downcast eyes, Belle projected an air of selfless modesty. "And to make it easier to care for him, I want to transfer his money into my account. That way, there isn't any waiting if I need to purchase something for him. Do you think you can help us with that?" Belle laid her hand on Mr. Todd's arm and raised her wide, pleading eyes to his.

Mr. Todd gave her fingers a reassuring pat. "Of course, Mrs. Gunness. La Porte Bank and Trust is honored to do business with such a fine Christian woman as yourself."

"Oh, thank you," Belle breathed with relief. "And if you could play along with the idea that I'm his wife? Call me Mrs. Barber. I know it may strike you as unseemly, but it's easier than trying to coax him back into reality."

"Of course, of course." Giving her hand one last pat, he escorted her back into his office. Settled into his desk chair, he uncapped his fountain pen and said with a wink, "Now then, I understand you want to make a deposit, Mrs. Barber."

"Joseph, why don't you give Mr. Todd the check?" Belle said. He'd shown it to her earlier, made out to "cash" in the amount of $1,764.00, and told her it was all the money he'd saved over the years.

Joseph withdrew the check from his breast pocket and handed it to Mr. Todd. "I want to deposit this."

"Very good, sir." Mr. Todd inspected the front and back of the check and had Joseph sign it. "It will take a few days for the check to clear the bank in South Bend before this money is available."

"Oh, that's fine," Belle said. "We don't need it now. Joseph just wanted to put it someplace safe."

"Very smart," Mr. Todd congratulated them. "The bank is the safest place for your money."

"That's exactly what I said," Belle said. "Didn't I, sweetheart?"

"That you did, wife. That you did."

"Now come along, Joseph. Let's get those rocking chairs."

Joseph had arrived home tired and cold from their trip to town, and Fidelia had put him to bed for a nap with a hot water bottle. "You rest now and warm up, Joseph," she'd said. "I won't have you catching your death. That's the last thing I need is you coughing and sneezing all over the place, and moaning about how miserable you feel." Joseph had to chuckle as she fussed over him and turned her concern into scolding.

He drowsed and woke, achy but refreshed, and made his slow way downstairs to end the day admiring the world from the new porch rockers. The light was fading and the chill in the air deepening.

Fidelia followed him out front. "What are you doing out here? You'll catch your death." She had her breeches on and stood over him, fists on her hips.

"Nonsense," he said. "Take a load off, woman. Sit with me awhile."

"You think I have nothing better to do than flap my gums sittin' on the porch?" Her words were rough, but her tone was gentle, and as she spoke, she sank into the other rocker.

"Shush, now. Lookit that sun." Low on the horizon, a glowing orange orb rested in a mackerel sky. Gray clouds stippled peach and pink veiled the sun as it descended. A companionable silence spread between them. The sad song of a mourning dove floated over the evening air. He never tired of watching sunsets with his beloved.

"Enough of this lollygagging," Fidelia said, rising suddenly. "I'm going in to finish supper. You come on in shortly, you hear?"

***

Ray pounded in the last nail and stepped back to survey his work in the small bit of light that lingered. Without Helgelien as a second set of hands, repairing the fence line had been a lot harder. Belle had helped some after the roof and her bedroom were finished, but her focus had shifted to what she called her "correspondence," and she spent a lot of time inside at her desk in the library, bent over pen and paper, and traveling into town to post letters and check for responses. Then the old fella arrived, and all her energy went to doting on him, leaving Ray to finish the project alone.

So when he stretched the last length of barbed wire to the final post and fastened it in place, he had no one to shake hands with on a job well done. Not that he'd have enjoyed shaking Helgelien's hand. Instead, he patted the last fence post with satisfaction. Then he packed up his tools and headed back to the house.

Barber sat in one of the new rockers on the front porch. He had a heavy blanket across his lap, and a wool hat and mittens knitted with Belle's selburose pattern protected him from the chill. His chin rested heavily on his chest, a soft snore buzzing his lips.

Ray had expected to feel jealous of the new arrival, but when Belle brought Barber to the house, all he felt was pity. Was Belle really going to marry this old codger? he'd wondered. To look at the fellow, so shrunken he almost looked like a child, Ray didn't think the man had much time left.

"Evening, Mr. Barber," Ray called as he neared the house.

The old coot jerked his head up. "Heh? Who's that?"

"It's me, Ray, the handyman." Ray came up on the porch. "Are you warm enough, Mr. Barber? It's getting colder."

"Oh, this is nothin'. A little cold can't keep an old soldier down."

"That right? What war did you fight in?"

"I was at the Battle of Palo Alto and the Battle of Resaca de la Paloma. Fought door-to-door for three days in Monterey. Lost a third of our company there. A lot of close calls in that war. But it wasn't until Mexico City that Lady Luck took her eye off me."

"What happened?"

"Took a ball in my ass is what happened. Left me with this limp. But I got home to my Fidelia, so maybe Lady Luck didn't desert me."

"Fidelia?"

"My wife. Married seventy-five years. I'm a lucky man. She takes awful good care of me."

Takes? Ray was sure Belle had told him the man was a widower, and the only one taking care of Barber was Belle.

"Made these mittens for me." Barber held up his hands, showing off the pattern Belle liked to knit on everything.

"Your wife made those?"

"That's right." He folded his hands in his lap with contentment, very much like a proud and satisfied husband.

The old man was clearly a couple bubbles off plumb. Poor fool.

Ray went inside to search out Belle. He found her not scribbling away at her desk, as she so often was now, but in the kitchen chopping vegetables. A mound of carrots was piled to her left, and a heap of potatoes grew to her right as her big knife flashed through the white flesh of potato after potato.

"Hello, Ray." She glanced up and smiled as he entered the kitchen. "There's a pot of beans there if you're hungry." She pointed her knife at a pot bubbling gently on the stove.

The smell of brown sugar and spices wafted to him, reminding him that it had been hours since he'd eaten. He scooped some onto a plate and, between mouthfuls, said, "Finished the last of the fence line. Your property is completely enclosed now."

"Wonderful! Well done, thank you." Her knife paused, and she looked up at Ray with a beaming smile before returning to the task of turning potatoes into cubes.

"Talked to that old fella on the porch," Ray said.

"Mr. Barber?"

"That's the one. Nice old fella. A little batty. But nice."

"He is sweet."

Ray waited for her to say more, but she didn't. "Thinks you're his dead wife," he added.

"Oh, that," she said dismissively. The knife kept up its work, whisking easily through potato flesh.

"Got me thinking," Ray said.

"Yes?"

"Well, he's an old fella. Real old. He's losin' his marbles." Had already lost them, as far as Ray could tell. "His time is comin' on. Can't be long now, right? What is he? Ninety?"

"Joseph is ninety-one years old and deserves great care."

"Listen, Belle," Ray said. "Do you really need to go through with the whole routine? He's so out of it, you've got him thinking you're his dead wife—"

"I *am* his dead wife." Her glare sliced through him as easily as her knife through the potatoes piled on the cutting board.

"All right, all right." Ray swallowed. "But maybe this time you could, well . . . maybe you could let nature take its course? Can't be long now. Don't you think?"

The flashing knife stilled. Belle pinned hard eyes on him. "Ray." She pointed her big blade at his chest. "I don't want to have to tell you this again. I am running a business here. Men come to me to get something they desperately need. Something they can get nowhere else. That old man out there"—she thrust her knife toward the front of the house—"is a war hero. Think of what he gave up for our great nation. More than a pound of flesh! Look at the way he walks! Before he came here, he woke up every day knowing he'd never see his darling wife, his one true love, again in this life. He was wasting away in misery. And now look at him. He's stronger, and he's happy. He will die with the love of his life by his side. That's all he wants. And we will give it to him." The knifepoint swished back to Ray. "Do you understand me?"

The tip, aiming dead steady at his chest, drew Ray's eyes. Was she threatening him? What about all those nights they'd spent together before Barber came? And between Gunness and Helgelien? She didn't have to lie with him; he wasn't a rich husband. She didn't have to seduce him into giving her his money. She *chose* to come to his bed. She wouldn't give him the same deadly treatment she gave her husbands.

"I understand," he said. The plate of beans had cooled in his hand, and his appetite had fled. Unsettled and confused, Ray walked out, leaving the plate in the sink.

Belle would never harm him, Ray knew that. He was sure of it. Wasn't he?

26

oseph's eyes blinked open sometime in the night when everything was still. Fidelia breathed quietly next to him. When they'd lain down for the night, he'd fallen into a slumber that was deep but not restful and didn't last. At his age, it never did. His many aches and pains sang loudly. It was a toss-up whether it would be better to lie there and suffer through it or get up and suffer standing. He opted to stand. At least it was a change.

Fidelia stirred. "Are you all right, sweetheart?" she said.

"I'm fine. Go on back to sleep. I'm just achy in my bones."

"Here, now." She pushed herself out of bed. "You don't need to suffer alone. Come sit in the kitchen. I'll make you a soothing tea."

She planted a kiss on his forehead, then rose and helped him get downstairs to the kitchen. She stirred up the fire and boiled the water. Filled the pot, poured their mugs, stirred in the honey.

"Here you go, sweetheart," she said, handing him his mug. "I put in something extra special tonight. It might taste a little different. But it will help you sleep."

Joseph took the hot beverage, drinking it down slowly, sip by sip, as Fidelia sat next to him by the fire. The concoction did soothe him, and his eyelids grew heavy. Maybe he'd just have a little cat nap here by the hearth. He let his head droop to his chest as sleep claimed him.

When he awoke, it was to a rumbling in his gut. That was another thing about getting old. Used to be he could eat a leather boot and horseshoes for supper and feel fine. Then somewhere in his midlife, his stomach began to get finicky. The same things Fidelia had cooked him all their married years began to run through him like a flood. He went as quick as his old legs would move him to the water closet off the kitchen. He barely made it to the toilet before his innards exploded into the bowl.

"You all right in there?" Fidelia called.

"I'll live. Just got the shits is all." He cleaned himself up and came out.

"What's wrong?" she asked. "You don't like my cooking?"

"Ain't that. It's just these old guts. They don't work like they used to." His innards rumbled again. "Hang on."

He spent more time on the toilet, emptying his bowels of runny green shit. It smelled to high heaven and burned his asshole on the way out.

"Holy hell," Fidelia said when he opened the door. She brought her hand to her face and covered her mouth and nose. "That smells somethin' awful."

With the mess out of him, Joseph felt like a new man. A young man. He reached for his wife. "C'mere, woman. Don't know how much time we have."

He led her to the library, shucking his night clothes as he went, then took a seat on a wingback, his erection a proud salute to days gone by. "Hop on, sweetheart."

Her eyes grew wide as silver dollars. But after only a moment's hesitation, she whipped off her nightdress and climbed aboard, just as willing as she had been in their early days.

"Hoo boy!" Joseph called out. She sure was a gift, this wife of his. He hadn't felt this good in a dog's age. She rode him like a wild woman, and he could feel the explosion building. But then his guts rumbled, threatening a different kind of explosion. "Uh oh," he said. He could only hope his climax would beat out the eruption from his ass.

Fidelia paused her gyrations. "You all right? You need to stop?"

Belle couldn't believe she was straddling a nonagenarian, let alone one who'd just downed a cupful of rat poison. The diarrhea hadn't been a surprise, but the raging erection certainly was. She had assumed that part of Joseph's life with Fidelia was far behind him. But she was a businesswoman and she prided herself on her customer service.

"Don't stop, don't stop," he panted.

"All right," she said, adding to herself, *Just don't shit all over my new chair.* She resumed bouncing in earnest. She had to bring him home before his bowels let loose again. With one hand, she held a breast, squeezing and massaging it and pinching her nipple. With the other, she reached behind her and took hold of his balls, gently rolling them in her fingers. Increasing the speed of her bouncing, she cried out, "That's right! That's right, Joseph. Oh! You're so big, so big! I can't— Yes! Now!"

"Jeeeee-rusalem crickets!" Joseph shouted. His eyes closed, and he was still.

Was that it? Belle leaned down and kissed Joseph's cheek. Dear Joseph. What a wonderful way to go.

His eyes blinked open. "Jerusalem crickets," he muttered.

"Oh!" Belle exclaimed. Not dead yet, it seemed.

"Who are you?" Confusion clouded his face and a storm of fear and anger swept over his features. "Who the hell are you? Where's my Fidelia?" He pushed feebly at her, trying to raise himself and get out from under her. As his fingers scrabbled weakly, he kept up a whimpering litany. "Who are you? Where am I?"

Belle disengaged herself and stood, thoughts racing. Poor old fool. Why did he have to regain his memory now?

Joseph clambered off the chair, falling in an awkward heap to the floor. He was sobbing, chanting, "Where is my Fidelia? Where am I?"

Belle tried to help him up, cajoling him with a sweet voice. "It's all right, Joseph, don't you recognize me? It's me, your Fidelia, your sweetheart."

He pushed her off, shouting, "Get away from me! What have you done with my wife? Kidnapper! Help! Help! I've been kidnapped!" He charged out of the room toward the front door, his deflated penis flapping against his leg. He yanked open the door and, framed in the doorway where anyone could see, shouted into the night, "Help me, someone, help me! I've been kidnapped!"

Son of a Benjamin! Belle raced over and yanked Joseph back and slammed the door. Sweet pleading didn't work, what about some of Fidelia's gruff command?

"Joseph Barber," Belle barked, fists planted on her hips. "Get yourself in here. What are you thinking, showing yourself to the whole neighborhood? You're going to get yourself arrested for indecency. I never in all my days!"

Stunned into silence, Joseph stared at her. His hands crept down to cover his privates. Then his face washed green and he clamped his knees together. "Ungh," Joseph groaned. "Here she comes again."

Belle slung an arm around his shoulders and helped him hobble down the hall to the water closet in short, shuffling steps, his knees clenched tightly. He shut the door, and Belle immediately heard groaning and splashing. Then, nothing.

Long minutes went by and Belle paced, waiting for Joseph to emerge, pausing to press her ear to the door, straining to hear something. Was he huddled inside, confused and scared? Or had the rat poison finally worked? Was he dead? Just when Belle reached for the handle, the door creaked open. Joseph tottered out, pale and trembling.

"Are you all right, old man?" Belle asked, hoping that if she stayed in character, Joseph would go along. She watched his face, anxious to see which way his mood would go. Then she noticed movement and glanced down.

His penis was gaining an astonishing second life. A grin spread across his face.

"C'mere woman," he said. "Can't seem to get enough of you tonight."

Who knew the old goat would be so hardy? Keeping up her Fidelia persona, she said, "All in good time, sweetheart. But let's see if we can do something about that belly first. I don't like to see you in pain."

"And let this go to waste?" He pointed down at his growing cock. He dragged a chair over next to the water closet door and plopped down, then wrapped his hand around his johnson and said, "Have a seat, madam."

The smell from the water closet was overpowering, but Belle was going to give Joseph his happiness. She just hoped she could give it to him before the next wave hit. She swung a leg over his lap and, hooking her heels on the rungs of the chair for purchase, began pumping up and down.

"That's it, my girl," he cried.

As she raised and lowered herself in a quick rhythm, Belle felt her thighs beginning to burn. "You're— so— big," she gritted out. "Can't— hardly— take— it."

"That's right, my girl. Take what I got for you."

She leaned forward, pushing her breasts into his face. "Give— it— to— me," she panted.

He scrunched his eyes closed. Pain crowded his features. "Ungh," he groaned.

Belle stilled. "Are you gonna be sick?"

"Nope," he grunted. He gave one big thrust and clutched her hips, then relaxed. His hands dropped to his sides.

Now what? Belle watched his face.

His eyes sprang open. "Yeee haaaw!" he hollered. "Fidelia, my girl, you put new life in a man. Ha ha!" His face changed. "Urgh."

She scrambled off him, and he scooted into the water closet.

Belle threw her nightdress on and fled to the stove, where she put more water on to boil. Surely a second dose would get the job done.

When Joseph came out of the bathroom, he was a little pale, perhaps, but otherwise healthy as a horse. With a grin, he looked down and said, "He's startin' to grow again."

Better make it a triple dose.

"Now that's enough of that, Joseph Barber," Belle scolded him. "You sit right down in that chair. I'm going to give you something for that belly, and you're going to take it. Then we'll see about Mr. Johnson."

"Yes, ma'am," Joseph laughed. He sat in the chair, naked as a jaybird, and waited patiently for Belle to mix the tea.

She served it in the largest mug she had and sweetened it with extra honey to hide the taste. "There you go, my sweetheart," Belle said. "Drink that down and see if it don't ease that belly."

"Thank you kindly, darlin'." He beamed at her. "You take good care of your old man."

Yes, I do. She was earning this payday in ways she never imagined. She scooted a chair next to Joseph and laced her fingers around his, pressed her lips to his cheek. "It's a pleasure to do for you," she said fondly. "I love you, Joseph."

This time it didn't take long.

When the knock came at his door early in the morning, Ray wasn't surprised. He opened it, and Belle said, "It's time."

The old soldier, just a bag of bones, was easy to carry out to a spot Belle had chosen in the field behind the house. Ray gently lay the fragile body on the grass, feeling a strange sorrow. What a waste, to murder an old man who surely didn't have much time left. But the echo of Belle's anger when he'd suggested letting Barber die a natural death reminded him to keep quiet.

Ray dug a hole, a deep one this time, and carefully lowered the old man down into it. He covered him well and tamped down the earth.

"God bless you and your life savings, great uncle Joseph." Ray caught the glee in Belle's tone but didn't have time to ask what on earth she meant by "uncle" before she patted his arm and said, "Another satisfied customer." She turned on her heel and strode toward the house, calling back, "I have letters to write, Ray!"

27

Asle Helgelien didn't like to leave the saloon, even for the afternoon. Matilda was fully capable of running the business end of things; she was better at it than he, in truth. But pulling pints and pouring whiskey and aquavit could be difficult—not the work in itself, but the men who came to enjoy the spirits. Their neighborhood was a decent one and most of their clientele law-abiding folk who simply wanted to relax with a glass or two. But there were also rough characters who liked their aquavit a little too much and had to be shown the door. Matilda was no shrinking violet, but she couldn't physically throw a man out.

However, it had been months since Andrew's last letter, the one in which he'd announced he'd met a woman and was off to see her. That letter had come in November, and now it was March. Even accounting for disruptions due to winter travel difficulties, such a gap in letters was unprecedented. The situation was urgent and getting more so every day.

Matilda shared his concern. "Go, Asle. See the police. It is so unusual not to hear from him. You must ask the police to investigate."

"I can't leave the bar, Matilda. What if there's a brawl?"

"We haven't had so much as a dustup in weeks. You worry too much. And I can ask Lars here for help if I need it. Isn't that right, Lars?"

Lars occupied the far end of the bar, standing hunched over a half-full pint. He was a slope-shouldered, potato-shaped mountain of a man whose back end would never fit on a stool and would probably break it if he tried. He was a gentle fellow, always polite, and very protective of Matilda. But his size was enough to convince most men to retreat. He spent his days at the bar, nursing a pint or two, because an accident in a machine shop had left him with only one working hand. And nobody hires a man with one hand.

"Of course," he answered. "You have a problem, you wave to me, I'll solve it. Don't worry, Mr. Helgelien, I'll watch over your wife and your bar. In that order."

Asle inspected the giant. He had a knack for sizing people up at a glance, and he'd always had a good feeling about the quiet but immense fellow who spent the lion's share of his time at the left end of this bar. "All right, Lars. Thank you. Your rounds are on the house today."

Lars nodded and raised his glass to Asle, then drained it. "I'll take one more, if you please, Mrs. Helgelien."

Asle kissed his wife goodbye and waved to Lars, then set off for the local precinct station.

He made the short walk in a few minutes and took the stairs into the squat building two at a time. He'd had dealings with the police on and off over the years, some good, some not so good. But he'd never had to communicate over such a ruckus.

"On Sunday night 'tis my deLIGHT and PLEASURE, don't you SEEEEEE," crowed a reedy tenor. "Meeting all the girls and the boys that work downtown with MEEEEEE."

The voice echoed from a hall to the right of the sergeant's desk, down which Asle could see a line of barred cells on either side. The invisible singer was likely the worse for drink. Another fellow allowed to consume more than he could handle.

"Good afternoon, Sergeant," Asle called over the man's caterwauling.

"THERE'S an organ in the PARlor to give the house a TONE,"

the drunk man droned the end of the chorus, "And you're welcome EVEREEEE evening at Maggie Murphy's HOOOOOME."

"Mornin' to you," shouted the desk sergeant. "What's your trouble?"

"My name is Asle Helgelien. I'm here on a difficult matter."

The drunk man launched into the next verse. "SUCH dancing in the PARlor, there's a waltz for YOOO and I, SUCH mashing in the CORNER, and kisses on the SLYYY." He collapsed into laughter, snorted, and was silent. Probably unconscious.

Grateful for the quiet, Asle said, "My brother seems to have gone missing. We received a letter several months ago, but have heard nothing since."

"That ain't unusual, sir. I go months without hearing from my sister back east. Up to a year, even."

"True, sir, very true. However, this is quite unusual for Andrew. He usually writes to us a few times a week, so even if a letter or two are held up somewhere or lost, we will get multiple letters from him in a month. But we have had nothing in four months."

"OH! BLESSED leisure hour!" The drunk man resumed his song. "That working-people OWNNN."

"Shut that howling, Hemmings," the sergeant bellowed toward the row of cells. He shook his head.

"See here," Asle continued, fishing out Andrew's last missive from his pocket. "His last letter says he has met someone. Perhaps she knows his whereabouts."

"Lemme see," the sergeant said, reaching for the letter. Asle handed it over, and the sergeant read it, muttering the words to himself. "'Fingers crossed that she's all she claims to be. I'm heading to her tonight, sun at my back and hope in my heart.' Well, there you have it." He handed the letter back to Asle, who pocketed it. "He found a woman and decided to stay awhile."

"Perhaps, but why has he not written? The next line says, 'I'll write to you in a week to tell you all about it.'"

"I'd say he's busy doin' other things." The sergeant winked. "You should be happy for him."

The drunk in the cell roused again and revived his favorite verse. "SUCH dancing in the PARlor, there's a waltz for YOOO and I, SUCH mashing in the CORNER, and kisses on the SLYYY."

Asle didn't waste time commenting on the sergeant's suggestive observation. "If my brother has found the right woman he . . . he would want to marry her, and he naturally would invite us to a wedding. Write us of the happy news, at the very least."

"Listen, Mr. Helgelien. Where did that letter come from? Somewhere in Illinois?"

"Indiana."

"Indiana. A whole different state. That is not my jurisdiction, Mr. Helgelien, and I'm not sure what you think I can do about it. You should talk to the authorities in the county where you last heard from your brother. But if you want my advice, you should just relax. There's probably a letter on its way to you right now, bearing glad tidings."

Asle wasn't surprised at the futility of his visit to the precinct station. He stalked the three blocks back to the saloon.

There was only one avenue forward. Asle would have to take matters into his own hands.

28

Robert Brophy had thought things would be easier in America. He wasn't fool enough to believe life would be trouble-free once he and Bridget brought their three children to Chicago, but he hadn't expected the relentless discrimination.

The crowded sidewalks jostled him, the noise and bustle loudest at midday. He continued walking, head down, hands in pockets, the prim voice of the landlady ringing in his ears. "No Irish," she'd said, turning up her nose at the cash in his hand. Sure, she wasn't too good to rent to immigrants newly arrived from England and Wales and even Scotland, but the moment she heard him speak, his money was no good.

His fist curled around the wad of bills in his pocket. Now what? Continue living in the one-room apartment where the eight of them—he and Bridget and their three oldest, plus the three more she'd birthed since they arrived in America three years ago—were crammed in?

The new place on Sacramento Street had three rooms—a living space plus two to sleep in, one for him and Bridget and the baby, and one for the other children. He had scraped together the rent plus a deposit equal to two months' rent, carefully saved over a year, Bridget scrimping with the household budget, making do on next to nothing and taking in extra sewing until she got too ill with this last pregnancy to do it. The midwife said Bridget was lucky to survive that birth. Sweet Jesus, so much blood. They'd had to throw the mattress away and slept with blankets on the bare floor. Even five months later, Bridget was still weaker than she ought to be.

Head full of troubles, Robert rounded a corner down a quieter alley, at the end of which lay the Windy City Horse Car Company barn. The smell of hay and manure was strong, and Robert found it almost soothing. Horses didn't care what kind of English you spoke. And neither did his bosses, as long as he showed up for work and ran his routes on time.

Robert's footfalls echoed against the buildings on either side of the alley. Something niggled at him, but he was still caught up in his worries and didn't realize what it was until he entered the wide doorway of the barn.

The space was almost empty.

There should have been horses in stalls, drivers tromping to work, laughter and talking, the jingle of harnesses. Instead, what Robert had heard as he approached was the clomp of his own boots. "Halloo?" he called.

Fat Farnsby came out of the darkness at the end of the barn. "Who's that? What do you want?"

"It's me, Brophy. I've come for my shift. Where is everybody? The horses?"

"Brophy, right." Fat Farnsby brought his namesake girth over to Robert and said, "We're all done with horses, Brophy. Switching over to motorcars. Less mess, easier to take care of, and faster."

"Oh. That's fine, then. Where d'you keep 'em? My shift is starting now."

"Not necessary. We don't need horsemen anymore."

A cold fist seized Robert's guts. He didn't like the turn this conversation was taking. "You need motorcar drivers, surely?"

"Got 'em," Fat Farnsby said. "With the motorcars moving faster, we expanded the routes. Don't need as many motorcars as we did horse cars. You can g'wan home, Brophy. You're not needed."

"But— I'm— You're saying I'm fired?"

"If you want to put it that way, sure. Sorry, Brophy. We just don't need you. Best of luck to you." Fat Farnsby waddled his bulk back into the shadows.

Robert reeled out of the barn, down the alley, and stumbled into the crowds on the sidewalk. "Watch it, buddy! Get out of the damn way," a man snarled and elbowed by. People pushed past on both sides, jostling him roughly. He shoved his way against the stream to the nearest wall and leaned against it. The tall buildings all around made a tunnel, and the wind whistled through it, cutting through his worn wool coat.

Sweet Mother Mary, what would become of them?

On the street, carriages, buggies, delivery vans, omnibuses, all pulled by horses, fought for space with vehicles powered by motors. When he'd arrived three years ago, transportation was mostly horse-powered. Now it seemed split almost evenly. The transition had happened before his eyes without him noticing it. Before long, it would be all motors.

What would he do? How could he go home to Bridget and explain? No larger apartment, and now no job either. How was he to keep feeding his family?

People on the sidewalk swept by, heedless of Robert's plight. Across the street, on the other side of the sea of traffic, a pub beckoned. He needed a drink to clear his head. Something would come to him.

He pushed through the people to the edge of the sidewalk and sought a break in traffic. Horses drawing a delivery van trotted by, followed by a honking motorcar. Robert darted out behind it, dodging a buggy and another motorcar and two hansom cabs before he made it safely to the other side.

Inside the saloon, it was dark. A fellow played a rolling tune on the piano. Robert didn't know it, but it filled the room in a pleasant way. Two men sat at a table and another read a newspaper at the bar.

"Whiskey," Robert told the bartender and dropped onto a stool. The man on the next stool looked up when he heard Robert's voice, and with a barely concealed sneer, he shifted off his perch and moved to a table, leaving behind his half-read newspaper. Sweet feckin' Jesus. The bartender set down his whiskey and Robert tossed it back. "Another." He sipped the next one slowly and picked up the abandoned newspaper. *Don't mind if I do.* It was folded to the classified ads. He scanned the columns for another apartment, but they were all too expensive or plainly stated "No Irish," "No Poles," or "No Irish, No Poles, No Negroes."

He finished his whiskey and asked for a third. It wasn't as smooth as good Irish whiskey, but it was doing the job. A softness was starting to envelop him. What did it matter he'd lost his job? He'd find another. He ran his finger down the columns. Welder, experienced bricklayer, factory hand. He'd have to learn the first two, and anybody could do the last, but again, there were the words: "No Irish." America was the land of opportunity, they said, but apparently only for some.

He raised his finger at the bartender. "You got money?" the bartender asked.

Robert plucked a bill from his pocket and slapped it on the bar. "Keep 'em coming."

The bartender snatched up the money and poured another whiskey.

"What's this now?" Robert said to himself as he returned to the classifieds. His tongue felt large in his mouth. "Lonely hearts, eh?" He read down the lonely hearts column. "'I would like to correspond with some refined and wealthy lady.'" Wouldn't we all, fella. "'Spinster at home every afternoon age 30, fair complexion medium height. Fond of sports and theater. Would very much like to meet gentleman of leisure. View matrimony.'" Good luck to you, darlin'. "'Comfortable widow, young, with good appearance, seeking partner for 42-acre farm. View to matrimony.'" Wouldn't that be a fine thing. Forty-two acres and a rich widow. Not a care in the world. Land enough to breathe on. No screaming babies, no need for a job. Where was this place?

Robert heaved a sigh and finished his whiskey. He placed the glass on the bar and—steady, now—made his way outside with the newspaper tucked under his arm. He ambled along the avenue, the whiskey's glow leaving him unconcerned by the jostling of those in a hurry to get to their destination. Idle thoughts of life as the pampered husband of a grateful and wealthy widow buoyed his spirits and clouded his reasoning. He paid little attention to the direction his path took him, and when he found himself in front of the newspaper office, thought *Why not?* and pushed through the door.

He told himself he was just curious, only wanted to know where this forty-two acres and rich widow were. The man at the front desk directed him to the classifieds office, and when the man there asked Robert if he wanted him to write down the address, Robert again thought *Why not?* He took the slip of paper and read the name of the town: La Porte, Indiana. "How far away is that, do you suppose?"

The helpful man at the classifieds desk said, "Maybe an hour by train, east of here."

Just an hour away. Imagine that. Forty-two acres and a wealthy widow—of good appearance, no less—only an hour away. He could just see it. Kick back, live the life of Reilly. He pictured himself riding the train out to this place, La Porte, and finding that rich widow. She'd take him in and feed him good beef and smooth Irish whiskey, make sweet love to him every night, and he'd never have to work again.

Aloud to no one in particular, Robert said, "Why not?"

Belle was more than a little put out.

Men didn't just send a telegram stating they'd be arriving that very day. That wasn't how it was done. This one hadn't even signed a name. Really, the nerve of some people.

She filled the teapot with hot water and set it on the tray next to her new china cups and saucers. Decorated with a pattern of yellow and blue flowers, the cups were made of porcelain so thin you could take a bite out of them. The set was perfect for afternoon tea or luncheons, and for dinner service, she had found an elegant, heavy white china with golden rims. All thanks to her brilliant business.

But this was not how her process went. It started with the ad placed in newspapers across the Upper Midwest, precisely worded to appeal to just the right type of man—a wording she had perfected through trial and error over the last several months. After that came the letter-writing campaign, which might take five or six missives spread over a matter of weeks. The correspondence allowed Belle to vet her pool of suitors and control the pace of their interest. She moved them along from curious to interested to eager until finally she selected one—and only one—to visit at a given time.

This process had worked four times now. After Joseph, there was Bruce King, a cobbler from Fort Wayne, shortly before Christmas. Then, soon after, came Kenneth Stegman, a tailor from Saginaw.

She should be preparing for the evening arrival of her next suitor, a well-set-up gentleman from Cheboygan, Michigan. He would be her first since the winter's bad weather had cleared up and allowed travel. She had too much to do to entertain a drop-in from who knows where. Did he even have any money? Belle would have to hustle him along— tea and conversation, and then, "Thank you kindly for dropping by, here's your hat, let me get the door."

It wouldn't do to have two men at once at the house on McClung Road.

Belle sawed through a loaf of bread with rough strokes, then cut each slice into small triangles. She arranged the triangles on a china plate and put it on the tray with little dishes of butter and jam.

She would have put off the man from Cheboygan, but she had developed a fine-tuned sense of when her men were ripe, and this one was a plump strawberry ready for plucking.

And while Bruce and Kenneth had both been wise business decisions, each bringing a reasonable nest egg, the librarians at the University of Chicago hadn't been at all helpful with easing their passing. Cyanide and strychnine were no better than arsenic, she'd learned the hard way. She had a vague memory of reading about a new machine to put down cows without suffering, but the details escaped her. If only she could remember where she'd seen that . . .

When the knock came, Belle opened the door to reveal a man whose appearance was less than awe-inspiring. His clothes were shabby and frayed and his hair a little longer than was fashionable. It was thick and dark brownish-red and sprang out from his head in unruly waves. His beard and mustache followed suit. Belle's ire spiked. His appearance said he didn't have two pennies to rub together.

But there was something about him that captured her attention. A soft, deep brown, his eyes held a sadness that Belle immediately recognized. Take away the man's growth of beard, the well-worn work boots, the beginnings of crow's feet, and his eyes were those of a lost little boy. Here was a man with more on his plate than he could handle. She supposed she could carve out a couple of hours for the fellow.

"Come in, sir," Belle greeted him warmly. "Be welcome in my home."

"Thank ye," he said, with a soft Irish lilt. His eyes widened as he entered the hall. Belle felt a deep pride that her house was finally living up to its promise. The hallway was completely finished. The floors glistened, a fashionable wallpaper with gold fleurs-de-lis on a field of blue hung on the walls, and the grand staircase had been fully repaired. The man's eyes landed on the painting of the home. Instead of contrasting oddly with the ramshackle interior, as it had once done, it matched and enhanced the beauty of the imposing entryway. "What a beautiful home ye have."

"Thank you, sir." Belle installed the man on the sofa in the parlor. She poured him tea and buttered him a corner of bread. "Jam?" she asked, and spread it thickly when he said yes.

"Beautiful country around here," he said, taking a bite of the bread and jam.

"Isn't it, though, Mr. . . . ?"

"Oh, er, apologies. I'm Mr. R— um, George Murphy."

"Well, Mr. R.M. George Murphy, I'm pleased to meet you. My name is Mrs. Belle Gunness. Have you come a long way? Your telegram came from Chicago."

"Aye, Chicago."

"And before that, Ireland, I'm guessing?"

"Aye," he said, shoulders slumping. "Is that a problem?" Heaving a sigh, he downed a swallow of tea and set the cup on its saucer, half rising as if to go.

"Not at all," she said with a reassuring smile. "Your accent is lovely. I, myself, am from Norway. More tea?" She refilled his cup with the steaming liquid. "It's funny how some accents are so pleasing, like yours. And some are so harsh. Take German, for example."

German! That was it! Belle suddenly remembered where she'd read about the livestock slaughtering device. In the newspaper, back in Indianapolis. What was the inventor's name? Heinz? No. Heiss! Dr. Hugo Heiss and his captive bolt pistol.

29

Robert sat back and felt a bit of the tension gathered in his limbs fade away. He wasn't going to be chased off. Imagine that.

A small brass clock ticked on the mantel. Outside, Robert heard birdsong. "I haven't heard birdsong since coming to America." In the city, the noise of carriages and motorcars and a million people working, living, and dying filled the ears day and night. "It's peaceful here. Just like I imagined." Another coil of tension loosened. He took a sip of tea.

"Mr. Murphy, I hope you won't think me too forward for saying so, but you seem a man of a great many cares." Mrs. Gunness encouraged him with a kind smile. She had such a welcoming and expressive face.

Robert hadn't planned to give a fake name. Then again, he hadn't planned any of this. After the newspaper, he'd gone straight to the telegraph office and the train station.

"Ha!" Robert let out a bitter laugh. "You could say so, Mrs. Gunness, you could say so."

"Well, they say there's nothing a hot cup of tea won't make better," she said. "So sit back and relax for a moment."

The smile she gave him was so warm, and her eyes met his unflinchingly. Robert felt that she saw him, Robert. Not the nameless horse car driver, not Bridget's husband, not the lousy Irish not good enough to rent to. Just Robert. He felt understood, not judged. He told her about arriving at the stable that morning to find his job had disappeared, about being turned away from the new apartment, cash in pocket.

She listened quietly, her eyes never leaving his, encouraging him with small murmurings of understanding and occasional questions. "Didn't it worry you to walk around the city with so much money in your pocket? I hope you put it right back in the bank."

"Sure, I should have. But it's still right here"—he patted his right hip—"every cent I have."

"I see," she said.

She rose to light some lamps. It had begun to get dark, and Robert realized he had stayed far longer than he had intended. He only wanted to take a peek into a life so alien to his own. Just to try it on for an afternoon. "I should be getting along," he said, rising off the sofa. "You've been gracious with your hospitality."

Mrs. Gunness showed him out, saying, "It has been a delight spending time with you this afternoon, Mr. Murphy." Just as she reached for the door, a banging came from the other side, causing the lady to startle. "Goodness, who could that be at this hour?" When she opened the door, a scrawny fellow hovered on the porch. "Ray! I wasn't expecting you."

"Sorry, Miz Belle. You got a telegram. I was in town and the telegraph operator asked me to bring it out to you."

"Thank you, Ray," she said, sliding her thumb under the envelope flap. "Excuse me just a minute, Mr. Murphy."

Belle gripped the rectangle of paper and reread the words from her suitor from Cheboygan, incredulous at his message: "Darling regret to say can't come. Collarbone broken horse threw me. Letter with details forthcoming."

That infernal man! What was he doing riding horses when he was supposed to be coming to her? Such foolish thoughtlessness. Did he have no respect for her, for her time? All that effort put into grooming him to be her next husband, all gone in a tumble from a horse. And now what? Her next candidate was at least another two weeks away from being ready for the final push. Fury crackled in her heart while Mr. Murphy hovered at her elbow and Ray dithered on the porch.

Why did Ray always have to look at her like that, like a whipped dog, always seeking approval and attention. Why couldn't she have a business partner who was as strong and smart as she was? Why must men always be such a disappointment?

The telegram in her hands suddenly spread into a great, flapping sail that wrapped Ray up like a mummy, his muffled cries as real to her as the clothes on her back. The telegram squeezed Ray ever tighter, crushing him into silence—until Mr. Murphy's words about the money in his pocket came back to her: "every cent I had," several months of Chicago rent.

Her fury evaporated and her vision with it, leaving cold, clear logic in its wake. While the sum wasn't enough to qualify a correspondent to move ahead in her process, considering it had walked up to her door and laid itself at her feet, she would happily take it. What had at first seemed a terrible inconvenience was suddenly a stroke of good fortune.

If Robert didn't know any better, the telegram had made Mrs. Gunness very angry. The look that flashed over her face reminded him of the one his mam used to get when his da crossed her. It sent a chill right down Robert's spine and made him glad he was on his way out. But as quickly as it came, it was gone again. It disappeared so completely, in fact, Robert wondered if he'd really seen it at all. Because in the next instant, she smiled sweetly at the man on the doorstep, thanked him, and closed the door.

Then, linking her arm in Robert's and drawing him back to the parlor, she said, "You know, Mr. Murphy, you've had a long and difficult day, and it's too late to head back now. Why don't you stay the night? I have a guest room all made up. Have a good night's sleep, and tomorrow you can look at your troubles with a fresh eye."

A good night's sleep. He hadn't had one of those in a decade. What would be the harm in staying one night?

There was a ruckus going on when Robert woke up. The sun was high, judging by the amount of light coming into his room. He rolled over in the sheets. So clean and white, they were. And he was clean too. Mrs. Gunness had shown him the bathtub in her water closet and set the taps running with steaming hot water. She'd left him in there with lavender soap and a stack of freshly laundered towels. "Don't come out until you're good and ready," she told him. When he came down more than an hour later, smelling of lavender, she'd fed him a beef stew and sent him to bed. He'd fallen into a sleep so deep and dreamless, he felt he was waking from the dead.

She'd left a pile of clothes for him, neatly folded on the seat of the rocking chair in the corner. A shirt and trousers, even underclothes. Everything clean and fresh and in good condition. His own clothes were nowhere to be seen.

He dressed slowly. The suit was quality, better than any set of clothes he'd owned, and fit him fairly well in length. But the girth of the trousers was such that he had to cinch up the belt, and the suit jacket gaped around his middle. Feeling like a boy dressing up in his father's clothes, Robert found his way downstairs.

Mrs. Gunness was out front, standing next to the man who'd brought the telegram the day before. He was a scrawny fellow, with ropy arms and a diffident air. In the driveway, a wagoner was backing up to the house. He cursed at his two teams of powerful Belgian workhorses. The wagon, filled high with crushed stone, heaved slowly to a stop.

"Ray, tell him to drop the load in a few piles," Mrs. Gunness said. "It will make it easier for you to rake it out."

"You want any stone goin' over to the carriage barn?"

"What do you think? We probably ought to. I don't know if I ordered enough."

The scrawny man consulted with the wagon driver.

Robert approached his hostess. "Good morning to you, Mrs. Gunness."

"Good morning, Mr. Murphy! Don't you look refreshed."

"Yes, ma'am. Slept like the dead in that fine bed of yours. Thank you again for your hospitality. And these clothes. It'll be a shame to put my own back on when it's time for me to leave."

"Oh, you won't be putting those clothes back on. I burnt them. Don't fret, now. That suit is yours to keep." She examined him from top to toe. "It fits you quite well, if a bit loose in the middle. It belonged to my husband, may he rest in peace."

A twinge of something like guilt nibbled at Robert's conscience. How would he explain the clothes to Bridget? How would he explain any of this? *Think about it later*, he told himself.

"What's going on here?" he asked.

"I'm adding a layer of crushed stone to my driveway. Every time it rains, it turns to mud."

The scrawny man finished his consultation with the wagon driver and came over to Mrs. Gunness. Robert gave him a friendly nod that was ignored. Odd fellow.

"Driver says you ain't got enough for anything more than the driveway."

"That's fine, then," Mrs. Gunness said. "I'll have to order another load. Ray, this is Mr. Murphy." To Robert, she said, "Ray is my handyman."

"Pleased to see you again," Robert said. "That was you that brought the telegram last night, wasn't it?" Ray just nodded. Not too friendly at all.

"You need some help raking?" Robert offered. "I could man a shovel for a couple hours before I have to go."

"I won't hear of it," said Mrs. Gunness, just as Ray said with surprising enthusiasm, "You ain't stayin'?"

Robert looked from one to the other, perplexed at their different responses. "I have to get back home. But I don't mind swinging a shovel for a time."

"You are a prince among men, George Murphy, to offer to help. But I won't hear of it." Mrs. Gunness took his arm in hers and drew him toward the house and into the kitchen, where the cook stove had the room toasty warm and the smell of fresh-baked bread filled the air. "You work hard enough in Chicago. No need to wear yourself out here. On my honor, as long as you are here with me, you will not lift a finger."

She pushed him to a seat at the kitchen table and began to set a spread. She cracked three eggs into a pan on the stove, and while they sizzled, she poured him a cup of hot coffee, then carved several generous slices off the fresh loaf cooling on a breadboard. The eggs went onto a plate next to the bread, which she brought him with a pitcher of cream and dishes of butter and jam.

"Now," she said. "Eat."

Robert ate. The food was delicious and plentiful. Might as well enjoy it. And then take the train home both well-rested and with a full stomach.

Belle settled Mr. Murphy at the kitchen table with breakfast and excused herself. "If you don't mind, I have a little correspondence to attend to. I'll be in the library."

"That's fine, then," he said, wiping his fingers on the linen napkin by his plate.

Belle was feeling quite chipper about how things had turned out. Her plan to place her ad in so many papers had paid off in Mr. Murphy arriving just in the nick of time. And dear, loyal Ray, who thought nothing of bringing her that telegram, so that she received it right away. Imagine if it had come after she had dismissed Mr. Murphy!

Yes, everything was going her way, and she couldn't be more pleased. With Mr. Murphy's money already in hand and his clear desire to relax and do absolutely nothing, she probably wouldn't even have to bother marrying him.

Belle unlocked her rolltop desk and took pen to paper. She wrote a careful letter to Dr. Heiss, explaining her need for his invention as the proprietress of a small abattoir in Indiana and due to the difficulty of finding good help. "More than one beeve has endured a grisly, painful death due to the incompetence of my hires. A poleax in the hands of a neophyte is a recipe for tragedy. I need a modern, efficient tool that will terminate the animal reliably, with little to no distress to the animal." Would he send her a prototype of his invention, she asked and promised to relay to him her experiences using it in the field in order to further his research. "Sincerely yours, Mrs. Belle Gunness," she finished.

She sealed the envelope and addressed it to Dr. Hugo Heiss, care of the University of Berlin in Germany. Now, if Dr. Heiss agreed to send her what she asked for, her future husbands would be granted a much kinder end.

Somehow, morning came and went, and Robert stayed. The hours slid by, talking with Mrs. Gunness, who listened to him in a way no person ever had in his life. She didn't offer advice or judgment but simply listened. She listened to not only his words but what went unspoken as well. He found himself telling her things he'd never told anyone, not even Bridget, the dreams he'd had as a young man in Ireland, imagining a life of plenty in America. Dreams that seemed foolish and naive to him now.

At midday, she coaxed him into taking a picnic with her into the fields behind the house. She packed a basket, and he carried a blanket. They sat next to a small brook that crossed her land. It was chilly, but the air was fresh and clean. So different from the thick, dirty air in

Chicago. They ate sandwiches of thick slices of ham on her good bread and drank a bottle of wine she'd tucked in the basket. He lounged with his head in her lap and dozed while she stroked his forehead. When he woke, she was gazing down at him with a little, secret smile.

He wished he could stay there forever.

As if reading his thoughts, she said, "I wish you could stay here with me." She leaned down and tenderly kissed his forehead, and he sighed with utter contentment.

Robert again spent the night. The next day got away from him, too, dozing and talking with Belle—she asked him to call her by her first name—and in the evening, as he got between the fresh sheets on the bed Belle called his, he promised himself he'd leave the next day. But another morning came and brought with it more hours of conversation, rest, wholesome food, and fresh air.

Three days passed, and Robert remained at the house on McClung Road.

Asle set down his bag and wrapped his arms around his boys. Crowds of restless travelers swarmed the station platform as a massive locomotive steamed to a stop. A conductor disembarked and bellowed down the length of the platform, "Gary, Michigan City, and South Bend! All aboard!"

"That's me, I'd better go." He pulled his boys closer. Harry, the oldest, stiffened and backed away, embarrassed by the display of affection. But Gordon, his sweet middle child, buried his face against his father's coat. "It's all right, son. I'll be back before you know I'm gone."

"You said we could play baseball together." Gordon's words were muffled by the wool coat he pressed into, as if to keep Asle fixed in place.

"I said it and I meant it, Gordon." Asle cupped Gordon's chin and tilted his face up. "I'll be back, and we'll play. That's a promise." Gordon's eyes shone with barely held back tears. He nodded once.

"What about me?" Christina, ever impetuous, fists on hips, glared at her brother, impatient for her share of attention.

"Come here, my girl, and let me kiss you before I go." Christina ran to him, jumping into his outstretched arms, and Asle swung her in circles until she giggled. He bussed the plump apple of her cheek and held her close. It was impossible to say how much he would miss these three small people.

Finally setting his daughter down, Asle turned to his wife. "You're sure you'll be all right? We can hire someone to search and I can stay."

"No, no. You go." Matilda stood there, strong and beautiful, unfazed at the prospect of running a home and a business while her husband went off on what could be a wild goose chase. "You know you won't be satisfied unless you do it yourself. Besides, it's much cheaper to pay Lars to help me at the bar than to hire a detective. I'll be fine. The children will be fine. The bar will be fine."

Asle, mute with gratitude and love and already missing her terribly, hugged Matilda close.

"Now go," Matilda said. "Before the train leaves without you."

She tipped her head down so he could kiss her forehead. Asle retrieved his bag and made for the train, where he found a seat on the station side and peered out the window. He waved at his family until they saw him and waved back. The train screamed and chugged and swayed out of the station, Asle still waving while his family receded from view.

30

obert was in an alternate universe. The world he'd known before was dark, strict, narrow, and disapproving. He'd worked and worked and never got any respect. He couldn't rent an apartment just because of how he spoke English. He loved his children, but they were anchors on his feet as he tried to keep his head above water.

Here, he felt he'd woken from a nightmare into a world of light and color, of cleanness and hope and freedom. Here, he was George, single, childless, and free to do as he pleased. He could breathe.

So when he announced he would take a late morning nap and Belle followed him upstairs to his bedroom, he found himself debating whether it was a sin to have sex with her. For the Robert from the old, dark, disapproving world, the answer was definitely yes. But for George, in this new world of hope and pleasure and freedom, sex with Belle was only natural.

He needed only fertilize his carrot with the same confidence, but it seemed content to stay buried in its garden. Perhaps because it knew all too well its own power. How many children had it already produced? And both he and the carrot wanted not a one more, thank you very much.

"Here, sit," Belle said, guiding him to the edge of the bed. She knelt in front of him and began unlacing his boots. Robert hadn't had to take off his own shoes in days. As she pulled off the first boot, she looked up coyly. "George, I suspect you won't be heartbroken if I confess to you that I'm barren."

Desire flared in him, and his carrot reared up out of its garden, growing hard as a rock in the Giant's Causeway.

Belle grinned when she saw his pants bulging. "Hello there." She gave him a playful shove, and he fell back on the bed. "Don't move. Remember, I said you'd never have to lift a finger as long as you live here."

First, she removed her clothing. Next, she removed his, piece by piece, tossing his shirt, his trousers, his underclothes toward the rocking chair.

Finally, they were naked together. Belle's curves were soft—soft and warm and strong. Kissing his bare chest, she murmured sweet nonsense against his skin. As promised, she brought their union to consummation without Robert having to lift a finger. He climaxed with an explosion of blissful intensity.

When it was over, and they lay side by side, out of breath, she said, "I love you, George."

Without hesitation, he replied, "I love you, Belle."

He'd found a happiness he didn't know existed. *I'm George now.* He vowed never to leave this house, this life.

The fire in the library hearth was getting low and the chill of March was creeping back into the room, but George was so comfortable in his armchair, he didn't want to stir. Just then, Belle swept in, bearing a steaming cup of tea. She set it on the table at George's elbow.

"Are you comfortable?" she asked as she built up the fire so it roared and crackled. She lifted George's feet onto a small hassock. *How do you like that?* He didn't even have to lift his own feet. George was swaddled in comfort, his every need taken care of from morning till night. What had he done to deserve this heaven on earth? He didn't know, but he'd take it.

"Perfectly, thank you, my dear," he said.

"George, the day you came, you mentioned the cash you were carrying." Belle lifted his feet and settled them on her lap as she sank onto the hassock. As she spoke, she stroked and kneaded the arch of one foot and then the other. Heaven. "Before I burnt your clothes, I found that money in the pocket of your trousers. It's quite a sum. I think it's best if I take it to the bank for safekeeping."

"Mm-hmm," George sighed, contentment flowing up through her gentle fingers, from his soles to his ankles and legs, up his torso and down his arms to his own fingertips. Soon a deep languor pervaded his whole body. It made no difference to him where she put the money. What need did he have of it?

"I won't say that anyone around here is not to be trusted," she continued. "But you can never tell about some people."

George thought he understood Belle perfectly. She was too polite and kind to come right out and say that Ray might pilfer the money. But he was the only other person on the property, so who else could she be referring to?

"All right," he agreed amiably. Money was superfluous in his life as George.

Belle rose, gently resting his feet back on the hassock, and kissed his cheek. "I'll be off, then. You have a restful afternoon."

Once Belle had gone, George stretched his toes toward the fire and nestled into the cozy wing chair. The heat soaked into his toes, his feet, and upward, making him almost hot. He welcomed the sensation, so different from the perpetual cold discomfort of winters in Chicago. He would sit by the fire and leisurely drink the tea Belle made for him. Perhaps later, he would take a turn around the house. Or not, as he liked. He picked up the teacup and blew on the steaming liquid before taking a sip. A very good mint blend. He would have to compliment Belle.

Ah, Belle. She cooked his favorite foods and glowed with health and good humor, greeting him always with warmth. He couldn't help but compare her to Bridget, who was forever pale and tired and in a low mood. How much more pleasant life was with a woman who had roses in her cheeks and put them to good use with a smile. He'd had more joy in his three days with Belle than in all the years with Bridget.

From time to time, he heard the whisper of guilt, scolding him for abandoning his family, but he turned a deaf ear to it.

George awoke, feeling a slight peckishness, and wondered where Belle was with his afternoon tea. She usually brought a biscuit or a slice of her good soda bread before he even knew he wanted it. He went in search and found her in the kitchen.

"Hello there!" she sang out. "I was just about to come find you. I have your tea here. And a slice of bread. I made a fresh loaf this morning. I hope you like it. Raspberry or strawberry preserves today, George?"

"I'm of a mind to have raspberry today, my dear." George pulled a chair up to the kitchen worktable. She passed him a plate with two pieces of bread thickly slathered with butter and jam.

"And your tea," she said, setting the cup and saucer next to the plate.

The bread and jam was delicious. Belle was a fine hand in the kitchen, no question about it. He washed the bread down with a sip of tea and winced at the sharp flavor. "A bit bitter today, isn't it, my dear?"

"Oh, is it? Did I forget to put the sugar in?" She passed him a sugar bowl and a spoon.

He ladled in two heaping spoonfuls and stirred. "That's better."

Belle pulled up another chair and sat across the table from him.

"Isn't it time to begin making dinner?" George asked, surprised to see her sitting down. He wondered what kind of feast she had planned. Every night was something wonderful. Last night was a roast beef, with potatoes roasted in its juices, crispy on the outside and perfectly tender on the inside. Creamed corn, fresh bread with butter, and gherkins rounded out the meal. And apples baked with cream for dessert. His mouth watered in anticipation of what tonight's meal could be.

"In a bit," she said.

There's nothing a little rest won't cure, and George was living proof. Belle glowed with the satisfaction of it as she sat across from him at the kitchen worktable. When he'd arrived, he was shrunken inside himself, thoroughly bound up and burdened by his worries. It was as if his very soul was in a cage. And now look at him. Shoulder to shoulder, he was a straight line, not the bowed wretch he had been when he came to her. He had filled out, although Charles's old suit still hung on him, and his face bloomed with good health.

She beamed at her newest client, and he grinned back around a mouthful of bread and jam. He washed it down with the last sip of tea. She was as proud of what she'd accomplished with George as any business owner could be. She came around the table to his side and kissed the top of his head. "Are you happy, George, my dear?" She already knew the answer, of course. They wouldn't be at this stage of her process if she didn't.

He wrapped an arm around her hips and squeezed. "Couldn't be happier, my dear."

"That's good, then." George's arm on her hip tightened suddenly, jerking her closer. "That's a bit tight, George."

His arm dropped away. "Unngh," he groaned. His arms and legs and even the muscles of his face and neck began to twitch uncontrollably. Suddenly, a massive spasm gripped him. His arms went rigid, and his hands froze into claws. His legs jerked against the chair legs.

"Oh, George!" Belle exclaimed. He was experiencing convulsions just like Andrew. Dammit!

His muscles loosened, and he sagged in the chair, groaning and panting. But before he could say anything, another spasm seized his body. His legs and arms strained. The muscles in his neck corded, and his jaw clenched.

"George!" Belle cried, alarmed by his obvious pain. "Does it hurt?"

His eyes were wild in his frozen face, and his teeth ground together, making a terrible noise. When the attack passed, he slumped down and let out a sob. "God Almighty," he said. "What is happening to—" His words were cut off by another seizure, the worst so far. His entire body froze, every muscle clenched tight, a grimace of agony etched onto his face.

This wasn't at all what Belle had wanted for George. She had created for him a sanctuary of rest and peace, and she wanted that for his end as well. She hated to see him like this, frozen in agony. But what could she do? She cast about, desperate for a solution, a way to end his suffering.

Bang! Bang! Bang! A thundering knock echoed down the hallway from the front door.

Belle froze. Could it be Ray? He didn't usually knock like that. His knock was a timid tap, followed by a shy "hello?" as he entered.

Bang! Bang! Bang!

Belle's eyes darted wildly, as George was gripped by another seizure, trapped in place by ever-tightening muscles. The grinding of his teeth was like rock grating against rock. If only she had Dr. Heiss's captive bolt pistol! Her frantic search landed on the heavy meat grinder in the hutch. She heaved it off the shelf and raised it as high as she could, then dropped it on George's head. The grinder smashed into his skull, knocking him out of the chair. As he crumpled to the floor, his muscles relaxed, and he lay quietly, serene and at peace at last.

Bang! Bang! Bang! The knocks were followed by muffled shouting, "Mrs. Gunness? You in there? It's Deputy Hofstetter."

Terror swamped Belle. She had a dead man on her floor and a man of the law at her front door. Ray was nowhere close by, unable to help her move the body. She felt as frozen as George had been moments ago.

But then a strange calm descended on her. With measured steps, she moved around George's body to where the hutch rested atop the buffet, a separate and unattached piece. One tug set it teetering, the dishes shifting as if on a storm-tossed ship. Another tug sent the thing on a long arc to the floor, dishes crashing and wood splintering over George's limp form. Only his stocking feet were visible.

Belle smoothed back her hair and calmly exited the kitchen. She swung the front door wide to find Little Jimmy on her porch, hat in hand. She greeted her unwelcome guest with a composed smile. "Good afternoon, Deputy Hofstetter. What an unexpected pleasure."

"Afternoon, Mrs. Gunness," he said, giving her a polite bow. He peered past her, eyeing the foyer and stairs, craning his neck to see farther into the house. "Everything all right in here? I thought I heard a crash."

"A crash?" Belle repeated, thinking fast. "Probably Ray. He's around here somewhere, working."

"I see," Little Jimmy said. To Belle's relief, he accepted her explanation without question. With brusque officiousness, he went on, "The reason I dropped by is we've gotten some reports of strange activity here. I wanted to check that you are all right. Safe and sound."

"Strange activity? What do you mean?"

"Oh, it's probably nothing. Your neighbor, Hank Philips, came to see me. He's one you might say always has something to complain about. Claims he's seen lights at night. A lantern in your yard, maybe some digging. Ol' Hank, he sure has a wild imagination. But I thought I'd come on by and check that all your livestock are accounted for." Deputy Hofstetter filled her doorway, a gentle and somewhat dim giant.

"Why, Deputy, aren't you the kindest man." Belle smiled up at him under her lashes and was rewarded with a blush. "I feel so much safer knowing you are looking out for me. But I can assure you, all my hogs are accounted for, and no one has been digging in my yard. Day or night."

***

Jimmy didn't put much stock in old Mr. Philips's claims of midnight digging. In fact, his questions belied his true intention: he was still as lovestruck as the day he met Belle Sorenson. He'd been crushed when she married that music tycoon. When the man passed, Jimmy wanted to give Mrs. Gunness time to grieve. After that, it had taken him a while to screw up the courage to visit her. When he finally did, it occurred to him he could use Mr. Philips's complaints as an excuse to come by, even if they were a few months old.

Now that he was here, he wasn't about to be turned away. He'd heard from men who'd worked for her what a fine cook she was. Maybe she had something good in the kitchen. "I'll just take a little look around," he said. "Just to be on the safe side."

He strode down the hallway toward the kitchen, but Mrs. Gunness scurried past and came to an abrupt halt in front of the kitchen door. She leaned casually on one arm against the door frame, blocking his entry. What was she doing?

"Don't be silly, Deputy. You think I have a nighttime digger hiding in my kitchen?"

"Ha ha," Jimmy laughed. Suddenly very curious, he gently shifted her aside and pushed open the door. Feet stuck out from under a mess of broken shelving. "What in the . . . ?" He turned to Mrs. Gunness. "What's going on here?"

She grabbed the knob and yanked the door shut again, then heaved a sigh, leaning toward him. Her breasts brushed against Jimmy's arm. He froze.

"I'm so embarrassed. You've caught me in a little fib, Deputy. The truth is, Ray is not working, and this is the crash you heard. And now you know my burden. Poor Ray. I've tried to help him. He's a good man, you know. But he can't hold his liquor." She sighed again, and her bosom expanded.

He didn't mean to, but he couldn't help it—his eyes dropped to her breasts. Gosh all Friday. He tried to look away, but every breath she took drew his eyes back.

"Now, Deputy, you watch those eyes." Mrs. Gunness laughed, winking and batting his shoulder.

"Um, er." *Stop stuttering, you fool.* He forced his eyes back to her face.

Before he knew it, she was ushering him out the front door. "I hope you won't spread any tales of what you've seen here today. We should pray for Ray, not judge him. Don't you agree?"

"Yes, ma'am." Jimmy nodded, more deeply in love with Mrs. Gunness than he'd been when he arrived. What a kind and understanding woman. He should ask her if he could court her. "Mrs. Gunness, I—" The door closed in his face.

Jimmy looked at the slab of wood. He looked at the porch floor. He set his hat back on his head. Descending the steps, he saw Ray Lamphere far across the yard, raking stones on the path to the carriage barn. Jimmy waved.

He untied his horse from the railing. Guiding his mount back to the road, Jimmy made himself a promise. Next time, he would ask her.

Belle watched out the parlor window as Little Jimmy rode away. Once he was gone from view, she went outside and crossed the yard to where Ray was evening out the load of stone for the carriage driveway.

"Let's go, Ray," she called to him. "Work to do."

31

Asle arrived at the crossroads just as a man was locking up its only building. Black-painted letters over the entrance, spelling out POST OFFICE, gave him hope he'd found the right place. "Ho there, sir," called Asle, dismounting his horse and holding the reins in one hand. "May I trouble you for some information?"

"If I got it, I'll share it," the man replied. "Come on inside." He unlocked the door and beckoned Asle to follow.

Asle tied his mount to the horse rail in front of the building. The nondescript gray mare was turning out to be a good purchase. He didn't need a fast horse, he'd told the trader in Portage. He needed a sturdy one, able to walk all day for days at a time. After some discussion, Asle settled on a mare with strong legs and a placid eye, called Jenny.

"My name is Asle Helgelien. I hope I've found the right place. Is this Farbut?"

"If Farbut is the place you're looking for, you've found it," the postmaster said as he took his place behind the counter. He was tall and slender with blond looks that marked him as a fellow Norwegian.

"I'm searching for my brother, Andrew. I have reason to believe he mailed a letter from here last fall."

"Helgelien, you say? We don't have any Helgeliens hereabouts."

"No, he's not a local. He's a traveling salesman. You might have seen his wagon. Black, with gold letters saying W.T. Raleigh Company. He's a little taller than me, with darker hair that he combs back. Wears a black suit with a patterned waistcoat."

"That's ringing a bell, just give me a minute to think." The postmaster leaned his elbows on the counter and scratched his jaw thoughtfully. "He came through here last fall, you say?"

"Yes, in November." Asle took off his hat and wiped his forehead. He'd been riding since dawn, stopping only when nature forced him to relieve his bladder. Jenny was proving to be healthy and strong and content to walk as long as Asle required.

He was well aware this was the easy part of his search. He knew Andrew's letter came from this tiny post office, and getting here took only an hour on the train and a day's ride. And a night at the cheapest hotel he could find. And the purchase of a horse. But still, this was the easy part because it was known. From here on out, he would have to discover everything for himself—which direction Andrew went, which roads he took, where he was going, and to whom. Unless this postmaster remembered Andrew and knew where he'd headed from here. The postmaster was tapping the counter, staring off into space. Asle gave him the time he needed. Hurrying a man while he was thinking never paid off.

The postmaster straightened suddenly and brightened. "Say, did he get married?"

"Not that I am aware," Asle said. "What do you know of it? You remember Andrew?"

"Oh, he came through here last fall, like you say. Never seen him come through here before, but I remember thinking he was a fine fellow. He was floating on air and love. Saying he was going to meet the love of his life. We toasted his good news with my aquavit. I figured you were here for the wedding."

"No, we haven't heard from Andrew since the letter he sent from this post office. I'm trying to find him. Do you know which way he went?" Asle asked the question even though the moment he'd heard the man say "aquavit" he knew what answer he'd get.

"Sorry, no. We were pretty deep in the aquavit when he left. He could've flown to the moon and I wouldn't remember."

Jenny waited patiently at the horse rail as Asle reached in his pocket and found one of Andrew's sweets, unwrapped it, and held it out to the mare. Her soft muzzle brushed his palm as she lipped it up. Asle unwrapped another and popped it in his own mouth. He barely noticed the mellow warmth of molasses, so lost was he in his thoughts.

Did Andrew fly to the moon? If anyone could, he could. Asle's little brother had always been prone to flights of fancy. His imagination and wanderlust could not be contained by one small town. Asle couldn't remember when he and Andrew began to talk about leaving Norway behind and going to America. It was something they always knew they would do.

Asle stroked the horse's nose, and she nuzzled into him, snuffling for another treat. "That's enough now, girl. We have to make them last. Which way should we go?" Asle surveyed his surroundings. There were four choices at the crossroads: north toward Lake Michigan, south deeper into Illinois, west into the setting sun, or east toward South Bend. Asle sighted down each road. He had no way of knowing which route Andrew had taken.

He had to put himself in Andrew's shoes. God knew, his shoes were plenty big enough. His little brother had more charisma than he knew what to do with, but Lord above, the man had huge feet. Huge, and ugly. Asle chuckled, remembering the way he teased Andrew about his unsightly trotters. Then he shook himself. Think. Which way?

The postmaster exiting the post office drew Asle's attention back to the little building. The lowering sun warmed his back and glinted off the window, sending a bright shaft of light into his eye. Blinking against the glare, Asle was struck dumb.

What was it Andrew had written in his letter? "I'm heading to her tonight, sun at my back and hope in my heart." Asle spun around and squinted at the setting sun. "The sun at my back," he said, a slight grin overtaking his features.

With a gentle word to Jenny, Asle put the sun behind him and set off east, toward South Bend.

Belle lifted her face to the morning breeze as her sweet little mare, Gwen, trip-trapped along the road to town. It was chilly but with a hint of spring, and the wind carried the scent of fresh earth and growing things beginning to wake up. Belle tried to match her mood to spring's hopeful return. She had so many reasons to be cheerful, after all. The house was reborn into its proper glory, she had her right-hand man, Ray, to keep it that way, and she had found an ingenious way to bring in the oil that kept it all running smoothly: money.

And yet. Her recent business transaction had been a bit of a bust. With the man from Cheboygan abandoning her at the last minute, George had made a better-than-nothing replacement. But the money from that deal had been far below her usual fee, and there had been the loss of the dishes, crockery, and sideboard to boot. In her shopping basket, she had an order to Sears and Roebuck to replace much of what she'd lost, and the rest she could get in town today. But the truth was, when Belle tallied up the debits and credits of this deal, she'd barely broken even.

And then there was Ray's moping. The look he'd given her when he handed her up into the gig that morning was questioning. Belle knew what he wanted to know. When would she come back to his bed? With her pressing schedule these last weeks, Belle had barely had time to visit Ray at all. So many details to attend to when running a business. She'd have to remember to throw Ray a bone. Keeping him happy was an important factor in her path to success.

As she neared town, the road became busier, and Belle waved to a farmer in his hay wagon and then a lady driving a small gig like her own. The lady gave her a respectful nod that reminded Belle she was still a well-regarded woman in town. Don't forget, she told herself, many businesses suffer setbacks. What determines success isn't the setback, but the response to it. A savvy businesswoman will find a way.

In town, she left Gwen and her gig with Gabriel at the livery stable. She visited with him briefly. Despite his exaggerated manner, his fawning praise was always a balm to her.

At the post office she posted her Sears and Roebuck order and collected her mail, and then stopped at Fischer Mercantile. Saving the best for last, she dropped in to see Della Rose. Her dressmaker friend always lifted her spirits, as she was the only one who understood Belle's drive to be an independent woman.

And Della Rose was the only person who had any inkling about Belle's men—some of them, anyway. Belle had told Della Rose about her great uncle Joseph passing away, and when they had spent time together at Christmas, Belle mentioned marrying Bruce, but it seemed wiser to say he had left her. She'd stayed mum about Kenneth, and probably wouldn't bring up George either.

A customer carrying bundles wrapped in brown paper bustled out of the shop, nearly bowling Belle over in the doorway. When she saw who she'd bumped into, she retreated into the shop. "Oh goodness me! I'm so sorry, Mrs. Gunness. Please, come in, come in. How clumsy of me, nearly knocking over La Porte's dear Mrs. Gunness."

Nodding regally, Belle processed into the shop. The woman's admiration settled on her shoulders like an ermine robe. *As it should be.*

"Good morning, my dear Belle," Della Rose welcomed her as she came through the door. "Will you have tea with me?"

"I'd be delighted. And then I have a number of dresses I'd like to order. Perhaps even a bicycling suit."

The back room was homey in its busy, overstuffed way. It was much the same as the last time Belle had been there. Fabric pooled around sewing machines, in various stages of progress toward becoming clothing. Della Rose's assistant huddled over an embroidery hoop, stitching an intricate pattern of twining vines. She darted looks to Belle and blushed when Belle caught her eye.

"Carrie, take that to the other room. My guest and I will have some tea and privacy." Della Rose watched the younger woman gather her things and exit. When the door closed behind her, Della Rose leaned an ear against it. Apparently satisfied, she joined Belle at the small table.

"Eavesdropper, is she?" Belle asked.

"Naturally. Her little life is so dull. How else is she to find entertainment?" Della Rose poured them both some tea. "How have you been keeping? Did the frosty winter help distract you from the shock of having your man run off like that, and so sudden?"

"Oh, yes, I'm fine. One moves on." Belle busied herself removing her gloves and the fur-trimmed velvet cape she'd worn against the morning's chill.

"Ah. I see. Perhaps he was not the great love? Perhaps you had other reasons to marry him?"

Fingering the soft fur of her cape, Belle said, "I wouldn't say I didn't love him." Della Rose made no reply, merely fixed her gaze on Belle. Her expression held the wisdom of a woman who knew what it was like to be married and then not, who knew how to take care of herself. A woman like Belle. "All right, yes. I didn't marry him for love. I married him for money. Fortunately, I made provisions for my own security before he up and left."

"Oh?" Della Rose's eyebrows lifted in curiosity.

"Of course." Belle let Della Rose take her cape and gloves. "You think me greedy? A mercenary? Yes. I married for money. But I wouldn't marry just *anyone*, Della Rose. There needs to be something, some need that I can help a man with. It's a transaction, almost a contract. He is lacking joy or desperately lonely or needing care or a respite. And I give that to him. He gives me his money, yes, but not for nothing. I give a man the one thing he needs that he has never—*could* never—get anywhere else, from anyone else."

Della Rose tipped her head to one side and eyed Belle with a new curiosity. Admiration even. "I didn't realize," she said slowly. "You are a woman of commerce."

Quietly, Belle said, "And they all leave me. Every last one. Men cannot be trusted."

"Quite a run of bad luck," Della Rose replied, and her tone held a faint note of skepticism. But when she searched her face, Belle saw nothing more than concern. "Well, my dear Belle, this is not news, what you are telling me. Saying men cannot be trusted is the same as saying water is wet or the French are a superior race."

"You were married once, weren't you?"

"You could say that. And once was enough. Take my advice and remain a widow. Keep your freedom."

Easy for Della Rose to say. She knew as well as Belle that money means freedom, but she had a skill, an occupation to support her. Belle had her wits and business savvy. She didn't mention to Della Rose that her pipeline of suitors was full and she had no intention of ending her trade. She had found an occupation that meant security, and she intended to carry on.

32

*E*verything was about to change.

Belle worked Gwen up to a lather getting back home from the post office. She reined the mare to a halt in front of her door and hollered to Ray to unload the gig. She grabbed the box from Dr. Heiss and was about to rush it to her desk in the library but stopped. Ray was happiest and worked best when she paid him attention, and here was a perfect opportunity. She set the box down again, forcing herself into patience.

"Ray!" she called again, shifting from foot to foot until he came out of the house.

"Is something wrong?" he asked, wearing a worried frown. "Gwen all right? Those new shoes giving her trouble?"

"No, everything is fine. I need help unloading, that's all." She greeted him with a kiss, wrapping her arms around him. He resisted at first, stiff and unresponsive. "I've missed our nights together, Ray," she whispered against his ear. She felt the moment he gave in. Tension in his shoulders eased and his arms encircled her, drawing her close. He nuzzled her neck, making a line of kisses from her ear to the collar of her dress. "Mmm," Belle mumbled. "You know how to make me feel good, Ray." It did feel wonderful, Ray's lips on her skin, his hands molding her body to his. But her focus remained on the package from

Dr. Heiss. She couldn't wait to open it and finally examine this amazing contraption. Had she given Ray enough attention yet?

Ray stiffened and pulled away. "You're distracted," he said. "I don't want to keep you."

Belle grabbed Ray's collar and drew him in close, teasing his lips with hers before lingering in a tender kiss. There, that should do it. "Bring the packages inside and take care of Gwen, won't you please?"

Ignoring the way his face fell, Belle retrieved the box from Dr. Heiss herself and brought it inside. Unlocking and raising the roll top, Belle set the small crate on her desk. Prying the lid off, she found an envelope, and beneath that, a smaller box and an object swaddled in layers of fabric.

The envelope contained a letter from Dr. Heiss. "Dear Mrs. Gunness. Thank you for your interest in my invention. It is good to hear from a kindred spirit who understands the dignity due to all life. Please follow the enclosed directions and communicate to me your findings. The captive bolt pistol will bring revolutionary change to the meatpacking industry, and your offer to put the device to trial will help further the project. Yours sincerely, Dr. Hugo Heiss."

It would bring revolutionary change to the success of her business as well.

Since George Murphy, she had married four well-off suitors: Martin Burns, a brewer from Milwaukee, who wanted her to bathe him like a baby in beer; Laurence Harrington, a professor from Madison, Wisconsin, who divulged his fears to a sock puppet he gave her; Stephen Luther, a zookeeper from Chicago, who brought a pet monkey that ate at the table with them and slept in their bed and proved harder to kill than any of her husbands; and Aidan Davis, a blacksmith from Grand Rapids, Michigan, who only wanted the perfect sandwich.

Yet despite the happiness she provided each and every one of them, their deaths had been just as awful as those that came before.

Belle laid the burlap-wrapped object on the desk and unfolded its swaddling. Inside was a steel cylinder almost a foot long. Belle picked it up, weighing it in her hand. It was heavy, a serious tool. She turned it this way and that. On one end the tube was open, and the other end had a knob and a lever.

Belle placed the device gently back in its cradle and clenched her hands together. Excitement and awe thrilled through her.

Searching through the box, she found Dr. Heiss's directions, a four-page handwritten letter. It had a diagram identifying all the parts—the knob pulled the firing pin, and the lever was a trigger to release the pin.

The directions went into a long description of Dr. Heiss's experiments, which Belle skimmed quickly, gleaning that the captive bolt pistol was so named because it fired a bolt that was prevented from being ejected from the pistol by a mechanism inside, making the bolt captive to the pistol. The blow, applied directly to the head of the animal, was guaranteed to kill instantly as the bolt shot into the brain, preventing the distress of a faulty poleax strike that injured and caused pain but did not kill.

This was precisely what Belle had been searching for. She wouldn't have to watch her husbands die in agony—or clean up the disgusting dreck their inevitable vomiting and diarrhea left behind—ever again.

Skipping ahead, she found the description of how to use the thing.

She dropped the letter and, taking the pistol in hand, drew back the knob for the firing pin until she heard a click. Carefully pointing the tube away from herself and her desk, she pulled the trigger.

Nothing happened.

What on earth? She knew the bolt should come exploding out of the end. She quickly reread the directions, this time noticing an important detail. Of course. The charges.

Belle opened the small box she'd set aside. In it were neat rows of bullet casings, which contained blank charges for firing the bolt. With the help of the diagram, she found the chamber on the pistol and inserted a charge, then closed the chamber. Suddenly the tool felt weightier, more substantial, even though the tiny blank couldn't have added very much weight.

She again pointed it away from herself, drew the firing pin, and squeezed the trigger. With a great bang, the three-inch bolt shot out of the mouth of the pistol at terrifying velocity. Son of a Benjamin!

It was perfect.

She retracted the bolt and stowed the pistol and the blanks in a bottom drawer of her desk and locked it. She would give the device its inaugural trial in a matter of days. She was expecting her latest suitor on the midday train.

Belle wasn't sure the man was going to fit in her small carriage.

He came off the train like a cow down a steep hill—awkwardly, slowly, landing heavily on the platform. He was well over six feet tall, with wide, beefy shoulders and a head of dark unkempt hair that met with and blended into a long, unkempt beard. His features were all but lost in the brush.

Belle had heard of people looking like their dogs, but never of people looking like their professions. Had she ever met a cobbler who looked like a shoe? A carpenter who resembled an armoire? But here it was undeniable: this butcher could easily have been mistaken for one of the beasts he routinely carved up.

He paused, eyes roving slowly, searching the small crowd. Belle waved and he lumbered over.

"Mr. Brown?" Belle knew from his letters that his wife had passed away nearly two years ago, which at the very least explained his disheveled appearance. Another man who couldn't seem to care for himself in the absence of a woman.

Up close, his dark eyes were framed with unexpectedly long eyelashes, which should have given him a sweet demeanor. But some painful emotion clouded them. Belle sensed in him something almost frantic. Sorrow? Fear? Regret?

When Mr. Brown's eyes landed on her, that whisper of unidentified emotion transformed into a silent question. Belle allowed herself a moment of confident satisfaction that she would solve the riddle of Mr. Brown and answer that question: yes, she could help him.

Mr. Brown managed to wedge himself onto the carriage seat next to her, and the bench listed to the right under his weight, forcing Belle to lean left to stay vertical. The mist thickened into droplets as they rode, and a damp, meaty aroma steamed off the giant, not entirely unpleasant. They were greeted at the house by Ray, who took Gwen's reins while Belle and her suitor descended from the carriage.

"Mr. Brown, this is my caretaker, Ray Lamphere. He is indispensable to the smooth running of my operation here."

Mr. Brown nodded his shaggy head, and Belle took him inside, telling Ray, "Give Gwen extra oats, won't you, Ray? She hauled a heavy load just now."

Inside, Louis Brown stared, mouth agape. "Bison's bollocks," he swore. "I fell off my horse and landed in a patch of clover."

Belle reveled in the admiration. It was exactly the reaction her renovations and sense of style deserved. "This way, Mr. Brown. Let's get you settled in your room."

She led him up the staircase to the room on the left, pausing briefly to give an assessing look at her suitor's bulk compared to what until this moment she'd thought was a perfectly sturdy bed. She hoped it was up to the job. She showed him the water closet and said, "Wash up, Mr. Brown. Come down to the parlor when you are ready, and I will have tea and refreshments for you."

She pondered the source of his troubled eyes as she prepared a tray and brought it to the parlor. It occurred to her he might need a little lubrication to loosen up and give her the opening she needed to puzzle out his truest, deepest need, so she dashed back to the kitchen for one last item. Before long, she heard him galumph downstairs.

"There you are! Come, sit next to me." He eased himself down by her side, and the joints of the sofa creaked as they received his full weight. She handed him a plate piled with slices of bread coated with butter and jam. "You must be hungry after your trip. How do you take your tea? Milk? Sugar?"

"Both, please." He took a polite sip and held the dainty cup awkwardly by its handle. Her instincts had clearly been right; he needed something more.

"Or perhaps a little tonsil varnish?" She produced the flask she'd tucked in her pocket and poured an inch into an empty teacup. "You should see the look on your face. Don't be so shocked. Here, bottoms up."

He set the tea down and took the new cup with enthusiasm. "Here's how," he exclaimed and tossed the liquor back in a single gulp.

"Another?" she asked, filling his cup without waiting for an answer. "Tell me about yourself, Louis—may I call you Louis? And you'll call me Belle? In your letters, you said you were a butcher."

"That's right." He knocked back the second slug and cradled the empty teacup in his hand. "It's a real craft. Most people don't understand the skill it takes. I could slice the smile off the Cheshire Cat and he'd never know the difference. I just have a way with a blade, always have."

He set the teacup down and from his coat pocket plucked a leather bundle and unrolled it, revealing six knives, each in its own pocket. He withdrew one of the smallest, with a narrow blade. "This is a boning knife. See how flexible the blade is?" The steel bowed as he flexed the tip against his thumb. "That helps you get around the bones. This one is my butcher knife." He hefted a heavy-looking knife with a long blade that widened slightly before it came to its point.

"So many knives," Belle said. "I had no idea."

"Each with its own specialty. Its own *personality*," Louis emphasized. He pointed to each and named them one by one: the boxy cleaver, the skinning knife, a pointed breaker knife, the wickedly curved cimeter. "I learned to skin game from my grandpappy. Learned all kinds of skills from him. But the art of butchery I had to learn for myself. I went and found all the best butchers in the county. Wore out my welcome asking 'em question after question. I couldn't get enough, you see? People don't understand what an art it is, to take a side of meat and break it down to culinary perfection. We're not cavemen, are we? We're not hacking hunks of meat off and roasting them on a stick. I'm talking about pure craftsmanship—the marriage of tool, talent, knowledge, and execution in order to create a perfect cut."

"My word."

Passion lit his face, and he gesticulated animatedly with his knives. Clearly, he was talking about something vitally important to him. Here was the first piece of the puzzle that was Louis Brown.

"By the time I was ten," he continued, "I was doing all the skinning and butchering for my family, our neighbors, the whole town. I even got folks coming from all over the county, asking for the boy butcher."

"How proud your family must have been, and grateful, too, I imagine. Contributing to the family's fortunes at such a young age."

"That's a fact, ma'am. I've been making a good living my whole life." A shadow crossed his face, and Belle knew she'd found another piece of the puzzle. Why would the thought of making a good living cause him pain? Most people are proud of that. Perhaps the method of earning it?

What had Louis Brown done to earn the kind of wealth that no ordinary butcher would have?

"I'm in horse meat nowadays. Now, don't be offended. Horse meat is just as edible as beef. There's a glut of horses in the US. They just ain't useful like they used to be, now that we got automobiles and electric streetcars coming to the cities. No reason not to make use of 'em as food. Better than letting 'em starve to death or go to waste."

"Oh, I'm not offended. It seems like a sound business plan." A sound business plan, but certainly not the source of Louis Brown's wealth. What meat would be so much in demand it could form the foundation of his very successful business? He'd said he was in horse meat "nowadays," implying there had been something else before. And a phrase he'd used earlier tickled at her brain. *Bison's bollocks*, he'd said.

She tried to recall a headline she'd seen about the buffalo trade . . . what was it?

"And I'm not one of these old reprobates who pass horse meat off as beef. No, I'm an honest trader. I've got my sins—sins aplenty—but fraud ain't one of 'em."

"We all have our sins, to be sure." Louis was right, many found the idea of eating horse meat repellent. But if trading in it wasn't one of his "sins aplenty," what was? "I'm sure you're no worse than any of us."

Louis looked down at the teacup in his hand. He lifted it to his lips, as if trying to eke out one last drop.

"There's plenty, Louis," she said. "Here." She handed him the flask.

He unscrewed the top and tipped it up. As he threw the last few swallows down his gullet, the details of the newspaper story flashed into her mind. He wiped his mouth with the back of his hand. "Oh," he said, seeming to realize his bad manners. "Here you go." He handed her the empty flask.

She accepted it gracefully, leaving one hand to rest on Louis's own. "Louis, tell me. How long did it take you to earn your fortune from trading in buffalo tongue?"

"I—. What? I never said nothing about buffalo tongue."

"You didn't have to. I read the papers. I know how much demand there used to be for buffalo tongue. How much money could be made there. Before the decline of the buffalo."

And there it was. The look on Louis's face confirmed it: the final puzzle piece, slotting into place.

33

er words just about knocked Louis over with a feather and left him feeling lower than a gopher hole. How could she know he used to trade in buffalo tongue? He hadn't mentioned that bit in his letters.

Her hand on his was warm and soft, and when he met her eyes, he saw warmth there too. "You mustn't be too hard on yourself, Louis. You seem very troubled, like you are carrying a heavy load. I want you to know that here, in my home, it is all right for you to lay your burden down and rest."

Because his enormous size had alarmed people when he was a young man, Louis had developed the habit of careful, gentle movements. Some folks even called him slow. But when the spirit took him, he was prone to sudden explosions. Overwhelmed by Belle's kindness, Louis did something he hadn't done since he was a babe. He began to cry. And not subtle tears coursing silently down his cheeks. No, this was a torrent of grief. He sobbed and shook, his mouth open, ignoring the tears and snot flowing freely into his beard.

"There, there, now, Louis," Belle soothed him. "That's all right. Go ahead and cry. Get it all out." She patted his hands and stroked his back until his sobs quieted to hiccups. She smoothed his damp hair away from his face and took a handkerchief from her pocket and wiped his nose. "Blow," she said, and he did. "Doesn't that feel better?"

He bobbed his head.

"Now. Take a deep breath and calm yourself, and then you'll tell me all about it."

Louis accepted the handkerchief, now soggy with his snot and tears, and crumpled it in his fist. This woman was so kind and sympathetic. She had guessed not only his guilt but its source, and now she wanted to hear his story. He hadn't spoken of the buffalo since he left the plains. Maybe it was time.

"When I was eighteen, I set out for the west, to bu—to buffalo country." He had to choke the word out. "I'd heard tales of massive herds and great hunts where butchers were in demand. It's easy as anything to shoot a buffalo, but skinning and butchering those majestic beasts takes skill." A skill he had, in spades.

"Everybody wanted tongue," he forced himself to continue. "Soldiers wanted it, Indians wanted it, even the swells back East wanted tongue. I was making money hand over fist. Cecily—that was my wife—anything she wanted, she got. I bought her a big new house and all the furnishings to go with it. Trips to New York and Paris for clothes. Me, I never wanted much. But it made me happy to give Cecily her heart's desire."

"She was a lucky woman."

"Lucky? She would have been better off never—" The bitter words caught in his throat. Shaking off painful memories, he said, "You ever had buffalo tongue?"

"I'm afraid not," Belle said.

"Shame. It's a flavor you can't get with any other meat. And now you never will." Louis wished there was more in Belle's little flask, but he'd drained it dry. Outside, a mild rain pattered down, plinking on the windows and sliding down the glass in rivulets. "Anyway, that's my story. Working with those noble creatures was the highlight of my life. And now I butcher horses from sunup to sundown. Not the same thing. Not the same thing at all." Louis heaved a sigh, his thoughts wandering back to a place he hadn't allowed them in years: those glorious days on the plains.

Gentle fingers threaded into his beard, tugging his head to face hers. "Look at me, Louis," Belle said softly.

He slowly found her blue eyes.

"Louis Brown. You are not being honest with me."

"Wha—? Of course, I am. I've told you the God's honest truth."

"As far as it goes, yes." Her kind blue eyes had turned wintry and stern. "But you have not told me the whole truth. You are still carrying a burden of guilt. It weighs you down as heavily as a load of bricks. What do you think we should do about that?"

"I— don't. What?" Louis was so confused. If he knew how to lay down his guilt, he would.

"Perhaps you deserve to be punished?"

What did she mean? Punished . . . how?

"Wait here," she commanded. She was gone only a few minutes, and when she returned, she wore riding gloves and held a riding crop, snapping it against her palm.

Louis's thoughts were as balled up as a nest of snakes. He searched her face for some clue, but he came up empty as a sack of air.

She smacked the riding crop on his shoulder. "Get down on your hands and knees."

"On my hands and knees?" he repeated dumbly.

"You heard me, Louis. Do it. Now."

Curiosity warred with confusion, and he thudded awkwardly to the floor, his fingers sinking into the plush pile of the oriental rug. She towered over him, and he had to crane his neck to receive her next instruction.

"Gallop."

"Gallop? Like a horse?" There's was nothing he'd rather do less than imitate a horse.

"No, Louis. Gallop like a bison."

Oh. Well, then. That wasn't so bad. He lumbered forward, off the rug and around the sofa, feeling like ten kinds of fool. His heavy bulk bore down on his hands, and the wooden flooring pressed painfully into his skin.

"Faster, Louis. I said gallop, not trot."

She tapped his back with the crop as he passed her, and he picked up his pace. His hands and knees felt every floor nail and seam as he circled the parlor.

"Stampede!" Belle shouted as he came past her again, and the sting of the crop crashing onto his flank sent him racing.

The pain in his hands and knees receded as his breath became more labored. He balled his hands into fists like hooves and galloped across the room, knees thundering on the floor. He raced to the far wall and wheeled left, banking past the doorway. He clomped heavily up the sofa and over it. The house shook when he landed on the far side.

Every time he rumbled past her, Belle swatted him with the riding crop. "Stampede! Stampede!" Louis ran on, snorting heavily, drool dripping off his mustache. Inhibition gone, he *was* the bison, wild and free, king of the plains.

"Whoa, now," she called, and he roared to a stop.

"Louis Brown, what did you do?"

"I went west." Louis panted.

"Why?"

"To—to make a living."

She swung her leg over his back. *Whap* came the sting of the crop on his ear. "Wrong! Stampede!"

Louis reared up and galloped off, careering around the room with Belle riding him like a bronco. Louis's hooves pounded the floor. Teacups rattled in their saucers and framed pictures bounced against the wall at his power.

Around and around he went. Over his thundering hoofbeats, Belle demanded, "What did you do, Louis Brown?"

"I was the best at what I did," he panted.

"Wrong!" *Thwap!* She swatted him with the crop.

"Everyone wanted—" he gasped for breath, "more and more and more."

"Wrong!" *Thwap!*

"Times were"—*gasp*—"different then."

"Wrong, wrong, wrong, wrong. Now ride!" *Whap.*

"I loved"—*gasp*—"those creatures." *Sob.* "Loved them."

"Louis Brown, that is enough. Love had nothing to do with it. Ride!"

Louis's muscles begged for rest, but he kept galloping, Belle clinging to his hair like reins. "I did. I loved them. Loved every shank and sinew." *Thwap, thwap, thwap.*

"I loved their weight. I loved their grace. I loved their hides." He barreled around the parlor, tears gathering at his eyes.

"Goddammit, Louis Brown, you leave my house this instant, or you tell me—"

"I butchered them! I butchered them all! Every last one of them." The floodgates opened as his guilt poured out in heaves and sobs. He collapsed in a heap, Belle remaining on the pile of him. "Greed. Avarice. We just wouldn't stop. Thirty million. Thirty million beasts. Kings of the plains." He wept, and howled, and brayed. "Thirty million roaming free, and when we looked up fifteen years later . . . they were gone, gone. All of them! There used to be so many!" Sweat poured off him, and his sides heaved as he wept, but he wheezed out the painful words as Belle rolled off him. "Like stars in the sky, everybody said. Thought there'd always be more. And we were making so much money. You have no idea. I went west to join the buffalo hunt and after fifteen years of hunting"—*gasp*—"the great herds were no more. Only three hundred and twenty-five creatures remained by the time we stopped. Three hundred out of thirty million. How could we know?" His ribs shuddered with each sobbing breath. "Such a monumental disregard for God's creation. We should have known."

"Whoa there, Louis. Whoa." Her voice was gentle now.

She moved to her sofa, and Louis collapsed at her feet. She pulled his sweat-soaked head into her lap. Exhausted, he couldn't stop the tears of guilt and sorrow that seeped out of his eyes.

"It was the taste of their tongue."

"I know. I know." Belle's voice was soothing and warm.

"A thousand pounds and all we took was their tongues."

"Ssh, now. There, there." Light hands smoothed his drenched hair. "Shh. But there's still more to tell, isn't there, dear Louis? Why don't you tell me about your wife."

Oh, Cecily. The tale of her demise was almost as gut-wrenching as that of the buffalo. "She was so good. I didn't deserve her. She was a pure, sweet, tenderhearted woman. She couldn't bear to let me leave her for the plains, and I was too selfish to make her stay home where it was safe. She had an awful big soft spot for animals, could hardly stand the butchering. She'd go out walking on the prairie, away from the day's hunt. She was always bringing home lost and broken creatures. I told her time and again it wasn't safe to go walking out there by herself."

"It's easy to get turned around on the plains if you're not familiar with the territory." Belle stroked his temple. "Did she get lost?"

"No, not at all. Cecily had a mighty good sense of direction and never got lost. But this day, the very last hunt of the season, she came upon a young buffalo stuck in a wallow, its mother lowing nearby. Now, buffalo mothers are very protective of their young."

"Oh, no!" Belle gasped, jerking her hand away. "And she was gored by the very beast you were out there to butcher? How ghastly."

Louis scoffed and sat back on his haunches. "No, no. There ain't a nobler way to die than at the horns of such a kingly animal." Why did his beloved have to die in such a ridiculous way? He continued his story.

"No, Cecily gave that mama her proper respect, moved real cautious like. She could see the calf was struggling, that it was stuck in there real good. It couldn't get out, mama obviously couldn't get it out, and the little mite was getting tired. Cecily knew she didn't have a lot of time. Slow and careful, she got close to the lil' fella. She got right in there, up to her thighs in mud, and hauled the calf out of the wallow. She was a strong 'un, my Cecily."

He couldn't help but smile, recalling her vigor and might. She had the soul of a buffalo, he used to tell her.

"Well, as soon as she was on firm ground, the mother charged her. Cecily was no fool, she plopped that calf down and ran, hoofbeats thundering after her. She thought she was a goner. Only, after a few dozen paces, the hoofbeats stopped. But Cecily kept a-runnin'. She wanted out of there before mama had a change of heart. She looked over her shoulder, and remember, she's head to toe mud. Skirts sodden and heavy. She got tangled up, and she tripped and fell and hit her head on a rock."

"And died? I'm so sorry." Belle's eyes welled with sympathy. But she had it wrong again.

"No, ma'am. She made it all the way home to our tents. Told me all about it—she had a real way with words. Told a story like painting a picture. I wish I could tell it to you like she told it. Anyway, we had a big old copper bathtub, and I got some water boiled and filled it up for her. She hopped in, clothes and all. 'Might as well kill two birds with one stone, Louis,' she said to me. Those were her last words because she got in, fell asleep, and never woke up."

Louis's mane tickled his temple as he shook his head, and he pawed at his hair. "She died in the bathtub. Where's the honor in that? Now Cecily's gone *and* the buffalo are gone, and I'm stuck cutting up horses. I can't wield my artistry on horses. What do I do now? I can't go back to my old life." Louis looked up at the woman he'd just bared his soul to, the redeemer who'd taken and absolved his sins.

Her benevolent smile beamed down at him.

Louis and Belle wed the next afternoon. Rain had made way for a bright, sunshine-filled spring day, and she drove them out into the prairie, to a small church in a town called Door Village. The minister agreed to marry them outside, under the Indiana sky, which reminded Louis of the Great Plains. The minister's daughter picked a bouquet of blue lupine for Belle to carry.

Louis said his vows in a state of desperate relief. The events in Belle's parlor had exorcised his sins, and the chains of grief and guilt that had bound him had dropped away. They were replaced by adoration for his deliverer: Belle. She was the keeper of his salvation, and he attached himself to her with the devotion of the born again.

Once the ceremony was over and they returned to Belle's estate, Louis followed her upstairs to his bedroom. At the doorway, she stopped and gave him a direction. "Go inside and take your clothes off. I'll join you in a moment." She disappeared into her room across the hall.

Louis stripped and sat on the edge of the bed. When the door swung open, there was Belle, his new wife. She was naked. Except for her riding gloves.

She had loosed her hair, which cascaded in brown waves. Wide-hipped and full-bosomed, with luscious pink nipples and a little brown birthmark on one breast, she was like a goddess.

A goddess holding a riding crop.

Louis's body reacted instantly. His cock leaped up, rising out of his hairy groin like a sturdy oak on the grassy prairie.

Belle's approach was leisurely, her swaying movements hypnotic. So much soft flesh, obscuring the muscles beneath. He pictured the curve of brisket under her breasts, shanks flexing to bring her closer, the round of her buttocks, and the tenderest meat of her loin.

Belle towered over her hulking husband. Coarse dark hair covered his body—back, arms, legs, even the backs of his hands and tops of his feet. She stroked the crop down his cheek. "You know what to do, don't you?" He shook his great, woolly head, and she leaned down to whisper in his ear. "Stampede."

Louis obeyed promptly, dropping to all fours with a thud that shook her walls. Maybe she needed to start vetting her prospective husbands for size and weight. He galloped across the room, his penis bobbing with every thunderous step. She winced when he heaved up onto the bed, still uncertain of the abuse it could withstand. Better nip that in the bud. "Down!" she commanded, then added, "gently!"

As he shambled past her, Belle swatted him with the riding crop. She much preferred this version of roughhousing to what she endured with Charles.

When she judged he'd had enough—she didn't want him too sweaty—she called "whoa" and mounted his back. "I'm your bronco rider. Giddy up!" Belle rode Louis hard, whipping her crop against his flank and urging him faster.

He was as big as an ox and just as strong. It would take hours for her to wear him out, and after only a few minutes, it occurred to her why hair shirts were such an effective form of punishment. The tender skin of her nethers was suffering from the hairy saddle of his back. Enough of that. There was a limit to the lengths she'd go to to fulfill her contract.

She dismounted and sent him around the room a few more times before getting down on all fours herself. It was time for his reward. Casting a coy glance over her shoulder, she said, "Louis, ride me like a buffalo!"

Louis lifted his shaggy head and bellowed in triumph. He reared up, and with his paws gripping her hips, drove himself into her, mounting her like a king of the beasts.

34

Ray rose early, as usual, and looked out his kitchen window across the yard of sprouting grass to the big house. Inside that house, he knew, Belle was tending to another husband. Images of what that would mean flooded him. His Belle, sharing her smile with that Brown fellow, touching him, holding him. Lying naked with him.

Shittagoddam. Ray shoved the hurtful imaginings away. How many times had he gone through this? He cast his mind back to that very first husband, Gunness, and held up one finger. The zookeeper with his horrible monkey, that oughta count for two fingers, but Ray just put up one. Helgelien came after Gunness, then that Irish fellow. Two more fingers. No wait, Barber came after Helgelien, so he put up a finger for Barber. *Then* the Irish fellow, so Ray added a finger for him. Wait, didn't Irish come earlier that spring? And there were the two husbands right around Christmas and then that goddam zookeeper. Oh! And don't forget the brewer. He brought bottles of a mighty good ale—why'd Belle have to kill off that one? Plus that smart fellow that was a college teacher, and the blacksmith who helped re-shoe Gwen, and then a zookeeper. Ray looked down at his hands. He'd run out of fingers. Something wasn't right. Did he count the zookeeper twice?

Bah! He threw his hands up in disgust. It didn't matter exactly how many, Ray knew there were *a lot*.

He longed for his nights with Belle, the two of them curled in his bed, his fingers twining a lock of her hair as she slept. He would lie awake, watching her, breathing in her scent, wishing he could bottle the moments to last through the times when she would abandon him again.

Light crept into the day as Ray made his breakfast. He hadn't seen hide nor hair of the newlyweds since they got back from Door Village, what, three days ago now?

Ray knew what that meant. Very soon Belle would come knocking on his door, asking for help. He should be shocked at her actions, shocked at what he was prepared to do for her. But he wasn't. He understood better than anyone the gifts she gave her husbands, the gifts she gave him when he had her all to himself. He'd never believed in himself or found purpose like he did when he was with Belle. All he could think of was her returning to his arms, to his bed.

Belle's newest husband could eat a lot. He'd woken at dawn, ravenous in more ways than one, and after she'd worn him out in the bedroom— she used a blanket as a saddle this time—Belle had prepared breakfast. She'd fed Louis four eggs, half a loaf of bread, an entire jar of preserves, a mound of potatoes fried in beef fat, several slices of beef, and a quart of hot coffee with cream and sugar.

"Got any more bread?" Louis said around a mouthful of eggs.

"Of course." Belle rose from the table. Standing at the breadboard by the kitchen window, she sawed slice after slice for him. And he'd need another jar of preserves, too, it seemed. If his stay with her wasn't drawing to a close, he'd eat her out of house and home.

A flash of movement outside the window caught her eye. Damn coyotes. Belle glared at it as it trotted merrily through her yard. It better not be after her hogs. Wait. Something dangled from its mouth. Was that a . . . ? Son of a Benjamin!

It was a human foot. An abnormally large human foot.

Behind her, she heard Louis's chair scrape back. He sat facing the kitchen sink. If he rose, he would see right out the window. Belle whirled around, pressing him back into his seat. "Don't you move a muscle, Louis. Here's your bread, enjoy your coffee. I'll go fetch another jar of preserves." She refilled his cup, then bent over him, adding cream and sugar, and nibbled on his ear lobe. "You sure know how to treat a woman in the morning." A rumbling growl came in reply. "Actually, I have a better idea," she said, pushing his plate away. She drew him from his chair, steering him so his back was to the window. She coaxed him out of the kitchen, and he followed her down the hall like a dog on a scent. At the foot of the stairs, she said, "Go on up and make ready. I'll have a surprise for you."

Belle watched Louis thunder eagerly up to his bedroom. As soon as the door closed, she spun and dashed out of the house. She raced to the caretaker's cottage and banged on the door. "Ray! Come quick!"

The knock came just as Ray expected. It was time. He opened the door, but before he could say anything, Belle blurted, "Coyotes are digging up the hog yard. I just saw one with Andrew's foot in its mouth."

Now, that was a surprise. "How do you know it was Helgelien's?"

"Nobody has feet like Andrew."

"I s'pose you're right," Ray said, remembering the giant foot that wouldn't stay buried. But how could a coyote get into the hog pen? Ray had built it good and sturdy, the gate secure. And what about the sows? Were they safe?

"Ray! We've got to do something right now!"

Jolted from his musing, Ray ran the hundred yards to the rear of the house with Belle on his heels. He scanned the field to check the other men's graves. Relieved to see only grass coming up in those spots, Ray ran the rest of the way to the hog pen.

In the wallow, a sow enthusiastically gnawed on what looked like an arm. What on earth? As Ray investigated, he realized the coyote wasn't the culprit. The hogs had done the digging on their own. They'd rooted into the spring-thawed mud and managed to unearth Andrew's remains, ripping parts out of the ground and spreading them across their pen. There was the other arm, a sow nuzzling at its hand like a French lover with his ladylove, and that had to be his torso, and oh God, that was his head and it was nowhere near the rest of the body. As they watched, a sow took a run at the head and gave it a playful bump with its snout, sending it tumbling across the muddy pen like a ball.

Belle gaped. "Raaay!" she wailed. "How could you let this happen?"

Wasn't my idea to bury a body in a hog pen, Ray retorted in his head. He traversed the perimeter of the yard and stopped when he was on the other side of the fence from the sow in the wallow. "I think I found something," he called. "Look here. The wallow has spread." Mud squelched and oozed under the fence with the movements of the lolling sow. Pressed into the mud were paw prints and scratch marks around a deep hole under the fence. "Coyote," Ray said, pointing.

"How did this happen, Ray?" Belle asked again, puzzlement softening her tone.

He shrugged. "Maybe frost heaving brought the body up to where the hogs could get at it. And the wallow spread with all the rain we been gettin'."

"Ray, you have to fix this!" Belle cried. She had lowered her voice, but he could feel the fury sharpen her words. "I can't have body parts spread all over creation and coyotes coming here like a buffet! What would Louis think if he saw this? And what if that stupid sheriff's deputy comes by again? You better get Andrew buried again. And find that coyote!"

She marched away and Ray was alone. He surveyed the job

in front of him and scratched the back of his neck. "Shittagoddam, Helgelien. You're not the fellow I expected to bury today. Let other folks have a turn."

Louis had waited for Belle with bovine patience, admiring the tremendous cockstand he'd grown in anticipation. She was taking so long, it must be quite something she was planning. But when she entered the bedroom she seemed distracted rather than eager. "You still have your clothes on," he complained. "I thought you had a surprise for me? Never mind. Here, I have a surprise for you." He proudly wrapped his fist around his cock.

"That is the biggest *surprise* I've ever seen," Belle said, unbuttoning her blouse.

That was more like it. She sauntered toward the bed, dropping clothing as she went. His cock couldn't get any harder. When she was within reach, Louis grabbed for her. "How's this for a surprise," he growled. He flipped her underneath him and drove into her.

"Oh!" Her eyes flew open, urging him on. His every action drew a hungry reaction from his wife—her breath catching in his ear, her low giggle as he nipped at her neck, the way she cried out with pleasure as he rocked into her. Her eagerness echoed the passion and love between them, which built until it swelled and burst over them. With a groan of satisfaction, he collapsed onto his side, protecting her from his great weight.

"Oh, my mighty Louis," she whispered, snuggling into the crook of his arm.

He drew outlines with his fingertips on her skin. "This is your shoulder clod," he murmured. "Part of the chuck. Very big piece of meat in a buffalo."

Belle raised herself up on her elbow. "I am to be butchered, is that it?" she teased.

Louis laughed. "No, don't be silly. Nobody would butcher a human.

But the parts are similar. Look." He lumbered to the fireplace and dug out a cold piece of charcoal, then drew a line down the middle of his chest, curving under his pectoralis major and around to his side. "This is the chuck. There are some tender cuts in there, once you remove a vein of gristle. Good for ground chuck too." He drew more lines encircling his ribs, his side, his belly, naming each as he went. "Rib, loin, plate," he said. "Sirloin, very tender. Round."

Belle was fascinated watching Louis enthusiastically describe all the major cuts and their sub cuts, how to prepare each type of meat to produce the best flavor and tenderness.

"Here, feel this." He drew her hand to his upper chest, which he'd called the chuck. "Feel how hard it is? The closer you get to the chest muscle, the tougher the meat. But inside, under this layer, are some very tender cuts." He moved her hand to his side. "Now here, you can feel the difference, can't you?"

Belle wasn't sure she could, but she went along, saying, "It's more tender here, isn't it?"

"That's right! This is the tenderloin. One of the tenderest cuts. You don't need to do anything special to that meat for it to be soft as butter."

"Who would have guessed such tender meat could lay inside such a big, strong animal?" Belle said. As she spoke, a revelation flashed into her mind.

Moonlight fell into the room, draping a blanket of light across Louis's hulking form. Belle stood over her newest husband, her right arm weighted down by the captive bolt pistol, watching his barrel chest rising and falling. With every descent, a beastly snore ripped from his open mouth. He was about to get the redemption he so rightly deserved, the only ending that would allow him to fully repay his debt to the buffalo. A penance only Belle could help him achieve. She leaned down and kissed Louis's forehead, then his lips, cutting short the snoring.

"Wha—? Mm, Belle." He kissed her back.

Belle climbed onto the bed and straddled him, keeping the pistol low and out of sight. He gripped her hips, snugging her close to him. "Louis," she said against his lips. "Look at me." She held his gaze intently. "Are you happy?"

Louis brought his hands to her face and cupped her cheeks. He stroked his thick fingers against her eyebrows, his thumb against her lips. His eyes were bare, allowing her to see past his guilt and fear into the deepest parts of him. "Yes."

The contract was complete. "Good. That's good. I love you, Louis."

"I love you, Belle," he answered, tears spilling down the side of his face.

The captive bolt pistol hung cold and heavy in her hand. Powerful. Would it do the job right? She was about to find out. As she slid her hands up toward the headboard, a fever of excitement took her. She realized it wasn't the pistol that was powerful. It was her.

His eyes were intent on hers, unaware as she guided the captive bolt pistol above his head. She stroked his woolly mane with the muzzle, burrowing through the tangled layers to scrub his scalp. He rumbled contentment, eyes drifting closed, like a great mastiff having his head scratched. She slid the muzzle gently down past his hairline, kissed him on each eyelid, and said, "This won't hurt a bit."

Belle held her breath, willing the device to work as expected. The trigger bit into her finger as she squeezed. The report echoed in the dark room, followed by a complete silence: success! Louis's breath and spirit left his body, and he lay as if sleeping quietly, his body relaxed and still, his face tranquil. The grief and guilt he had borne like a heavy mantle had sloughed away. He seemed lighter somehow.

Louis was at peace.

Only a small dark hole on his forehead was any indication that death had visited. And this time, death had done so without a need for extensive cleanup.

Belle gazed at the pistol in wonderment. The bolt, so recently implanted in Louis's brain, gleamed wetly in the moonlight. It worked! The captive bolt pistol had performed perfectly. Her future husbands could receive their end of the bargain without having to pay an excessive price for it.

Giddy with the possibilities, Belle sprang up and spun in a circle, clutching the pistol to her breast. When she withdrew it, she noticed a bloody smudge left behind on the white cotton. No matter. The simplicity and ease were well worth a little laundry.

After dressing quickly, she wiped down the bolt and returned the pistol to its hiding place in her desk in the library. At the caretaker's cottage, Ray opened the door to her knock.

"Let's go."

The knock had awoken Ray from a light sleep. It was the summons he'd been expecting, finally. He followed Belle to the bedroom at the top of the stairs on the left, hoping this husband didn't have to be buried more than once. And that it wouldn't be so messy. He didn't mind hard work, but he didn't want more gore. Especially after spending all morning gathering Helgelien's separated remains and committing them to a deep hole outside the hog pen.

"Doesn't he look peaceful?" Belle asked. "He could almost be asleep."

"Except for that hole in his head," Ray said, pointing to a black circle above Brown's eyes. What had caused that? But even more perplexing were the markings. "What are the black lines all over him?"

"Louis was a butcher. He was explaining his profession to me. It's a fitting end for him. I want you to follow those lines and take him apart."

Ray frowned in confusion. She couldn't mean what he thought she meant. Could she?

"It's a fitting end for him," Belle repeated.

Maybe she could. "You want I should take a knife and—" He hesitated, unsure how to put it. He motioned in the air, as if he were carving.

"It's what he deserves, Ray. We've talked about this." Her voice was sharp, losing patience. "Men come to me in need. I give them what they need, what they deserve. I can't have a partner that balks at every instruction I give. Are you with me or against me, Ray?"

"All right, all right. I'm with you. You know I'm with you," he assured her, even though this was a mighty different kettle of fish from any of her other instructions. He surveyed the immense body laid out on the bed, the white sheets, the white and black comforter tangled at its feet. So much white. He imagined the blood and hoped he could use it as a way out of the predicament. "But . . . here? I'm not sure that's a good idea, Miz Belle. Your special quilt will be ruined. It's likely to be, uh, messy."

Belle's brow furrowed, and she seemed to be coming to her senses. "I suppose you're right, Ray." Relief flooded through him, until she continued, "We'll have to move him. Let's carry him to the downstairs water closet."

There was no getting out of it. Ray looked at the gargantuan man on the bed. He looked at Belle. He looked down at himself. That'll be a trick. He positioned himself at the head of the bed and reached under the man's shoulders. Shittagoddam! His head alone must weigh fifty pounds. "You take the feet, Miz Belle. On three. Ready? One, two, three!"

They heaved mightily, managing to shift Brown's head and feet a few inches, while the rest of his bulk remained rooted in place.

"Put your back into it, Ray." Belle got a fresh grip on Brown's ankles. "Let's go again. Ready? Heave!"

Ray strained again, trying to pry the massive corpse off the bed. It was like trying to move a sack of potatoes the size of a buffalo. "This ain't goin' to work, Miz Belle. Let's try rolling him off."

They teamed up on the side of the bed. "Ready, go!" Ray said. They succeeded in moving his head and feet again, but the rest of him remained stubbornly immovable. "We need to push where he's heaviest," Ray suggested. "Let's work together." Side by side at Brown's midsection, they pushed with everything they had. The body barely budged.

Out of breath, Ray and Belle collapsed, flopping over Brown's inert form. Scratchy chest hair tickled Ray's ear, and he sprang upright.

"This may not have been the best place to release Louis's spirit," Belle said. She was draped over Brown's midsection, her head resting on his abdomen. She looked wistfully up at the corpse's head.

"I've got an idea," Ray said and left the room. He went to a pile of leftover lumber in the barn and dug around until he found two lengths of two-by-four. He trotted back across the yard with a board in each hand, thinking about the task ahead—the moving of a large, heavy object over a distance—rather than the reality of what he was being asked to move.

In the bedroom, he handed one board to Belle. "Here. We gotta lever him off. You take the shoulders, I'll take the hips."

Ray shoved his board under Brown's midsection and pressed it into the mattress, worming the end as deep under the hips as he could get it, while Belle did the same at the shoulders. He gave her a nod to say "Go" and pressed down on his board with all his might. The wood creaked and bowed, threatening to crack in two. Shittagoddam, this man was a beast! Grunting and gasping with effort, he and Belle pried Brown up, rolling him onto his side. After making sure the body was stable and wouldn't fall back, they repositioned the boards and went again, rolling the body closer to the edge of the bed. All at once, momentum caught Brown, tipping him over the side. He crashed to the floor with a thunderous boom that shook the house.

"We did it!" Belle dropped her board and threw herself at Ray. "You're a genius!"

She kissed him soundly on the lips, and Ray wrapped his arms around her, burying his face in her softness. The past several weeks had been a desert of loneliness. He had longed for her desperately. Finally, he was back in her attention again, and he was so immersed in Belle that it took several minutes for a realization to dawn. It seemed to strike Belle at the same time, and they broke apart and skirted the bed to where Brown lay on the other side.

They were greeted by his monumental, hairy ass. The immense body lay inert, the man's face pressed into the floorboards, his arms flopped awkwardly. How on earth would they get him downstairs?

Louis's now-stiff body cascaded from one step to the next like he was soaring down a waterfall. His head knocked against the railing and risers as he slid down to the landing, his legs thunking after. The stairs shook and the railings groaned as he tumbled, and the whole trip sounded like the stampede of a million buffalo.

Belle followed him down the stairs with the stately calm befitting a solemn ceremony, even if his treatment was less distinguished than she'd intended. "Soon, Louis," she soothed. "You'll be fully at rest soon."

Moving Louis to the water closet required a fresh pair of boards, and Belle was thankful—and, frankly, astounded—that she and Ray got him into the bathtub.

Louis just barely fit. Belle perched on the edge of the tub and surveyed the markings on his flesh. "Go get a wheelbarrow, Ray. We'll use that to transport the cuts once you're done."

While Ray was outside, Belle retrieved Louis's knives. When Ray returned, she unrolled the leather wrapping and showed him the sturdy bone saw, the heavy butcher knife, the gleamingly sharp boning knife. "Use these, Ray. It's only fitting."

Ray turned the bone saw over in his hands. "I never done any butchering, Belle."

"Do your best, Ray. The lines are there to guide you." She drew her finger over a charcoal mark, remembering Louis's words. *Rib, loin, plate. Sirloin, very tender.*

Ray rested the gleaming serrations of the saw against Louis's knee. He took a breath and set his shoulders, then drew the blade. With heavy strokes, he sliced through flesh and muscle, and then bone. The blade sawed wetly, making a squelching sound unlike any Belle had heard before, and a heavy smell of iron arose. Was this really necessary? The sight, sound, and smell of the proceedings were beyond disgusting. Belle pinched her nose and breathed through her mouth. Certainly, this was the most fitting end for Louis, but would he even know if she didn't actually complete the contract?

But, no. Quitting now was out of the question. Her integrity required that she fulfill her end of the bargain, so she said nothing and reminded herself of her purpose in bringing Louis here: to give him what no one else could. Well, that and to earn the massive check she intended to write herself from his account.

She distracted herself from Ray's grotesque work with deep, even breaths, dreaming about how she would spend his savings—a lavish garden would make her grounds as much of a showpiece as her house was becoming. Versailles was known for its gardens, wasn't it? Maybe she should travel to Paris, as Louis's wife had done, and see it in person for inspiration.

When the last stroke of the blade freed the leg and it came off in Ray's hand, Belle was ready to receive it, her mind once again clear and focused on her work: she was fulfilling her commitment to Louis and earning her paycheck in the best way she knew how. "Keep going," she told Ray as she accepted the limb in two hands.

Unaccustomed though they were to being fed in the middle of the night, when the hogs caught the smell and heard Belle calling as she crossed the yard, they trotted to the edge of their pen. "Take this meat," she said to the closest one. The sow grunted and snuffled, then tugged the leg out of Belle's hands. Perhaps this would make up for denying them a meal of Andrew earlier.

Belle returned inside, where Ray continued his work, removing pieces of Louis with gritted determination. Belle named them one by one. "Here is the chuck," she said, "and here is the loin." Belle brought the cuts out to the hogs, each in turn. When the hogs were sated and refused to eat anymore, she stacked the pieces in the wheelbarrow.

Processing Louis's body took several hours. By the time it was complete, the bathtub looked like an abattoir and Ray a red ghost.

"That was a fair bit of work," Ray said as he wiped his brow, smearing blood across his forehead.

"You did a fine job, Ray. It was what Louis deserved, and he is at peace now. Rinse all this down the drain and get yourself clean too. Then we'll dig a hole."

Pink light bled over the horizon by the time Ray rolled the wheelbarrow to the edge of the small grave.

"Dear Louis. You were wild, strong, and all too human." As she spoke, Belle gently deposited the final chunks of her twelfth client into their resting place. "You had a great talent in life, and like anyone, you wanted to put your talent to good use. You used it to help with the expansion of the West. But you saw too late the destruction you were part of, and the consequences of that destruction. Because of you, and men like you, a great species has been reduced to a few hundred where there used to be millions. It was—how did you put it?—a monumental disregard for God's creation. Your failure grieved you and shamed you. But now you have been justly punished, and I gave you happiness when you thought that was no longer possible. Rest now, Louis. Peace be upon you."

The morning was quiet, as if the birds of the air and beasts of the field were holding silent council. Belle was sure they'd find no fault in how she brought Louis a fitting salvation.

"Do you want to say a few words, Ray?"

He looked at her incredulously. "Me? No, ma'am."

"Fill it in, then."

***

You're a fool, Asle Helgelien. A damned fool, Asle told himself as he and Jenny waited out a storm under the eaves of a barn in the middle of nowhere. The eaves offered poor shelter. Rain poured off the roof in sheets just inches from Asle's face. It spattered in the dirt and splashed mud up his pants. Jenny's pale gray legs were turned black.

Asle had been full of hope heading east from Farbut—hope that by following Andrew's direction, he'd come upon him sooner or later. But there were many towns and hamlets east of Farbut. Many towns, hamlets, farmsteads, crossroads where Andrew could have left the main road to make a sale or two as he traveled east. And east how far? Was his supposed beloved in Illinois? Indiana? Ohio? New York City?

Every town Asle came to was a wheel with two, three, five, or more spokes leading away, and he had no way of knowing which route Andrew had taken. Townsfolk were friendly, happy to give him direction when they knew, but often all they could say was which farm was likely next on Andrew's itinerary. "The Wilsons are a quarter mile that way," Asle would be told, and on he'd go to the Wilsons' place, where he'd be directed to the Carlsons and the Schultzes, or maybe the Beckers and the Lyons. It wasn't a wheel with spokes; it was an infinitely branching tree of possibilities. The only solution was to pick a direction and hope. And when hope proved unfounded, to turn back and try another branch on the tree.

Asle shivered under the overhang. His eyes felt full of sand and his mouth tasted sour. He hadn't had a decent bath since leaving Chicago weeks ago, and sleep was infrequent and fitful. Would it ever stop raining? He'd hoped the storm would pass, and he and Jenny could have a meal and bed down for the night, but it showed no sign of slowing, much less stopping.

"Come on, Jenny. Let's get something in our bellies," he said to his ever-patient mare as he unbuckled the saddlebag. A couple handfuls of oats for her, and a piece of stale bread with a bit of hard cheese for him. It wasn't much, but it would quiet his hunger pangs until he could get a full meal.

As he opened his mouth for a bite, the wind picked up, throwing the sheet of water pouring off the roof into his face and washing the bread and cheese out of his hand into the muck at his feet.

It was his last piece of each.

A sob of frustration gripped Asle's throat. He owed it to his little brother to keep looking, but how much longer could he search? *God, grant me the strength to carry on. Just one more day. Please, Lord, give me the strength for just one more day.*

35

The woman was not what Frank Devlin had expected. She had an unlined face and honey-brown hair swept into a soft pile at the back of her head. She was nothing like the widow who had lived in his neighborhood when he was a boy, a scrawny, white-haired crone who always wore black and seldom left her house.

She was, however, as deep in sin as her correspondence had indicated. She lived in grand excess—what need did a widow have for a large brick house with a turret?—and her dress, with its shockingly narrow skirt and tight bodice, was calculated to appeal to shallow men who cared only about appearances. He should have known, given her pursuit of a new husband and business opportunities, both shameless and immoral. A widow should retire from the world and accept God's plan for her.

She had requested he arrive on Thursday, and it was only Tuesday. But Frank had set off from Kansas City as soon as he received the letter, eager to bring the widow to the light.

As he'd approached the front door, his boots crunching in the driveway's crushed stone, a verse had come to him. It was one of his favorites—although there were so many he could call favorite—and filled him with joy whenever he recited it. It would surely open her eyes. He'd knocked and the door had opened and he'd raised his voice to glory, letting the words ring out: "'For God so loved the world, that he gave his only begotten Son, that whosoever believeth in him should not perish, but have everlasting life.' Everlasting life, Mrs. Gunness. That is what is at stake. That is what you ignore at your peril. Your *everlasting* peril. Do you not see that?"

He searched for signs of the effect of his words but saw only politeness, perhaps mixed with surprise, in her features.

"Mr. Devlin, I presume? Why, you're early, I wasn't expecting you until Thursday. But welcome." She swept her arm wide and ushered him in, and he followed her swaying skirt into a parlor at the front of the house. A tendril of hair had escaped the confines of its pins, and brushed against the pink skin of her neck. A faint scent of lavender and vanilla beckoned him closer to her.

Begone! he told himself harshly, pushing away the dangerous thoughts her beauty seduced from him. *Wide is the gate and broad is the way that leadeth to destruction.* Frank reminded himself of Matthew 7:13, and followed it with its next verse: *Because strait is the gate, and narrow is the way, which leadeth unto life, and few there be that find it.* He would be among the few, and he would strive to shepherd this wayward woman with him.

The woman sat on the sofa and gave him a look that reminded him he still wore his hat. He removed it swiftly and brought it to his chest, and said, "'Look unto me, and be ye saved, all the ends of the earth: for I am God, and there is none else,' Isaiah 45:22. Hear the words, Mrs. Gunness. There is none else. Know that Our Lord Jesus Christ is your savior. He is my Savior, and he is your Savior. 'Whoever believes in the Son has eternal life, but whoever rejects the Son will not see life, for God's wrath remains on him.' And in John 10:9, we learn, 'I am the gate; whoever enters through me will be saved.'"

Frank's words flowed with passion, and the sinner before him listened without interruption. Her beauty distracted him, but with admirable restraint, Frank kept his eyes from straying to her.

"Mr. Devlin, do sit down." She patted the seat next to her on the sofa. "You must be fatigued from your journey."

"Fatigued? But no, never fatigued. 'And let us not be weary in well doing: for in due season we shall reap, if we faint not.' That is what is said in Galatians, and that is what guides me. I must faint not, and I shall reap in due season."

"Of that, I have no doubt, Mr. Devlin. But I find it hard to follow your words as you traipse back and forth across my parlor. Please, have a seat, and I will bring us some tea and refreshments."

Pleased to learn he was making some progress with the woman, Frank perched on the edge of the sofa. She took his hat and left the room. The urgency of his mission drove him to his feet again, and he roamed the space, taking in the fine furnishings, the window draperies, the ornate gas lamps on mahogany end tables, and the floor covered with an oriental rug. He was right to come. This woman was far into the trappings of a comfortable life. Instead of advertising for a husband as if for a new sofa, she could provide for herself by selling off some of this unnecessary indulgence.

She returned before long, bearing a tray with a basket of muffins, a teapot, and cups and saucers. "It won't do to starve yourself and wear yourself down to nothing, Mr. Devlin. Come sit and eat. Isn't there something in the Bible about your body being a temple?"

"'Do you not know that your body is a temple of the Holy Spirit?' Yes, you are right, Mrs. Gunness. 'Glorify God in your body.'" Frank alighted on the sofa again.

Mrs. Gunness handed him tea with milk and sugar and a muffin on a plate. Frank ate, refusing to take pleasure in the offerings. The tea was oversweet, the muffin tender but cloying, and the sofa too soft. Decadence. The path to everlasting life was strait and narrow and all too easy to miss.

Frank sprang off the sofa and set to walking the length of the room again. He was indeed fatigued and sore but refused to succumb to the comforts of the body. A sip of the harsh liquid in his hip flask served to drive the sweetness of the tea and muffin from his mouth.

"Mrs. Gunness, you live in great comfort here in your large house," he said, "with its plush furniture and fancy teacups and clothes of the latest fashions. But I wonder. What good will these comforts do for you in Hell? For did not Paul write to Timothy and say, 'She that liveth in pleasure is dead while she liveth'? Dead, Mrs. Gunness. You think you live, yet you are dead already. You have forsaken your place as a Godly woman. And you will meet your end in the fiery pits of Hell, surrounded by demons and the wailing of sinners such as yourself. Paul wrote to Timothy and counseled him on the proper role of women in the church, of widows, saying, 'Let them learn first to shew piety at home, and to requite their parents: for that is good and acceptable before God.' Mrs. Gunness, why do you not return to the bosom of your family to do what is right and spend your days in prayer, giving glory to God, as you ought?"

The ball of rage that was Mr. Devlin burned across Belle's hundred-dollar oriental carpet, fueled by his faith and the liquor in his flask.

He'd appeared on her doorstep a full two days before his expected arrival, his tie askew and his shirt unironed. His jacket needed buttons, and his hat covered hair that hadn't been recently washed. He burst into her life mid-sentence, continuing their written correspondence in the flesh, and hadn't ceased preaching since. He'd been speechifying at her for a full forty-five minutes, and Belle was afraid there was no end in sight.

She thought of the bicycle she had bought just that morning with some of the money she'd earned from Louis. It had taken some practice to get his loopy scrawl of a signature right, but she'd done it, and Mr. Todd hadn't questioned the check she'd written to herself. Louis had never told her exactly how much was in his account, but she thought it safe to assume there was at least $5,000 available, and a bicycle was an exciting addition to her lifestyle. She was eager for the freedom of being able to ride to town on a moment's notice, without having to hitch Gwen up to the gig, and had planned to practice that very afternoon. The day was fine, bright and sunny, and the roads had begun to dry out from the winter thaw. It would have been a perfect day to be outside on a bicycle, but instead she was stuck inside, listening to a sermon.

Really, the nerve of some people, showing up early and unannounced. She remembered when George Murphy had arrived unannounced as well. Was this the way of things now? What was the world coming to?

She tried not to let her irritation show on her face. Composing her features into what she hoped was a pious, gentle, *attentive* smile, Belle gave her full attention to Frank Devlin. Not to the content of his sermon, but to his unspoken message. He was much smaller than she had expected, but wound tight with some intense emotion. A wild fire lit his eyes. He clenched his hands into fists, punching the air to emphasize his words, all the while stalking the length of the room. He spoke to her, but not *with* her in conversation. He looked everywhere but at her, at the floor in front of him and all around the high corners, as his sermon erupted faster and faster—more intense, more impassioned—so that the words ejected from his mouth with great force and a great deal of spittle. Sometimes when he reached the far wall and spun on the heel of his boot, in the same smooth motion, he would pull a flask from his pocket and down a swig as he stalked back to the doorway. The liquor only fueled his rage.

Poor Mr. Devlin. Such an unhappy man. Where did all that misery come from? "Mr. Devlin?" she tried, but the man carried on preaching.

"'For the Lord himself shall descend from heaven with a shout, with the voice of the archangel, and with the trump of God: and the dead in Christ shall rise first—'"

"Mr. Devlin!" Belle had to yell to get his attention, but the man finally stopped and faced her, his expression surprised, as though he had forgotten she was there.

His eyes bored into her with desperate intensity. "Yes, Mrs. Gunness? Please, if the spirit moves you, speak."

"Mr. Devlin, you speak with such passion and power. I'm moved almost beyond words. You have such a gift for preaching."

Stunned into silence, if only for a moment, Mr. Devlin gaped at her. "Thank you," he finally said.

"You are blessed by the Holy Spirit, I think. Your abilities are a gift from God."

Mr. Devlin bowed his head and clasped his hands together. "I am His humble servant," he said. "I have God to thank for every good thing that has happened to me. It is through God that I met the man on earth who led me to the light."

"Oh?"

Mr. Devlin returned to the sofa, this time sitting next to Belle. She poured him a fresh cup of tea and, when she handed it to him, exchanged it for the flask in his hand. It was almost empty. She set it aside.

"Tell me about this man," she said.

"He is a great man, a man of God, of such devotion and perception. He is truly filled with God's presence. The first time I heard him preach, I was captivated. I didn't know what I was seeing. I had not been raised in the church, you see. My childhood was a dark wasteland, and I had never seen or heard anything like it. That day in that tent was like moving from darkness into light. I came out of a long, black night into the blaze of day. And Pastor Edward White was the man who led me there."

The way Mr. Devlin spoke of this Pastor White reminded Belle of something. There had been a man back in Norway who lived alone in a cottage far outside of town and never married, despite being of good family, with means and an attractive face. It was said he preferred the company of men to women. When she was a girl, Belle didn't know what this meant. But living in Indianapolis, she learned of several men who had this preference, even a pair of men who made a home together, although on the surface they insisted to be mere housemates. It seemed it was something that happened the world over but was accepted no-where. Was Mr. Devlin of this persuasion? His manner of speaking about Pastor White seemed overly devoted. There was an intensity of feeling there. Was this the reason for his anger and misery? The inability to be with the one he loved?

"How beautiful. How blessed you were to meet someone you loved so," she ventured. "I understand, Mr. Devlin, and you will find no judgment here. How did it end?"

Up until this moment, Mr. Devlin had described his pastor while staring into her eyes without turning away or blinking, though she could tell he wasn't really seeing her. It was as if he were focused on a private vision all his own. But when he heard these words, his focus slowly found her. "No! No, you don't understand," he spat. "He wasn't a man of earthly desires. He was above that, beyond it. I can only aspire to that kind of devotion to the Word. I am all too prone to the sin of the flesh, the lure of Eve."

His eyes dropped from Belle's face and roved over her body, and she saw plainly that she was wrong about which way his inclinations lay. That made her aim all the easier to achieve. She smiled knowingly, but it did not have the effect she was used to. Instead of inspiring Mr. Devlin to words of love, her response launched him off the sofa, his face suffused with red rage.

"Seductress," he hissed. "Displaying yourself to me like the temptress you are. Do you know the story of Bathsheba? An instructional tale. Every woman should know it, and every man. Know it and learn the consequences that come to pass as the price of *unchaste acts*." He paused to let the words hang in the air, to let his audience apprehend their full weight.

"Bathsheba was the wife of Uriah, a military man in Jerusalem. One evening she displayed herself to her king, the great King David, while in her bath. He saw her and bade her come to him. They lay together, and a child was conceived. To hide his sin of adultery, he sent to the battle for Uriah to be brought home. You see, he wanted Uriah to lie with Bathsheba so the world would believe him to be the father of this baby conceived in sin. But Uriah would not take the comfort of his home while his men slept rough and battled on, saying his men 'are encamped in the open fields; shall I then go into mine house, to eat and to drink, and to lie with my wife?' Uriah was a man of honor. Do you know what David did when his plan failed? He followed sin with sin and had Uriah sent into the hottest battle, where he was killed. David then took Bathsheba as his wife. All this sin born from Bathsheba's vain temptation. From the very first woman, Eve, who seduced Adam into eating the apple, woman has been the downfall of man. From the very first, to every woman of modern times." He eyed Belle pointedly, and then continued, his voice gathering volume as he spoke. "'For the lips of a strange woman drop as an honeycomb, and her mouth is smoother than oil. But her end is bitter as wormwood, sharp as a two-edged sword. Her feet go down to death; her steps take hold on hell. Lest thou shouldest ponder the path of life, her ways are moveable, that thou canst not know them. Hear me now therefore, O ye children, and depart not from the words of my mouth. Remove thy way far from her, and come not nigh the door of her house!'" His final words boomed like thunder, echoing off the walls.

With that, Belle expected Mr. Devlin to leave. Didn't he say come not to the door of her house? But instead, he continued his pacing, muttering to himself. "Is it the vice that does it? The drink? Or is the drink the result of the sin? Eve's original sin. That is at the root of everything. Eve, how humanity has suffered because of you. The mother of all, and mother of all sin. *Mother*." He bit off the final word with such venom it took Belle aback. He continued his muttering and pacing, sinking deeper into his thoughts, while Belle was inspired by her own.

"Was it your mother who introduced you to the pastor?" she broke in, hoping to jar him back to the present.

He cut a look to her and said, "My mother couldn't rouse herself from her sinful ways long enough to introduce me to anything good or right or just. I had to find my way to the light on my own. Through God's will."

"Your mother was not a godly woman?" Belle prompted.

"No. Never. My father married a weak woman who fell into sin when he died."

"Your father passed away? You didn't mention that in your letters. How sad for you. How old were you?"

"I was a small boy of five. My father was a worker in a railway yard. I remember a man came to our house. Mother was baking a pie and singing. In those days, she sang often. Of course, not worshipful music, but the common tunes. I knew no better and loved to hear her sing. The man came to the door, and she put down her rolling pin and dusted her hands on her apron, and went to open the door. He came in, stood in the kitchen with his hat in his hands, and spoke to my mother. I don't remember what he said, except I heard the words 'rolling stock car.' My mother dropped to the kitchen floor like a puppet with cut strings. You know, before that man came, my mother laughed often. But after that man came, I never saw her smile again. It was replaced by the artifice of a Jezebel, with her face paint and false ways."

Belle was struck by how Mr. Devlin had moved so quickly past his mother's grief, her prostrate on the floor, to the story of Jezebel.

"It sounds like your father's death was very hard on your mother."

"I suppose she was sad that day. It didn't last. The next day she was back to baking pies and cleaning house."

"She had a little boy to take care of," Belle pointed out.

Mr. Devlin merely jutted his chin. "It wasn't long before she greeted her first *gentleman caller*." These final words dripped with scorn. "The gentleman callers became a regularity, which was soon followed by her descent into drink. Truly, I could not have witnessed a more ignominious slide into depravity. It was during one of these visits that I left the house, looking for somewhere else to be—anywhere else—and I stumbled upon the revival tent erected in what had been an empty field the day before."

"How tragic it all is. You were a happy family before that day. She loved your father. It was more than she could bear to lose him." Belle squeezed Mr. Devlin's hand, trying to convey her deep sympathy for him.

The effect was electric. He sprung off the sofa, clutching his hand. "Temptress! Still you try to lure me off the path of righteousness. You use my sad history against me! But you will not prevail, Mrs. Gunness." He brought out a small book from the pocket of his jacket. It was well used, the black leather covers softened and curling. He waved it in front of her. "I have all the shield I need. The word of God is my light and strength." He began pacing again, chanting to himself and nodding his head in rhythm to the words. "'The Lord is my shepherd; I shall not want. He maketh me to lie down in green pastures. He leadeth me beside the still waters. He restoreth my soul. He leadeth me in the paths of righteousness for his name's sake. Yea, though I walk through the valley of the shadow of death, I will fear no evil, for thou art with me. Thy rod and thy staff they comfort me. Thou preparest a table before me in the presence of mine enemies. Thou anointest my head with oil, my cup runneth over. Surely goodness and mercy shall follow me all the days of my life, and I will dwell in the house of the Lord for ever.'" He finished on a whisper, speaking only to himself. And then he burst into tears.

Belle watched the performance. It gave the impression of a child soothing himself with a favorite song, trying to convince himself everything would be all right. It was clear he didn't want to leave.

"Come this way, Mr. Devlin. It's time to rest." She guided her guest, who was now sobbing, upstairs to the room on the left. She put him to bed like a child. "Take your shoes off. Don't be muddying up my clean sheets now."

He huddled on the bed in a fetal position, his arms crossed over his Bible like a favorite toy. His sobs were softening to hiccups.

This boy needed a mother. A mother he never had.

36

The sun was well above the horizon, and Mr. Devlin was still abed. Belle had already started the day's baking and fed the hogs and the chickens, and she'd settled in the library to work on correspondence.

Mr. Nesbitt, from Muncie, a lonely widower with two children due to arrive in eight days, wanted to be certain that she liked children. She wrote back assuring him that she did, that children were a gift from God, and that she looked forward to their arrival. The lie gave her pause. She was no more looking forward to having to care for children in addition to a man than she was to dispatching them. But more importantly, Mr. Nesbitt was an executive at a large corporation and was likely to be her biggest deal to date, so she couldn't pass him up.

There was a letter from a new suitor in Traverse City who wrote to say that the assets he could bring to a marriage included the strength and stamina of youth, along with a lively sense of humor. Belle had plenty of each herself. She tossed the letter in the waste bin.

Her rows and columns were stuffed with correspondence; there was no shortage of men eager to find matrimony with a widow of property. She received so many responses, Belle had taken to recording their projected arrival dates in a journal. The prospects' arrivals were carefully scheduled, about a week apart, so the men would not cross paths with one another.

Belle flipped open the journal and reviewed the schedule for the coming days. With Mr. Devlin's early arrival, there was now a short gap. She drummed her fingers on the pages. How could she fill it? Perhaps she could get Mr. Nesbitt there sooner? Belle ripped up her letter to him and rewrote it, making much of her eagerness to meet his children and urging him to move up his travel plans.

Finally, she unlocked the bottom drawer of her desk. The captive bolt pistol waited patiently to be put into service again. After its successful debut, Belle had carefully cleaned it, removing the screws that held the barrel to the base and taking out the killing rod to wipe it clean of gore. After oiling and replacing the rod, she reattached the barrel with the screws and reset the device to be ready for its next use. Now, lying in her hands, its solid metal felt heavy and cool. And deadly. Its power was intoxicating.

She took a fresh sheet of writing paper and began, "Dear Dr. Heiss, the captive bolt pistol arrived safely last week, thank you. The first use was as you promised, a humane and painless way to euthanize livestock."

Closing out her correspondence, Belle tsked to herself. Still Mr. Devlin had not made an appearance. He was like a little boy who had overtired himself the night before. This would not do. She collected her outgoing letters, locked the pistol safely in its drawer, and rolled down and locked the desk's front. Dropping her letters in the silver tray on a table in the front hall, Belle went to rouse him.

She found him huddled in the bed, covers over his head. A little boy indeed. If he was going to act like a little boy, she would treat him as such. She drew the covers roughly back. "Frank! This is not a vacation resort! It is long past time to be up and about."

"I don't want to. I feel awful," he moaned. He had removed his pants sometime in the night and his shirt was twisted up around his midsection, revealing calico drawers.

"With all that hullabaloo yesterday, I have no doubt you feel quite miserable. You drank that whiskey like a babe with his bottle. But it's nothing a good meal and some fresh air won't cure. You will get up now. You will use the washroom to bathe, and you will dress and make yourself presentable. I expect you downstairs in short order." She spoke with firmness, in a voice that would brook no disobedience. Without waiting for a reply or giving the man-boy any opportunity to argue, Belle left him and returned to the kitchen to fix breakfast.

When Mr. Devlin came down, he was a different man. Contrite and subdued, he called her ma'am and seemed to want her to direct his activities.

"There's my good boy!" Belle greeted him. "Come, sit. You must be hungry." She put a plate of bread and slices of fried ham in front of him.

He ate quietly and wiped his mouth on the cloth napkin by his plate. "Thank you for breakfast, ma'am."

He rose from the table but hovered uncertainly until Belle said, "Clear the table, Frank. Don't leave your dirty dishes there. This isn't a restaurant."

Having received his orders, Frank took his plate and fork and coffee mug to the sink. "Shall I wash them?"

"What a good boy! Yes, thank you. There's soap right there and a dishcloth. Very good. Now dry them, and you can put them away in the buffet. Very nice. Now, I need to go into town to post some letters. You will drive me. We will also visit a pastor and arrange our wedding."

"Our w— wedding?"

"Yes, Frank. That is what you came here for. It won't do for you to stay here without benefit of matrimony. We must observe the proprieties. The pastor in Pinola should be able to marry us this afternoon, I would expect."

Frank gulped. "Yes, ma'am."

***

The marriage went forward just as Belle—she insisted he call her Belle—had proclaimed, and by evening Frank was in nervous agony awaiting what came next.

Frank had never been with a woman before, and his knowledge of marital relations was limited to what he had witnessed of his mother with her gentlemen callers. But this was different. There was no saucy innuendo and seductive looks. Belle took charge of their encounter and led him through it with a calm and reassuring manner.

"Take off your clothes, Frank." She sat in the rocking chair in the corner. "That's right, all the way off. You may fold them and lay them on the dresser."

Frank did as he was told. The cold air raised goose bumps on his skin and his penis hung small and inert.

"Come over here, Frank." He presented himself to her, standing naked like a supplicant. She ran her eyes coolly over his body. She lingered on his manhood, watching it take shape and grow. She reached forward with one hand and cupped him. His balls clenched and his penis hardened. Oh, sweet good night. Holding his gaze, she wrapped her hand around him, drawing slowly along his length. Somehow he knew he mustn't move, mustn't look away.

"Now"—she rose from the chair—"undress me."

Frank didn't know how to undress a woman. They wore so many layers, so many complicated fastenings. He stared dumbly at her.

"Don't just stand there. What do you say when I give you an order?"

"Yes, ma'am."

"That's better. Now do as I told you. Undress me."

"Yes, ma'am." He reached for her sleeve and gave it a tug.

"Not like that, Frank." He'd made her cross. Her sharp tone and baleful stare bored into him.

"I'm sorry, ma'am. I don't know how."

She took pity on him and guided him through how to remove her clothing piece by piece, how it was to be folded, and where he should lay it. He kept his eyes downcast, seeing only the buttons and strings before him, not daring to look at her naked flesh as it was revealed. He tried hard to do everything as she instructed.

"Good boy," she said. "You may look at me."

He was still hesitant to lift his eyes from the floor, but he didn't want to disappoint her or make her cross again. "Yes, ma'am," he said. Her feet were small, with dainty pink toes. He raised his eyes slowly up her legs, but moved swiftly past the juncture of her thighs; that was too much too soon. He diverted to her hands and arms and up to her neck, stopping at her face. Her beautiful face. It told him she knew his fear and understood. Gratitude filled him.

"Good boy, Frank. That's a good beginning." She crossed the room to the bed, moving as if she were created from air and water, not the hard earth that formed man. She reclined on the bed and beckoned to him. "Come to me, Frank."

"Yes, ma'am."

She spread her legs and he clambered forward, fumbling to fit his penis into her. Where was the opening? He pushed and pushed until her fingers finally guided him in. Oh, blessed God! Her softness sheathed him, held him tight, and he lost himself stroking in and out. His release erupted quickly, robbing him of sense.

"There, there, Frank. That's a good boy," Belle murmured as he lay in her arms, sobbing.

Belle established a routine for them. She woke Frank early and they prayed together on their knees in the parlor, under shafts of morning sunlight. After prayer, they broke their fast with a simple but wholesome meal Belle prepared. They spent their morning in Bible study, Belle urging Frank to instruct her and Frank eager to complete his mission to bring her to the light. Afternoons were for chores, because man was meant to work. As Frank taught her, "and the Lord God took the man, and put him into the garden of Eden to dress it and to keep it." And in the evenings, after a simple supper and more prayer, Belle took Frank to bed.

Each time he obeyed a motherly command, she saw a happier man, a man at peace.

Before dawn on the morning of the third day, Belle woke Frank with a kiss. "Frank, I want to pray," she told him. "I want to pray as the sun rises, and welcome the day with a prayer of thanksgiving."

"Yes, beloved," Frank said, his eyes gleaming with devotion and desire.

They rose and went out in the darkness. A blanket of frost sparkled in the moonlit grass. Belle led Frank out to the field, to the low rise topped by the cherry tree. As she walked, the heft of the captive bolt pistol in her dress pocket knocked against her legs.

Belle shepherded Frank to a spot under the cherry tree, not far from a hole that had been dug by Ray the night before. In the dark, Frank could not see the deep pit, six feet long and six feet deep, and Belle made sure he did not stray too close to it.

Belle took Frank's hands. "Let us kneel," she said, and they sank to the earth, face-to-face, knees touching. Frank's eyes were pools of blackness. "Will you lead us in a prayer?" she asked. Belle closed her eyes and bowed her head, and waited for Frank's words.

"Let us give thanks to the Lord our God," Frank said.

"It is right to give thanks," Belle responded, as he had taught her.

"'Oh come, let us sing unto the Lord. Let us make a joyful noise to the rock of our salvation. Let us come before his presence with thanksgiving, and make a joyful noise unto him with psalms.'"

As Frank spoke, Belle opened her eyes and watched him in the faint gray light that had begun to seep over the horizon. His hands were clasped over his heart, and his eyes were closed, his face rapt with sincerity and devotion. He rocked forward slightly to emphasize the words: let us *sing* unto the *Lord*, let us make a *joyful* noise to the *rock* of our *salvation*.

Belle leaned her forehead against Frank's. "Beloved Frank," she whispered and kissed his mouth before pressing her lips to his forehead.

"'For the Lord is a great God,'" Frank continued, eyes still fervently closed, the breath of his words puffing into her neck, "'and a great King above all gods. In his hand are the deep places of the earth; the strength of the hills is his also. The sea is his, and he made it: and his hands formed the dry land. O come, let us worship and bow down: let us kneel before the Lord our maker. For he is our God; and we are the people of his pasture, and the sheep of his hand.'"

Belle withdrew the pistol from the pocket of her dress, replaced her lips with its mouth, and depressed the trigger. The bolt's action was swift and loud, echoing across the field. Frank fell backward, his hands still folded over his heart. The features of his face held the serene repose of a man at peace. Belle straightened his legs and gently arranged his body. She gripped him by the shoulders and dragged him to the waiting pit. Frank was not a large man, and although the task stole her breath, she was able to lug him the several feet and roll him into the earthen chamber.

"Goodbye, Frank," she said. "You've found peace now."

37

A fresh breeze had come in the night and swept away the storm clouds that had hovered over northern Indiana for days on end, soaking the fields and roads in torrents of rain. The wind had howled around the little caretaker's cottage, making Ray's rest a fitful one. The springs of his cot squealed as he swung his legs to the floor. However restless his night had been, he was eager to be up and about his day.

As always, once the work associated with a husband was complete, Belle had more time for Ray. With that last one—Devlin, was it?—in the ground, Ray saw Belle constantly. She asked him into the house for minor repairs, came to visit him when he worked outside, and, best of all, spent the nights with him.

He dressed quickly and ate a plate of cold beans, then left his quarters behind to go ready Gwen and the gig for a trip to town. Sunlight caught in the raindrops that beaded on the grass, throwing off sparkles and reflecting his own sunny mood.

"Good morning, Ray!" Belle called as he brought Gwen and the carriage up to her front door. She stowed her shopping basket in the back of the gig and climbed into the driver's seat. "I don't know if you noticed, but those lilac bushes you pruned last summer are starting to bud."

"I did see that, Miz Belle." Ray settled onto the seat next to her. "Won't be long before you have some pretty flowers to enjoy."

"Well done, Ray. Thank you. Get up now, Gwen," Belle called to her mare and snapped the reins. Gwen set off at a lively trot.

"You expecting anyone to arrive today?" Ray asked.

"Not yet." She cast a glance back at her basket. "We have an extra two days before we have another guest."

Ray's heart swelled. Another two days of having Belle all to himself! He deserved it. He had accustomed himself to his role in what she called "the business." He just had to wait out the three days and nights she gave every husband, and once the work was complete, his reward was so glorious, he could forget those three nights. Or try to, anyway.

Belle was energized as they set off for town. In her handbag was a check made out to Mrs. Belle Gunness, signed in a very close approximation of Frank's crabbed signature. The two extra days in her schedule loomed ahead of her, but she hoped her letter to Mr. Nesbitt would convince him to come sooner. And if not, well, she would think of something.

The livery was busy. As they drew up, she saw Gabriel turn away a dray pulled by two strong workhorses.

"Gabriel, do you have nothing left?"

"Fear not, fear not," he assured her, taking Gwen by the bridle and stroking her nose. The mare nuzzled his palm, looking for treats. "Folks are taking advantage of this nice weather to come into town and get supplies and all the scuttlebutt. It's so busy I've got 'em packed tighter than two coats of paint. But I saw you coming, Mrs. Gunness. I've always got a stall for Gwen here. Don't I, girl?"

"Oh, Gabriel, you *are* an angel."

After passing off the reins, Belle and Ray navigated their way among the throngs to the telegraph office. Just as they reached the entrance of the train station, Alice Longacre rushed up, spots of color highlighting her pale cheeks, her hands clutching a book. "Hello, Mrs. Gunness, Mr. Lamphere! How happy I am to see you!"

The young schoolteacher's outsize greeting startled Belle; the girl had always been polite, but no more than that. But then she caught the way Miss Longacre mooned up at Ray, and all was clear. The girl had calf's eyes for her handyman. How quaint. Wouldn't that be something? Alice and Ray.

But no, that was ridiculous. Ray belonged to Belle.

"Good afternoon, Miss Longacre. Shouldn't you be teaching school right now?"

Belle's comment cut into Miss Longacre's mooning and she cut a look at Belle. "Oh, well, I gave them the day off. It's so lovely out, I thought everyone could do with a break. I've been reading my book." She held it up, showing them the title: *A Romance of Two Worlds*. "It's very exciting, by Marie Corelli. Do you like to read, Mr. Lamphere?" Ray didn't seem to know quite how to respond. He couldn't meet Miss Longacre's fawning looks and kept glancing away, but the young lady was not deterred. "Mr. Lamphere, there's a church dance on Saturday. Will you be going?"

"Oh, er," fumbled Ray. He sent a pleading look to Belle, but she was enjoying the scene far too much to rescue him. "I, er, expect I'll have to work, Miss Longacre."

"Oh, that's too bad." The light in Miss Longacre's eyes dimmed, but then something over Ray's shoulder caught her attention and she startled. "Lovely to see you, I must go! Mr. Lamphere, if you come on Saturday, I'll save you a dance!" And she was gone, darting off into the crowd.

"How sweet, Ray. You have an admirer," Belle teased. "It's all right with me if you take some time off to go to the dance. I would never want to stand in the way of your happiness."

Ray's face darkened and he opened his mouth to speak but didn't get a chance. Pastor Bauer bustled up, visibly angry.

"Did you see Miss Longacre just now?" he demanded, and then

checked himself. "I'm sorry to be so abrupt. Good day, Mrs. Gunness, Mr. Lamphere." He gave them each a courtly nod. "But I am looking for Miss Longacre. She is absent from the schoolroom."

Oh, ho, so that's how it was. The little schoolteacher was playing hooky. Belle enjoyed a secret glee at the drama the whey-faced girl had created, but feigned disapproval in her response. "Oh, my. Is she not settling in to her responsibilities?"

"Mrs. Gunness, I'll tell you, I pray for that young lady every day. She isn't what we expected at all. Not at all."

"Oh? How is that?"

"She's flighty, Mrs. Gunness. Flighty and not at all a serious Christian woman. Oh, she attends my sermons and always brings something for the church supper afterwards. But I can see her attention wanders during the service. And, do you know, she sends the children home early from school at least once a week. And some days, she doesn't show up to teach them at all. No one knows where she goes."

"Oh, my," Belle commiserated. "I never would have guessed."

"Indeed. The townsfolk are quite dissatisfied. We hired her to teach our children, and she is not meeting her obligations. Honestly, I would not be surprised to find that she had up and run away some day."

"My word, Pastor," Belle said. "Have you talked with her about it?"

"Until I'm blue in the face," Pastor Bauer said. "She nods and agrees and promises to do better, and the next day it's the same thing all over again. Excuse me, I must find her." And off he hurtled, his black coat flapping behind him.

"Well, that was a delightful little melodrama. I wonder how it will turn out. Remember, Ray, you have my permission to go to the dance on Saturday." Belle ignored Ray's scowl and, still chuckling to herself, entered the station.

Belle and Ray had finished sending her telegram to Mr. Nesbitt when a rumbling roar from outside drew everyone's attention. They and a crowd of others rushed out in time to see a motorcar come to a stop across the street in front of the saloon.

The machine was breathtaking, and its driver magnificent. The two-seater sported shiny brass lanterns at each corner, with button-tufted black leather upholstery and the wood painted a shocking scarlet. The driver's looks were nearly as striking: jet-black hair to match the upholstery and a strapping form as powerful as the vehicle's engine, clad in tawny trousers tailored to show off muscular thighs, a gold-striped black waistcoat under a long duster, and a scarlet scarf. He rested the tiller-steerer on the seat next to him and removed his cap and driving goggles. Readjusting his flat cap, he tossed the goggles on the seat with a cavalier air, seemingly unconscious of the stares his arrival in town was drawing.

Belle swayed forward, uninhibited by the awe that had frozen the gawkers on the street. "Good morning, sir. Welcome to La Porte."

"Is that the name of this little town?" He looked around, unimpressed, as he stripped off his driving gloves. His face was dusty where it had been unprotected by his goggles.

"What brings you to our corner of Indiana? Perhaps I can direct you."

"What?" He jumped out of the vehicle and circled to the rear. "Oh, not necessary. Everything I need is right there." He pointed at the saloon, then began to tinker with the engine, hidden inside a compartment.

Belle came alongside the car-driving Adonis and admired the works of the machine. "Oh, my, what a complicated machine! It must be so . . . powerful." The man reached into the engine with a wrench, nearly elbowing Belle in the stomach. "I said it must be such a *power-ful* machine," she tried again, adding a special emphasis to make him understand she meant more than his motorcar.

"Yes, yes," he said impatiently.

"How much horsepower?" Ray asked, having joined Belle in looking over the engine.

The driver's head emerged, and he stood up straight and looked Ray in the eye. "Hello, there," he said, sidling closer. "It's a four-horsepower engine. I built it myself. It gets up to almost twenty miles per hour."

"Why, you could drive all the way to Chicago in just a few hours!" Belle said, coyly laying her hand on the driver's arm. "My word!"

The driver extricated himself from Belle's touch and, with a tip of his cap to Ray, disappeared into the saloon.

Though befuddled by the man's blatant disinterest in her, Belle couldn't stop thinking about his motorcar. Twenty miles per hour! If she had one, she could go to Chicago for lunch! Wouldn't that be marvelous? She wondered how much a motorcar cost. Probably several thousand dollars. Frank hadn't been a huge windfall—only $1,000—but considering she was still sitting pretty on her earnings from Louis, and Mr. Nesbitt's nest egg sounded promising, perhaps she could consider it. She went about her errands in a blur of calculations and daydreams.

At the mercantile, their last stop before loading up the carriage and returning home, Belle turned to Ray while Mr. Fischer filled a sack with flour. Piled on the counter were butter, eggs, beans, rice, and coffee and tea. "Ray, what do you think? Should I get a motorcar? I wouldn't want that shocking red, though. Perhaps they could paint mine blue. Wouldn't blue be lovely? To match my eyes?"

"Sure, Miz Belle. Blue would be awful nice. You'd need a mechanic, though, I think. Someone who knows how to fix engines. Looks mighty complicated. And I hear they break down all too regular."

Belle ignored Ray's doomsaying. He always had to focus on the negative in a situation. "I'm sure I could find someone, Ray. Perhaps you could be my mechanic. I have no doubt that you could learn to fix it. Would you like that? I could get you a livery uniform. Something dashing, with a cap and brass buttons. That would be delightful! Don't you think? Although, I probably will want to drive myself, so perhaps not."

Back on the street with her packages and parcels, Belle was disappointed to see that the motorcar had disappeared. She would have liked another crack at its driver. Goodness, he was handsome. Belle wouldn't mind a truly handsome husband for once. And he must have money if he's building and driving a motorcar.

On the way out of town, Belle was still daydreaming about driving through the countryside in a splashy new motorcar. "But don't worry, Gwen," she cooed to the placidly walking white mare. "You'll always have a place in my barn. Oh, look, Ray!"

Up ahead, parked on the side of the road, was the black and scarlet motorcar, with its striking driver again bent over the engine compartment.

"Hello!" she called as they drew up alongside. "Do you need assistance?"

"Not necessary," he said over his shoulder. "Just a small adjustment."

Ray hopped down from Belle's carriage and joined him. "You built this yourself? That's quite a job."

The driver looked up and grinned when he saw Ray, who was studying the workings of the engine. Why was Ray getting a smile while Belle got ignored? "Well, I learned on bicycles. And when I heard about what Mr. Benz built in Germany, I couldn't get enough of reading about it. Before long, all the richest of the rich will own one of my motocars. Are you a fan of machining?"

"Not like you," Ray answered. "It would be a good thing to learn. Times are changing."

"I'm Simon Gladstone." He shook Ray's hand and held it for a long moment.

"Um, Ray Lamphere. Pleased to make your acquaintance."

Gladstone went back to tinkering with the engine, all the while explaining to Ray what he was doing. "Ah! That's got it. Come now, Lamphere. I'll show you how to get 'er going." Gladstone insert-ed a crank arm and gave it a few spins, bringing the engine to life with a growl.

"Oh!" Belle gasped and then giggled, seeing the chance to reinsert herself into the situation. "Listen to her go! I would love a ride, Mr. Gladstone, if you please."

"Sorry, but no." Gladstone shook his head. "If I say yes to one, I have to say yes to all. And if I gave a ride to every person who asked, I'd be going all day like some kind of carnival ride."

Did she hear him right? They were on the side of the road, sur-rounded by fields and farms, not another soul in sight. Where were all these clamoring ride-seekers he alleged? He could give her a ride, but clearly he didn't want to. Was she losing her touch?

Then it dawned on her. She'd been wrong about Frank, but this man's attraction to another man was plain as day. Ray was quite the attraction, it seemed. First Alice, now this fellow. Well, if she couldn't have the driver, she could still have the motorcar. Ray was clearly oblivious, but no matter. Belle knew just how to take advantage of the opportunity.

"Mr. Gladstone, it would be my honor to have you for dinner this evening. Perhaps you can show Ray everything he might want to know about your powerful engine. Ray loves big, strong engines, don't you, Ray?"

"Oh, sure, of course," Ray agreed with an awkward blush.

"That would be grand, thank you," Gladstone said, beaming at Ray. "Lamphere, why don't you ride with me, then."

So Gladstone was happy to break his no-rides rule for Ray? She had his number all right. Belle waved them off and followed slowly behind in her gig.

38

"**R**ight this way, Mr. Gladstone." Ray was surprised when Belle beckoned him into the parlor as well. "You, too, Ray, come have refreshments with us."

"Well, then," said Ray, unsure how to act when treated like a guest in the house he only ever entered as a handyman. He hovered awkwardly at the threshold of the elegant room. He was still unsettled from the attention he'd received from Miss Longacre. In a different world, Ray might have courted her. She wasn't bad to look at, and though she was a bit on the young side, she was almost the right age to make a good wife for him. But with her pale face and washed-out personality, Miss Longacre couldn't begin to compare with Belle.

"Ray! Don't just stand there." She gave him an encouraging smile. "Come, sit and relax. There, that's better," she said once she had maneuvered him onto the sofa next to Gladstone. "You fellows get comfortable, and I'll prepare a tray."

Ray felt self-conscious, sitting on the silk-covered sofa in his work clothes. They were clean, to be sure; Belle kept him supplied in good, sturdy trousers and shirts and saw that they were laundered regularly. But he felt like a country bumpkin next to Gladstone, who lounged with one foot, clad in a glossy black boot, resting on the other knee.

He seemed awfully at ease. Mere inches separated his thigh from Ray's own, and Ray perched forward, conscious of Gladstone's arm behind him and his eyes pinned on Ray's profile. Was Gladstone getting closer? Something brushed Ray's shoulders and he jumped. Gladstone's arm had dropped down the sofa back, almost like he was putting it around Ray. And now he was leaning in.

"So, Lamphere, what do you do?"

"I'm, uh, I'm the handyman for Miz Belle. I do whatever she tells me to." He tried to look Gladstone in the eye, like a man, but couldn't hold it. Safer to look at his boots.

"Really?" Gladstone leaned yet closer. "Do you always do *whatever* people tell you to?"

"Of course not!" Heat burned Ray's cheeks. Something about the way Gladstone spoke made him uncomfortable. Was the man teasing him for being too obedient? He wasn't a slave. It was his job to do what Belle asked, that was all.

Belle arrived with a tray arrayed with crackers and slices of cheese and meat, plates and glasses, and a bottle of whiskey. She poured Ray a generous serving and winked as she handed it to him, a special sign between the two of them. These were Ray's favorite times with Belle, when she was between husbands and they worked together, almost as equals. Though he wasn't exactly sure what she was up to by inviting Gladstone for dinner. She probably just wanted her own turn riding in his motorcar. He took a large swallow of the whiskey and enjoyed the warm slide down his throat. He took another swallow and leaned back on the sofa, bumping into Gladstone's arm. He immediately jumped forward. "Oh, hey there, sorry about that."

"Nothing to worry about, good man." Gladstone shifted his arm slightly. "Go ahead, lean back and relax. Tell me about your job here, Lamphere. This is a big spread for one man to run, isn't it?"

Ray eased back again. "'Bout forty-two acres, a few hogs, flock of chickens."

"Don't forget Gwen and my carriage," Belle put in gaily.

"No, course not. It's not too much. Miz Belle does her share too. She's not above hard work."

She smiled at Ray warmly, as if to acknowledge their special bond and their successful business. Not that he'd tell Gladstone about that. He finished his whiskey, and Belle immediately refilled it.

"Thank you kindly, Miz Belle," he said with a conspiratorial grin.

"Think nothing of it, Ray," Belle replied. "Why don't you tell Mr. Gladstone about the cattle." She refilled Gladstone's glass, too, and set the bottle on its tray. Rather than take her seat, she idly moved about the room, hands clasped behind her back, nodding while listening to the men talk.

"Cattle? You're a cattleman?" Gladstone had twisted his torso to fully face Ray on the sofa, his arm resting across the sofa back.

"Not yet."

Gladstone cocked his head and gave Ray a sly grin. "You seem . . . a little uncomfortable. You're not one of those fellows who's afraid of other men, are you?"

"No. No, of course not." What was to be afraid of? He was just sitting on the sofa, next to Gladstone, talking. Ray hadn't spent much time sitting on sofas in fancy parlors, having conversations. This must be how fancy folks sat together.

"That's good, I'm glad. I wouldn't want you to be afraid of me. I had hoped we could be friends." Gladstone clapped his hand on Ray's shoulder with a broad grin.

A wash of loneliness swept over Ray, quickly replaced by a spark of hope. Ray didn't really have any friends outside of Belle, and he wouldn't give her up for anything. He searched for her, craning his neck to see her wandering the room. She circled behind Gladstone and gave Ray a reassuring nod.

No, he'd never replace Belle, but maybe there was room for Gladstone too. Wouldn't that be something? To have a friend, a man he could talk to and spend time with? Maybe they could visit the saloon—

Bang!

A spatter of warm liquid hit Ray's face and his thoughts froze. Gladstone dropped forward into his lap, blood trickling from a small black hole in the thick of the man's dark hair. Shittagoddam!

Belle stood behind the sofa, a long black cylinder in her hand. What on earth was that? Ray had never seen anything like it. He looked at the device and then down at Gladstone, and he suddenly understood how Brown met his end. Devlin, too, most likely, though he'd only had to shovel in the dirt for that one.

Belle wiped blood off the deadly instrument and slid it into the pocket of her skirt.

"Come on, play time is over." She took Ray's drink out of his hand. "Let's get this done. I don't want him leaking blood all over my sofa."

Jenny was tired. Asle knew he couldn't ask much more of her. She had valiantly carried him on a circuitous path through the countryside of northern Indiana. They'd been through dozens of unnamed towns, visited hundreds of farmhouses, asked countless locals about Andrew. Now here they were some miles south of Michigan City, on a minor road that wended through pastures and farmland. Jenny plodded from foot to foot, barely moving forward. The poor mare was about done in, and Asle wasn't sure he could go much farther either. He had heard train whistles in the distance, and the thought crossed his mind that he could sell Jenny and ride the train back to Chicago. He pushed the thought away as unworthy.

Jenny came to a halt. Asle gently tapped the reins against her neck and whispered, "Come on now, girl. Let's go." But Jenny wouldn't budge. Asle sighed and dismounted. He couldn't blame her. He stroked her nose. "You're a good girl, Jenny. You've done more than I should have asked of you." He led her to the side of the road and removed her saddle and bridle. Perhaps if they had a little rest, Jenny could at least make it into town. He took a brush from his bags and rubbed down her sides. "I have to thank you for carrying me all this way in search of my brother. He is a stranger to you, but I think you would like him. Everyone does."

Jenny patiently accepted Asle's efforts to brush dust and debris from her coat. He stroked the brush down her gray flanks. "Andrew could never resist an adoring audience. Or a hot flame. He was caught more than once playing with matches. One afternoon, late in summer, Andrew took a pilfered box of matches behind the alderman's barn, where there was a large hay field. He and a crowd of children dared each other to see who could hold a lit match the longest. I know what you are wondering, Jenny. And the answer is, yes, I was one of those children."

Asle moved to Jenny's other side, trailing his hand along her neck as he crossed in front of her.

"Most of the matches were shaken out before falling to the ground. But Andrew, my stubborn, grandstanding brother—" Jenny stamped the ground. "Yes, exactly," Asle responded. "I see you understand where this is going. Well, my brother, determined to impress, hung on to his match until the last possible moment. The flame singed his fingers, forcing him to drop the still-burning match. Fire and dry hay being what they are, you can guess what came next."

Asle packed away the brush and fed Jenny a handful of oats as he finished his story. "It set the edge of the field alight. All the children ran, except Andrew, who tore off his shirt and began beating at the flames. But it had been a hot, dry summer, and the fire outpaced his efforts. In the end, the whole field burned, and the alderman's barn suffered damage before the town's fire brigade brought the fiasco under control."

Satisfied that his mount was taken care of, Asle lowered himself to the ground to rest against the saddle and folded his hands behind his head. Jenny nickered softly and began cropping at the grass.

"Now, the alderman was not a bad man. But he had suffered a great loss and wanted restitution. He demanded Andrew's arrest. 'But he's only a boy!' our parents protested. It was a great to-do, and my parents worried we would not be able to leave for America as planned." Asle eyed Jenny calmly snuffling in the grass, seeking tender shoots. "Are you not on the edge of your seat, wondering how it all came out? I confess, I am not the storyteller Andrew is. Do you know who talked the alderman out of making an example of my brother? Why, Andrew, of course. He went to see the alderman and wove his magic and somehow convinced the old man. And that, Jenny, is my brother in a nutshell. He can't resist playing with fire, and he can talk his way out of anything."

Jenny made no comment and continued her search for sweet grass. Asle settled back against the saddle and sleepily surveyed their surroundings. The country they'd traveled through was mostly good farmland interspersed with stands of trees, but here they had come to lowlands that were marshy on both sides of the road. Tangled brush and trees, newly green with unfurled leaves, obscured Asle's view. Bullfrogs galumphed and red-winged blackbirds had their say. Asle thought to let his eyes close and take a quick nap when something caught his attention.

Through the screen of branches and leaves, he spied something that shouldn't be in the woods. He sat up, and it disappeared behind leaves. He lowered himself again, and there it was: a black board with gold letters painted on it. Asle could just make out RAWL, with the rest of the word hidden under foliage. As he leaped to his feet, the letters vanished in the thick brush. Asle forced his way through the tangle while marshy ground squelched under his boots and wet began to seep through the worn leather at his toes. Undergrowth caught at his trousers and scraped at his hands as he pushed branches aside. Mosquitoes swarmed his face, their buzzing like needles in his ear. Finally, he came upon a mound of tree limbs. Not a bush, but branches that had been deliberately cut and piled. He pushed some aside and discovered a black wagon. He frantically dragged the branches down, tossing them aside. Painted on the boards in gold letters were the words W.T. RAWLEIGH COMPANY.

Thank God. Finally, something concrete.

But what did it mean? Asle didn't want to jump to conclusions, but it seemed ominous to find Andrew's wagon hidden in the woods. One possibility was that something had indeed befallen Andrew, and his wagon was hidden by the perpetrators. But another possibility was that Andrew had hidden the wagon himself, for some mysterious reason, and was perfectly healthy in an unknown location.

Asle cleared the rest of the brush off the wagon and set to work examining what was left inside it, waving mosquitoes away as he searched. There wasn't much. The compartments held Andrew's bottles and tins of cures, salves, tinctures, and whatnot. A lot of it rubbish, in Asle's estimation. There was no luggage, no sign of Andrew's suitcase of clothing. Just some bits of trash and an old discarded newspaper, abandoned under the driver's bench.

Asle fought his way through the bracken back to the road and Jenny. Frustration boiled over, and he slammed his fist into the nearest tree, then cursed loudly at the pain. He clutched his hand and inspected the knuckles. They were red and beginning to swell. Stupid.

But, dammit! He'd come so far! What a stroke of luck to find Andrew's wagon, and what a crushing disappointment to find nothing inside it to help point the way.

Jenny nickered softly and went back to searching the roadside for greens. Asle lowered himself to the saddle and used a stick to scrape mud out of the seams of his boots. Now what?

Asle knew he was being unreasonable. Locating the wagon was an incredible clue, not to be sneezed at. He knew for sure that Andrew had been to this very spot. Perhaps he was close by. Perhaps he had taken his suitcase and stashed his wagon because he had no safe place to keep it where he was staying.

And perhaps Asle was grasping at straws.

Still, while Asle might not know when Andrew had been here or where he went after, he at least had a starting point. He had a location and a—

Of course! You fool, Asle cursed himself. The newspaper. It would have a date! With a date, he could narrow down the time frame when Andrew had been in these parts. Perhaps that would jog people's memories.

He heaved himself to his feet. "Hang on, Jenny. I'll be right back."

Asle pushed into the thicket, thrashing at the undergrowth to make his way back to the wagon. Mosquitoes descended upon him in welcome. He clambered up into the front, reaching under the driver's seat for the newspaper. He felt a tickle on his ear and slapped at it, his hand coming away with a smear of blood. Damn mosquitoes. He snagged the newspaper and climbed down. The paper was yellowed and wrinkly, but the masthead was clearly legible.

It was the *Chicago Tribune*, and the dateline proclaimed October 4, 1890.

October? But that didn't make any sense. Andrew was still in Chicago, staying with Asle and his family then. Why would Andrew have an outdated newspaper with him? Unless he discarded it and never realized it was underneath his seat? Which would mean the newspaper meant nothing.

Mosquitoes swirled around Asle, angling for their share of his blood. He swatted at the pests with the folded newspaper. They scattered, only to cloud around him as soon as he stopped. Asle abandoned the wagon and made for the dry and relatively mosquito-free road, waving the bloodsuckers away with the paper in one hand and pushing branches aside with the other.

"No luck, Jenny," he greeted his horse. Her only response was to continue cropping at the grass. "We'd best be getting on. There should be a town close by. We can ask around and maybe stay a night or two and rest up."

Asle let the newspaper flap to the ground and bent to pick up his saddle. As his fingers touched leather, his eyes landed on the back of the paper for the first time. He immediately burst out laughing.

***

"Start it up, Ray," Belle called gaily as she loaded a picnic basket into the small open compartment above the engine in the rear of the motorcar. When nothing happened, she turned to check on Ray. "What's wrong?"

Ray surveyed the vehicle from the back, hands on hips. "I don't know where he stowed that crank arm." They searched around the picnic basket, checked under the driver's seat, and looked for hidden compartments. Finally, Ray got down on the ground and peered up at the undercarriage. "Ah ha! Got you, you son of a bitch." He emerged holding a metal bar bent on both ends. "It rests in a bracket under there." Ray fitted the gear end of the bar onto the crankshaft and turned the handle a few times.

"Off we go!" cried Belle over the rat-a-tat-tat of the engine, as Ray hopped in. She pressed the accelerator pedal, and the motorcar lurched forward. "Hurray!"

At the end of her driveway, she pushed the steering tiller hard to the right, and the wheels veered left sharply, sending them careening into the road. The force shot the vehicle up on its right-side wheels, the left side hovering in the air. They hung there for a moment, and Belle screamed in terrified glee. Then the motorcar crashed down on all four wheels again, and they sped off down the road.

The breeze on Belle's face as they raced through the countryside was electrifying. Even at a full gallop, Gwen pulling the gig could never produce this kind of pace.

To think, not even a year ago, Belle was desperately trying to get Mads to listen to her ideas about how to make the candy shop successful. Oh, how he had dismissed her and belittled her. And yet here she was, the mastermind of her own business, successful beyond anything she dreamed of in that dingy, old candy shop. Plus, she was the owner of a *motorcar*. Only the richest, most successful people owned motorcars.

A little twinge reminded Belle that she had taken it without her usual contract. She hadn't solved anything for Gladstone or given him his heart's desire. That contract was her trademark, her warranty, and she had skipped straight to its termination. It was as if she had delivered an empty crate but still collected payment.

Belle pushed the unwelcome thoughts away. Never mind. She would have married him if she could have. Was it her fault he wasn't interested in her, or any woman? She gave him Ray for a little while, wasn't that enough?

"It's marvelous, Ray! Don't you think?" She had to raise her voice to be heard over the noise of the engine and the wind.

"Marvelous!" Ray agreed.

"It's good to see you smile so!" Belle cried. He gripped the side of the seat with white knuckles but couldn't hide his glee.

Belle drove them to the same spot where she had picnicked with Charles Gunness, in the meadow by the lake. Ray helped her unload the basket, and they spread it all on a blanket in the grass. Belle fixed a plate for Ray, piling it with cold fried chicken, and poured them both a glass of wine.

"Here's to us," Belle said, raising her glass. "We've built something real, Ray. I've built a glorious life here in La Porte through hard work and perseverance. You've been beside me every step of the way. I couldn't have done it without you. Here's to many more years of happiness. *Skål.*"

39

Asle Helgelien sauntered along Washington Street in downtown La Porte, saddlebags slung over his shoulder and the newspaper tucked under his arm, happily calling himself ten kinds of fool. Why hadn't he immediately flipped the paper over and checked the back side? Asle could only blame his fatigue and hunger. Either that, or he had always been thickheaded, which he didn't think was really the case.

The paper hadn't been thoughtlessly abandoned; it had been purposely folded to the classifieds section and saved, with one ad circled in ink: "Comfortable widow, young, with good appearance, seeking partner for 42-acre farm. View to matrimony. Write to Mrs. Belle Gunness, care of this newspaper."

Things were beginning to make sense. Near where he'd found the wagon, a passing farmer had given Asle directions to the nearest town, La Porte, just five miles away.

Suddenly Asle had many clues: a place, a time frame, a name. And he wasn't about to waste time writing to the newspaper to receive her address. No, if Andrew's wagon was in the woods outside La Porte, he must have stopped somewhere close by to meet this mysterious "comfortable widow."

It was a charming little town, sidewalks busy with friendly folk.

Asle found a livery for Jenny and walked to the train station. The stationmaster seemed as good a place as any to start asking around. The office was inside the station, which also held a restaurant and hotel. Asle thought longingly of a hot bath and a good meal.

Asle knocked and entered the stationmaster's office, which was small and stuffy, filled with clouds of pipe smoke. The man himself sat behind his desk, a briarwood pipe clenched in his teeth.

"Good morning, sir," the stationmaster greeted him, pulling the pipe from his lips. He wore a pleasant expression under his peaked cap. A bottlebrush mustache neatly topped his upper lip.

"Good morning to you," Asle said. "Do you happen to know a Mrs. Belle Gunness?"

"Of course, of course." The stationmaster frowned at his cold pipe and searched his desktop, landing on a box of matches that hid behind a pen stand. "Everybody knows Mrs. Gunness."

Asle experienced a satisfying feeling of pieces thunking into place. She was here, in La Porte. "How do I find her?"

"That's easy enough. Now, you just go out there on Washington Street, make a left at the corner and follow it until you get to the McClung Road. Her mansion is out there about two miles. On the left. You can't miss it."

"Mansion? Mrs. Gunness is a wealthy woman?" Asle hadn't put much stock in the details of the lonely hearts advertisement.

"Oh, sure. Wealthy, beautiful, kind. Everybody loves Mrs. Gunness. Such a shame she lost her husband." The stationmaster gave a sad shake of his head. "But she took in her great-uncle, suffering from dementia, I've been told, and has welcomed a few other guests to her home over the months, perhaps family coming to pay their respects before the old man dies."

"Indeed," Asle said politely. So that part was true too. She really was a widow, really was attractive and wealthy. This was promising. If she was honest in her ad, wasn't that a good sign? "Do you recall seeing a traveling salesman come through town, heading out to her place?

The wagon was branded 'W.T. Rawleigh Company' on the side. Have you seen that come through any time in the last six months, around November, perhaps?"

The stationmaster gave the question due consideration and finally said, "Can't say I have, sorry."

"I see. Thank you."

Asle took a room in the hotel, and after a scorching hot bath and a very decent meal at the restaurant, he settled down at the desk in his room to write home to Matilda. He'd sent her a few telegrams over the last weeks to let her know he was all right, but this would be his first chance to write a letter. Putting pen to paper didn't come naturally, but he knew Matilda would appreciate hearing from him.

Early the next morning, just before dawn, Asle visited Jenny in her stall at the livery, and with apologies for making her work again so soon, saddled her up and followed the directions given to him by the stationmaster, through the dark streets and out into the farms and pastures on the north side of town.

The widow's residence appeared before him in the gloom of breaking dawn, as big and ostentatious as the word "mansion" implied. The house was fronted by a circular driveway of crushed stone wrapped around a plot of grass. A small but neat caretaker's cottage stood off from the house a ways. New-looking barbed wire fencing stretched along the road to both sides. Asle rode past and found a stand of trees farther down the road, from which he could observe the house without being seen. From his angle, he could catch glimpses of a barn and animal pen behind the house.

Before long, he saw signs of life—first an upstairs light, presumably a bedroom. Then after a time, a light in a downstairs room in the back: the kitchen, most likely.

Matilda had lately taken up the newly popular hobby of birdwatching, so on her last birthday, Asle had given her a pair of fine binoculars from France. They were quite expensive, costing more than he should have spent—if Matilda knew how much, she would be cross with him.

They were made of brass and leather with superior optics, and Matilda had delighted in sighting and identifying the feathered creatures that populated their neighborhood.

Asle used them now to bring the figure moving within the kitchen into clarity. A woman, with brown hair swept up in a style that Asle recognized as fashionable. Mrs. Gunness, no doubt. Asle watched her performing the familiar chores of any home kitchen: stoking the stove, boiling water. She came out the back door and tended to what his binoculars revealed to be hogs in the pen behind the house and then went into a coop with a basket, emerging with her head bowed over it counting eggs, Asle surmised.

A man then appeared in the yard, walking toward the barn. In an instant, Asle knew it was not his brother. The man was too short and too slight, and his gait was nothing like Andrew's loping stride. Judging by this man's dress, he must be a hired man of some sort. Asle couldn't see the front of the caretaker's cottage, but the man had come from that direction and was headed toward the barn. In short order, the lanky man led a white horse hitched to a small gig to the front door. Asle knew it was time to move.

Nothing he had seen indicated that Andrew was living there, or a great-uncle. Had Andrew arrived and met Mrs. Gunness, only to discover the match would not suit, and moved on? A flicker of hope lit within him. For a moment, he imagined Andrew on his way back to Aberdeen, perhaps even now arriving to find Asle gone. How he and Matilda would laugh!

But then why would his wagon be abandoned in the woods? Asle's fantasy evaporated in the strong light of logic. Did Andrew abandon the wagon, or was that the work of someone else? Asle tried desperately to find innocent explanations for the facts he knew, but it was a struggle.

Mrs. Gunness bustled out the front door and took her place at the reins. She waved off the man and called her horse to a brisk trot. Asle let her drive off before following at a distance.

It wasn't hard to track her down in La Porte. The widow strode along the main street, brightly greeting her fellow townsfolk, a basket swinging from her arm. Her jaunty stride and proud chin gave her the demeanor of a very self-satisfied woman.

Asle returned Jenny to the livery and followed after Mrs. Gunness.

Her first stop was the post office, which Asle observed from the corner opposite. He purchased a paper from a newsboy and held it up in front of his face, flipping pages slowly and lowering it to look about from time to time, a man interested in the news of the day as well as the world around him.

Mrs. Gunness remained within the post office for a quarter of an hour and emerged with a handful of letters that she sifted through as she walked along the sidewalk. Stuffing them in her basket, she entered Fischer Mercantile next. This stop was longer, perhaps a full hour. A stock boy followed her out with a tower of parcels and bags in his arms. A delivery van with Fischer Mercantile stenciled on the side arrived, and Mrs. Gunness directed the stock boy and driver in loading her purchases inside. Far from chafing under her direction, which couldn't be necessary—surely these two had loaded many a delivery wagon in their time—the two men seemed eager for the attention and praise of the woman.

Very interesting.

In the midst of the project, Mrs. Gunness suddenly stilled. She scanned her surroundings as if trying to locate a sound. Asle shook out his paper, holding it high to cover his face. Next time he checked, the wagon was loaded, and Mrs. Gunness was bidding her helpers goodbye. They tipped their hats with besotted grins and returned to their work, the stock boy inside the mercantile and the wagon driver up on his bench, ready to command his team.

It appeared Mrs. Gunness had more to do in town. Asle let a distance open up between them before folding his paper, tucking it under his arm, and sauntering after her.

At the train station, she pushed through the double doors. Was she taking a journey? Asle allowed a couple minutes to pass and then entered. The lobby was empty. Mrs. Gunness was nowhere to be seen. Asle legged it straight through, passing the hotel and restaurant, the telegraph office, and the deserted baggage room. Out on the platform, no train had arrived yet, and Mrs. Gunness was not among the waiting travelers. Returning to the lobby, Asle checked at the ticket counter. Both offices held lines of two or three parties, none of which were Mrs. Gunness.

Where could she have gone? The only other businesses within the train station were the hotel and the restaurant. Approaching the restaurant concierge, Asle spotted Mrs. Gunness at a table in the dining room beyond, sitting across from a stylishly dressed woman.

"Good afternoon, sir. May I show you to a table?"

"No, thank you. But I wonder if you could send a message for me." Asle searched his pocket for one of Andrew's candies. "Please give this to the lady at the table there. The lady sitting on the left."

"Yes, sir. And the message?"

"That is the message. She'll understand."

"Of course."

Asle watched the man place the candy on a small silver tray, with the distinctive I.R. brand facing up, and approach Mrs. Gunness. The instant her glance landed on the little sweet, an unmistakable flash of recognition lit her eyes.

Belle smiled quizzically at the waiter as she plucked the candy from a small tray he extended to her. Her breath seized as she recognized the I.R. on the pale-brown wax paper. *Andrew.* Where did this candy come from? Why would someone send it to her? What did they know? Her eyes darted to the host's desk. "Who sent this? I don't see anyone."

The waiter turned. "He's gone now, ma'am. Can I get you anything else?"

"No, thank you."

Belle fingered the molasses drop as the waiter departed. What could this mean?

"What is it?" asked Della Rose. "You are distressed."

"Oh, nothing," Belle said. "A token from an admirer. Just another man who will doubtless make promises and then break them." Belle dropped the candy in her handbag as if she didn't have a care in the world.

40

"Hello, good afternoon, I'm Morris Nesbitt. Morris Nesbitt of Muncie, Indiana. Perhaps you recall our correspondence. I'm Mr. Nesbitt. Morris." The rabbity man introducing himself on Belle's doorstep took off his bowler to reveal a shiny, bald pate ringed with a soft, mousy-brown fringe. His mustache needed trimming.

Belle could already tell their wedding night would be tame, which was only fair since she was saddled with caring for his two children as well.

The boy and girl, with pale eyes and fine blond hair, flanked him to the left. They looked very much like what their father had described in his letters. The little boy in short pants, just five, stood at smart attention in a burgundy velvet suit of the Fauntleroy style, complete with a white linen shirt decorated with flounces of lace ruffles at collar and cuff. The older child, a frail-looking girl of eight years, was dressed immaculately, from her shiny black boots and stockings to her butter-yellow satin dress. Her serene face was framed by a fringe of bangs and rag curls hanging from a black bow so large it posed on her head like a giant butterfly.

The girl held a leash attached to a small dog, some kind of mixed breed, with wispy hairs sticking out at all directions and an unfortunate overbite. It was perhaps the ugliest dog Belle had ever seen. It sat on the porch with an attitude that implied the leash was attached to it, not the other way around.

Setting aside the dog's uncomely appearance, the trio made a charming picture, a credit to poor Mr. Nesbitt, who had written that he'd lost his wife only months ago.

"Yes, of course, Mr. Nesbitt. I've been expecting you. Please come in. Ray will get your bags." Belle was pleased to see that Ray was already unloading the mountains of luggage the family had brought with them from Muncie. "These must be your darling children. You must be Winnie?"

"Pleased to meet you, ma'am." The young girl curtsied, then looked down at the dog. "This is Beauty. Even though he's ugly."

"I see," said Belle, then addressed the boy. "And you are young Master Melvin?"

"Yes, ma'am." The little boy performed a stiff bow, one hand on his waist and one behind his back.

"Come in, please." Belle gestured them inside. "You must be tired and hungry. I have refreshments in the parlor."

"Er, thank you," Mr. Nesbitt said. "Come along, children."

Winnie gave the leash a sharp tug, which dragged Beauty forward on his paws and was wholly unnecessary.

Belle brought them into the parlor and settled them with tea and slices of fresh-baked coffee cake. Winnie set Beauty free from his leash, and he proceeded to nose around the room. He sniffed Belle's feet and jumped up, resting his front paws on her skirt. His soft, brown eyes gleamed with an intelligence Belle didn't expect. "Is he friendly?" she asked, scooping him up.

"No," the children and Mr. Nesbitt chorused.

But Beauty had settled into Belle's lap and was licking her fingertips. "Oh? He seems quite gentle and sweet."

"He was Mama's dog," Winnie explained. "He doesn't like anybody else. Usually."

"Well. I can tell Beauty and I will be great friends. Tell me, Mr. Nesbitt, how was the trip from Muncie? Uneventful, I hope?"

"Er, yes, fine. We have no complaints. Er. Do we, children?"

"No, sir," the children replied. They sat together on one of Belle's sofas like two portrait subjects, posture straight, expressions fixed, their hands clasped in their laps. But as Belle and Mr. Nesbitt made pleasant conversation about the trip and the recent weather and the news of the day, the children slowly lost their polite, well-mannered veneer.

First Belle noticed the foot swinging. Melvin's feet didn't quite reach the floor, and he took to swinging them to and fro, gently at first, but when his foot accidentally brushed the rung underneath the sofa, producing a whisper of sound, it proved irresistible. The boy did it again, louder, which prompted another try. He swung his feet back and forth, tap-tap-tapping on the rung beneath him until his sister nudged him with an elbow and whispered, "Quiet, Melvin."

"Of course, glass is a fascinating medium to work with," Mr. Nesbitt was explaining, seemingly unaware of the growing restlessness of his offspring. "As vice president in charge of gift development at the Ball Brothers Glass Manufacturing Company, I am in charge of, er, gift development. It's an exploratory new wing of the company."

Melvin nudged Winnie back and hissed, "I *am* being quiet."

Winnie gave Melvin another elbow to the ribs, with a little pepper behind it. "Stop kicking the seat. You're being a horrible pest. Let the grown-ups talk."

"I'm not stopping them. Blah blah blah. They'll talk all day. C'n we go outside?"

"You see," Mr. Nesbitt droned on, taking no notice of the brewing hostilities, "the idea is to, er, explore the possibility of branching into glass gift items."

"Not now, Melvin," Winnie chided. "Remember what Mama always said. Children should be seen and not heard. So *be quiet!*"

"Oh! That reminds me. We have gifts for you." Mr. Nesbitt's attention finally shifted to the other sofa where the children sat, hands folded neatly in their laps, obediently facing forward, while their elbows jabbed viciously sideways, digging into each other's ribs. "Children! Er, um. Stop that right now." Mr. Nesbitt's admonition was sadly ineffectual; a few sideways kicks joined the flailing elbows.

It was clear to Belle that Mr. Nesbitt had never had much of a hand in raising or disciplining his children. In all likelihood, the late Mrs. Nesbitt had single-handedly ruled the domestic front, feeding and clothing Winnie and Melvin, teaching them their letters, and instructing them on good social behavior. How successful she had been, Belle couldn't say, but clearly Mr. Nesbitt had lost any authority he might have once had.

Despite their father's attention, the children's fighting escalated. Melvin unclasped his hands and reached behind Winnie's head to take hold of her rag curls. He gave a mighty yank, which drew a shriek of pain and outrage from his older sister.

"Well, now!" Belle commanded, rising from her seat. The children froze, wide eyes pinned to Belle. "That is enough of that. Melvin, Winnie, you may be excused. Go outside and play. I will call you when it is time for dinner."

"Oh, er, is it safe?" asked Mr. Nesbitt. "That is to say, are there ruffians about? Or, er, wild animals?"

"Of course not, Mr. Nesbitt. It is perfectly safe. Not a ruffian for miles around. If the children stay on my property, they will be just fine. Winnie, you are the eldest, so you are in charge." Winnie shot Melvin a smug smirk. "My property is quite large, so you have plenty of space to roam and explore. Whatever you do, stay out of the hog pen. Now, off with you!"

The children didn't need to be told twice. They ran from the room and out the front door. Their footsteps clattered off the porch and were gone.

Mr. Nesbitt watched them go with perplexity. "Er, their mother raised them properly. I can't account for their behavior today."

"Don't be silly, Mr. Nesbitt," Belle reassured him, though she was already regretting her decision to accept a suitor with young offspring. "They are but children, children who have spent the morning in the confines of a train compartment, children who have lost their mother only recently. It will do them a world of good to spend some time in the out of doors, playing freely."

"Perhaps. I fear for their upbringing now that Penelope is gone. Every day it seems the children move further and further away from me. I—"

A high squeal cut through his words, along with frantic yipping and barking. Belle leaped to her feet. "Pardon me, Mr. Nesbitt." She raced after the terrible sound and banged through the kitchen door to discover a torture scene at the hog pen. Melvin perched on the slats with one hand gripping the rail for balance, and in the other he held a pitchfork aloft like a spear. Next to him, Winnie poked through the slats with long-handled lopping shears. She snapped the shears at the hogs, nipping at their backsides, trying to get hold of a tail. How dare they threaten Belle's carefully procured and tended livestock!

Beauty apparently agreed with her. He raced back and forth along the fence, barking wildly. He dove at Winnie's ankles, nipping and racing away again when Winnie turned the shears on him.

Ray raced up from the far side of the enclosure. "Get down from there! Get away from them hogs!"

"Stop it right now!" Belle shouted at the children. "Winnie and Melvin, put down those tools!"

Melvin glanced over his shoulder at Belle and let loose with the pitchfork. Beauty abruptly went silent, his nose arcing as he followed the pitchfork's trajectory. It sailed toward the sow, who skittered away just in time, and the sharp tines thunked into the mud. Why, that little . . . !

Ray hauled Melvin off the fence by his shirt and shook the boy.

"Ow, help!" Melvin screeched as he squirmed. "Quit it! Father, Father! This man is trying to kill me!"

Belle snagged Winnie by the wrist and yanked the shears out of her hands as Mr. Nesbitt appeared on the kitchen steps.

"Oh, er. My golly. What is going on here?"

"Father, that man is trying to hurt Melvin, and Mrs. Gunness is hurting my wrist!" Winnie twisted her arm, trying to release Belle's grip. "And we didn't do *anything!*"

So they were liars too. Belle was hardly surprised.

"All we were doing was standing here watching the hogs, and then they came and attacked us!" Melvin said.

"Why, you little—" Ray started.

Belle had to regain the upper hand, with Ray and these little savages. "Ray, you can let Master Melvin go now," she said calmly, as she loosed Winnie's wrist. "Here, take these farm tools back to the barn."

Ray reluctantly let go of Melvin and accepted the shears Belle handed him. "I better not catch you near here again," he warned the two children, fixing them with a stern look. As soon as Ray's back was turned, Melvin stuck his tongue out.

"Now, now, son. That's no way to act," said Mr. Nesbitt. "Go on and play nicely, now. The grown-ups are still talking." He went back inside.

No wonder these children didn't listen to their father. He never held them to account. The children started to run off, but Belle snagged them each by an ear. "Now listen here, you two. Those hogs never did anything to you. You leave them be. If I catch you harassing them again—"

"Oh, yeah?" Melvin said. "What are you going to do?"

"Yeah, you can't do anything," chimed in Winnie. "You're not our mother."

Belle bent down so her face was inches from the girl's. "Do you know what hogs like to eat?" she whispered, her eyes flashing ominously from Winnie to Melvin. "*Everything.* Kitchen slops, the mice from the traps. They'll eat anything at all. Even children."

The children's haughty indifference faded to uncertainty and then darkened to fear. Belle released her grip on their ears. "Now, go. Play, like your father told you. And remember what I said." She snapped her teeth at them, and they ran off toward the pasture like rabbits from a fox.

Belle scooped up Beauty and stroked the mongrel's back. Underneath the bedraggled fur, she felt the little dog's heart pounding. "There now, it's all over," she soothed.

She found Mr. Nesbitt pouring himself fresh tea in the parlor.

"Er, what a ruckus," he said.

"That was more than a ruckus," Belle said, her anger boiling just under the surface of her words. "They could have hurt my hogs, don't you think?"

"Oh, I don't think they would have done any harm, really." He swiped a hand over his unkempt mustache. "Er." He cleared his throat. "The truth is, I worry that I am not up to the task of raising them properly." He took another bite of cake.

In her mind's eye the morsel grew and grew, stuffing his mouth and choking off his breath. Expanding quickly, it forced his jaws apart and stretched his cheeks. His face turned red, then purple, and his eyes popped wide open, bulging out of their sockets. His head was a big cake-filled balloon.

Belle stifled a giggle and took her seat. She poured herself some tea, using the ritual of stirring in sugar and milk to regain her composure while Mr. Nesbitt went on munching, blithely unaware of his hostess's visions. This little family were her latest clients, and she needed to put that first. The warm liquid was calming as the first sip passed her lips, and she rested her cup in its saucer before setting it down and facing her guest once more. She rested her hand on Mr. Nesbitt's arm and gently squeezed. "You must make some allowances for them, of course, as they are still grieving. But a firm hand is what children need. I will help you, Mr. Nesbitt, fear not."

Mr. Nesbitt gripped her hand in thanks.

"Now," she said. "I must turn my attention to preparing our evening meal. Come, I will show you to your room. Ray has already brought in your luggage."

Belle escorted Mr. Nesbitt upstairs to the bedroom on the left with the selburose quilt.

"How very inviting," he said.

"The children will sleep in the room at the end of the hall. Freshen up, take a rest if you need to, and I will see to the children when they come in from playing."

"Thank you, Mrs. Gunness. You have no idea how grateful I am to have found you."

As he should be. At least it was clear what this man and his children needed from her. Belle got busy in the kitchen, and before long, Winnie and Melvin appeared at the back door, hungry and looking for handouts. Their faces were flushed and hair windblown, and they looked just like children should: healthy and vigorous. But also filthy. The yellow satin of Winnie's dress was begrimed with dirt down the front and along the hems of her skirt and lace underskirts. Melvin's lace cuffs drooped over his hands, soaked in mud. Both children's hands were dark with caked mud, and their shoes were sodden. Their footsteps as they came into the kitchen left thick, muddy prints. That wouldn't do.

"Stop right there!" Belle instructed. The children came to a halt. She was still angry for their mistreatment of the hogs, but she set it firmly aside and addressed them in a kind and curious tone. "My goodness, what have you been up to?"

"We found a stream! It was full of frogs! We built a castle for the frogs with mud and sticks. It's beautiful! You must come see it!" The words tumbled out of little Melvin.

To tide them over until mealtime, Belle handed them each an apple, then allowed them to guide her to their masterpiece in the brook out in her pasture. They described how they caught the frogs and built them a castle, regaling her with a story about knights and princesses trapped in frog form. They had a creative side in addition to their malicious one, clearly.

When the tale had ended, they traipsed back to the house and she gave them a bucket of water to rinse the mud off their shoes. She directed them to leave the bucket outside and put their wet shoes and socks and stockings by the kitchen stove to dry.

"Now, go upstairs and wash up. Put on something clean and bring me your muddy clothes. And, children, tomorrow when you go out to play, perhaps you should choose more practical attire."

"All my dresses are the same," Winnie complained. "All fussy lace and pink or white or yellow. Mama always said a lady should dress in delicate colors. But I'm not a lady! I don't want to be a lady!"

"All I have are these dumb velvet suits," wailed Melvin.

"At least you get to wear pants! I want to wear knee pants like Melvin gets to!" The outburst seemed to surprise Winnie, and she abruptly clamped her mouth shut.

"I'm sure your mother knew what she was about, Winnie. But perhaps we can find both of you some clothing that is a little more suitable. Now, come along. I'll show you your room and the water closet where you may get cleaned up."

Asle sank into a seat at the restaurant to ponder his findings over a steaming cup and a fresh roll. After Mrs. Gunness's lunch with the elegant woman, the two had walked to a business called Della Rose. It appeared to be a dressmaker's shop. Mrs. Gunness spent an hour there and emerged with a parcel wrapped in brown paper. She spent another fifteen minutes inside the bank and fifteen minutes standing in front of it chatting with a pale young woman. As he was not schooled in following a person undetected, more than once he'd had to duck into a doorway or abruptly walk the other way when it seemed Mrs. Gunness had spotted him. She was, for all appearances, a woman of means. Earlier, at the mercantile, she'd purchased enough food for a crowd. Was she expecting guests?

He took a sip of coffee and winced at the bitterness. As he stirred in a teaspoon of sugar from a small bowl on the table, the clink of metal on china reminded him of the way Andrew would tap his spoon three times on his mug rim. His brother was a vagabond and impulsive, but Asle missed him terribly.

A thought that had been swimming in the undercurrents of Asle's mind leapt into his consciousness, clear and concrete and brooking no doubt. It sent a black wave of despair washing through him.

Andrew had never made it farther than La Porte.

Which left Asle with a clear course of action.

Inside the cramped sheriff's office, he found an old man in a tan uniform slumped at a desk, his hands draped over the arms of his chair. White hair flowed away from his forehead and swept over his collar. Asle was not one to dismiss a man just for being old—he based his judgments on a man's actions, not the whiteness of his hair—but it soon became clear that Sheriff Johnson's prime was well behind him.

"Good afternoon, Sheriff, my name is Asle Helgelien. I am visiting from Chicago, Illinois."

"Noise? What noise?"

"No, sir, I said, 'Illinois.' The state."

"The state? This here's Indiana." In a mutter that carried perfectly in the small room, he added, "What kind of fool doesn't know what state he's in?"

Asle let the comment go. No point arguing with a deaf man. Asle spoke loudly. "I'm here to ask some questions."

"Hah? Questions? About what?"

"About Mrs. Belle Gunness."

"Who? Never heard of him."

"Not him, her. Mrs. Belle Gunness. She lives on McClung Road."

"McClung Road?"

"Yes, the redbrick mansion on McClung Road."

"That's old Judge Quilleran. Been dead, what, fifteen years now."

"Sheriff, I'm asking about the current owner, Mrs. Belle Gunness."

"Hah? Who?"

Just then, a man came in from the street, clad in the same tan slacks and shirt as the sheriff. He stooped under the door lintel and removed his hat. At his full height, his head nearly brushed the low ceiling of the room. The star of a sheriff's deputy was pinned to the left side of his shirt, and Asle was relieved to see this man appeared hale and hearty and hoped he'd be someone to reason with.

"Good day, Sheriff," the man said. "Good day, sir."

"Hello, perhaps you can help me. My name is Asle Helgelien. I'm from Chicago, Illinois. I'm looking for information on Mrs. Belle Gunness."

"Are you now? Well, she's a fine, upstanding civilian. La Porte is proud to have her."

"I see." Asle felt some relief to hear that the widow was on the right side of the law. Perhaps his conclusions were in error and she would be able to help him track down Andrew. Asle speculated that if Andrew's hoped-for romance didn't pan out, he might have gone off in an embarrassed sulk. Mrs. Gunness could shed light on his state of mind when he left.

"Yes, sir, a fine lady," the deputy was continuing, a slight flush coloring his neck. "An upstanding civilian, kind and generous, honest to a fault. Folks around here think the world of her. A great beauty, they all say. Never seen a lovelier lady . . ." The deputy let out a sigh far too wistful for a professional lawman. He sounded like a lovestruck schoolboy.

"You've never had reason to suspect her of any wrongdoing, then?" Asle pushed.

"Well, gosh all Friday! No, sir. Why, Belle—I mean, Mrs. Gunness is a perfect specimen of the womanly virtues. She is all that is kind and good, sir. Her morals are above question."

Was that so? It seemed to Asle that no one's morals were above question. And the judgment of the lovelorn deputy was now in question itself, as far as Asle was concerned.

"I'm searching for my brother, Andrew Helgelien. He was on his way to meet Mrs. Gunness. I found his wagon hidden in the woods a few miles outside of town." Asle didn't know the name of the road it was on, but gave the deputy detailed directions to find it. "This would have been last fall, sometime in November. He is a traveling salesman, tall like me, with darker hair. Always wears a patterned waistcoat. His wagon is unmistakable, black with gold lettering: W.T. Rawleigh Company. Did you see him or his wagon?"

The deputy's eyes lost focus, concentration screwing up his face. "No," he said slowly. "No, I don't recall seeing anyone of that description coming to town. Haven't seen any traveling salesmen in over a year."

"But what about his wagon? Don't you think that's odd?"

"I suppose, yes. It is a little odd to call it W.T. Rawleigh when your name is Andrew Helgelien. But to each his own, I always say."

"No, I mean that the wagon is hidden in the woods. Abandoned."

"Oh, that. Well, I suppose your brother grew tired of being a traveling salesman and settled down somewhere."

"His letter says he was going to visit Mrs. Gunness." Asle didn't muddy the waters explaining his conclusion came from the newspaper ad he'd found. "But I see no sign that he's there now."

"Mrs. Gunness is a very discerning woman. Perhaps she sent him on his way. I can tell you any man would be happy to win her hand. Anyone who wants her . . . well, get in line."

The implication behind the deputy's claims was unmistakable. Get in line . . . after me. Seeking help from the man was pointless. Asle thanked him for his time and left.

The street outside was clogged with carriages and farm wagons trotting by in the May sun, which provided a mild warmth in the middle of the day. The pleasant conditions caused him a wave of homesickness. Was Matilda planning a flower garden as she usually did? Were the boys playing ball after schoolwork and chores were finished? And little Christina, how much had she grown in his absence? Asle wanted desperately to find the truth about Andrew and return to his family.

In a break in traffic, Asle spotted the pale young woman Mrs. Gunness had chatted with in front of the bank. She was strolling along the sidewalk, a book in one hand, looking in windows. She stopped in front of a bakery, eyeing the cakes in the display, and Asle seized on the opportunity.

He took a position next to her and admired the selection of confections. "They all look so good, I don't know how to choose," he said as if to himself.

"Mmm, me too," she sighed, then shook herself. "Not that I'll be having any of them. Schoolteachers don't have money to waste on fancy cakes." Another beleaguered sigh escaped her. "I wish I'd never come to La Porte."

"It seems a fine town," Asle offered. "Although I've only just arrived myself. Is there something I should know?"

She pulled her attention from the cakes and turned watery gray eyes to him. Up close, Asle realized she was just a girl, probably no more than fifteen or sixteen. "Oh, it will be fine for *you*. You won't be stuck in a schoolhouse all day every day with rude farm boys. I'd much rather be reading my book. It's called *Thelma*, by Marie Corelli. Do you know it?"

"I'm afraid not," Asle said.

The schoolteacher carried on in a glum tone, "I wish I'd never come here. Won't they be in a fix if I up and leave. See if I don't." The mulish set to her jaw made her look even younger.

Loath to be drawn further into the girl's discontent, Asle ventured, "Perhaps you know the lady I've come to La Porte to see, Mrs. Belle Gunness?

"Of course, everyone knows Mrs. Gunness." She turned back to the cakes and muttered wistfully, "One day I shall live in a fine house and wear beautiful dresses."

"She's quite wealthy, I suppose. Have you known her a long time?"

"We arrived in La Porte on the same train. So I've known her longer than anyone in town." The girl said it with an air of self-importance. She seemed quite immature, moving quickly from her sulk over her situation to envy of Mrs. Gunness to this odd pride in how long she'd known her. If she moved on from her teaching situation in La Porte, Asle felt sure the town's children would be better off.

"It sounds like you are quite close with Mrs. Gunness. I have not yet had the pleasure of meeting her. Tell me, what is she like?"

"Oh, she's just wonderful," the girl gushed. "She is beautiful, of course. She is everything I wish I could be. No one tells her what to do."

"There you are, Miss Longacre!" She startled as a pastor came striding up, his black coat flopping open with each step. "I've been searching for you for over an hour!" The pastor took a deep breath and visibly calmed himself. He went on in a quiet, pained tone, "Miss Longacre, you can't keep shirking your duties like this. The children have been waiting for you to return from the dinner break. Most of them gave up and went home. Come along home now and we'll discuss this." He took Miss Longacre gently by the elbow and guided her away.

Asle watched the confrontation transpire, unacknowledged by the pastor and without so much as a glance from the young lady he'd been speaking with. His whole conversation with her seemed a waste of time. He'd learned nothing of value about Mrs. Gunness and more than he wanted to know about the tribulations of a small-town schoolteacher.

4-1

At dinner, Morris and the children assembled around Mrs. Gunness's table for a meal of roast pork, pickled beets, and baked potatoes. Beauty was outside playing fetch with the handyman, who appeared to have taken a shine to the little dog. Morris couldn't understand why, though Penelope had found something to love in the mongrel too.

Winnie and Melvin devoured the food on their plates. Even Morris, who hadn't had much appetite since Penelope's passing, found himself tucking in with enthusiasm. There was something about Mrs. Gunness's house; it had a homey, restful quality. He felt at peace here, and safe.

If he and Mrs. Gunness married and he and the children made their home here, it would mean giving up his position with Ball Brothers in Muncie. This did not give him the pause it perhaps should. Penelope had obtained the situation for him through her family's connections. If he allowed himself to admit the truth, he'd never fit in well there. His ideas were dismissed and he had never made the contributions expected of him. In fact, it would be a relief to give up the position and all the pressure that went with it.

He chanced a look at Mrs. Gunness as she cut small bites of roast pork and slipped them into her mouth. She caught his eye and smiled, triggering a stab of—was it desire? It felt disloyal to Penelope to notice Mrs. Gunness's soft features and stylish hair. But oh, my, what a picture she was. Would such a captivating creature be interested in him?

As the meal was winding down, Melvin burst out with, "Can we now, Papa? Can we give her the gifts?"

"Oh, er, yes, Melvin. Good idea. Have you got them with you?"

"We left them in our room," Winnie answered.

"You may be excused to go fetch them," he said, and they wasted no time scraping back their chairs and dashing for the door. "Oh, Winnie, one thing . . ." he called after his daughter.

She poked her head back into the dining room. "Yes, Papa?"

"Please bring me my satchel. It should be with the luggage in the corner of my room. You know the one. It has my initials on it."

"Yes, I know the one. M for Morris, H for Henry, N for Nesbitt. I'll go fetch it."

"Walk, children," Morris called after them. "Well, er, I suppose . . ." His words faded as they thundered up the stairs. He must be firmer with them.

Belle was watching them go with what seemed like amusement. "Don't worry, they can't hurt anything by running in the house. Reminding them of the manners they learned from their mother will take some time. And I will help you, if you let me."

"Mrs. Gunness, I would be grateful for your help in that, er, arena."

"Of course," she said. "You know, it sounds so formal when you call me Mrs. Gunness. Won't you call me Belle?"

"Oh, er. Why, yes, er. If you like."

"And may I call you Morris?"

Discomfited by the flush of embarrassment—and, perhaps, excitement?—heating his cheeks, Morris could only nod. Would it be too forward, too precipitous, to ask her to marry him so soon?

"Morris"—the sound of his name coming from her plump lips elated him—"I've been thinking. I hope you won't think me too forward. But I find myself quite charmed by your children . . . and you. And you came here with the idea of matrimony, as we said in our letters. Would it be too soon to think of . . . taking that step?"

Was she suggesting what he thought? Could it be true, that she felt the same way he did? He hadn't dared to hope. "Er, I think. That is, er. I would be honored, er, Belle, if you would be my, er, wife."

"I'm delighted, Morris." She rose elegantly, rounded the table, and dropped a delicate kiss on his cheek. "I know of a lovely little chapel east of town. We can drive there in the morning."

"Here, open mine first," Melvin exclaimed as he burst into the room. He stumbled to a halt at Belle's side and pushed a small box into her hands.

"Why, what a surprise," Belle said, resuming her seat. "I never expected to receive gifts from you like this. Shall I open it now?"

"Open it, open it!" Melvin hopped up and down on his toes, barely able to contain his excitement.

"Settle down, young man," Morris admonished. "Your bouncing is disturbing our peace." There, that sounded very firm, and an approving smile from Belle confirmed it.

Melvin stopped for half a second and then began bobbing again. Belle wrapped her arm around the boy's shoulders and squeezed. "Melvin, you are like a bunny rabbit! I'm afraid you will bounce right into my lap!"

Apparently inspired, Melvin started to hop a circuit around the table with his hands curled up in front of his chest like rabbit feet, drawing laughter from Belle and Winnie. Morris was surprised to find a chuckle or two escape his own lips.

"You are a fine rabbit, Melvin! Now bounce outside and around the house three times," Belle instructed him, and off he went. "That ought to settle some of the energy out of him."

"How clever," Morris observed. Yes, this was going to work out very well. He blessed the day he saw the ad in the Muncie newspaper. It might be the best thing that could have happened to him.

"Mama used to make Melvin do jumping jacks in the kitchen,"

Winnie said, having returned to her seat at the table. "She would say she didn't think he could do twenty, and he would do twenty. Then she would say he couldn't possibly do any more. And he would just keep doing them and doing them until he was all worn out."

"Your mother was a special woman, Winnie. You must miss her."

Winnie dropped her eyes to the red smears of beet juice remaining on her plate.

Melvin bounced back into the dining room just then and presented Belle with the glass figurine of a cat he'd chosen from the Ball Brothers showroom. "How adorable," Belle exclaimed. Winnie's delivery of a delicate glass rose was more subdued, and Belle responded with great care. "Beautiful, Winnie, thank you."

"Did you bring down my satchel, Winnie?" Morris asked when it was his turn.

"No, I didn't find it, Papa. It wasn't with the luggage."

Morris tsked with irritation. "Foolish girl, of course it must be." He pushed his chair back and plodded up the stairs to search for himself. In his room, his suitcase lay open on the quilt with the remarkable black-and-white pattern—what had Belle called it? Something "rose," he thought. It did look rather like a rose, with eight petals. His cases sat on the floor next to the rocking chair in the corner, waiting to be un-packed. His satchel, the one Penelope had given him when her brother had hired him, was not on the bed with the open suitcase. It was not on the floor. Not on the rocking chair, and not on the dresser.

Oh, bother. He'd have to return to the train station to see if he'd left it there. But that could wait until after he and Belle were wed.

Belle poured herself a dram of whiskey and sank into a chair at the kitchen table. It was late, long past time to be asleep. The Nesbitt fam-ily were upstairs, dreaming in their beds. Belle had tried to sleep, but her anxious mind couldn't settle down. After an hour of tossing and turning, she gave up and came down to the kitchen.

Going about her errands earlier that day, she'd felt almost as if someone was watching her. But whenever she searched the faces of townspeople around her, all she saw were folks going about their own business. And then came the mysterious gift of the molasses drop. Who had delivered it? Why? *Had* they been following her? Did they know something?

She was startled from her thoughts by a faint scratching at the back door, followed by a quiet tapping. Belle rose to find Ray on the stoop.

"Evenin' Miz Belle, sorry to bother you. I saw the light and got worried. Everything okay?"

"Oh, Ray, I'm glad to see you. Will you come in? Everything is fine, I just couldn't sleep."

Belle really was glad to see Ray. She didn't usually like to be interrupted when she had a suitor in the house, but tonight she was feeling overwhelmed and alone. And Ray was the only other person who understood her business. She settled him at the table with his own glass of whiskey and listened as he talked about what was going on with the farm. She didn't register his actual words, but the cadence of his voice made a soothing backdrop to her restless thoughts.

She eyed Ray as he nattered on about what seeds they should be putting in the ground for a kitchen garden, completely oblivious to her worries. Ray knew about Andrew's candies, didn't he? Could he be playing a prank on her?

"That sounds perfect, Ray," she cut in to his explanation of soil temperature and germination times. "Why don't you go ahead and do that."

"All right, Miz Belle, I will."

"Ray, were you in town today?"

"No, remember I just said I was turning over the earth in the kitchen garden?"

"That's right, silly me." She tried a different tack. "Ray, do you remember the candies that Andrew always had with him? Did he ever give you any?"

A slight crease formed between his eyebrows and he said slowly, "I suppose I do remember. They were . . . sassafras? Or sarsaparilla?"

"Molasses."

"Oh, that's right. Molasses. I only ever had the one he gave me when we were stringing barbed wire. But it was good. That's a funny thing to bring up. What made you think of that?"

Belle studied Ray as he spoke. He was so guileless. She didn't think he was capable of lying to her. "Oh, nothing. Just reminiscing, I guess." Belle took a sip of her whiskey and let it burn on her tongue a moment before swallowing. "You know, the strangest thing happened to me earlier, Ray. When I was in town, I felt . . . I almost felt as if someone was watching me. I know it sounds crazy, but I kept feeling eyes on me, everywhere I went. Isn't that odd?"

"A might bit odd, I guess. Did you see anyone?"

"No, just the same townsfolk as always." Belle shook off the uncomfortable feeling, not wanting to dwell on it. Diverting the conversation, she said slyly, "I ran into Miss Longacre. I think you'd better strike while the iron is hot, Ray. That girl won't be in town for long, mark my words. She hates teaching so much, I wouldn't be surprised if she ran off in the dead of night sometime."

Ray blushed and stammered a quick goodbye and headed out the kitchen door.

Ray fumed as he stomped across the yard back to his cottage. Belle sure did like to get his goat, teasing him about Miss Longacre. She knew full well he had no interest in the schoolteacher but couldn't resist joshing him about it. And he fell for it every time. Maybe next time, he would tease her right back. Make some comment about how many husbands she'd had.

Somehow, he didn't think she'd laugh.

He shook the rain from his hair as he crossed his threshold and toed off his boots. He'd sleep a bit easier now that he'd been up to see Belle. The fact was, he'd been lying restless in his cot when he caught sight of the kitchen light. A hum of worry had set up in his belly. Was it time already? The Nesbitts had only arrived that day. Was she really going to go through with the whole thing with these folks—even the children? The hum of worry had hardened into a sour ball lodged under his breastbone, making it hard to breathe. Ray didn't like the idea of Belle shifting her "business" to include children. That didn't seem right.

So he went up to the house to see, and after listening at the back door a few moments and reassuring himself nothing was happening, he knocked. And it was nice. She gave him a whiskey and they had a good jaw about the kitchen garden where she listened carefully to his ideas and told him to go ahead. They sure did work good together.

He'd been working himself up to asking her about the Nesbitt children when she'd gone and teased him. Feeling the heat creep into his face he'd clammed up, unable to come up with anything sharp to say back.

He shucked off his clothes and climbed under his blankets. Next time, he'd say, "At least I haven't had dozens of husbands." No, that was no good. What could he say? He drifted off, searching for wit and coming up empty.

42

The children were blooming in the fresh air of the country. Only a day after their arrival, their cheeks were rosier and their moods seemed lighter, more free. Their improved health confirmed Belle's opinion: the Nesbitt family needed her, needed her business. Morris and his poor motherless darlings deserved some happiness, and Belle congratulated herself on providing it.

The morning had dawned clear and bright after a few showers overnight. After breakfast, Belle took her house guests for a walk along the brook, into the adjoining woods. A breath of wind sent droplets pattering down from the canopy of leaves. Winnie strolled at Belle's side while Melvin ran ahead, bursting with boisterous spirits. Beauty trotted along after the boy, exploring the landscape on his own schedule. And Morris trailed behind them all, seemingly lost in thought.

Twined into Belle's satisfaction was a loose thread of unease she just couldn't shake. Who had brought that candy to the restaurant? She tried to recall all the people she'd seen in town, most of whom were residents of La Porte she had met at least in passing. But there were a few unfamiliar faces as well. Was it possible one of those strangers had some interest in her?

"Are you to be our new mother?" Winnie's words cut into Belle's worries. The girl marched briskly next to her, her black-stockinged legs kicking her yellow satin skirt ahead of her. Her directness surprised Belle, but she had to admire it. The world needed more girls who spoke their minds.

"Yes, Winnie," Belle replied, answering directness with directness. "Your father and I agreed you three would come for a visit, and if we all suit, then he and I will be married. Last night, we decided marriage is best for all of us."

The girl stayed silent for a few paces, then said, "How do you know you suit? We've only been here a day. What if you decide you don't like us?"

Up ahead, Melvin had found a long stick and was using it to thrash the underbrush. He waved it over his head, flourishing it like a sword, and hollered, "Avast, ye scoundrels! Take that!" The stick crashed down on the poor plants, tearing off leaves and breaking stems.

"Why would you think I wouldn't like you?"

"Melvin is a pest, for one thing."

"Melvin?" As far as Belle was concerned, "pest" could easily apply to both little Nesbitts.

Beauty bounded ahead and then dropped his hindquarters in a sit, observing Melvin with his head cocked to one side. "Hey there, boy," Melvin greeted the dog and held out his hand to invite Beauty closer. When he was within reach, he scooped up the mongrel, crying, "Got you, you scurvy weasel." He climbed onto an old stump, Beauty squirming against his tight grip. "Time to walk the plank!" he shouted, and tossed the dog to the ground.

Beauty landed awkwardly and shot away from his tormentor. "That's right, scurvy scalawag, run away. The next time you won't be so lucky!"

"Melvin!" Belle called sharply. First the hogs, and now this? She strode angrily toward the boy, Winnie close on her heels. "What are you thinking? You could have hurt Beauty."

"Aw, he's just a dog."

"Melvin, he's a little defenseless animal, and he looks to you to care for him."

"I feed him every morning!"

"Every *other* morning," Winnie put in. "We take turns."

"Caring for an animal means more than feeding it. Dropping him like that could have broken his leg."

"Aw, he'll be all right. See? He's running fine." Melvin was right. The little dog was running as fast as he could—away from Melvin.

"You mustn't be so callous. Would you like to be dropped from a height like that?"

"It wasn't that high. I could jump from higher than that."

Belle threw up her hands. There was no getting through to the boy. She craned her neck, looking for Morris, who had fallen far behind. "Wait until your father hears about this. Perhaps a few licks of the paddle will remind you of your responsibilities."

Melvin shrugged and scampered ahead. He stomped his feet and in a low bellow shouted, "Fee fie foe fum! I smell the blood of an Englishman!"

"He doesn't seem at all concerned about a paddling," Belle remarked.

"He knows he won't get one," Winnie said. "Father never paddles us."

"No? Then how does he discipline you?"

"He doesn't. Mama always told him things we did, but Father could never decide what to do. Mama would say, 'Use the paddle,' and Father would hem and haw and say, 'Er, I suppose,' and then wander off to his study to read about glassmaking."

Belle was beginning to get a pretty clear picture of Morris Nesbitt. He wasn't the take-charge company executive he had portrayed in his letters. She compared him to the powerful, controlling personality of Charles Gunness, who had built his musical instrument business from the ground up. She doubted Charles had left many decisions up to others.

"Where did Beauty run off to?" she asked. "We need to make sure he's all right."

"Oh, he'll come back. He always does," Winnie said, apparently no more concerned about the little dog than her brother was.

"Well, we need to be getting back. It's almost time to leave for the wedding. We'll take my motorcar. Wouldn't you like that?"

"I suppose, yes. We always take our motorcar at home."

Disgruntled at the girl's blasé response, Belle quickened her pace. The sooner she was married, the sooner she could be rid of these pests.

Jenny clomped wearily toward town, her heavy footfalls echoing Asle's dismay. He'd spent the day riding the length of McClung Road, speaking with Mrs. Gunness's neighbors. When he didn't find the answers he needed, he expanded his search to include Clear Lake Road and all the other roads in the area, in case Andrew had traversed any of them. He discovered that the distance from Mrs. Gunness's house to the road he'd come to La Porte on was less than two miles. And he'd found Andrew's wagon only a few miles down that road.

But at house after house, farmstead after farmstead, Asle was told the same thing. "No, never heard of him." "No, haven't seen a wagon like that." If Asle hadn't seen Andrew's wagon in the woods with his own eyes, he'd be convinced his brother had never made it to La Porte.

There was only one house left to try. When he'd stopped at the small, simple cabin with unpainted clapboards and no porch earlier that morning, his knock went unanswered, but he saw a man out in the field beyond, following a plow drawn by a single horse. Now the field was plowed, and Asle caught a glimmer of light coming from the windows. He was weary and hungry and wanted to pass on by—what were the chances that this household, out of all the others, had something different to tell him?—but a voice inside wouldn't let him.

Asle reined Jenny into the yard and dismounted. He gave her a pat on the nose and asked her to wait, knowing her well enough after all these miles together to be confident she would stand patiently until he returned.

His knock was answered without delay, and Asle recoiled when he came face-to-face with a small troll of a man. His head barely reached Asle's chin, and he was almost as wide as he was tall. He was bald but for long gray wisps that sprang away from his scalp, and the hair of his eyebrows spiraled crazily above beady black eyes. Asle took a small step back, then steeled himself. He'd come here for a reason and he was going to see it through, even though the man's fierce and slightly crazed appearance gave him little hope of finding answers. "Good afternoon, sir. My name is Asle Helgelien—"

"Hey now!" Surprised glee burst across the man's face, revealing snaggled teeth, widely spaced. "Come in, come in." He beckoned Asle into the one-room home and insisted he take the only seat, a ladder-back chair next to the fire. Asle sat, his head now just below the troll's. An iron pot of something mysterious hung over the fire, and the man ladled some into a bowl and pushed it into Asle's hands. "Take it, take it," he said, hovering over Asle until he accepted the bowl and spooned up a mouthful. It was piping hot and scorched the roof of his mouth, but flavorful.

"Thank you," he said, realizing the man must be terribly lonely.

"Where's yer wagon?" the man asked.

Asle almost dropped his bowl. "My wagon?"

"Yar, yar. Ain't seen you in months. I need more o' that liniment. Where's yer wagon?"

"Black wagon, with gold writing? W.T. Rawleigh Company?"

The crazy eyebrows drew together in puzzlement. "You don't know yer own wagon? 'Course that's the one I mean. Where is it? You got some liniment?"

"I'm afraid you have me mixed up with my brother, Andrew. He's the one with the wagon."

The man leaned down and peered at Asle's face. "Thought you looked different," he finally said. "What you doing here, then? Where's your brother? You got any liniment?"

"I'm trying to find my brother. He's missing. When did you see him last?"

"Months ago," the man said. "Months ago now. Mebbe last fall? October . . . no, no. November it was. Came rattling down the road in the middle of the night. But I can't sleep, y' know, on account of the rheumatism. So I heard 'im. Looked out the window. Skinny little moon that night, barely enough light to piss by, but I saw the wagon. Ran out after him to see if he got any cures. That liniment, mm-hmm, worked good. I'm all out now. You got some?"

The man was so eager to tell Asle what he needed to know—what he'd been seeking to learn for days, weeks, even—that he didn't want to risk losing his goodwill by mentioning he had no liniment. "Tell me, how did he seem?" A blank look. The fire crackled and the stew bubbled. The bowl in Asle's hands had cooled some, so he tucked in, giving himself time to think of a different tack. "Did he say anything to you?"

"Yar, yar. I told him 'bout my rheumatism and he said he had some liniment. Sold it to me for sixty cents. C'n you believe it? 'That's a steal,' I said. He said, 'My name is Andrew Helgelien,' and asked me my name and I told him and he said, 'Mr. Karsten'—nobody talk to me like that, respectful. Most folks around here call me Dirt Troll, but he—Mr. Helgelien—he call me 'Mr. Karsten.'" The odd little man affected a pose, placing his hand over his breast, and it caught at Asle's heart. It was just the way Andrew stood when performing. Karsten went on, "He said, 'Tonight I go to meet my love. In honor of this momentous occasion, I wish to give you this discounted price. If I thought it wouldn't offend your honor, I would give you the liniment for free.'" Karsten nodded once, sharply.

The man gave a fair imitation of Andrew's florid way of speaking. He seemed to have very good recall. Asle had no doubt the words were exactly how Andrew would have spoken. "And then he carried on down the road?"

"It were late and he been so good to me. I told him to bed down in my barn."

"Did he say where he was going? Who he was meeting?"

The crazy eyebrows crowded together, and he pursed up his mouth. "Yar. Over to the widow Gunness. Down the road there."

When he said nothing more, Asle asked, "Do you know Mrs. Gunness?"

A shrug.

"Did he make it to her house?'

Another shrug.

"And you haven't seen him or his wagon since?"

One short shake of the head.

Asle sighed. "Thank you very much for your time and this wonderful stew. I should be getting on now." He handed Karsten the empty bowl and crossed the small room to the door.

"Hope you find yer brother," Karsten said as Asle opened the door. "Hope he got to her house and kept on goin'."

Asle froze. "Why is that?"

Karsten's mouth had a grim set to it. "Ghosts. There's ghosts up there. I see 'em. In the night. Lights dancin' in the yard." He shook his head. "Ain't no good up there at the widow Gunness's. No good at all."

Morris was a very mild man, Belle noted as she lay next to him on their first night as a wedded couple. He'd been content with a short interlude of hugging and kissing and then performed the act itself in a very straightforward way, with Belle on her back and Morris breathing into her ear. In a few minutes it was over, and Morris was asleep. Even his snores were mild. If only his children were.

Belle huddled underneath the selburose quilt, eyes wide open in the dark. A wild breeze chased around the eaves outside, and she was keyed up, too, filled with some indefinable emotion that was preventing sleep. It was a mixture of intense satisfaction and a powerful sense of accomplishment, tainted by a niggling tendril of dread.

Here she was, a girl from a tiny backwater town in Norway, come to America with nothing, hastily—foolishly—married to a man who couldn't appreciate anything she might offer. But on her own, less than a year into her new business venture, she was by any measure a tremendous success. She had vowed to restore her home to its proper glory and had done so. She earned more than enough money to support herself, and Ray too. She was able to buy any little thing she had a mind to. People in town loved her. And there was no end in sight to the successes she had accumulated. She had every reason to feel proud of what she, and she alone, had accomplished.

Was she going to let one trifling candy ruin it all?

Asle entered the train station lobby lost in thought, pondering old Karsten's last words. He wasn't one to put stock in ghost tales, but midnight lights? What could be going on in the middle of the night at Mrs. Gunness's property?

Absorbed with puzzling out the significance of Karsten's words, he strode across the lobby, intent on getting to his room and having a rest. In his fatigue and inattention, he misgauged the position of a chair, smacking his hip into its back and dislodging it from its position in line with its mates. So clumsy! He rubbed the sore spot and carefully positioned the chair back in line. As he did so, he noticed a satchel sticking out from under it. Left behind by a traveler, presumably. Asle would bring it to his room and give it to the stationmaster in the morning in the hopes it could be returned to its owner.

He bent to retrieve it, and the sides fell open. It wasn't even latched. How careless.

As he grasped the sides to close the bag, his eye caught sight of something, a word. *Belle.* A twinge of guilt advised Asle to close the bag without investigation. The satchel wasn't his property, and its contents were not his business.

And yet.

Asle propped the open satchel on the chair and withdrew a small box carefully wrapped in elaborately designed paper and tied with a bow. Dangling from the bow was the tag Asle had seen, labeled in large script with the words, "To Belle, with fondness, from Morris."

Once his initial hesitation was overcome, Asle had no qualms about digging further into the bag. He found a pair of white cambric hand-kerchiefs, one neatly ironed and folded and the other crumpled. Asle pushed it aside and wiped his fingers on his pants. Beneath that were a notebook, two fountain pens, three return tickets to Muncie, and a silver case containing calling cards engraved in black ink:

Morris Nesbitt
Vice President, Gift Development
Ball Brothers Glass Manufacturing Company
Muncie, Indiana

At the very bottom of the bag was an envelope, torn open at the short edge, addressed to Mr. Morris Nesbitt. The return address was for Mrs. Belle Gunness of McClung Road.

The lobby was silent, but Asle couldn't help checking over his shoulder as he withdrew the letter from its envelope.

43

Two children are heavier than you might think, Belle thought as she wheeled the young Nesbitts across her yard. The boy, especially: he was small, but dense. Their little blond heads were facing up, and two pairs of pale blue eyes stared at her, almost accusingly. She set the wheelbarrow handles down and turned their faces away.

They rolled right back, their eyes piercing though lifeless.

"Honestly," Belle muttered. She twisted them away again, and again they rolled back, determined to stare at her for the whole journey to their final destination. She angled the boy's face to the side of the wheelbarrow and shifted the girl's head right next to it. Then she found a rock and wedged it next to the blond curls. "There. Now stay."

She leaned her weight on the wheelbarrow and shook out her hands. The well-used farm cart had smudged dirt on her palms, sleeves, and across the dark blue cotton of her skirt. It wasn't her best dress, by any means, but it was finer than any she'd had in her old life. Maybe it was time she hired a laundress.

It had been a very stressful morning. After three days of refurbishing Morris's fallen pride—seeking his advice and praising whatever he came up with, allowing him to make plans for future ventures on the farm, and complimenting his intelligence, wit, and strength at every opportunity—and three days of mothering these ungrateful children, Belle had fulfilled her end of the contract. Things had gone downhill from there.

She'd brought the children to Ray's cottage to keep them out of the way while she took care of Morris, only to find that Ray had left for town earlier that morning. There was nothing to do but dispatch the children then and there. Fortunately, she had her captive bolt pistol in the pocket of her dress and was gratified to discover it worked as effectively on small brains as it did on larger ones. That would be useful information to report to Dr. Heiss.

She'd left the children's bodies in Ray's cottage, hoping he'd return in time to help get them in the ground, and gone back to the house to attend to Morris. After, when there was still no sign of Ray, Belle had used the time to fetch Morris's checkbook. At least that part of her plan had gone right.

Belle stormed back outside, ready to tear into Ray for leaving her to do the hard work alone. But he still hadn't appeared. How could he go off and leave her like this? He had to know today was the day. What could he need in town, anyway? She provided him with everything. And this is what she got for thanks. Just like any other man, letting her down.

Belle reached her hands over her head and leaned back, stretching her aching back. It was a perfect May day, a light breeze carrying the sweet scent of her lilacs, but it gave her no delight.

Hearing the clop of horse hooves, she looked over her shoulder. It was about time Ray got back.

Only it wasn't Ray. A man on horseback approached from the direction of town, his animal plodding along at a patient pace until the rider reined it to a stop at her driveway.

Dammit to hell and back!

There was something familiar about the visitor, but Belle couldn't think. Her heart pounded in her ears. He was still a hundred yards away, but Belle knew she had only moments to get the children out of sight. She hesitated, trying to judge the amount of time it would take to get the wheelbarrow hidden, either ahead to the rear of her house or back inside the barn. Indecision trapped her. She wanted to keep going, away from the road and the approaching man. But the barn was closer.

With an agonized plea to an unidentified power—*please let this work*—she chose the barn.

She set to the wheelbarrow, bumping it over the rough ground of her lawn. The children's heads knocked a rhythm on the boards of the barrow, loosing the rock holding them in place, and slowly rotated to staring back at her again. Just as disobedient in death as they were in life. "Stop looking at me," she hissed. The children continued their silent judgment. "You never once minded me," Belle accused. "Not once."

Reaching the barn, Belle wrenched open the wide door, pushed the wheelbarrow through, and slammed the door shut behind her. She took a moment to catch her breath, leaning against her motorcar and letting her eyes close.

Who was this man? He looked strangely familiar.

Her eyes snapped open.

She *had* seen him. She hadn't taken note of him at the time, but seeing him now she realized she'd caught sight of him several times the other day when she was shopping: when she came out of the post office, when she went to visit Della Rose, and again when she was buttonholed in front of the bank by the tedious Miss Longacre.

What did he want? Whatever it was, she had to keep him out of the house.

Belle opened the man door a crack and peeked out. The visitor had dismounted his horse and was on the porch, knocking on the front door. A satchel rested at his feet. After a moment, he approached the parlor window and peered inside. If he did the same on the other side of the door, he would have a clear view of Morris's body slumped in a chair in the library. Dammit!

She burst out of the barn, calling, "Hello there! How can I help you?"

The man pivoted and eyed her coolly as she crossed the yard. "Good afternoon, ma'am." He tipped his hat and leaned his tall frame down to retrieve the satchel.

"Why, hello!" she greeted him, striding up the steps and, tucking her hand in his elbow, guiding him down to the driveway. "What an unexpected surprise! We hardly ever have callers and now here is a new and friendly face! It's such a delight. To what do we owe such a pleasant surprise? No, let me guess. Have you brought me a delivery from town?" Belle kept up a distracting patter as she led him back to his horse, which was placidly cropping her grass. "No? Hmm, perhaps a request from the pastor's wife? She does love my apple pies. You'll have to tell her I'm fresh out. Thank you ever so much for coming by."

Asle allowed Mrs. Gunness to lead him back to Jenny. Her manner was bright, but brittle. She deposited him and turned back, trotting briskly up her steps. When her hand was on the door handle, he called in a stern voice, "No, ma'am. No messages from town, or packages, or requests for apple pie. I have an entirely different purpose." She froze.

He paced slowly toward her, taking in her appearance as he neared. She held her composure as she waited, but she seemed on edge, as if she were a racehorse quivering at the starting gate, ready to bolt at the gun. Her blue dress was plain, but the fabric and workmanship were fine. Dark smudges dirtied the skirt, and her face was flushed and bore a sheen of sweat. What labor was this fine lady performing? Surely she had people to do these chores?

The letter Asle had found in Nesbitt's satchel was enlightening but devastating. Whatever qualms he felt at reading someone else's correspondence fled under the outrage and horror provoked by the words contained within the letter.

"Dearest Morris," she had begun. "I can wait no longer to lay eyes on you and meet your darling children. Say you will come to me on the next available train. Can I hope for you to arrive by the 17th of May? Please say yes. Remember, tell no one of our liaison. It is too precious to bear the scrutiny of outsiders. And if you will remember to bring your checkbook, our plans to improve the farm can proceed without delay. Yours in fond anticipation, Belle."

Asle had remained awake the rest of the night, torn apart with anguish over what had likely happened to his brother. He was certain this was the same type of letter that had lured Andrew to the house on McClung Road. Asle felt almost completely sure that Mrs. Gunness's aim was to bring Andrew, and now this man Nesbitt, to her home and marry them for money. And then murder them.

He only had to prove it.

Asle had approached the stationmaster the next morning. Without mentioning his discovery of the satchel, he confirmed that a Morris Nesbitt of Muncie, Indiana, had arrived by train and taken a hired carriage to Mrs. Gunness's house. Even more chilling, Asle learned the man had two children, a boy and a girl. From their descriptions, they seemed to be close in age to Asle's children. When Asle asked the stationmaster if the family had taken the train home again, he'd said no.

Asle had returned to his vantage point up the road to watch Mrs. Gunness's house for several hours. His observation confirmed she had visitors: a man, two children, and a little dog.

The family was clearly of some means. The children wore expensive clothing, even when out playing in the yard and fields. They were loud and rambunctious, shouting and screeching at something they found in the brook, the boy chasing after the girl with it. Their little mongrel followed them closely, despite the fact they treated the thing poorly. At one point, Asle witnessed the boy shove the dog with his boot. It wasn't quite a kick, but it wasn't far from it either.

But all was silent now.

Mrs. Gunness slowly descended the steps. "Oh?" she said. "And what is your purpose?"

"It seems you have been doing some gardening," he observed. "I'll only be a moment and you can get back to it."

Her brow furrowed.

He gestured to her dress, and she looked down. "Oh, yes," she said, brushing at the brown marks, "just trying to get my garden planted."

He inspected her face closely, saying nothing. He let the moment stretch out. She shifted on her feet and looked away. If this woman, in her plain but expensive dress and fancy house, did her own gardening, then Asle was the king of France.

"If only every seed we put in the ground produced a crop," he offered.

"Hope springs eternal." Mrs. Gunness's eyes finally found his. "How can I help you, sir? I don't even know your name."

Asle's lips tightened as he ignored her question and thrust an object toward her.

"I have come to return this satchel," the man said, holding out a leather bag. It was embossed on the side: M.H.N. Belle heard Winnie's high-pitched words in her head: "M for Morris, H for Henry, N for Nesbitt." Son of a Benjamin. She tried to keep the panic out of her expression.

"I'm in town to find my brother," the man went on, his eyes still boring into her. "I've been asking around, seeking information. In the process, I found this satchel. I did a little digging and learned that the owner arrived here with his children not long ago. It seems that your friend left it at the train station."

"I . . . am not sure who you're referring to," Belle hedged. A bead of sweat gathered between her shoulder blades and crept down her spine.

"I examined the contents of the satchel, hoping to find a clue of where to return it. It seems your friend, a Mr. Morris Nesbitt, works for the glass company in Muncie and was bringing something for you." He withdrew a small box from the bag and held it up for her to see. The box was beautifully wrapped and Belle saw a tag attached to it with a ribbon: "To Belle, with fondness, from Morris." Son of a Benjamin!

"He had your address in here, too, so I figured I'd catch up with him."

"Do you make it a habit to paw through people's belongings?" Belle snapped. "In any case, I'm afraid you're out of luck. The man and his children decided to return to Muncie."

"Already? A long way for a short visit, I would think." He eyed her a long moment, making Belle feel weighed and measured to the ounce. She bit her tongue and said nothing. "All right, then. That's on my way, as it happens. I'll bring it to him in Muncie. Unless you're expecting him back? And you'd like to hold it for him?"

"It's neither here nor there. We parted on rather cool terms, and I'm sure I don't care—" The gift. It had her name on it. And who knew what other personal effects might be with it. He wouldn't have been daft enough to bring their correspondence, would he? Affecting nonchalance, she said, "That is, it's of no consequence to me if you bring it to him or leave it here. But you might as well leave it. He was my guest, and I'll see that it is returned to him."

"I really don't mind," the man insisted. "As I said, I'm heading to Muncie anyway."

Belle reached for the bag. "No, I must insist. You are a stranger to him and he will not thank me for letting a stranger take responsibility for his personal items." She tugged on the bag, but the man refused to release it.

"Say," he said, "do you receive many men visiting your lovely home?"

With a sharp tug, she wrenched the bag from the man's hands. "I'll have you know—"

But he didn't let her finish. "I'll get out of your way now. Have a good day, ma'am." He tipped his hat again, mounted his horse, and the animal moved off at an unhurried pace.

Fury steamed inside Belle. How dare this man come here and make accusations? Just who did he think he was? She called after him, "Who are you? You never gave your name."

The man reined his horse to a stop and swiveled in his saddle.

"My name is Asle. Asle Helgelien." And then he reached into his pocket and tossed her a piece of candy.

Part IV

Exit Strategy

44

If the dog would just shut up, she'd be able to think. But Beauty darted about close at her heels, yapping incessantly as Belle thrust the shovel into the ground again and again. "Hush, Beauty," Belle told the little beast. How long did it take to dig a hole big enough for three? This was taking forever.

Her mind traveled over and over the conversation she'd had with Asle Helgelien. Could it be called a conversation? It felt like more than that. A fencing match, or an interrogation, or a game for which she didn't know the rules.

So this was the brother Andrew had mentioned, the saloonkeeper. What had Andrew told her? She cast her memory back. He told her about the family donnybrook he'd witnessed, where he snuck around back to give the little girl a book. And he told her about the old couple who were so in love. What had he said about his brother? Something about rescuing Andrew from a fire. A brave man, apparently.

What game was he playing? Following her, sending her the candy, coming here to confront her—but never coming right out and asking her about Andrew. What was he up to? How did he come to have Morris's satchel?

What did he know?

The shovel bit into the earth, doing its work. Belle pitched the dirt over her shoulder. Beauty yapped and Belle nudged him away with her foot. Damn dog.

"Hush, Beauty!" Dig, pitch. "Ow, dammit!" The dog had gotten ahold of her ankle. "Let go! That hurts!" Belle shook her foot, trying to loose the pest. "Let go, or you're next!" Belle swung the shovel at the mongrel, and just as she was about to connect with his little head, the dog danced away and Belle struck her ankle with the hard metal blade. "Son of a Benjamin!" Tears sprang to her eyes. The shovel had cut through her stocking and into the thin skin covering her ankle bone. A trickle of blood seeped into the edges of the fine cotton lisle. Ruined. She tsked. She had really liked this pair of stockings. They were black ribbed, with delicate lavender embroidery up the shin. Some of the lavender threads were loose now and stained with blood.

"Dammit, Ray! Where the hell are you?"

She scanned the road, hoping to see the wagon. Nothing.

Belle stabbed the shovel into the earth again, cursing the hole that was ever so slowly getting larger. The skin of her thumbs turned red where the rough wood of the shovel rubbed against them as she dug. She should have gotten her work gloves, but she didn't want to spare the time. She had to get these children and their father into the ground before someone else came along.

The hot spots on her thumbs blossomed into blisters, bubbles of fluid pressing against the shovel handle and threatening to burst with every dig and pitch. Beauty wouldn't quit worrying at Belle's ankles, making the job nearly impossible. He lunged at the shovel and barked. "Watch out, or I'll give you a taste of my captive bolt pistol." She kicked at Beauty's head, striking a glancing blow. The dog let out a small yip of pain and scampered a few yards away. "Serves you right, you little rat."

Belle hefted her shovel again only for Beauty to take another lunge at her ankles. "Oh no, you don't." Belle wound up the shovel to send the troublesome thing into next Friday. She swung the heavy blade around and down, but Beauty nimbly sidled out of the way and it whistled through the empty air, its arc throwing Belle off balance. She toppled into the grave, her bottom smacking the hard earth much the way she'd wanted to discipline Winnie and Melvin. The shovel crashed in after her, its blade striking the ground just an inch to the left of her head.

"Well, I . . ." She was too stunned to say more, her view of the world suddenly constricted by the short walls of her resting place. Then Beauty leaned his ugly head over the hole, tongue lolling from his open mouth. Belle could swear the dog was smiling. She sat up, coming eye to eye with him. "Better run, little Beauty. Next time I catch you, you'll see the business end of my captive bolt pistol."

Beauty turned tail and made for the woods on his stubby little legs.

As Belle clambered out of the hole, the sides crumbled and collapsed so that she was head-to-toe dirt by the time she was out. She didn't bother brushing it off.

"Let's get this done," she commanded herself. She retrieved the wheelbarrow from the barn and heaved it over the uneven yard to where she'd been working. She hoisted the handles up and the bodies of her erstwhile children slid unceremoniously into the hole. She swiped her hands against one another, briefly satisfied, then wheeled the empty barrow to the kitchen door and went inside to fetch Morris. It wasn't easy dragging him across the floor, through the kitchen door, and into the wheelbarrow, but achievable in a way that moving Louis had not been. "All my husbands should be this small," she noted to herself for the future.

Belle muscled the wheelbarrow out to the hastily dug grave and heaved her latest late husband in after his children. Filling the hole took far less time than digging it had. When the ground was relatively level again, Belle stood back to view her work. No denying it; it was a sloppy job. But it was done.

Belle was easing herself into a kitchen chair for a cup of hot tea when the kitchen door slammed open and Ray tripped in. He looked back at the top step as if surprised by its height.

"Your timing is impeccable," she said, not bothering to hide the annoyance from her voice.

"What?"

Ray's dumb confusion grated on Belle. "Never mind," she said. "Where have you been? It's past noon. I thought you would be back sooner."

"Oh, well, sorry about that," he said. He wiped his mouth with the back of his hand. His face was flushed, and as he came closer, Belle caught a familiar whiff of ale. Visions of drunken Mads popped into her mind. "Lonnie was off sick and Peacham's wife is having a baby— No. That's not it. Other way around. Lonnie's wife is the one having a baby. Or is it?" Ray trailed off, brow furrowed in concentration. Suddenly he brightened. "Yup, yup. It was Lonnie's wife, I guess she—"

"Ray! I don't care whose wife it was and I don't care if she's having a litter of kangaroos! What is your point?"

"Oh, sorry. Point is, it was real busy at the lumberyard and only one young fella to do the work. So it took a while."

"Well, it's about time you got back."

"Sorry 'bout that, Miz Belle. But I got the supplies loaded up with the help of the nicest fellow. We got to talking, and he said he ought to buy me a beer after all that. So we went into the saloon and had a good jaw. We got along like a house afire."

"Did you, now," Belle said. Leave it to Ray to get drunk in town while she was left with the dirty work.

"He was a friendly one, all right. New to town, name of Asle something or other. Didn't catch it. Fine fellow, he was though. Fine fellow."

Belle's stomach dropped. Asle Helgelien just happened to be there when Ray needed help loading the wagon? That was more than a coincidence.

"Ray, how many drinks did you have?" He wasn't exactly the sharpest tool when sober, and the idea of him babbling away after a beer made her blood run cold.

"Not that many." Ray raised one finger, then two. He thought a moment and added a couple more fingers. "I guess I lost count."

Belle had a sudden vision of plummeting into a hole, a deep, deep hole dug with her own two hands. Much like she'd done not an hour ago, but this time falling and falling, dirt pouring in after her, all her hard work and planning buried in an avalanche of prairie dirt.

Carefully, she asked, "And what did you talk about with your new friend?"

"Oh, this and that. Told him about how I grew up here in La Porte. Told him about the farm, and working for you—"

"Dammit, Ray!" Belle exploded, jumping out of her seat. "What were you thinking, blabbing about what we do around here?"

Ray reeled back. "Belle, I—"

"Don't 'Belle' me! What were you thinking? What did you tell that man?"

"Nothing! Nothing, I swear," Ray insisted. "I only told him the truth. How coming here and working for you was the best thing that ever happened to me. How you're the most wonderful, kind, beautiful creature ever to walk the earth, and any man would be lucky to be near you."

Ray hung his head. Belle wanted to feel bad for lighting into him, but she couldn't. His carelessness may have cost her dearly. How was she going to fix this? Everything was crashing down at once. She had worked so hard to create security for herself, and now her world was falling apart. She had to find a way out of this mess, but she didn't know where to begin.

One thing she knew for sure. She couldn't afford to alienate Ray. He may not be the sharpest tool, but he was the one she had. She would find a way to use that. "It's all right, Ray." Belle forced kindness into her voice. "I'm sorry. I shouldn't have yelled at you. I know you wouldn't knowingly do anything to ruin our operation here." With two fingers, she gently tipped his chin up. He still wouldn't meet her eyes.

"Ray," she murmured against his lips, ignoring the smell of beer on his breath. "Ray. I need you."

His arms came around her, and with a needy groan, his lips found hers. He pushed his hands into her hair and hugged her to him desperately. Belle was swept into his passion, momentarily forgetting her purpose. Ray's hands moved down her body, and he walked her back until she was pressed against the kitchen door. He dragged her skirts up and nudged her legs apart with his knee. He had her drawers off and was inside her, her knees gripping his hips, her back sliding on the wood behind her, when a plan flashed into Belle's mind.

At first, she rejected it. She had built so much here; she couldn't see it all thrown away.

Ray worked toward his climax, bringing her with him. Desire coiled and unfurled, stealing thought, threatening to unweave the threads of her idea, leaving her mind a blank. But as the pleasure expanded to fill every corner of her body and soul, finally bursting forth, dragging a desperate cry from her throat, the plan appeared in her mind, fully formed and perfect.

It had to work.

45

On the porch, Belle let the early afternoon sun warm her cheeks, admiring her beloved property. With a plan of action in mind, her spirits were buoyed. Ray crossed the yard, rake in hand. She was glad to see his earlier drinking hadn't impeded his work ethic. "What are you up to, Ray? Didn't you rake the leaves last fall?" The mighty oaks behind the barn had shed what seemed like millions of leaves, but Ray had cleared them all away before the first snow fell.

Ray laughed and pointed to the bushes fronting the house, where mats of brown leaves hid under the branches. "There's always a few that escape," he said. "But don't worry, I'll get 'em raked up."

"I'm certain you will. I'm going into town now. You be good," she told him. "What am I saying? You're my true blue, reliable Ray. You're always good!" Belle tinkled a laugh and planted a kiss on his cheek.

She slid kidskin gloves over the blisters she'd earned from digging. The gloves were new and matched her cycling suit. Very likely, this would be her last chance to ride the bicycle. *Don't think like that*, she counseled herself. *You can always buy a new one.* She retrieved the bike from the barn and deposited her things in its basket: her handbag with money and her bank numbers, a brush and a few extra hairpins, and a hand mirror.

The divided skirts of her bicycling suit made it easy to step over the top tube of the machine and straddle its seat. She pushed off and sailed down the driveway onto the road, turning the pedals over swiftly to gain speed. The breeze created by her progress blew at her hair, and a wisp tickled her cheek.

She sped along until she was well out of sight of her house, but not so close to town that someone was likely to come along, and braked to a stop. In order for her plan to be effective, she needed to create some evidence. She needed to be injured, and obviously so. Nothing elicited a response from a man like a black eye on a woman.

Belle curled her fingers into a fist. She took a couple slow practice swipes toward her eye, then, with as much force as she could muster, punched herself in the face. It hurt, but not much. The leather of her gloves, even fine as it was, acted as padding. She stripped them off and tossed them in the basket. She drew back and tried again.

"Ow! Oh, son of a Benjamin!" Belle checked the injury in the hand mirror and was disappointed to see little more than a red mark that would likely fade by the time she arrived at the sheriff's office. Maybe a split lip would do the trick. She hauled back with her fist and landed one square on her mouth.

"Son of a Benjamin!" This one hurt, too, and she tasted a little blood. But the hand mirror revealed only a slight bump where she'd cut the inside of her lip. This was proving harder than she'd anticipated. She needed a weapon.

A scan of the woods alongside the road rewarded her with a knobby stick, a few inches long and the thickness of two fingers. She whacked herself in the face several times but couldn't get the leverage to do much damage. She tried running into a tree, and while that did knock her on her backside and set her head ringing, it failed to yield a black eye or busted lip.

Belle rode her bicycle a little farther along until she came across a rocky ditch. She set her bike down on the roadside and crossed to the far side. Taking a running start, she flung herself down, tumbling over and over. Lying in a heap on her side, Belle took stock. Her cheek pressed into the dust, and rocks jabbed her ribs. Her body communicated a number of hurts. Ribs and shoulder felt bruised; a sharp and cold sensation on her knee told her that her stockings were probably ripped and her knee cut. Overall, she was feeling rather abused.

She slowly pushed herself to sitting, and after gathering her wits, got to her feet and gave herself a going-over. Dusty smudges marked her shoulder and hip. Her left stocking was indeed shredded and her knee was bleeding, but her cycling skirt, albeit shorter than a traditional skirt, was long enough to hide that damage. Besides, no one was going to call the cavalry over a scraped knee. She fetched the hand mirror from her bicycle basket and inspected her face. Nothing but pale prairie dust.

"Son of a Benjamin," she swore softly.

She remounted her bicycle and pedaled toward town, more slowly now thanks to her skinned knee, mulling over her dilemma. Belle cycled past spring-blooming flowers she took no heed of, her feet pushing at the pedals, her mind worrying over how to give herself a black eye. A flash of darkness on the edge of the road caught her attention as something crashed through the brush. Her front wheel slammed into the thrashing forms of—

Belle sailed over the handlebars. Her head met the ground with a thud and her right shoulder scraped the dirt. Her short flight came to a halt, leaving her stunned and immobile.

Was that—

Her mind barely had time to form the question before she was being pummeled over her head and upper body. Blows landed on her neck and jaw, falling with brute force and tearing at her skin, as angry squeals and grunts filled the air. Then silence. Belle lay in the road for a time, dazed, then raised herself up slowly. The trees lining the road swooped in her vision, making her stomach reel along with them.

Stumbling to her feet, she looked around for the culprits and saw a pair of feral hogs tussling in the field. The terrifying creatures had taken their fight from one field to another, tearing across the road and viciously trampling her along the way. A sob bubbled up from her gut at the thought of what could have happened if those beasts had turned their tusks on her.

Breathing heavily through the pain, Belle cast about for her belongings. Everything was scattered across the road, flung from the basket. She collected her handbag and her hand mirror a few yards away from it.

She took stock of her body. Her palms were scraped and bloody, and her cycling habit was torn at the right shoulder and covered in dust and road debris. Her face throbbed. Belle raised the mirror. The glass had shattered, and through the web of cracks, she inspected her face. What she saw made her wince. A purple goose egg was blossoming on her cheekbone, and a bruised scrape decorated her jaw. More bruises purpled her neck. The most grisly injury, though, was the tear that split the shell of her ear in two.

Belle did not cry. She was a mess, ugly with bruises and scrapes, and hurt in a way she hadn't experienced since the devastating kick she had received from the father of her unborn child back in Norway as a girl.

No, Belle didn't cry. She looked at her wrecked visage in the mirror and smiled triumphantly.

If Asle had once harbored doubts about Mrs. Gunness's involvement in Andrew's disappearance, they were dispersed to the four winds now. He sat in the sheriff's office, holding tight to his impatience while he waited to speak with the deputy. Asle had plenty to say about his "perfect specimen of the womanly virtues."

"Mr. Helgelien." The deputy finally greeted him. "How can I help you today?"

Asle raised himself up off the chair to his full height and extended a firm handshake. "Good afternoon, Deputy Hofstetter. Thank you for seeing me. I have some pertinent information for you regarding the goings-on at the home of Mrs. Belle Gunness."

"Oh? You still on that kick? Didn't you say you're looking for your brother?"

Annoyance clouded the young deputy's features, and Asle bit back his own. "Yes, sir. And I have reason to believe something nefarious happened to him, here in La Porte."

"Is that right? What makes you think he even came to La Porte? I've never seen the wagon you described."

Asle stared at the man. "I told you I found the wagon abandoned in the woods. Did you even try to find it?"

"Now, see here," the deputy said. "I searched all up and down that road. You're lucky I'm not bringing you up on charges. Wasting the sheriff's time like that."

Asle cursed himself for not taking Hofstetter there himself. "I assure you the wagon is there, and I can show it to you."

The deputy gently clasped Asle's shoulder. "I understand, Mr. Helgelien. I understand the fear and uncertainty you are going through. Have you considered taking up a hobby?"

Asle stepped back and the deputy's hand fell away. In a low voice, Asle said, "A crime has been committed. And you need to do your job and investigate that crime. My brother wrote to me and told me he was going to see a woman. In his wagon was a newspaper with Mrs. Gunness's classified ad circled." Asle held up a finger as he enumerated each fact. "I found a leather bag in the men's waiting room of the train station. In the bag were items identifying the owner as Morris Nesbitt, of Muncie, Indiana. A letter from Mrs. Gunness directed Nesbitt to come to her farm, bring money, and tell no one. The stationmaster confirmed that Nesbitt and his two children arrived on the train and took a carriage to Mrs. Gunness. I spoke with her just this morning and she claimed at first not to know Nesbitt, and then claimed that the family had gone back to Muncie. But according to the stationmaster, they have not returned to the train station."

A perplexed frown creased the corners of the deputy's mouth. "Classified ad, did you say?"

"That's right. Mrs. Gunness advertises for a partner in matrimony and business. At least two men have responded, that I know of. My brother, Andrew, and this Morris Nesbitt."

The effort of rational thought worked on the deputy's face. "Nothing wrong with that, is there? Nothing illegal in taking out an advertisement. It's a free country, isn't it? And she's a young woman still. Bound to be feeling lonely in that big house all by herself. Although, you'd think she could find someone closer to home . . ."

Who is he trying to convince, thought Asle. *Me? Or himself?*

The deputy gathered himself and asked, "And this leather bag you say you found, where is it?"

"Mrs. Gunness insisted on keeping it." Asle kicked himself for allowing her to take it.

"I see," the deputy concluded, a little too triumphantly. "So you have no proof, then? This whole tale is just your word."

Asle reached into the depths of his soul for more patience and carefully said, "If you will perform the smallest part of your duty and ask questions—ask the stationmaster if Nesbitt came to town. While you're at it, ask him if the man went back to Muncie! Come with me and I will show you my brother's wagon. Speak with her handyman, Ray Lamphere. Surely he knows something. Speak with Mr. Karsten, who saw Andrew the night he arrived in La Porte."

"Well, gosh all Friday! Now you're bringing the Dirt Troll into it, the craziest coot in La Porte. That old fella sees ghosts and goblins in the night. You know he wanted me to go out there to check on nighttime ghost activity? Now, I'll tell you. Hank Philips thought he saw lights out there at night, and I checked it out, and nothing came of it."

"Deputy Hofstetter," Asle tried once more. "I believe Mrs. Gunness was involved in the death of my brother, and now it seems likely another man—and his children—are missing, perhaps murdered. I implore you to open an investigation to get to the bottom of these goings-on."

"Murder? Don't be ridiculous. Where is the body?" Deputy Hofstetter cast about as if searching for a corpse. "You need to be very careful throwing around accusations against one of La Porte's most solid citizens like that."

"Deputy." Asle's hands had curled into fists, and he deliberately loosened them, coaching himself to remain calm. "If Nesbitt went back to Muncie, why were his return tickets still in his bag? I know Mrs. Gunness has been a seemingly good and kind woman, a model citizen of La Porte, and you are loath to suspect her. But if you will stop and think for a moment—"

And that was as far as Asle got. The deputy had grown very still, seeming to occupy more space than he had a moment before. His indignation was gone, replaced by a dangerous cold. Without a word, he seized Asle's elbow and ushered him to the door. Twisting the knob and jerking the door open, Hofstetter said, "Think very carefully before you broadcast any more nonsense accusations. Good day to you, sir."

Belle hadn't expected the gasps. She'd been so focused on envisioning the shock and outrage she would provoke in Deputy Hofstetter when she entered his office, wincing and weeping, and creating the picture that would elicit that reaction, she had forgotten that to get to the sheriff's office she would have to walk down the streets of La Porte.

As she progressed through town, the same women who typically greeted her in admiration murmured to one another, hiding their comments behind sturdy farm-hardened hands. Belle composed an appearance of patient suffering for her audience, holding her head high and her countenance regal. A path parted as La Porteans made way for her, opening up a view of the sheriff's office. Where Asle Helgelien stood.

Belle spun a quick U-turn, her heart rattling a rapid tattoo. Her plan did not include convincing Andrew's brother that she had been attacked.

Defeat swamped Asle's confidence as he descended the steps of the sheriff's office. He'd been away from his family for more than a month. He wanted to kiss his wife and hug his children and sleep in his own bed. He felt a white-hot flash of anger at Andrew for putting him in this position. But as quick as it came, it snuffed out when he remembered: Andrew was surely dead.

Oh, Andrew. Why did you have to turn east at that crossroads?

As he headed toward the train station, up ahead the swaying form of a woman reminded him of Belle Gunness. As she disappeared around the corner, Asle kicked himself. Now he was imagining her everywhere. Time to go home, surely.

Belle had performed a circuit of the block. Peering around the corner, she searched the street and sidewalks for her nemesis, but could see no trace of Asle Helgelien. When she was confident he was gone, she approached the sheriff's office.

Deputy Hofstetter greeted her with exactly the chivalric horror Belle had envisioned. "Gosh all Friday, Mrs. Gunness, who did this to you? Tell me who it was. I'm going to pound that son of a no good you know what. Don't you worry. You'll never have to see him again. I'll lock him up good for you." His face was stony and a muscle in his jaw clenched and unclenched. "Just tell me who it was."

Belle blinked and let the tears in her eyes slip down her cheeks, then brushed them away angrily. "I won't stand for it, Deputy. I won't be attacked on my own property. I refuse to be afraid of him."

"Of course not, Mrs. Gunness," the deputy said firmly. "There's no excuse for this. Nothing you could do could justify this kind of abuse. Whoever did this has to be brought to justice. He's a menace to any woman. We can't let it happen again. Just tell me his name."

Belle raised her eyes to Deputy Hofstetter and said clearly, "It was Ray Lamphere."

46

*W*here Deputy Hofstetter's reaction was all heat and fiery masculine bravado, Della Rose's response was more subdued. "So. It has come to this." Belle held still so Della Rose could take in the full glory of the bruises, swelling, and smears of blood. With a philosophic dispassion, she fingered the tear at the shoulder of Belle's cycling costume and tsked. "Come to the back, then."

Belle let Della Rose install her at the little table in the sewing room. The seamstress's demeanor was brusque and businesslike. She clapped her hands sharply and dismissed Carrie with firm words. "Out, out. Don't come back until the morning."

But her touch was tender, her fingers light on Belle's chin as she tilted it this way and that to take in the damage. "Sweet lord above," Della Rose whispered. For the first time ever, Belle saw Della Rose become unsettled. She had always had an air of equanimity, as if she were above petty little concerns. But now she was visibly upset. "My poor, dear friend. Look at your ear. The tear has gone through completely. Who has done this to you? No, don't answer. I am being selfish, wanting answers when what you need is care. Why are you not home in bed? Shall I fetch the doctor?"

"No, no, I don't want a doctor. I'm too ashamed," Belle said, letting tears infuse her voice. It wasn't difficult, given the pain of her injuries. "Please, just sit with me."

"Yes, of course. Sit, and we shall have tea." Della Rose picked up the kettle but set it down again. "I think something stronger is in order." She dug around in a cabinet and found a bottle and two small crystal glasses. "A little cognac, I think." She filled each glass with the reddish-brown liquid and handed one to Belle. The liquor warmed her tongue and soothed her mood. She eased back in her seat, as Della Rose regarded her once more. "I'm so sorry for your pain, my dear friend. Can I assume the perpetrator was a man?"

Belle nodded. "Ray, my handyman. He has always had a bit of a mash for me. It seemed quite sweet for a long time, but lately he has gotten very jealous. I told him how sad I was about M—" Belle tried to think. Which husband had she told Della Rose about last? "About my last husband, and it set him off. It was awful."

"Is that so? I wouldn't have thought the meek Mr. Lamphere had it in him," Della Rose mused. She gave Belle an assessing look, holding it for an uncomfortably long moment. "But who can say what lies inside the heart of a man—or woman—when pushed to the brink." Then, after one of her gallic shrugs, she raised her cognac to Belle.

Yes, Belle had chosen well when she had identified Della Rose as a fellow soul. She lifted her own cognac, and they touched glasses. "I suppose you are right," Belle agreed. "We all do what we must."

Now that she was seated and the drama of the morning was past, the pain of her cuts and bruises began to intrude on her senses. Every time she moved, a new sting or ache announced itself. And the intense, searing pain of her torn ear made it difficult to think of anything else.

Della Rose made appropriate soothing noises. "Your ear," she ventured. "It must be seen to." She drew her chair next to Belle and leaned in to inspect the injury. "Sweet lord above," she whispered for the second time. "You want me to stitch it up?"

Belle nodded.

"You understand it will hurt a great deal."

Belle nodded again, determined to show no fear.

"You are strong," Della Rose said with approval. "Drink up your cognac, and I will boil some water. Then we will get it over with. I will be as quick and gentle as I can."

Della Rose was quick, and she was gentle, but the procedure still hurt terribly. Belle gritted her teeth through every puncture into the sensitive tissue. She could hear the thread sliding through her flesh and cartilage, and it made her wince.

The seamstress kept up a genial stream of chatter while she worked. "This is not my first time stitching up a cut, I'll have you know. I never told you about my husband—because he is not worth the breath—but I will tell you now. He was a rough man. Prone to fighting. I put more stitches in that man than the finest gown." Della Rose paused to adjust her position. "No, not my first time. It's not something I ever got used to, seeing these ugly cuts. But I did learn to harden my stomach. Are you doing all right, my dear?"

Belle held her head very still and muttered a simple, "Mm-hmm."

"Good. I'm almost done. Very soon I will finish this little bit of piecework you have given me. And then we will have another cognac. This day calls for it. There, that's the end." She gently clipped the thread with a pair of dainty embroidery scissors. She laid her needle and the scissors on the table and refilled their glasses.

"Thank you, my friend, but I cannot stay," Belle said. "I must go home and rest, but I want you to know I appreciate your friendship. You will never know how much you have done for me."

As she returned to the showroom on her way out of the shop, Belle was surprised to find Carrie had not gone home as she was instructed. The assistant moved hastily away from the door as Belle came through and made herself busy inspecting a bolt of fabric. The bored seamstress was doing a little eavesdropping, was she? Belle departed the shop, hiding her pleasure. She couldn't have planned that better. Between Carrie and Little Jimmy, soon the whole town would be talking.

* * *

The beans were hot, and Ray was famished. He scooped a portion from the pot on his small wood stove—not a fancy cookstove like Belle had, but it got the job done for simple things like heating up the leftover beans she sent home with him. He settled down to fill his belly, spoon in fist, when the knocking began. More of a pounding, really, that rattled the door and sent thunder through the tiny cottage. "Ray Lamphere, you in there?" came a booming voice.

Ray dropped his spoon into his beans and scraped back his chair. The pounding kept on going, between shouts of Ray's name. Whoever was out there, he was in a damn hurry.

"I'm comin', I'm comin'," Ray hollered. "Keep your shirt on."

When he opened the door, he found Little Jimmy on the other side, fist raised, about to pound again. Ray had known the deputy since grade school, just a couple years behind him and already a head taller than even the oldest boys in the school. Little Jimmy had filled out a lot over the years, and the man on Ray's front porch was not one to dismiss easily. And he looked damned angry, to boot.

"What's this about?" Ray asked.

"Ray Lamphere, you are under arrest for assault." The deputy hauled Ray out onto the lawn by his shirtfront.

"I'm what?" Ray jerked his shirt out of Little Jimmy's grasp. "That's crazy! I haven't touched a soul!"

"Resisting arrest, is that it?"

"What? No! I—" Ray's words came to a halt when they met with Little Jimmy's incoming fist. Ray reeled back, cupping his nose as warm blood dripped through his fingers. "Shittagoddam!" Suddenly he was spun around and his hand yanked from his face, as Little Jimmy clicked a set of handcuffs around Ray's wrists. The blood from his nose poured freely down his mouth and chin, spattering his shirt. "Little Jimmy, what the hell is going on?" Ray's voice sounded nasally and he wished he could touch his swollen nose. "I've been here working on Belle's property all afternoon—"

"Oh, so you admit it, then?"

Ray stumbled over the uneven ground as Little Jimmy steered him to the waiting paddy wagon. When he lost his footing, the deputy let him fall roughly and his already-broken nose smashed into the turf. "Shittagoddam!"

"Watch your language. Now I'll add disturbing the peace to your charges." Little Jimmy hauled Ray to his feet and all but threw him in the back of the wagon. Ray landed on the floor between two benches that lined the walls. His nose had swollen shut, and he could feel the pressure building in his eyes. But the pain was the least of his worries. "Who on earth said I assaulted them? I haven't been to a saloon in months. Well, except to jaw with that fellow earlier, but all we did was talk—"

"As if you don't know," Hofstetter cut in. "You beat Belle Gunness to a bloody mess." He slammed the grated door shut and snapped the lock. "And don't call me Little Jimmy. That's Deputy Hofstetter to you, Lamphere."

Ray rode into town in a state of frantic bewilderment. Had he heard the man right? Belle had been beaten?

When they got to the sheriff's office, Little Jimmy dragged Ray inside and threw him into a jail cell. Ray stumbled and went sprawling on the floor, his chin skidding across the rough wooden planks. The door clanged shut behind him, and the deputy said, "Stay on the floor all night if you like, but if you want those handcuffs off, get over here."

With his hands bound behind him, Ray awkwardly got to his feet and shuffled over to the iron bars that locked him in the tiny room. Little Jimmy loomed on the other side, glowering.

"Turn around," he barked.

As the deputy unlocked the handcuffs, Ray said over his shoulder, "Who said I beat up Belle? Go ask her, she'll tell you it's a mistake."

"She's the one who made the charge, you animal. She came in here beaten and bloody, but brave as a lioness. Said she wouldn't be beaten and nearly killed on her own property, that she wasn't afraid of a no-account son of a drunk who couldn't get a job without her."

The words slammed into Ray with brutal force. He remembered every whispered conversation they'd had in the blissful nights they'd spent together—the blissful days too; it was just this afternoon they'd last made love. What did he do to make her so angry?

"She was right as rain when I saw her a few hours ago."

"Save it for the judge, Lamphere." Little Jimmy removed the hand-cuffs and gave Ray a final shove before he left the cell room.

Ray sank down onto the wooden bench affixed to the wall. What was going on? How could Belle have claimed he'd beaten her?

Still hurting but somewhat revived after her visit with Della Rose, Belle set off from the seamstress's shop to complete the next step in her plan. She limped stoically through the streets of La Porte to the bank, ignoring the stares and whispers that followed her, wondering how many of them already knew she'd been viciously assaulted by her handyman. Mr. Todd visibly winced when he saw her but was too polite to ask any impertinent questions. "My dear Mrs. Gunness, come into my office where we can have some privacy. Make yourself comfortable. I'll have my assistant bring us tea."

When they were seated at a small conference table in his office, two steaming teacups in front of them, Belle told the bank manager her purpose. "I need to withdraw some cash from my account, please."

"Of course, Mrs. Gunness. I'm happy to help you do that today. How much do you need?"

"All of it."

Slowly, it dawned on Ray that Little Jimmy had seen Belle's injuries. "Beaten and bloody," he'd called her. Even if Little Jimmy didn't believe him, Ray knew he hadn't hurt Belle. Could never hurt Belle! But then, who had? That person was still out there. Was Belle in danger?

Her tale of feeling watched in town the other day came back to him. Maybe she really was being followed. He had to warn Little Jimmy! He had to get Belle some protection!

"Little Jimmy! Little Jimmy!" Ray hollered, trying to bring the deputy back. Remembering Jimmy's admonishment when he'd locked Ray up, he tried again. "Sorry, Jimmy! I mean Deputy Hofstetter! Deputy Hofstetter, come quick! It wasn't me, I swear!"

No answer. Nothing but silence.

"Deputy Hofstetter, you've gotta listen!" Ray shouted. "It wasn't me! But I think I know who it was! And I'm worried for Belle's safety! You've gotta listen to me! She's in danger!" The door to the cell room began to swing open. "Oh, thank goodness you've come back. Listen, I—"

But it wasn't Little Jimmy. It was the night jailer, who went by the name of Fanciful. He entered with a lantern and held it high. "Quit yer caterwaulin', Lamphere. The deputy's gone home for the night, so you might as well kick back and relax. Yer not goin' anywhere tonight."

"Fanciful, you've gotta get a message to Little Jimmy! I know who did it. I know who beat up Belle."

"Do ya now? That's good. Cuz it's no secret it was you. Belle swore out the complaint herself. Now, I can't say as I blame you, that gal is a handful, no doubt."

"What? No, she's not, I mean. She's wonderful. I mean. No, listen—"

"Thing is," Fanciful went on, ignoring Ray's protests, "you gotta know how to treat her right. There's a right way to go about it. And leavin' her with bruises from tit to tail ain't it. You follow me?"

"No, of course not. Hitting a woman is not—"

"Exactly." Fanciful sidled closer and checked over his shoulder. At what, Ray couldn't say because the sheriff's office was deserted. "Now, you want to discipline yer woman, you gotta do it right. No one the wiser, eh?"

"No, of course—what?"

"Leave no trace. Never hit the face, is my advice to you. Bruises too easily, and then it's there for all to see. Now, a good tug of the hair will do wonders. Hurts to bejeezus, but there's no mark."

Ray stared at Fanciful. What the hell was the man talking about?

"There's just no call for hitting the face, Lamphere. Ladies wear an awful lot of clothes. That's a lot of ground to cover, plenty of territory to make your point, see? A jab to the belly will teach her who's boss. Don't need to be a hard one, neither. A gal's belly is soft. She'll get the point right away."

"No, that's not—"

"Now, one that's fun for everyone is a good spanking. Get her over your knee and give her a few swats. That can lead to some wild times." A far-off gleam came into Fanciful's eye. Ray didn't want to know what he was thinking of.

"Fanciful, you've got a lot of advice."

"Yer welcome to it, Lamphere." He nodded and laid a finger by his nose. "'Member what I said."

As Fanciful sauntered away, Ray shook his head in disbelief. Fanciful was a nut.

But with Fanciful gone, Ray was left with only his worries. He thought over his last few encounters with Belle. There was the companionable late-night visit they'd had, planning the kitchen garden. And while she did get heated about his talk with that Asle fellow, they'd made up instantly, making love right there in the kitchen. How could she go from clinging to him and crying in his ear to swearing out a complaint against him? There had to have been some kind of crazy misunderstanding.

Belle found Miss Longacre at the schoolhouse just after the children had left for the day. The teacher was at her desk at the front of the one-room building, stowing books into a leather satchel. Her habitual sulky demeanor vanished when she caught sight of Belle. "Mrs. Gunness! Whatever happened to your face?"

"Nothing for you to worry about, Miss Longacre. It looks worse than it feels." This was a flat-out lie; Belle was acutely aware of every scrape and bruise, and her ear was on fire. "I've been thinking about your situation, Miss Longacre. Is it true that you have found that teaching is not best suited to your ambitions?"

"Oh, Mrs. Gunness. I *hate* teaching. I would do almost anything else, if I could."

"I might have a solution for you."

"Really?" Miss Longacre clasped her hands to her breast, her eyes gone wide and pleading.

"Yes, really. But before I tell you, I have to know you can keep a secret."

"I promise, I promise! You can count on me to keep quiet."

Belle hesitated, drawing the moment out, as if considering whether Miss Longacre was truly trustworthy. The girl bounced on her toes, fairly quivering with anticipation.

"All right," Belle relented. "Pack a bag and come to my house tomorrow night. Late, after everyone is asleep. No one must see you. I will explain everything then."

Despite making his livelihood in a saloon, Asle had never been much of a drinker. The occasional glass of wine or port, nothing more. So the fifth of whiskey he'd purchased from the saloon and brought back to his room was quick to do its work.

He tipped the bottle up and took another swig. The harsh liquid burned all the way down his throat to his empty stomach. He couldn't eat, couldn't sleep. He paced the small room he'd been renting for what, a week? It was two and a half strides from door to window. He'd made the trip countless times now, unable to sit or sleep. What time was it?

Two in the morning? Three? He took another slug of whiskey, only to find the bottle empty.

"Gosh darn it!" He flung the bottle across the room, expecting a satisfying crash. But the bottle only bounced off the wall and fell to the floor. "Gosh darn that Belle Gunness!"

The woman was responsible for Andrew's death, Asle was certain. She was dangerous, with her fancy airs and flawless reputation. Underneath that oh-so-warm smile and surface charm was a conniving, murderous, soulless devil. Asle knew it the way he knew the sun would rise in only a few hours. Her evil was even infecting him, turning him into a dissolute scapegrace. She had him drinking and swearing. And when was the last time he wrote home? Matilda would be worrying, but he couldn't make himself put pen to paper.

His tongue felt fuzzy and full in his arid mouth. He should have a drink of water and put himself to bed.

Should, should, should.

What he should do was hold that woman accountable. Was he going to let her get away with what she did to Andrew?

47

In the morning, Ray paid his fine to the judge and started walking home. Whispers dogged his footsteps. Folks who usually had a friendly wave for him turned away. And when he passed old Farmer Nilson leaning on the railing outside the saloon, Nilson shot a stream of tobacco at Ray's feet, barely missing his boots.

"Hey, watch it!" Ray exclaimed.

"What I hear, it's you that needs to watch himself," Nilson said, giving Ray a dead-eye stare.

Ray moved away, striding out of town as fast as he could. People must have heard about the accusation against him. Damn that Little Jimmy. He couldn't keep it to himself for one day? Give Ray the chance to clear up what had to be a misunderstanding?

Ray made it to McClung Road and eased up his pace. He took a deep breath and wiped sweat off his brow. Disbelief and confusion burned through him, raising an unfamiliar and very uncomfortable feeling. He was angry. At Belle. By the time he arrived at the property, Ray was ready to light into his mistress. He knew just what he would say. *After all the bodies I've buried for you, this is how you repay me? By lying about me? Having me arrested! How would you like it if I told some stories to the sheriff?*

That ought to get her attention.

He pushed through her front door without knocking. "Belle!" he hollered, all his anger and frustration erupting into that one word. The door slammed into the wall behind him. "Belle! Where are you! What the hell were you thinking?" He stormed farther into the house, pushing against habits formed over the months of never being invited inside unless it was to work on something. But he didn't care. He was so damn angry with her. What right did she have to accuse him?

All of a sudden, she burst out of her room upstairs and hurtled down the stairs in a flurry of trailing skirts and unbound hair. "Oh, Ray, you're back!" She threw herself into his arms. "Thank God!"

Ray stumbled back, catching her as she flung her arms around him, kissing his neck and face over and over. This was not the reception he expected.

"I've been so afraid, you have no idea." She clung to him, and Ray had to hold himself in check not to sink into the embrace. His anger stiffened his spine, and she must have sensed it because she said, "Oh, Ray, you're not angry with me, are you?" She squeezed him tighter. "Please say you're not mad. You have to understand, I've been so afraid. I didn't know what else to do. Please don't be angry with me." She pressed more feverish kisses along his neck and cheek as she spoke.

The words didn't register. She thought a few kisses would make up for a night in the pokey and a tattered reputation? Well, she had another think coming. Ray pried her arms from his neck and set her back, but the words he'd practiced died in his throat when he got a good look at her face. A purple bruise near her eye pushed against the tender skin, closing the lid halfway. Scrapes on her cheek blazed angry and red. Her bottom lip was split and swollen. A seam of fine thread held together two parts of her ear.

All his anger slipped away like a fish off a line. "Good God, Belle. What happened to you?"

"Oh, Ray. It was awful. That man, Asle. You met him? At the saloon? He caught me on my way into town. I was riding my bicycle and he shoved a stick in the spokes. I fell and then he hauled me up and shook me. It was awful! He was so angry! He was asking me questions and I didn't know what to tell him. So he hit me! He just kept hitting me. I was afraid for my life. Finally he threw me to the ground and stormed away. Deputy Hofstetter found me. Of course, I couldn't tell him what really happened. That would expose everything. I said the first thing that came into my head, the first thing I thought the deputy would believe. I'm so sorry, Ray. Can you ever forgive me?"

Belle reached up and gently laced her fingers through his and pulled his hand to her heart, imploring him with shining eyes. "Please?" A tear welled up and spilled over, sliding down her cheek. "You know I'd never hurt you, don't you, Ray? You're the only one I can trust. It's always been you." She turned away abruptly, wiping at her face.

Suddenly his anger shifted. That Asle! He'd seemed like a decent fellow, buying him drinks and asking him questions. Now Ray could see the man was only interested in pumping him for information about Belle. What the hell was wrong with the man? Assaulting an unsuspecting woman!

"Aw, Belle," Ray said. He folded her close and gently brushed his lips over the bruise near her eye. "That son of a bitch! Beating on a woman like that. I oughta show him what's what. I oughta give him a taste of his own medicine!"

"No, Ray, you can't! What if he hurts you . . . or worse, kills you! I couldn't bear it. Please, don't leave. Stay with me."

Belle pressed her mouth to Ray's and kissed him deeply. All his fiery anger flamed into passion. Her eyes drifted closed as he moved his mouth down her neck. Her breath came in pants of pleasure.

"Take me upstairs, Ray," she murmured. "Don't leave me. I need you."

If Asle never had another drink, it would be too soon. His head and stomach warred over which made him feel worse, and his tongue felt like sandpaper. But his physical discomfort paled in comparison to the fury that drove him from his room and out onto the street.

His drunken fit last night hadn't dimmed his certainty that whatever happened to Andrew, Belle Gunness was responsible for it. And the overbright light of morning illuminated what he must do next. He would be leaving this Godforsaken town soon, but before he did, he would hold Belle Gunness accountable.

Striding purposefully to Fischer Mercantile, Asle plotted just how he could do that. What punishment was fitting for such a vile, callous person?

Inside the mercantile, Asle waited impatiently for his turn at the counter. It seemed the shopkeeper and the patron ahead of him had a lot to say to one another. Occupied with his own schemings against Belle Gunness, he paid them little mind, until he caught mention of her name.

"It's shocking is what it is." A stout young woman dressed head to toe in houndstooth check—did she think she was Nellie Bly?—leaned over the counter to make her point. "I ask you, Mr. Fischer, what is the world coming to when a woman is so savagely attacked by her handyman? Poor, dear Mrs. Gunness."

"Indeed, Mrs. Cochrane," Mr. Fischer replied. "Couldn't agree more. One night in jail isn't enough for him."

What was this? Lamphere attacked Mrs. Gunness? Asle gleaned a few more facts as he eavesdropped: Lamphere had beaten her face to a pulp, broken some of her fingers, and left her for dead. Asle couldn't credit it. The man he'd spoken to in the saloon just yesterday was head over heels in love with the woman. He couldn't see that reedy, lovelorn man viciously attacking her.

"Pardon me," he interjected. "I couldn't help but overhear. How did they come to settle on Lamphere as the culprit?"

"Why, from her very testimony," the Nellie Bly acolyte announced.

My left foot, thought Asle. Far more likely, it was some nefarious plot by Belle Gunness herself, and she was using Lamphere as a scapegoat. His skepticism must have shown on his face because the woman bristled and exclaimed, "Do you doubt her word, sir?"

"Lamphere doesn't seem the type, if you ask me. Why would he attack her? Isn't she his employer? Now he is out of a job. And a home, too, yes? He lives on the premises."

The lady's face darkened, and outrage simmered in her words. "The 'type'? What type is that? You can see into a man's soul and know what he is capable of? Hmph. It must be nice to be so sure of yourself." She turned her back on Asle. "Good day, Mr. Fischer."

The bell tinkled merrily as she yanked open the door. In the chilly silence that was left in her wake, Mr. Fischer cleared his throat and said, "How can I help you, sir?"

"I need to buy a length of rope." To push past the awkwardness left behind by his heated exchange with the departed Mrs. Cochrane, he offered a pleasantry. "Fine day out there, isn't it?"

"Indeed, indeed. Spring has sprung, as they say. Don't mind Mrs. Cochrane. We are all a bit unsettled by the news."

Asle didn't doubt it. He was unsettled too. More than unsettled. Was there no depth Mrs. Gunness wouldn't stoop to? Hanging would be too good for the woman. But it was pointless to argue with the shopkeeper. "Of course."

"Now, right this way. What will you be tying up?"

"Excuse me?"

"That's to say, what kind of rope do you need? How sturdy does it need to be?"

"Oh, of course. It needs to be quite sturdy . . . um. Strong enough to lash baggage to a horse's back ought to do it."

The merchant selected a spool of thick rope and measured out a few feet. "That seem like enough?"

Asle eyed the rope, picturing what he had in mind for it. "More. A couple more feet."

Mr. Fischer payed out some more and at Asle's nod cut it and coiled it before bringing it to the counter. "Anything else today?"

"No, that'll do."

Fischer took payment and wished him good day. Asle collected his rope and turned to leave. Before long, he would be quit of this place. Just as soon as he held the devilish Mrs. Gunness to account. His hand on the doorknob, a thought occurred to Asle. "Come to think of it, I need more than this rope."

The amber light filling the guest room told Ray the sun was setting. He lay next to Belle, tangled in the selburose quilt, restless thoughts chasing each other through his mind.

He and Belle had made love all afternoon and into the evening, passion driving them from room to room. They'd had sex on the chair in the library, again on the kitchen table. When Belle had gone to use the powder room, he'd cornered her there and they'd done it leaning against the sink. She'd straddled him on the stairs, and by the time they made their way into the spare bedroom, they'd collapsed, spent, on the hardwood floor.

She curled against his side, her head cradled on her arm. Sinister bruises marred her skin. Poor Belle. The thought of what she went through at the hands of that Asle bastard tugged at him.

And yet, a small voice whispered at the back of his mind, now that he wasn't distracted by her words and body. Ray rolled away from Belle and got up. She could have thrown blame on anyone—a neighbor or a passing tramp. She could have made up a story about falling on that crazy two-wheeled contraption she loved so much. But she had pointed the finger of blame at Ray, her closest confidant, her business partner—her partner in crime, literally. After all he had done for her.

Silently, Ray returned to his cottage in the descending twilight. He sat for the rest of the evening, thinking.

50

"Lamphere! Lamphere! Get out here! The house is on fire!" a voice called.

Ray sat bolt upright with a gasp. An eerie red hue lit his dark room. His heart pounded in his chest, echoing a pounding on the door.

The house on fire? God Almighty! Ray threw off his covers and stuffed his legs into pants, hopping on one foot as he looked out the window. Horror seized him. The big brick house that he had labored so intently on these past nine months, the house that held the woman he loved, was engulfed in flames. Scarlet and gold danced from the brand-new roof, and a reddish-yellow glow illuminated the upper windows like eyes. "Belle!" he cried.

Barreling through the door, he almost ran into the Dirt Troll. "Come on, Lamphere! Hurry!" the squat man hollered.

The pair ran out into the yard that separated Ray's cottage from the main house. A line of townsfolk was assembling to pass buckets of water hand to hand from a water wagon parked in the yard, its two sturdy workhorses protected from their fear of fire by blinders.

Ray snatched a bucket and bounded up the porch steps and inside. The line of water-bearers led up the stairway to the second floor, where the blaze raged. Ray dashed up the stairs and joined the front of the line, flinging water at the flames pouring out of the main bedroom. Belle's bedroom. He tossed the empty container to a waiting child who ran back down the stairs. Ray grabbed the next bucket and flung more water. He tried to get closer but the heat pushed him back. Everything in the room was on fire. Flames consumed the bedding of the big four poster and licked up the bed hangings. The posts were torches. Tendrils of flame crawled up the walls and across the ceiling, even starting to burn into the attic.

"Where's Miz Belle?" he yelled to the man behind him, taking the bucket of water. It was fat Fred Roman, the bricklayer, his face glowing red in the light of the conflagration. "Have you seen her? Is she safe?"

"Ain't seen her," Fred said, turning back to receive the next load of water from his brother Ed.

Ray held the front of the line and poured bucket after bucket, hour after hour. Dawn was breaking when the last of the fire succumbed to the dousing and the crew of neighbors and townsfolk began to dissipate. Ray collapsed onto the lowest step of Belle's grand staircase, barely noticing the others who were lingering in the downstairs of the ruined house or out on the lawn. He leaned his weight on his arms, his hands dangling loose between his knees. He could hardly lift his head. He didn't *want* to lift his head. Didn't want to see the smoking ruins above and behind him, the destroyed bedrooms. The destroyed bed. And what, presumably, lay in it.

He wanted to stay right there and stare at the floorboards between his feet. He wanted to go back to sleep and find out this had all been a nightmare.

Two feet, encased in heavy black boots, came into his view, and a hand fell on his shoulder. "Are you Ray Lamphere? I'm Tony Godwin, captain of the volunteer fire brigade." Ray squinted up at the man. His eyes stung from a long night of being enveloped by smoke. "I understand you're the caretaker here. What happened, man?"

Ray shrugged. "Dirt Troll woke me up and the place was already burning."

"What time did it start?"

"After midnight? I don't really know."

"Anybody been around here, strangers? Suspicious characters?"

"No, nobody," Ray answered quickly. "Just me and Miz Belle."

A commotion broke out by the front door, where Ray saw Little Jimmy trying to block a man from entering. A stern voice carried over their heads. "Let me through, man! I have a right to see what happened!" Through the volunteers in the entry hall, Ray saw the tall man who'd bought him drinks at the saloon the other day. Who'd attacked Belle. Asle.

That son of a bitch. Without benefit of conscious thought, Ray was off the step, barging past the fire captain. He launched himself at Asle, his hands seeking the other man's throat. "You did this! You did this, you son of a bitch!" Arms grappled him and held him back. Ray struggled against them, desperate to reach the bastard who had killed Belle. "She's dead, and it's your fault. Monster!"

"Me? That's madness. I had nothing to do with this," Asle said. "My name is Asle Helgelien."

Helgelien? All strength escaped Ray, and he sagged into the arms that had been holding him back.

"My brother Andrew was corresponding with Mrs. Gunness last fall and disappeared," Asle went on. "I have reason to believe she killed him. Let me through."

Ray lunged again. "That's a damn lie! Belle never killed no one!"

Just then, a hush fell over the crowd clustered in the hallway. Something drew the attention of the men standing in front of him, and the hands holding him back loosened. Fearful of what he would see, Ray chanced a look over his shoulder. Two men made their way down the staircase, bearing a sheet-draped stretcher between them. Under the sheet, a form was visible. Ray broke free, and his faltering steps brought him to the foot of the staircase as the stretcher-bearers descended. They reached the bottom and lowered their burden.

"We found her on the floor, by the column. Looks like she must have got out of bed but was overwhelmed by the smoke," one of the stretcher-bearers said.

Ray tore the sheet back. "Oh, Belle." He crouched over her body and moaned, tears cascading down his face. She was curled on her side, like she was asleep. Ray thought of all the nights he'd held her just like that. He brushed his fingers through her hair, singed and blackened. "My poor, dear Belle," Ray sobbed. He rolled her on her back so he could see her face and reeled back at her charred, disfigured skin. A gag rose in his throat. "Oh, God," he moaned. He didn't want to see her like that, but couldn't tear away. Flames had meandered senselessly over her body, ravaging her face, burning away her hair, and singeing her dress, but leaving other parts untouched. At her wrist, Ray noticed a loop of scorched rope—had she been tied up? It *was* that Asle fellow! If he had suspicions about Andrew, he'd have every reason to want to harm Belle.

Ray was about to call him out when his eyes landed on the creamy, unscathed skin of her chest, revealed where her dress had fallen open when he'd rolled her.

Suddenly, he hid his face in his hands. Not to cover his tears, but to cover his unexpected relief and joy.

This was not Belle.

This woman, whoever she was, had perfectly clear skin over her left breast. Belle's distinctive and alluring birthmark, the reddish-brown patch that reminded Ray of angel wings, was nowhere in sight.

Raising his head to say a prayer of thanks to the Lord above, Ray's eyes fell upon another strange sight. Belle's beloved painting of this very home, the painting she had asked him to hang that first day—it was gone. He stared, the possibilities of what this meant swirling in his mind.

"What are you looking at, Lamphere?" asked Captain Godwin.

"Nothing," Ray said. "Nothing at all."

He stumbled past the crowd of people, through the kitchen, and into the backyard. His elation bubbled up inside him, flooding out in a cry of sobbing laughter.

As weak sunlight fought through the foggy dawn, Beauty, the little dog that had arrived with the Nesbitts, trotted up to him and sniffed his ankle.

"Hey there, little fella." Ray greeted him with a pat. "Where've you been?" Beauty yipped and danced at his feet. He barked a couple times, trotted away, then turned back and yipped again. "Aw, you want to play fetch, don'tcha? Maybe later, little fella." As if he understood, Beauty gave one last yip and trotted off.

If Belle wasn't dead, where was she? Would she send for him? Would they finally be together?

"Lamphere." A voice broke into his thoughts. It was Little Jimmy, covered in soot and sagging with exhaustion. He must have been here all night too. His face seemed to have aged overnight.

Across the yard, Beauty began yipping again, scratching at the earth and barking excitedly. Somebody was going to have to take in that dog, Ray supposed. Maybe he'd do it. He kind of liked the little mongrel.

"Lamphere, Jesus. What an awful thing. I can't believe—can't believe she's gone." Little Jimmy's voice broke.

Ray nodded, not trusting himself to speak.

"She was something else, wasn't she?"

Ray nodded again.

"I never knew anyone like her. Probably never will." The deputy eyed the smoking ruins of the second floor of the house. "What the hell happened here, Lamphere? How did it all start?"

"Hell if I know," Ray answered, and it was the God's truth. How did she do it? He hoped he got a chance to ask her.

"Whose dog is that?"

Beauty's yip had become frantic. He was head-deep in the hole he'd dug, wrestling with something.

"What? Oh, that's B—" Ray was about to say the dog's name

and caught himself. "I don't know. He's been hanging around here this morning."

"All worked up about something, isn't he? You got a mole problem here? Ground squirrels?"

A creeping dread was building in Ray. He didn't recall a rodent burrow in that spot.

Little Jimmy's brows drew together. "What's he got there?" He started toward the dog. "It looks like . . . it looks like he's pulling something out of the ground. And it's not a mole."

Ray followed with rising alarm.

"Is that . . . a hand?" the deputy hazarded. He broke into a run.

Ray trailed in slow motion, dazed with a blind panic. *No, no, no, no,* his mind chanted. He reached the spot a few steps behind Little Jimmy. Beauty was tugging on something, hauling his full weight backward. His teeth had a grip on a piece of tweed, a hand flopping out the end as Beauty tugged again and again.

The deputy knelt next to Beauty. "What did you find, little dog? Here, give it. Give it!" He wrestled the dog away from what was now clearly an arm sticking out of the ground. Beauty sat on his haunches almost in triumph, as if waiting for praise. With his tongue hanging out and panting, he looked like he was smiling.

"What the hell is this, Lamphere?" Little Jimmy boomed. "Who's buried here?"

"How the hell should I know?"

"Only two people occupy this property, Lamphere. And one of them is dead."

Ray cast around for something to say and came up empty. He stared at the deputy. Ignored by the two men, Beauty went back to nosing around. He sniffed the earth and pawed at it, scraping away more dirt, widening the hole he had begun.

Just then, Captain Godwin strode up. "Deputy Hofstetter, we discovered the remnants of rope tied to one of Mrs. Gunness's wrists. It would seem she was tied up in her bedroom before the fire was started."

Little Jimmy sputtered, "Tied up? You mean . . ." He spun toward Ray and grabbed him roughly by the bicep. "Ray Lamphere, I'm arresting you on suspicion of murder." He eyed the hand sticking out of the soil. "Two counts."

Beauty yipped, and the deputy looked down. Another hand had come unearthed, this one smaller and obviously not a pair with the first.

"Three counts."

5-1

Asle returned to the ruined house on McClung Road after
briefly checking on Jenny down at Mr. Karsten's. He'd
used his new length of rope to hitch her to the man's
fence, so she wouldn't be scared off by all the commotion outside Belle
Gunness's house. From the gossip he'd heard in town, his plan for ven-
geance on Mrs. Gunness was now moot. Tomorrow, or perhaps the day
after, he'd use his new rope to load up Jenny for the trip home. Taking
stock of the crowd, he thought it seemed the whole town had gathered
to witness the removal of the bodies from their shallow grave. Would
Andrew's be among them?

An acrid burnt smell hung in the air. As Asle neared the front yard,
a sharp elbow jabbed him from behind, and a pair of boys jostled past.

"I heard it's bodies of kids that she ate," the taller boy said. "That she
tricked children into coming inside her house. Gave 'em candy. Then
she ate 'em. Cooked 'em and ate 'em."

"That don't make no sense," the other argued. "If she ate 'em, then
there'd be no bodies, you dummy."

"It's just bones," came the retort. "You're the dummy. You can't eat
bones, can you?"

Asle followed the children as they bullied their way through the crowd. He came upon Deputy Hofstetter, who watched as a crew of men carefully worked the dirt at the gravesite.

"Deputy," Asle greeted him. Hofstetter nodded. "I wish you had listened to me, Deputy, and investigated this woman."

"You're not quite as smart as you think you are, Mr. Helgelien. It wasn't Belle who was responsible for this."

Next to them, men reached into the grave and lifted out the first body, a man in his middle years. They laid him on the grass. The crowd collectively leaned forward, stretching to glimpse the soul who'd met his end here.

"No? What makes you say that?" Asle asked. A craning onlooker stumbled into him, and Asle turned him back with a pointed stare.

"A little bird's been singing a fine song." Deputy Hofstetter pointed to a group of men gathered just beyond the swine enclosure; outside the fence, stiff and solemn, slouched the skinny man Asle had seen through his binoculars and coaxed stories from in the saloon. He was handcuffed, guarded by a deputy, while the other men set to with shovels. "Ray Lamphere, Mrs. Gunness's handyman. He knew all about the bodies buried here."

"Did he?" Asle wasn't all too surprised. Gawkers pressed around him, straining to get a better view of the gruesome spectacle being unearthed. He took a small step forward to create space. "What happened to the hogs?" When he'd been here before with his binoculars, she'd had a passel of three or four.

"Neighbor took 'em to his farm," the deputy said, edging away from the crowd and toward the grave. "Of course, Lamphere spun a merry tale about Belle being behind it all. Some kind of money-making scheme, he claimed. Said her desk was full of letters from men and some kind of journal or schedule, but when I checked, there was nothing. Just a copy of a ladies' romance novel. *Thelma*, I think. My mother is reading the same book."

"Popular book," Asle muttered. That was the novel young Miss Longacre had with her in town the other day.

The deputy nodded. "But we've got Lamphere dead to rights. After all, who's left behind? Not Mrs. Gunness. We think he killed her so he could take her money. Set the fire to throw off suspicion."

On the face of it, it sounded plausible. But Asle knew it was wrong. And so would the deputy, too, if only he'd examine the evidence Asle had collected.

The workers carried another body out of the ground. It was a child. Her dress of yellow satin told him this must be the girl he had seen playing in Mrs. Gunness's yard. A shocked murmur rolled like a wave through the crowd, as viewers in the front passed the news to those behind.

"There's another one in here," one of the diggers said. They carefully removed earth from around the body and lifted it out. The boy.

Children. Asle shook his head in disgust. The two children and their father, each forehead marred by a single black hole, all wearing an expression of complacent surprise, as if the end had come in the form of a poorly prepared meal. May the Lord bless them and keep them. Even Asle hadn't expected such depravity.

The crowd surged again, forcing Asle another step forward and Hofstetter back.

Near the hog pen, the diggers began to lift out more remains. From where Asle watched, only one thing was visible—an obscenely large and gnarled foot. Something between a sob and a gasp of laughter escaped him.

"Good gosh all Friday, look at that foot!" Hofstetter exclaimed. "Who could that be?"

That foot could belong to only one person, and Asle's terrible suspicions were confirmed. Poor Andrew was dead.

The fear and worry he'd endured these last weeks swirled into a storm of fury. Asle thrust himself forward, squaring up to the taller man. Hofstetter's heel, which had been pushed to the lip of the grave, sank suddenly, pitching him off balance. He threw a panicked look over his shoulder.

"That, *Little Jimmy*"—Asle poked the man's chest—"is"—*poke*—"my"—*poke*—"brother"—*poke*.

Hofstetter's arms windmilled, and the earthen wall beneath him caved, sending him flailing into the now-empty hole.

Leaving him floundering in the grave, Asle pushed his way through the surging crowd toward the diggers. "Make way, make way," he cried. "That's my brother."

"Wait, I've only got a foot." The digger held it aloft, shoeless and dirt-covered. "Where's the rest of 'im?"

Unattached to a limb, Andrew's massive foot and knobby toes looked even more freakish than Asle remembered them.

"Hell if I know, Clyde," said the head man. "Keep digging."

Asle stood by in horrified anticipation as the three men poked their shovels here and there, searching for more of his brother.

"Hey!" one exclaimed, feverishly working something out of the earth. "I got something!"

A long arm emerged, fingers dangling. But there were only three fingers . . . and were those gnaw marks?

"Jumpin' Jehoshaphat, lookit this," the one called Clyde blurted. He looked at his digging partners incredulously and with two hands hefted something round. "It's a bleedin' head."

Asle gasped and leaped forward, wresting his brother's head away from the callous digger. "What the hell happened here?" he roared. He scanned the crowd. How he hated these fools. "Do you see what your precious Belle Gunness did to my brother? Can't you see? She fooled you all!"

Some of the gawking townspeople frowned at him, unwilling to believe their idol could be responsible. Others looked away with guilty faces.

Asle gently brushed dirt from his brother's face. "Oh, Christ, Andrew. Your silver tongue couldn't get you out of this one." He pointed to the diggers. "You. Bring me a wagon. I'm taking my brother home. You two: find the rest of him. And have a care. He was a man, not a circus sideshow."

Cradling Andrew's head, Asle turned on the townspeople. "You deserved her. The lot of you. So impressed with her money and her surface charm. 'Our dear Mrs. Gunness.' Ha! She had you all fooled. Every last one of you. Especially—" Asle paused, searching for Hofstetter, now near the front of the crowd, brushing dirt from his backside. "You. Some lawman. What did you call her? 'Kind and generous, an upstanding civilian'? The evidence was there for you to see, but you refused." He felt a sneer of contempt twist his mouth. "She wasn't good. She wasn't kind. She was a con artist and a murderer.

"She was a monster. Belle Gunness was a monster."

Afterword

This is a work of fiction. The story it is based on, however, is all too real.

Belle Gunness was born Brynhild Paulsdatter Storseth in Selbu, Norway, in 1859. The youngest of eight children born to a stonemason and his wife, Brynhild had a hard childhood.

One unverified story is that as a teen she became pregnant and went to a country dance where a man attacked her, kicking her in the abdomen and causing a miscarriage. The man came from a wealthy family and was never prosecuted. It was said that after that experience, her personality underwent a significant change, and the man who attacked her died shortly afterward. His cause of death was said to be stomach cancer.

Brynhild emigrated to the United States in 1881, where she changed her name to Belle and traveled to Chicago to live with her older sister.

Belle's first marriage, in 1884, was to Mads Sorenson. The couple owned a candy store, which failed to turn a profit and was destroyed in a fire. Some years later, their home was similarly destroyed. Both losses resulted in insurance payouts. Later, a life insurance policy on Mads was set to expire on July 30, 1900, with a new policy to begin the same day. Mads died of a cerebral hemorrhage on that very day, granting Belle a double payout of $5,000.

With this money, Belle moved to La Porte, Indiana, about 60 miles away, and bought a property of some forty acres and a large house.

In 1902, Belle married Peter Gunness. Less than a year later, Peter died from an injury to his skull. Belle was granted $3,000 in insurance money.

Children did not fare any better under Belle's care. Two babies died in her home when she was married to Mads Sorenson, and Belle collected life insurance on both children. Shortly after her wedding to Peter Gunness, his infant daughter died in Belle's care. Belle also adopted a girl named Jennie, who disappeared as a teen.

In 1905, Belle began placing marriage ads in Norwegian-language newspapers in Chicago and other midwestern cities. Her habit was to tell her correspondents to keep their connection a secret and to come to her farm with money.

Among the many men who fell prey to her scheme was Andrew Helgelien. During a months-long correspondence, Belle cajoled and flattered Andrew, finally convincing him to come to the farm in La Porte in January 1908. Andrew obeyed the admonition to keep their relationship a secret, telling his brother Asle only that he would return in a week or two. But that time came and went, and Asle began to investigate. When he found some of the letters Belle had sent Andrew, his concern turned to suspicion.

With the walls closing in, Belle fired her handyman, Ray Lamphere, and hired a new handyman, Joe Maxson. Soon after, a fire gutted the farmhouse on McClung Road. Four bodies were found inside the house, including that of a woman whose head was missing.

Asle Helgelien arrived in La Porte shortly after the fire, seeking information about his missing brother. Joe Maxson reported that Belle had instructed him to bring loads of dirt to a large area near her hog pen. Asle and Joe began digging and soon discovered Andrew's body.

Over the course of several days, officials found more than a dozen bodies buried throughout the farm, including Belle's adopted daughter Jennie.

Ray Lamphere was arrested in May 1908 for arson and murder. He denied the charges and insisted Belle had lured men to her farm through marriage ads and then robbed and murdered them. He claimed the body of the headless woman was not Belle but a victim, placed at the scene to mislead investigators. Ray was acquitted of murder but found guilty of arson and sent to prison.

Estimations of the amount of money Belle garnered through her schemes are as high as $250,000 (more than $9 million in 2024 dollars).

The body of the headless woman was laid to rest as Belle, next to her first husband. But the belief that Belle survived the fire and escaped persisted for decades, with alleged sightings being reported from Chicago to San Francisco to New York, and even a town in Mississippi in 1931. In 2007, the body was exhumed and its DNA tested. It was hoped that the flap of a sealed envelope found at Belle's farm would have enough DNA to finally lay the case to rest, but testing was inconclusive.

The mystery of what became of Belle Gunness remains unsolved.

Other books by
EDEN FRANCIS COMPTON

Emily
A world-famous playwright becomes obsessed with Emily Dickinson,
believing she has left clues of her personal trauma in her poems. He is
forced to come to terms with his own difficult past as he begins losing
his grip on reality.

Death Valley
In the dark and seedy part of Las Vegas that tourists never see, two
brothers with a volatile past battle over a woman they both love—and
the money she wins at a casino.

Catch and Kill
Angie has retreated from the world because of debilitating depression
and anxiety. When her beloved movie star sister commits suicide,
she is compelled to find answers. But in Hollywood things are never
what they seem. It will take a newfound inner strength for Angie to
confront the dangerous forces at play, in this thriller set in the gilded
world of Hollywood's elite players.

Stay up to date:
Follow Eden on Amazon

https://www.amazon.com/author/edenfranciscompton